Don't

Her

Jane Kirwan

After all this time!
best wishes
Jane

Published by Blue Door Press
Copyright © 2016 Jane Kirwan
Cover design by Pavla Ezeh
ISBN-10: 1530940125
ISBN-13: 978-1530940127

CONTENTS

2013

The taxi dropped Jess near a goods entrance blocked by dead trolleys. The airless heat of a town centre August. A café at the corner of Fishmarket where she had bunked off from school was gone – Fishmarket was gone.

On the other side of the dual carriageway, dwarfed by a windowless seven-story building, were six recycling bins hiding a railed off patch of grass with a few grave-stones. Leaning against the railings, a young woman tapped at her smartphone.

It had to be Rose.

The only thing was to brave the traffic and run across.

'You could have got killed. You must be Jess?'

Jess bent to catch her breath. 'I am.'

Rose was tall, slim, wearing expensive jeans and an expensive silk top. By her feet a bulky parcel and a box of seedlings.

'Connie told me you had red hair,' said Rose. 'And you do.'

Connie had said that Rose was mixed race, but not that she was beautiful. And she was.

What were they doing here? They made to shake hands before it became an extended hug. It was consoling to be held, and Rose was almost a relative.

Jess took two glasses and a bottle of Jameson from her bag, while Rose dropped the parcel and box over the railings.

'Shall we sing something?' said Jess. 'No one will hear above the traffic.' They toasted each other, the graves, the busy road. 'You start.'

'I can't,' said Rose. 'I sound like a frog.'

They stared at the blank headstones.

'Tell me how to help.' Jess refilled their drinks.

'Let's get on with it.' Rose collected a trowel and bottled water from her bag, climbed over.

Jess put away the whiskey and with an ungainly jolt, joined her among the graves. She waited while Rose scooped out earth, tucked in a few plants, then helped her unwrap the parcel; it was full of small grubby stones. Rose started pushing them into the soil. Jess crouched down, pressed in a few more.

'How many?' said Jess.

'Fifty.'

They took their time. Rose dug in two rosemary seedlings and watered them. They argued over the best places, kept changing their minds.

'We're probably too pissed,' said Rose.

The alcohol had been an excellent idea.

Rose bedded in some lavender. When they got to the remaining five stones, they counted together; linked hands as they pushed down the last one.

'Do you have the ashes?' said Rose.

'I do.'

PART ONE

1963

1963

1

A sea of white linen tablecloths, the hotel dining-room had been abandoned. Connie finished off her rashers and tomatoes, she needed more toast. She poured the dregs from the silver coffee-pot, examined her hands. Freezing outside, the knuckles red from her morning dash to get cigarettes. She must buy gloves.

The waiter grabbed her plate in case, God forbid, she had plans for more. There was a phone-booth in Reception, she dialled Liam.

The poor man sounded exhausted. 'The girls are asleep but I managed to dress Rory.'

Her sister Pat might imagine they were in London to get credits towards their diploma; she was here to have a break from the practice and the children. Pat's idea to get more strings to their bow, in general practice they'd always be assistants, always second fiddle to their husbands – must repeat that to Pat when her sister returned from praying.

Liam would leave the girls to sleep until Mrs M came.

'The house is freezing. I've no chance to get more than the kitchen fire lit. Rory was up most of the night.'

The man was a martyr. Well, about time – she must investigate more excuses to escape.

Apparently her niece had been reading to Rory and Claire before bedtime, got carried away.

'Nell scared them half to death.'

'She's on holiday too, give her some treats.'

Nell was only visiting for a few days, Liam had better not take advantage. Connie smiled soothingly at a woman waiting to use the phone. She had an hour before the first lecture, would pop into Dickins and Jones.

'I've been abandoned. Pat's flown off on a carpet of sanctity to hear Mass in the Oratory.'

'I must go, Con, Rory is screaming. Enjoy yourselves while you can, only two more days.'

He was counting the minutes.

*

Nell was trying to get away from the panting – someone was chasing her, her feet stuck in treacle. She opened one eye; she was in a bed by a window. The ceilings were high, the room huge and cold, she could see her breath. She was visiting her cousins, sharing Claire's room. Claire was making those noises.

Her sheet and blankets were twisted in a knot and it was hard to wriggle free. The room filled with a milky light when she opened the curtains. Circles of frost covered the glass. Outside was white like yesterday, and still snowing. Magic.

But Claire was making strange noises, had thrown off her eiderdown. The kind thing would be to put it back, tidy up Claire's bed. It would be the responsible thing to do, she was four years older. The lino would be freezing, her slippers were at home. She couldn't mention it or she'd be told off.

'You are very calm and thoughtful,' Aunt Connie had said two days ago, before leaving for London with Mum. 'Claire is so energetic. And I don't think she'll stop being crazy even when she gets to be fifty.'

More fun being noisy like Claire and untidy and only six.

Nell straightened Claire's bed. Her cousin made a cross face but at least she was now breathing normally. She looked sweaty and her black curly hair was stuck to her head. 'I was being boiled in an enormous pot with carrots.' Claire glared at Nell. 'It was you. You were going to eat me.'

'Don't be silly. That was Hansel and Gretel – I read it to you and Rory last night.'

Claire looked doubtful, wrinkled up her nose. 'I want my mum.'

Uncle Liam was cooking porridge in the kitchen, Rory in the high-chair making a yucky mess with some bread soaked in milk. It was stuck all over his face and bib.

Her uncle ran up the two flights to the bedroom and looked down at Claire. 'Good morning, Missus Grumpy.'

He took Claire's temperature, felt her pulse. Nell stood by the door, trying not to be noticed. Uncle Liam was very different from her aunt. He was quiet and serious, Nell was always worried he'd get angry.

'You should remain in bed today, young lady.' Uncle Liam patted Claire on the top of her head.

He smiled at Nell and his look said, you are going to have to be responsible. 'You stay here, Nell, I'll get breakfast for our patient.'

'Lucky you. A whole day doing nothing.' She went to plump up Claire's pillows, Claire kicked her away. It hurt and Nell pinched her leg, Claire began to howl.

'I'm sorry,' said Nell. All these promises she'd made after confession to be good, then forgot. But Claire was spiteful.

'My head feels funny,' said Claire, suddenly calm. 'You keep getting bigger and smaller.'

Nell fetched a glass of water from the bathroom, helped Claire sip it. Uncle Liam came and put a tray on the bed-side table. 'Eat something, drink the orange juice and try to sleep, Claire.'

'Sorry, this is a bit of a let-down, Nell. I'm late for surgery but will be back mid-morning. I know Rory's no fun to play with.'

When he left, Nell tried to feed Claire but she closed her mouth so tightly, porridge went all over the eiderdown. Nell began to scrape up the mess but it was impossible, she was making it worse.

'What's going on?'

It was the daily woman, Mrs M. She had on her outdoor coat over her overall. 'You go and see to little Rory, Nell. I'll sort this young lady.'

Nell looked back just at the moment Mrs M bent to straighten the bed and Claire was sick all over the sheets.

Once Mrs M had finished clearing up after breakfast, she wrapped Nell and Rory in scarves and coats and sent them out to the garden. At the very first snowball, Rory started to cry and ran inside. Nell tried to read to him but he wanted to play with his train. She took paper and crayons from the play-box and did some drawing. Claire was more fun, even when ill.

Nell crept into the bedroom and Claire opened an eye and grinned. 'Tell me a story.'

Before Nell could say anything Claire was out of bed and on her lap with a copy of a Secret Seven mystery. Claire sank down, all hot and heavy and in a few moments was asleep. Nell carried on reading very quietly and staying very still, then Mrs M came in with soup and put Claire back to bed and shooed Nell out.

The day had lasted forever. The house had gone dark and cold and silent except for the clock in the hall. Seven thirty. Claire and Rory were asleep and, if she could avoid it, Nell didn't want to go upstairs at all. Mrs M had made her a bed in the guest room which was full of boxes and big trunks that left shadows on the walls. A fat priest had come to the door with a thin nun. They'd disappeared with Uncle Liam who had forgotten all about her.

It was horrible to go into the dining-room with no one there. It was usually her favourite bit of the house, full of noise, people talking. Aunt Connie sliding dishes through the hatch, screaming at everyone to stop being polite, start eating. The long polished table was empty. Ten chairs waiting for supper.

In the bay window was the Christmas tree. It was nearly as high as the ceiling, much bigger than theirs. Mum said it was all a ridiculous waste. Nell lay down beside it; the smell was of stale food, not the pine forests Dad always wanted inside their house. She could shuffle right under the branches. Yesterday she and Claire had tried to see who could get in furthest. Claire had won.

The brown layer of needles on the carpet scratched Nell's legs. One of the coloured balls had fallen, Claire must have knocked it. It had a hole so you could see the silver paint on the inside; the clasp was still hooked to the tree. Two chocolate soldiers were stuck to lumps of cotton-wool snow and out of reach. And lots of dust. Well, Mrs M couldn't be expected to sweep under there.

'What I would give for her, she's a treasure,' her mother had said last summer. 'Adores the ground your uncle touches. The woman does everything for that family.'

Mrs M did seem to do more than Mrs Billings, their daily at home in Newcastle, who was always rolling-out her tobacco and muttering behind Mum's back.

Nell wriggled out. Yesterday Claire had got upset – said the big gold star on the very top of the tree was crooked. It *was* crooked.

Aunt Connie had given her a hug – they'd be back in four days. 'Will you be a darling, help me get rid of these decorations?'

Then Nell had to go home with Mum to Newcastle and school, to Sister Elizabeth and her ruler on the back of the hand. Another term in Miss Murphy's class who didn't like her and insisted on calling her Eleanor. She hated the name Eleanor. Mum said she just had to put up with Miss Murphy, who had her own problems.

Laughter from the sitting room. Driving through the snow on New Year's Day to spend time with her cousins had been exciting. It had almost not happened. Her mum thought Aidan should come because he was closer to Claire's age and they liked playing together. And Rory would prefer to have a boy around. But Aidan had a cold. Anyway Aunt Connie liked her best. She always said that Nell was her true guardian angel and obviously intended for her. It was God who got the address wrong. That it was lovely when Nell came to stay, they could run errands and Nell could help entertain Rory and Claire and tell them ridiculous stories. But Mum had dropped her off and gone with Aunt Connie.

'Through that weather, God help us,' said Mum.

They were doing a course and it was not to be missed. Mum and Aunt Connie were both GPs like Dad and Uncle Liam. 'We are discontent,' Aunt Connie had said last summer. 'Aren't we Pat? We need a break from these men, their adoring patients, bossy receptionists.'

It was impossible to make out words in the mumble from the sitting-room.

'Bugger,' Uncle Liam had said when the door-bell rang.

He had told her to carry on reading *The Bantry Boys*. But Rory was playing with his toy monkey, pretending it was a train, and Claire was in the next bedroom asleep. Her uncle had taken Claire's temperature and given her some medicine. He'd told Nell to be very quiet, let Claire rest. There'd been no point reading to Rory. Nell had come down here to the book-case to look for something more exciting.

The telephone rang in the hall and her uncle picked it up. Nell crawled across to the door. He was talking very quietly, he mustn't want the priest and nun to hear.

'Everything is fine, she's sleeping. I'll try, yes I'll try. Nell is keeping an eye.'

What would he try? Why should she keep an eye? On what?

'I'll get shot of them. Enjoy yourselves.'

Her uncle put down the receiver and went back to the sitting-room, closing the door. The phone was next to the Black Baby Box. Mum would pick the box up and shake it when they first arrived. 'Stingy visitors to your house,' she'd said two days ago.

'You with a surgery in the home, Pat. All the grateful patients filing past. Why not shell out for our poor abandoned thing?'

Did Aunt Connie mean the abandoned African babies? In the pictures on the box they were chubby and smiling.

'And have you raiding it, Con, for the milk-man?'

Keeping an eye. What did he mean? Nell went slowly upstairs. Mrs M had gone home to her daughter; she'd be back in the morning to cook breakfast. Rory was fast asleep, his monkey tightly gripped in both hands. It was a grubby red monkey with a torn waistcoat. Who would want to take it?

Claire had pushed off her eiderdown, was lying flat and her breathing sounded scratchy. It was like the way Dad breathed when he was chasing them round the house, pretending to be scary. Claire was always full of energy.

'Cheer-up, Nell, be more like Claire,' her father would say. Nell couldn't cheer-up. Claire was born cheerful. That's how it was.

'That Claire is exhausting,' Mum had said last summer.

But now Claire looked sweatier than before. Would Uncle Liam get angry if she interrupted them and told him? What would Aunt Connie do? Nell ran down the stairs and called her uncle.

'I'm Sister Anne,' said the nun, as Uncle Liam went off with Claire into the snow and dark in the fat priest's car. 'The canon is helping your uncle take Claire to hospital. We have to contact your aunt.'

The nun pushed the Black Baby Box to one side, placed the phone in the middle of the mantelpiece. Then she dialled and waited and spoke to someone. 'We'll say a few prayers, Nell. After that I'll try again. Any clue what your aunt planned?'

Claire had been wrapped in an eiderdown, Uncle Liam was holding her much too tightly.

After a few minutes and three muttered Hail Marys, the nun phoned again. She frowned. 'Come, let's find somewhere quiet.'

They went into the dining-room. They walked round the table

and looked at all the pictures on the walls, then they stood in front of the tree.

'Let's go next door,' the nun said.

They knelt in front of the painting near the sitting-room fire. Why didn't the nun kneel by the crib on the sideboard? But she didn't. 'It's a beautiful painting, isn't it? It's by Raphael. The original is in Florence. Do you know what it's called?' Nell didn't know. 'It's the *Madonna of the Chair.*'

The baby in the picture was fat and ugly. The child looked nice and could be a boy or a girl, but it had the goodie-goodie look some children had when queuing for communion. The woman was pretty. The chair was like the one in the hall at home.

It would be hotter in the room if there was more coal on the fire. It was nearly ashes, Nell's teeth were chattering. She'd probably be told to keep quiet if she said anything, Aunt Connie always let her take coal with the tongs and put it on the fire.

Every few minutes the nun would try ringing the London hotel. There was a rug on the sofa. Nell wrapped herself up in it. The nun didn't tell her off. They were in the middle of the litany, Nell sort-of joining in with 'Thanks be to God' when the phone rang.

Sister Anne came back. 'Little Claire is very poorly. Your uncle will stay with her. I'll stop here until he comes. Maybe you should go to bed now, Nell?'

The nun paused as if not sure of something. 'I can tuck you in.'

2

Liam pushed closed the bolts of the garage door, walked back through the garden to the house. The quarter-moon was hidden by cloud but the snow on the lawn was luminous; he wanted to lay himself flat in the white innocence of it.

He held firmly to the railing going down the icy steps to the scullery. The patient didn't live far, he had driven slowly but it felt dangerous, even though the Humber was solid enough.

His partner Gerry had been doing the visits. Connie was out of action, the assistant away for a long Christmas break and they hadn't managed to find a locum. Gerry had looked relieved when Liam said he'd take the night calls.

The phone had rung at 3 a.m. and Liam raced down the stairs – not wanting the house wakened. Connie hadn't stirred; there was no sound from Rory or the guest bedroom where his brother and sister-in-law were sleeping off the effects of too much consoling. The patient was an elderly woman he'd seen a few times before, frail and confused. She had fallen on the way to the bathroom, probably fractured her hip, so he had to wait with the woman's daughter for the ambulance.

He stood in the kitchen watching for the kettle to boil. It would soon be dawn; it would soon be the day his daughter was buried. He'd never witnessed the burial of a child. He had seen them die, there'd been plenty when he was a student in Dublin. Whether initially heartbroken or stony-faced the parents had looked at the solidity and stillness of death as if astonished. He had not been able to look at Claire.

'It's because children are so alive, so vital, Liam,' a house-surgeon once said. 'The minute that energy is gone, they seem made of marble.'

Liam was made of marble. He looked round for the packet of

tea. Pat, his sister-in-law, had put everything in unlikely places. He had wanted to take Claire's coffin over to where his mother was buried in Howth but Connie had said he was mad. 'What's the point, Liam? The woman's been dead twenty-five years. Sailing over there in the middle of this freezing winter? Will it put the clock back? We'll get a resurrection, will we?'

'It would feel more like Claire's gone home.'

'Home! For God's sake, Liam, the child is dead.'

Pat had intervened, said it was a bad idea. 'There's no travelling anywhere in this weather.'

That was several days ago, since then Connie had said nothing. She'd stopped talking.

The kitchen was cold and it was too early to start a fire. Liam held his hands over the gas then turned off the stove. He didn't want tea, he wanted nothing except for all this to be a nightmare. That any minute he'd wake up.

Connie was a sleeping mound of eiderdown at the edge of their bed; Pat had probably given her a pill. He turned on the electric fire and slid in quietly, he wouldn't be able to sleep but it was marginally warmer under the blankets. For a moment he was tempted to shift over and hold Connie. He changed his mind.

There was daylight in the now-yellow sky, more snow on its way. So he had slept. Liam could hear noises from downstairs, voices in the hall; the alarm clock said a quarter to nine. Connie's side of the bed was empty. He got dressed, went downstairs. Pat was in the basement kitchen giving Rory porridge, Mrs M upstairs using the Ewbank on the sitting-room carpet. Dermot was reading the *Daily Telegraph* in front of the dining-room fire – Connie nowhere to be found.

'I haven't seen her at all,' said Pat. 'We thought you were both sleeping in.'

Connie had disappeared. Her car was gone from the garage. All morning, as they had breakfast, answered the phone, got ready for church, he kept checking the front door, the garden, no sign of her. She disappeared on the day her daughter was being buried.

*

Connie walked into Perkitts department store, straight past the make-up ladies gossiping behind their counters, to the lift. The relief to get out of the cold, she should have worn gloves. Don't think. Get on with it. Now she was in the warm, she'd remember what she needed. The car would be safe parked where it was, she'd only be a few minutes.

The lift smelt of Chanel No. 5, had mirrored walls. The lift-boy refused to look up at her, kept his eyes on the ground. She checked: she was a sight, black rags of hair loose over her fur collar, she looked like a witch. The boy had gold-braid on his cap and jacket and barely reached her waist. He was much too short, far too young. They were hiring children illegally and dressing them up, Pat would have it reported immediately. Her sister's face the night she and Dermot arrived, the pious concern – Pat could be unbearable.

'This is the third, Madam,' he said for the second time. The boy looked anxious, as if Connie might not ever get out. All those people on the other floors banging on the bell would be extremely angry. Could he smell the drink? She'd only the smallest tot.

The third floor looked wrong, but she couldn't decide why.

'Can I help you, Madam?' The assistant had appeared from nowhere.

'A black coat. I need a black coat.'

The woman was trying to be helpful but was clearly confused. 'For you, Madam?'

17

Of course for her. The sales assistant stood there, a great lump of gormlessness. Connie waited. Then they both looked around: racks of children's clothes, rows of them. A whole floor of children's clothes.

'Well, for goodness sake,' said Connie. Everything was so difficult, people were impossible. 'This is no help to me at all.'

The assistant didn't seem contrite, was still looking blank as Connie marched off towards the stairs. When she caught her heel in the carpet, a small boy following his mother stopped to stare; Connie made a murderous face. He scuttled off.

On the ground floor was a booth selling watches. That's what she needed, she could never hold on to a watch. 'It's twelve-thirty, Madam,' said the bald man behind the counter.

They would be going into the church. The house would be empty.

3

The town had put their cemetery on the road to the reservoir, crows cawed in the oaks that lined the central avenue. This place was beyond dismal. Liam pulled his scarf more tightly, he was freezing. A teddy bear, perched on a wall, was lop-sided and he straightened it. The children's graves were in a separate section away from the adult plots, red and blue balloons tied to bare branches bobbed against the snow. He had to get through this day, look in control. Move around, keep the blood flowing, stop shivering, nod when people speak. And he must not wail.

Pat was convinced that even if Connie didn't turn up at the church for the Requiem Mass, she'd come to the cemetery. 'We have to let her do as she wants.'

Miss her daughter's funeral?

Liam had nearly said: 'What will people say?' Thank God, he'd stopped himself.

'The whole of Westport loved their wakes,' Connie had told him soon after they met. 'The relations dragged us to the whole fecking lot, even when Pat and I were tiny: kiss the ancient dried-out body, smell the moth-balls, a sip of whiskey, listen to that keening. On your knees praying for hours. Oh, the stench of death and candles, a mawkish celebration of grief, the famine years deep in them all. I vowed the day I left for college, never again.'

Someone was behind him: Dermot, his brother-in-law, stamping snow from wet boots. He and Pat must be appalled at Liam's neglect. They were both competent doctors, would immediately have seen what was happening to Claire.

Dermot put a hand on his arm. 'I was thinking to ask if you're ready, Liam? We could go back to the house, give this lot a warm drink.'

This lot were not many, people had slipped away after the

church – surely his daughter deserved more.

'Connie will be at home,' said Dermot. 'The family can't bear funerals. The mother-in-law always said she couldn't take another.'

Connie's parents hadn't come, blaming the weather. His own father had pleaded bronchitis but that was forgivable; Papa had been grieving since Mamma died all those years before.

What would she have said about her son's neglect? Papa talked of Mamma's passion for medicine, about the patients who adored her. She wouldn't have missed the diagnosis.

'Do not blame yourself, Liam,' said Dermot. 'It could happen to any of us.'

'It was text-book meningitis.'

'Isn't there no such thing.' Dermot pulled up the collar of his tweed overcoat. 'We could all have been fooled. If you'd spotted it earlier, what then?'

Snow gusted around, flakes settling on the grave. Pat couldn't be arguing with the canon about the pope after her niece had just been buried? Gerry stood talking to the new headmistress; next to them was the pile of fresh earth waiting to be dumped over his child. They had all of them taken the spade, let icy earth drop like pebbles on the coffin. What else was there to do?

He should thank the headmistress for coming.

'Will you both join us back at the house?'

'I have a list of visits, I'll pop in when I'm done,' said Gerry.

'Can you give me a lift?' said Sister Anne. She reached into the depths of her black habit, took out an envelope. 'I'd like to give this to Connie.'

The nun must have come by bus. Why had she not asked at the church for one of them to drive her?

To everyone's profound relief, Connie was at the house, sitting at the kitchen table with a glass of whiskey. Liam could breathe again. She'd made egg and cress sandwiches, wouldn't look him in the eye. All he could feel was the need to be held by her and forgiven; instead he was sent upstairs with Pat and Dermot, Sister Anne staying downstairs.

Gerry turned up at the house in the middle of the afternoon. Mrs M had taken Rory and it was a struggle to keep from breaking down, Dermot and Pat trying their best to distract him. Liam could now give up, Gerry knew them well, would carry the conversation.

'Will you have a whiskey?' said Pat.

'No, thanks.' Gerry perched on the edge of a chair. 'Did the headmistress stay long?'

'She's down in the kitchen with Connie,' said Pat.

Connie certainly wouldn't be praying. Or would she? It wasn't possible to predict anything.

'You're a school governor, Gerry. What's such a young woman doing as a Head?'

'She's a gamble, Pat.' Gerry passed round a silver cigarette case. 'Not yet thirty, Oxford, an only child. She lost her parents before the war to TB, grew up in an orphanage run by nuns.'

Dermot was still wearing his heavy overcoat.

'Are you cold?' said Liam.

'Don't mind him.' Pat shovelled coal from the scuttle onto the fire. 'He likes showing off his new Foxford tweed. You should get rid of the crib, it's after the Epiphany.'

He would never get rid of it, had watched Connie and Claire unpack the figures from the attic. Rory had helped glue the cotton wool – he'd got in a right mess.

'The school's moving to the edge of town, she's the angel of change,' said Gerry.

'Would someone ever tell me who'd sign on as a nun in this day and age?' Dermot collected an ash tray from the sideboard.

'Losing your parents?' said Gerry. 'The convent is her family. Isn't it the same for all nuns?'

'So?' Dermot lit Pat's cigarette. 'We can safely say she has nothing in common with Connie. Then what have they found to talk about?'

*

Anne gazed out of the window into the night, at the steps leading up to the garden and the back gate. Everywhere was thick with snow. So dark out there, so still and peaceful. She closed her eyes, lowered her head, whispered. 'Hail Mary full of grace…'

'Stop.'

Anne turned, startled. Connie's voice was sharp. 'Don't mutter. And do sit down.'

'Will you at least try to pray with me?'

Connie stretched across the table for the bottle, poured herself another glass of whiskey.

'It would calm you, Connie.'

'I don't choose to be calm.'

Anne glanced at the red tiled floor, if only Connie would kneel next to her. That was what she could offer, otherwise she was of no use. Connie had noticed, looked down at the tiles and shrugged. 'There's no keeping them clean.'

Hard to imagine this beautiful young woman mopping any tiles. She looked Spanish, those brown eyes. Connie's expression was furious, as if she wanted a fight.

Anne picked up her cup, took it to the sink, started to wash the pile of dishes, stack them in the rack. There was no tea-cloth for drying. The place was chaos, she'd no idea what belonged where.

Connie had put her head back between her arms, was again rocking side to side. Her long black hair had come free from its plait; her nails against the black sweater were painted red, her long fingers clawing at the sleeves.

At least Connie was sitting, when she stood up she made Anne feel small and inconsequential. Oh, to get back to the quiet of the convent. She'd drunk the tea Connie had made, there was nothing more to do here; she could go straight to the chapel, offer prayers for this family.

This woman opposite was a child herself, so sloppy and untidy and over-emotional. And the crowded kitchen was unsettling, full of Liam and Connie's life: the Irish landscapes, the Mayo calendar of a market day in some town. Not a crucifix or holy picture anywhere except for Christmas cards stuck behind pots and vases and along the mantelpiece over the fire. Bottles of milk, open packets of cheese, sliced bread, discarded quarters of tomato, egg shells; there were dirty dishes next to Anne's Mass card that had been thrown into a corner of the dresser.

A few nights ago, walking round with Nell clinging to her hand, the house had seemed full of family and warmth. Now it was a mausoleum.

Anne went to look for a yard brush; in a small room off the scullery was a toilet. A salvage bag hung from the door and a stack of boxes with empty bottles filled the corner; over the sink was a calendar with a picture of the Sacred Heart. It was from two years before.

She took it down.

Connie watched her put the calendar on the dresser. 'Ah, I meant to get rid of it, then reprieved the thing. No one uses that toilet except the few of us.'

They stared at each other.

'I should go, Connie.'

'No, no, you can't. They'd all be down, I couldn't take it. Pat wanting a rosary, preaching acceptance. My brother-in-law having me believe it was my fault. No, please stay.' She paused. 'But I cannot pray.'

'Do you wish to talk?'

Connie shook her head. She'd started to cry again, not like tears at all but guttural choking noises.

'Your faith will help you, Connie.'

There was a clatter, someone coming down. Connie gripped her glass as if to hurl it at the intruder.

It was Liam; he leant over the bannister. 'Gerry is leaving and we were wondering about lifts.'

'Get out,' growled Connie.

Liam didn't move. He was a child too, she felt so old compared to the two of them. 'Sister Anne, do you want Gerry to drive you home?'

'Go, for fuck's sake,' Connie screamed. 'Get out.'

She'd raised the glass as if she'd indeed hurl it. Anne shook her head; Liam hesitated then turned and went back up. There was talking in the hall, goodbyes, and the front door banging shut.

Connie had put her head again in her arms. Those dreadful sounds were unbearable to listen to; Anne found her gloves, went out and took the shovel to clear the steps. Once that was done, she swept them clean.

It was a fine night, showing off a half-moon with hundreds of stars. A relief to get out of that hot, airless room; the only active thing Connie had done since Anne arrived, apart from making tea and pouring whiskey, was to get up whenever the fire needed coal.

Anne paused once she'd finished sweeping and murmured: 'My soul has magnified the Lord...'

When she had finished the Magnificat, she went back inside. After brushing her habit, kicking snow from her shoes, she sat again and waited. Connie lifted her head, her face swollen and blotchy; she examined Anne as if she was a stranger then rested her forehead once again on the scrubbed wood table. Anne reached out to touch Connie's arm then pulled back, slipping her hands into her sleeves. What this grieving woman needed was to be held.

Connie looked around the room. 'I can't do this.'

Anne wanted to help but could only think in clichés. 'Why don't you drop into the school when you have time? We could talk.'

Upstairs was Connie's sister; Connie had a husband and child. Sorting out the school was going to take every minute Anne had.

She couldn't possibly resent Connie? Still, the thought lingered: this woman had a family, a career, a lovely house. Connie would survive this, have more babies.

But Connie had no faith. Anne had, surely that was more than enough. 'Why didn't you come to the funeral?'

Connie hesitated, then shook her head as if it was an absurd question. 'She's so small. And she was so cold. I couldn't watch them put my baby into that icy ground.'

4

Connie dumped the potatoes on the tray with the cabbage and gravy, carried it up to the dining room. Liam was at the far end of the table hacking at the shoulder of lamb, Rory at the other in his high-chair bashing a spoon against an empty bowl. He was too big for that chair, but he seemed so comfortable.

'This is madness,' said Connie. 'We should stay downstairs.'

When she had set the places, she'd left her glass on the sideboard. The bottle of gin had gone, now there was a jug of water. What did he imagine?

'I'm not eating in the kitchen on Easter Sunday,' said Liam. 'Is there no mint sauce?'

'If there is, I'm not getting it. Up and down like an idiot.'

Liam looked over, caught her eye, and smiled. She could feel the familiar clench in her stomach. Her husband turned back to the roast, carried on with his carving.

'You were happy enough with this room when we had visitors, or clergy, or Pat and the family. Gerry was at Mass, you could have invited him.'

'Yes,' said Connie, taking the skin off a potato and putting it with some meat into Rory's bowl. 'I was happy enough.'

The old Liam had gone. This tall, sad man carving lamb, red hair combed and brylcreemed but still sticking up, lips pursed as if he was doing the most complicated surgery, was too far away.

The two of them had stood in the pews that morning at High Mass, kneeling and standing then sitting for the sermon, diligently making the sign of the cross, muttering the Creed, while Rory squatted on the kneeler playing with his toy lorry. Connie had even taken communion, queuing with the others as if she was one of them, and they must have looked a normal couple, she in her fur, Liam in his father's old winter coat.

This man was a stranger; they had both committed a crime and would be eternally estranged. And Connie's was not just the crime of being away when her daughter needed her, but of consuming a bereft Liam in those following weeks, pulling him into the centre of her body in the desperate hope that would erase the emptiness. And of course he was guilty of nothing.

'One minute you can't stand me,' he'd said one morning when she'd dragged him back to bed. 'Then this.'

'Not true, I need you. I want to be wiped out.'

It hadn't worked. She'd tried, done her bit. She would leave the two of them, disappear and no one would suffer. Her feelings for this man were too confusing, too unhealthy; they would destroy him, destroy Rory.

Except for one small thing, she'd missed two periods and her breasts were tender. She couldn't have been so stupid. Connie leant over Rory and mashed her son's potato in with the cabbage. He took a dollop in his fist and hurled it at the wall.

The store windows were full of mannequins – padded-out breasts, headless, leg-less, waiting to be dressed in pastel twin-sets, tweed costumes, jersey frocks, sensible blouses. Strings of pearls and leather handbags were scattered at the feet of the torsos, ready to be hooked to their owners.

Connie stumbled past: thank God none had heads, no staring eyes.

Where had she left the car? That pub, the Old Drake, was somewhere; it must be open already for the evening – use their phone, have a small tot.

The next window was lined with glittering rows of fountains pens, boxes of oil-paints, note-books. There was a pile of geometry sets. Was this it, she was here to buy a geometry set? Who for? Would Claire have looked forward to opening her first one as eagerly as Connie once had, play for hours with the protractor, compass, set-square? Hers had arrived in her Christmas stocking and instead of brand-new she recognised it as a reject from Pat, the missing parts replaced so some were shiny, others scratched, but she'd loved it.

She leant against the window; she'd go in this minute and buy one. Oh, boo hoo, weep over the pavement, you pathetic woman.

'Are you all right?'

Some stranger was hauling at her elbow; the face was blurred, everyone's face was blurred as they scuttled past, moving away to the edge of the pavement, not wanting to be contaminated.

'Let me help.' It was that nun, that headmistress.

'Leave me alone.'

'I saw you through the window. You look unwell.'

Unwell? She was fine. What was the woman up to, dragging her along like this?

'I was buying blotting paper, next week's the start of term and we've run out. I'll find you somewhere to sit.'

Tell her to feck off, but you can't swear at a nun. God, the woman was strong, pulling her fast down the street.

'We're coming up to Fishmarket, we'll go in the back gate.'

Hustled. Connie was being hustled like a stubborn heifer. Stop this, she had to buy whatever it was. A grip like steel on her arm, the woman half her size and an Amazon. She was pushing Connie past people and through a gate and onto a bench and then nothing: cool spring air, open space, peace. No more buses, cars, only bird song.

Even the nun had vanished, something about getting coffee. Get out of here, where was that entrance?

A blackbird was belting away in a tree, warming up for the evening seduction. There must be a nest in the maze of overgrown roses; the garden gate was probably beyond all that. Get home. She did not want any bloody coffee. Find that exit. Why didn't they clear away these weeds and brambles? She'd ruin her nylons.

The ground gave way – Stars. Fuck. A sharp pain shooting up her right leg. She'd banged her head.

Everything hurt. At least she hadn't lost consciousness. Or had she? A black-out? Had she fainted? Totally dark. She'd gone blind.

Ah, well. Connie paused, took several deep breaths, leant back against the wall of earth and looked around. She wasn't blind at all, had fallen into a hole; beside her were a few stone steps. What had possessed her to go wandering in this jungle?

There were more steps going down. She was bleeding from everywhere, had grazed her palms, wrecked her stockings, both knees scraped. Below through the gloom she could see a figure. Her heart raced then she realised it was a statue; this was a grotto dug out of the ground with a statue at the back. She felt her way towards it and leant on a ledge, above her was some saint, face raised to heaven.

This was exactly the place she'd imagined, she'd been sent here. She needed to mop up the blood, find a hankie. Where the feck was her bag? It was here, still being gripped for dear life in her left hand as if her left hand didn't belong to her; the bag was her amulet, her life-belt. She still had it, a miracle. Inside, the quarter bottle of whisky unbroken, an envelope of tablets. Get on with it.

There were a couple of stones in the bottom of the bag, Connie took one, slipped it into her coat pocket. What about the nun? She'd never think of Connie stuck down in this hole, would assume she'd gone home. But who would find her? Not a child, surely. Not one of the girls?

They'd be back soon, the holidays nearly over. No, she couldn't do it here; she'd have to stop this wandering, drive well out of town, get to the sea, go for a swim. That was the best – but the tablets looked so inviting, so easy.

Someone was calling her name.

'Connie, what are you doing?' The bloody woman was peering through the entrance; all Connie could see was the white of Anne's wimple. The nun made her way carefully down the steps holding out a blue and white striped mug as if it were the holy host.

Connie stuffed the envelope back in her bag next to the bottle. She must sound coherent, get away quickly.

Anne settled next to her on the slab below the saint. 'Are you all right? Your forehead is bleeding, your leg's bleeding.'

'These gardens are a menace,' said Connie, taking the coffee.

'It's all going, the pupils are not allowed anywhere near.'

Had Claire come here? It would have been so tempting.

'I'm glad you've found Teresa, Connie. She's my favourite.'

And she and her superiors will demolish all of it. The ghosts covered by shops and a bus station, all urged on by the good sisters. The coffee was undrinkable. How could she sit with this woman, make small talk when life was beyond bearing?

Somehow she was being held, the nun was stroking her back and holding her. They were both crying.

'I see no reason to carry on, Anne, the whole performance.'

'Hush, hush, be still.'

They seemed to stay like that for hours, Connie being held in the dark of the cave below a statue with its face turned up. Instead of heaven, it would see only darkness, and a ceiling of earth.

Of course she wasn't going to do anything. What kind of madness did she think she was playing at?

'I'm pregnant.'

Anne sat back. 'How come?'

'The usual.'

After a short silence, Anne said: 'A blessing, a gift from God.'

'It's a punishment. I'd like to cut the thing out, be done with it, abandon Rory and Liam. They'd be better off.'

'Mother of Jesus.' Anne crossed herself then knelt down.

'Liam is sure I'll get rid of it. I heard him talking to Pat.'

'Connie, listen to yourself, please.' Anne grabbed Connie's hands. 'Is that why?' The nun paused. So she had seen the tablets.

Too bloody cowardly. Of course she wouldn't top herself, and wouldn't have an abortion. Or, maybe she wouldn't. Not to please any God, but because she didn't want to. And of course Liam and Pat would think she'd followed her conscience. Maybe she had but it was her choice. The important thing was to do no more harm than she'd already done.

The saint above them was saying nothing.

'Think of Liam and Rory, what they have suffered. How could you even consider this?'

What idiots she and Liam had been. Why bring more innocents into this hideously unfair world. She'd get rid of it, only a few cells, nothing really.

'Connie you have to make a promise that if you get this desperate again, you'll let me know first.'

Connie looked up at the saint. She had always liked Teresa. Not the little flower Thérèse, the one the sadistic nuns at school in Sligo had liked, but this one, Teresa of Ávila, the mystic, the ecstatic.

She stuck her hand in her pocket, touched the stone.

'Anne, in that case, I've a favour to ask.'

5

Liam paused in the shade of the wall then clicked the gate shut behind him. So far the summer had been miserably wet but today was hot, the cool of the convent garden a relief after the heat of the town.

It was a surprisingly big space, tennis courts with no nets, a lawn that was more like a meadow with wild flowers and knee-high grass. The air full of bird song. The sweetness of honeysuckle. On his left, an extensive neglected wilderness that sloped up at least a hundred yards as far as the wall to Lords Lane; small hills and humps of ground obscured by overgrown bushes and unpruned trees. It looked impenetrable. There were statues partly covered by brambles, heads of saints stuck out from the undergrowth.

Claire had said there was a wild part they weren't allowed near, but some of the naughty ones tried. Well, they wouldn't get far.

Gerry was away with his family for a three-week holiday, had advised Liam to keep straight down the path to the side-door for the enclosed part of the convent. 'Our new headmistress wants us in the back entrance like tradesmen. Not the same as your day, the front door off the High Street, a pot of the best tea.'

Liam pushed his way through rhododendrons, nearly his height – avoiding the brambles, nettles – under an arch into a separate garden. A nun traipsed back and forth filling up at a tap. Surely they had a hose? It was Sister Raphael; she watched as he went over to what had once been a pond. Almost empty, the smell sickly. Liam squatted down, pulled out strands of newspaper caught among the dead water lilies – he took off his jacket, sat back, lit a cigarette.

A shadow blocked the sun, a bat dropped from some roost, arms tucked into each black sleeve.

'You're dangerously quiet when you creep up on a man, Sister.'

'In future I'll whistle a warning, your patient is waiting.'

'Where's the pond water?'

'The hose was stolen. What are you doing? Come along now.'

Liam stubbed out his Woodbine in a pile of sodden paper, retrieved his jacket. Sister Anne was walking swiftly ahead to a door in the convent wall. The woman said jump and he jumped. He followed her into the cool darkness, along the polished corridors. The air was soft and enclosing. Stripes of blue, gold, purple, red from stained glass windows set high in the walls flashed on to the nun's black habit, across his face and grey suit. Her skirt swished rhythmically, revealing flashes of ankle in thick white stockings.

Now that his patient, Sister Jude, was without her black veil, the white linen enclosing her head made her seem already a corpse. Liam looked blankly at the crucifix at the head of the bed as he took her pulse. It was fast and weak.

Anne had left, closing the door gently.

They smiled at each other like conspirators. 'You'll get used to her,' Jude said.

He didn't intend to, would have nothing to do with the school once Gerry got back.

Liam took a stethoscope from his bag. 'Can you lean forward?'

He helped Jude pull herself up then listened to her chest beneath the cotton vest. The room was muffled in a heavy quiet. A relief after the day he'd had – a waiting room of patients wanting his permission to be ill. The few who were desperately sick, he couldn't help. He palpated a back that was all spine and ribs.

Jude had slumped forward, almost asleep. Liam adjusted the earpieces of his stethoscope. 'Do me a couple of coughs.'

'Oh, I've missed you,' Jude said. 'I do understand, but it's been nearly a year since we lost Claire.'

'Not even seven months.'

'And you vanished. I must have been one of your first patients, seven years ago?' It wasn't even four. 'Gerry's all right but he hasn't your touch.'

Liam held out his hands; they both studied his long fingers. He should trim those ginger hairs bristling from his knuckles.

'Connie says I'm hairy as a werewolf.'

'Well I've seen a fine few of them, tell her from me you're not, none have red hair. How is Connie?'

Liam took her wrist again. 'Your pulse is fast, Sister.'

'I'm hardly surprised, this is the most I've talked all week.' He helped her settle back on the pillow. 'Has Connie gone to the seaside with little Rory?'

'They'll stay all summer. Her sister Pat and the children are there; the brother-in-law, Dermot, will be with them soon.'

'So when do you go?'

Liam tightened the strap of his watch. So peaceful in this room.

'You know, Jude, I'd never seen your gardens before, didn't know the extent of them.'

They both looked at the white-painted wall as if expecting a window. Most of the convent and school turned in on itself, only a few classrooms faced the playground and gardens.

'You should get away, Liam, weren't you brought up by the sea? Sister Anne thought you might be missing it, we wondered how you were.'

He could well imagine. Everyone assuming he was unreliable, might vanish back to his childhood. 'Well, that's really dandy.'

'Really natural, Liam. She is pushing it along, you know, none of this gradual move. They'll not be back in September.'

Jude closed her eyes again. He doodled on his prescription pad, letting time slip into the quiet. He hadn't thought about Howth in a long time. He'd not been a content child, his father doing his best on his own. Connie's family were so noisy, so intense, fierce rows and fiercer making-ups. But they seemed happy.

They will never forgive him.

Liam leant forward, kissed the nun on her forehead then pressed the buzzer. Sister Anne appeared immediately and briskly straightened Jude's blankets. Jude ignored her, winking at Liam as he waved goodbye. He handed over the prescription, useless, but better than nothing. The headmistress tucked it into her habit, closed the door and walked quickly past.

'Could you put flowers in her room, Sister?'

'Flowers?' The nun turned and stared. 'What for?'

'Would a couple of blooms be missed from the chapel?' He had to raise his voice, she was again racing ahead.

The nun walked back, was going to punch him. Liam flinched.

But instead she looked amused. 'Of course not. Do you have time, Doctor, for a cup of coffee?'

He had all afternoon, only Mrs McInerney's cold lunch and smell of beeswax which Mrs M simply wiped around the front door. No evidence of shiny polished wood, just empty rooms and abandoned toys in the bedrooms.

Liam followed the nun to a small kitchen, watched her pour warm water from an ancient kettle. Despite her protest that she could manage, he took the tray with two cups, milk jug, fig rolls, followed her outside to a bench. So this had been planned.

A veranda stretched the opposite side of the playground; glass doors and floor-length windows separated it from each of the classrooms. In the gloom beyond would be tiny desks and chairs, a blackboard, a Sacred Heart. In one corner of Lower Kindergarten, a picture of a lady on a cloud. Only there a term and five-year-old Claire had been sent to that corner for what she said was hours.

The Nescafe was weak, the water hadn't boiled, there was no sugar. Gerry said this nun had been sent to put dynamite up the governors' backsides. Plans for the move to the new girls' school were well advanced but there'd been resistance.

'Has it been hard, Sister, getting them on your side?'

'Oh, I forgot sugar. Do you want it?'

Liam shook his head.

'It's you, the parents,' she said. 'And the bishop and the canon.'

'The bishop is harmless.'

She was right to look doubtful. Liam would switch off when Connie had clergy to the house. They ignored him anyway. Connie would be sipping and mixing, pouring out sherries and whiskey, flying around the kitchen calling Mrs M 'darling' to her face and 'that faggot' as soon as Mrs M laboured downstairs for another tray of food for what Connie called the 'holy gullets' or 'those gannets'. The bishop had a strong heart and good blood pressure despite being overweight: a solid, calm, unflappable, devious man, partial to crystallised ginger.

But that had been in the past, before Claire.

'You never come near the school,' said the nun. 'I need someone to advise me. It's hard to get anybody this time of year.'

What gall the woman had. And to expect him to sit here staring out at the playground, looking over at those classrooms.

Liam stood up. 'Do you mind if we walk around? Gerry's the governor, I've nothing to do with the school.'

She paused. 'I've already asked Connie. I thought it a distraction but she wasn't interested.'

The last thing Connie would want was distraction.

The nun kneeled, made the sign of the cross, kissed the crucifix on the heavy wooden rosary looped round her waist, picked up the tray. 'I must get on.'

Liam turned when he reached the gate, looked back at the mess, neglect. Somewhere in there was honeysuckle or wild woodbine, his father's favourite. A blackbird belted out a song from the bushes; the headmistress had disappeared, he couldn't go home.

He started on the first pond, tearing out dead lilies and weeds with an abandoned rake. Out of the corner of his eye, a shadow moved behind some bushes. This was crazy. The shadow turned into the reassuring bulk of Sister Raphael filling her watering can. No ghosts of dead children. His heart slowed to normal – the nuns could have bought another hose. Raphael didn't respond to his wave but he could sense her spying as he went to another, larger, pond near the high brick wall that separated the convent from Silver Street, but the water looked too rank, weeds too consuming to tackle today.

Sweat trickled down his neck, dampening the edge of his shirt collar. Raphael was dragging herself to the tap, her heavy serge habit sweeping the ground. If she could work in this, so could he. Raphael had diabetes, was addicted to gob stoppers and acid drops; her blood pressure was erratic, sugar levels even worse. She must be dizzy in the heat.

A bee snuffled through clematis. Was it clematis covering those low walls circling that ivy-covered saint? By a six-foot high crucifix, long-dead daffodils drooped in clumps from dry earth. He looked round for a compost heap. Where did Raphael put her rubbish?

For the next two hours he worked his way further into the wilder section. Traces of paths became a little clearer. They must have once connected what was now the remains of grottoes and shrines. He'd made little headway with the brambles, left small heaps of weeds, dead plants, rubbish, like a mole. The scratches and nettle stings were welcome but next time he'd bring gloves. Even without including the nun's cemetery by the chapel, the whole garden must be nearly an acre, his effort insignificant. He'd have to visit the McInerneys, raid the old man's shed for a shovel and rake and good cutters. A wheelbarrow was what he needed.

For the next few days the surgery was busy. People had come from the factory-week break with diarrhoea and vomiting and fervent vows never again to stray from home. There were first-degree burns from those who had gone to Spain. The factory owners had stayed under umbrellas on the French Riviera.

The wheelbarrow was too big for the boot of the Humber; he had to find a rope to tie down the back and needed to visit Dunson's hardware for a hose-pipe. Thursday was his half-day, Martin, the locum for the summer, on call.

Liam let himself in at the back gate, balancing his medical bag on the sack of tools. He'd found a rusty mower stored in a shed but most of the grass he would leave as meadow. He stowed everything behind the grotto to St Anthony and caught Raphael as she was about to vanish like a white rabbit behind the biology lab. His question about compost threw her into a frenzy of anxiety so he calmed her down, let her scurry off.

Sister Jude was impatient.

'She said I'd to wait for your say-so. I've been with this old body long enough, know it well enough. It's between God and me when I go. Not you lot, forgetting all about me.'

Was Sister Anne a tyrant? 'Calm down. Your blood pressure. Are you taking the tablets?'

'You are having a holiday, Liam? You are going to join the family?'

6

The sea sneaked over Connie's legs and around her hips leaving her belly a marooned island. How absurd it looked. Seagulls would perch on her Pacific atoll. People would name it: Tierra del Total Balls-up, await immediate evacuation.

The sky was so far above, the water so stealthy. It was cold, but her body was used to holidays – daily dunking in freezing water.

Children's voices in the distance: Pat's lot running wild and Pat screaming, but it wasn't them. It felt early, too early. Another night of not sleeping and she couldn't even have a drink, she'd promised Pat. Her sister had some wild notion that a few days ago Connie had been rushing up the track to the main road at three in the morning in her pyjamas.

'You were out of your mind, Con,' Pat had said the next day. 'Looking for Claire. If you weren't pregnant I'd have shot you full of Largactil.'

Her sister over-dramatising as usual.

Connie's hair was soaked and full of sand. She stretched and rolled her bottom in the water. In that vast belly was a baby.

'Now that you're welcoming it, it will save your marriage,' Anne had said on a gusty blue-sky day when they'd been chatting in the convent garden.

Welcoming it? Hardly. But had she really stopped complaining?

Everything had the cheek that May afternoon, as they'd struggled through the bushes, to look new and hopeful. She'd examined all the crazy abundance: the overgrown rose-bushes that would soon be in flower, the lilac dizzying, and decided that the one thing possible, since she hadn't the courage to end the pain, was to leave Liam.

She might not save the marriage, but she could save him.

Liam thought Connie wanted a child to replace Claire, how

obscene was that? Replace her curly-haired darling? The stupid eejit. Even Pat and Dermot realised she'd got pregnant by mistake.

They'd all been worried, even Anne, that Connie would break the law, get it removed somewhere, commit a mortal sin. But she went to Mass. Occasionally. She was a Catholic in all important senses of observance – it was the faith bits that niggled.

The truth was she couldn't face an abortion, so she didn't have one. 'My prayers have been answered.' Anne had said. Maybe they had, that initial urge to cut the bloody thing out had been so strong.

'You do want this child, Connie. I know it.'

No, she didn't. She'd leave it with Liam and Rory and vanish.

They'd been sitting on the steps in their usual place that led down to the cave with St Teresa, Anne had fought through the brambles holding two mugs of undrinkable tea. As usual, Anne had been telling Connie off. Anne had plans. What was it with nuns? Anne really did think that symbolic acts and prayers would help.

A larger wave swept over her and Connie spluttered out salt water, pushed herself to her feet – what an elephant already. She picked up a pebble, skimmed it over the water, then squatted again.

She had to stop the images flooding in: the end of last summer and a late heat-wave, a neglected sand-pit, box of poster-paints, a jam-jar with brushes and dirty water, scrap-paper, a line of sheets. They were mainly sheets, and she was on a deckchair pretending to be asleep and the girls on a rug. Claire hugging herself with glee, rolling over as if she were being tickled but not being tickled, just the pleasure of sunlight and how it caught them one minute then was hidden by washing. Nell was watching, as always shy, too reserved for a nine-year-old. The sheets were flapping and Claire kept jumping up, hiding behind them and giggling. She had lent Nell a few of her precious stones. Nell was looking at them mystified. 'Paint them,' Claire ordered. 'Now. And don't let *her* see.' And the child was off again in peals of laughter.

Connie had kept her eyes closed.

There was the postman by the veranda waving a letter. 'Leave it on the porch,' Connie yelled.

She bent over and pushed a few pebbles into the sand. She must go somewhere away from family, away from all that was familiar. They had all been here at the beginning of last summer, this place was haunted by Claire.

The postman had clambered back on his bicycle. No sign of anyone. Pat or Mrs P had probably gone for bread. Connie splashed into the sea, swam briefly then lay on her back, buffeted up and down. She took a deep breath, screamed as loud as she could. No one around, she could make as much noise as she liked.

She raked through her hair with her fingers, that would do instead of washing. She had better get out, couldn't laze all day. She grabbed a sandy towel, walked slowly up to the house.

The envelope was in Anne's neat handwriting; Anne had clearly taken it on herself to keep an eye on Liam. That was easier than it seemed, since Liam had practically moved into the convent. An image of Liam in a nun's habit, it would suit him.

What a relief not to be going into that bloody surgery every morning: Mrs Citric Lemon pursing her lips and handing over a stack of the worst patients. It was beyond the woman to call Connie, 'Doctor'. Instead, Connie was Mrs Dillon, some minion who knew nothing and should be home cleaning and making tasty meals for lovely Dr Liam, and not neglecting her children.

Connie settled herself into a deckchair: Anne was bothered by Liam's obsessive gardening; he seemed to think that by pruning a few rhododendrons he'd go back in time, had insisted that Sister Jude needed the garden to keep her alive. 'I told him, all she needs is the chapel. When we take that, she'll follow it to the new place.'

Typical of Liam to think he could advise Anne on how to care for the older nuns.

What would Anne do about the nun's graveyard? How pretty it had been, that low brick wall surrounding fifty or so headstones; the grass was cut, flowers weeded in contrast to the rest. It would have been a much kinder place to put Claire.

'Oh my god,' Connie screamed. Aidan had jumped out, the little devil had been hiding behind the porch door.

'Sorry,' said Aidan. 'I was just going for a walk. Everyone is asleep except Mum and Mrs P.'

Well, hardly everyone. Asleep? It was earlier than she'd thought.

'Then scram,' said Connie, wrapping the towel more securely around her. Aidan paused and stared.

'Do you need anything, Aunt Connie?'

What did he imagine she needed, a scrawny kid and so twitchy?

Connie settled back again as Aidan grabbed his plimsolls and raced off. Make the most of the peace. She picked up one of her discarded novels: *The Unlikely Fate of the Adulteress*.

*

There was a note by the phone in the hall. Mrs Dillon had called to ask Liam when he was joining them. Why couldn't Mrs M say Connie or your wife or the mother of your children, your child rather? Or the lady doctor, or that aauld bitch from Westport, which were certainly her words to Mr M.

Liam tucked the note under a dried-out pot of tradescantia. Once Gerry was back, there'd be no excuse.

It was while dealing with the boiler, taking the ashes to the bin at the top of the yard stairs, that Liam realised what he could do with the garden. He was hanging the brown shop-coat on its hook, about to hunt for coloured pens, when he heard the door-bell.

Rolling down his sleeves Liam ran up from the kitchen, a cuff-link dropping to the hall floor. 'Hold it a moment.'

The canon joined him, pacing the polished parquet, until they found the link Connie had given him at Christmas. 'A small one then,' said the canon, leading the way down.

Liam poured two glasses of whiskey with a splash of water. He knew what would happen. They would briefly argue about how dangerous De Valera was as president, how inept Macmillan was as prime minister, then spend several minutes on Malone's excellent black pudding and sea fishing in West Cork. They'd not mention the sad loss of the pope: John XXIII was far too radical. They wouldn't mention the night the canon turned up with Anne.

'A roomy Kelvinator and nothing in it, Liam. Wasted on you.'

Liam found rashers of bacon and broke eggs into a pan. Once the canon had finished his food, he'd be gone. In the old days, if Connie had been around, they'd have had to encourage him out the door well after midnight.

'Haven't seen you at Mass for a while.'

'Oh, I slip in at the back.'

'That young nun is going great guns getting the new school sorted. We're told you have her ear?'

So the headmistress had been having a word with the clergy.

'They are cute, those ones. That's a great order for managing money.' He mopped up the last of his eggs. 'Liam? We've never spoken, not in a fair while. How are you, really?'

The canon wanted his confession? Liam put the bread back in the bin. 'I'd a long day. I've letters to write.'

'Fair enough, fair enough.'

Connie thought confession a farce, never went, whoever asked was told she'd got pregnant during finals. Immaculately. They'd married as soon as she knew. Liam took over most of Claire's care; once Connie had finished her house-jobs they came to Moreton. If anyone didn't approve, Connie didn't give a toss.

The canon drained his glass and shook himself like a Great St

Bernard back from a snow rescue, glad to get that over with.

'I'm sorry for troubling you, Liam.'

Like hell he was.

'Well, I'm off to face the wrath of Mrs Moss and her abandoned stew. When are you going to join the family?'

'We're very busy.'

At last the man was gone and Liam could double-lock the front door, close the curtains in the small study. He unscrewed his fountain pen, drew in the boundaries: the High Street along the front of the convent, the wall that separated the gardens from Silver Street, the graveyard and chapel to the left of the school. Fishmarket ran almost all along the back before it joined Lord's Lane, the garden hidden there from the town by another high wall. He'd taken a ladder from the shed, climbed up, made notes.

With mounting satisfaction, he marked the grottoes built into the slope, others piled on mounds of rocks, earth, the occasional circle around simpler shrines. It was as if his thoughts were flowing unedited. He pencilled in class rooms, the upper school, he'd made the tennis courts too near the old science block. Tomorrow he'd pace out measurements. Under all the overgrowth there had to be a pattern. He sat back, looked at the blank space in the middle; before giving up for the night, he would colour in the playground, the verandas around it, the kindergartens.

7

Nell looked up at boarding-house ceiling, at the gaps between the wood. She had done something wrong;. A lump in her head pushed down to her heart, like the brass weight her mother used when pressing cooked tongue.

Colum was asleep in the bunk by the door. He snuffled as he slept. If she could only remember what it was, she'd apologise, or explain, or hide the evidence.

A yell from downstairs, an answering cry from the veranda, someone calling Aidan. Mrs Podrowski had gone swimming. Had Mum joined her? More likely Aunt Connie, with her belly straining at the seams of that old blue swimming costume. Aunt Connie lying flat on the wet strand, arms stuck out like a starfish waiting to be covered with water.

Nell's lips tasted of salt. Yesterday had been normal. It had rained, yet again, just like last year. No one had been angry with her. Aunt Connie, had screamed at Mum and Mum had screamed at Colum. He had stormed off, been away all day, was still fed up when they did the dishes. She washed, he dried. Her brother always grabbed the cushy option just because he was the oldest. Her with her arms in dirty luke-warm water trying to ignore the soft lumps of food she should have scraped into the old zinc bucket. Nell hated that bucket. No one cleaned it. But when she asked Colum where he'd been, he said to mind her own business.

No, it was Tuesday yesterday. The day the fish-man came, fresh fish on Mrs Podrowski's kitchen table leaving blood dripping all over the wooden floor. They'd had plaice. A treat, Mum said. It hadn't many bones, which was good. Nell knew what happened when you choked on fish bones. It would be more practical if the fish-van came on Friday, no meat allowed on Friday. A mortal sin.

Maybe yesterday Colum had visited the tents. There was a line of them a mile further up the beach. Enormous and brown. Old army ones, Colum had said.

The day after they arrived, Nell had walked there. A man had told her about a flood ten years before. It was dark inside the tent, his shadow on the canvas walls making him twice his height as he moved up and down, talking and talking. He'd told her of losing his house-boat, everything swept away, seeing a wall of water higher than a skyscraper. When she'd told Colum, he said the man repeated that story, year after year.

There was something about the way the man kept describing the water, his shadow moving over the sides of the tent. But that wasn't the reason for her feeling so bad.

Her bed was bumpy, a truckle bed.

'Flimsy,' Mum had said. 'So be careful. Draughtiest room in a draughty old house.'

Some blankets were on the floor covered in dust and muck.

The wind made a funny crying noise through the cracks in the roof. She hated being so close to the rafters with only one small window – the latch should hold it open but didn't. Claustrophobic, Dad would say. 'Around your mother, Pat, I'm claustrophobic.'

The glass was dirty, a square of deep blue. Aunt Connie said the horrible smell was the oil they put on the wood.

It was like when she was small – that morning feeling of having done something bad. Funny, it was always there, then suddenly gone. How many weeks since confession? This year there was no boat to Ireland to stay with Granny. So, nearly two weeks since she'd tried to remember sins for Father Rogers.

Had she lost her temper, hit Aidan? Aidan was a sneak, always running to Mum or Aunt Connie. He'd soon be going away like Colum. School, according to her father, would 'sort Aidan out'. Why did she not need sorting out? Colum had been different before going away. At Easter he was sent to a prep school where they wore floppy grey hats, had cold showers. Colum said it was because the parents were panicking.

About what? Colum wasn't happy, his eyes had a bruised look, but he wouldn't talk. He was obstinate and nearly as tall as Mum. Soon, he'd hit Mum back.

He was now making snorting noises. Sun already filled each dusty corner leaking through the wood slats, the walls bending with each gust. If she could think into the weight in her head, remember whatever, break it up, then she could breathe.

She had escaped yesterday. Not for as long as Colum, but she had got away; had hidden behind the shed where Mr Bronks repaired old fishing boats. She'd spied on the boy living in the bungalow. Alexander Lloyd. He was born in 1952, one year older, his birthday in April like hers. She'd never seen Mrs Lloyd, and Mr Lloyd only once. He had the same blonde hair as his son, a fat stomach and baggy shorts that finished below his knees.

Alex spent most of the day sitting on the edge of his veranda, scratching with a twig in the sand. Sometimes he'd race up and down the slope on his bike but mainly around in circles, pulling the front wheel off the ground, then he'd try on the dunes, but always fall spectacularly.

The weight on her was not to do with Alexander. The first time she'd passed him, they did talk. He'd asked where her cousin was. He said, the little one who won't stop chatting, the one with all that crazy black hair.

He said Claire looked so happy, that's what he had said. As if all the rest of them were sad and had always been and it was Nell's fault, Claire wasn't here. But she didn't reply. She didn't tell Alex that her mother insisted no one was to mention their cousin.

Her book was under the bed with the cobwebs, spiders, dead flies and fluff. She closed her eyes. The sun was getting higher, slabs of bright red across her eyelids. The tarry, woody smell was getting stronger.

The metal ribs under the mattress seemed even sharper. 'Oh Nell, no princess and pea could survive this contraption. Look at those wonky legs,' Aunt Connie had said when she helped make it. And it sagged. 'Ok, it's a dodgy bed, but you're no weight. There's nothing of you, love.'

The racket downstairs was probably the milk man, Nell had heard the float rattle and clink up the lane. Someone had been sent to ask for more. The milkman was cheerful and very tall. There was always a faint smell of sick. He'd stoop down whenever she was sent for cream or eggs, give an enormous smile. One single tooth in the middle of his bottom jaw and nothing else – when she'd mentioned it to Mum, Mum had smacked her on the head.

If yesterday had been Monday then Mrs Podrowski would have washed the sheets, filled the lines in the yard. Monday was the day before. Mum had fed the mangle, dragging out clothes from the hot water with wooden tongs. Nell had helped, collecting the slabs of shirts and shorts, putting them into a basket. Then she'd pegged out everything with Colum. Except the sheets. Aunt Connie had managed to pull herself from her deckchair, to help Mrs Podrowski with those. Hanging out wet clothes with Colum – when the sun was shining, they were by the sea, and not much to do – makes it all right. Out in the sun with that flap and dazzle. But it had started to rain, someone must have taken everything down.

Colum was making different noises. If he could only keep it quiet. The house, Aunt Connie said, was a plywood box.

She'd nearly finished her book, the end of her pile from the library in Hunstanton. She didn't want it to finish even though she'd read it already. Marianne was crouched in a hollow, the heather and tall grass hiding her. The sound of a horse, the rider getting down, approaching footsteps. He knew Marianne was there.

She should push the story to earlier, but it was late, from the sounds below of banging frying pans, Mrs Podrowski was back from her swim.

'Colum! Stop.'

Her brother leapt out of bed. 'Ok, Ok.'

He scrabbled around, looking for his glasses then pulled on a T-shirt that had escaped the wash. Colum was skinny, his black hair sticking out in a halo. He kept his eyes shut as he sat on the edge of his bed, wriggling up and down as he pulled on his shorts. When she'd grumbled yesterday, Aunt Connie had laughed.

'A total pain, aren't they, Nell? You'll be glad to get home to your own room.'

Colum knocked into her bed. 'Sorry', he said as he charged around looking for a missing plimsoll.

Crash, crash, as he went down the stairs.

'Shut it.' A wail from the kitchen. Aunt Connie.

Alex did see her. She was in the sand dunes behind Mr Bronk's shed – well out of sight – when he'd suddenly disappeared. A minute later and he was above her, looking down. His legs were brown but his knees scuffed and white. He was wearing a yellow aertex shirt and grey school shorts, a belt with a red dragon clasp. He'd said nothing. He should have said something.

That first time he had wanted to know about Claire. It was as if he thought one of them had buried her somewhere and he was the hero, would find the villain.

Nell sat up, knocking her head on a beam. That was it. Claire. She'd dreamt about that nun and Claire. They were on the beach. It was hot, the sun blinding. Nell was behind a sand dune watching Claire and the nun make a sandcastle. Claire was wearing the old elasticated swim togs that she'd worn last summer, she and the nun were giggling.

So that was the reason for the heavy feeling. Nell had never dreamt about Claire, had only met Sister Anne once. That had been awful, having to get down on her knees and pray while this nun recited prayers asking God to listen – which he didn't.

The nun had got muddled in the dream with Uncle Liam, the Uncle Liam who yelled at her the day Claire died. He'd been making lunch. Aunt Connie had gone to the hospital with Rory, but by then Claire wasn't alive. No one said Nell should go. Mrs M was dusting and saying things like 'It's God's will'.

Nell had asked Uncle Liam why had it happened if God knew everything. He had yelled 'God does what he damn well likes.' Then Mrs M had turned on the hoover and Uncle Liam got even angrier and threw the frying pan full of fried eggs on the floor. Then he suddenly said, very calmly, that Nell should skip lunch, have a lie down. As if she was the one making all that noise.

She'd gone up to Rory's bed and fallen asleep immediately, just like that, in the middle of the day. When she woke, her mother, Aunt Connie and Rory were back from the hospital.

When they drove home, Mum had told her there was not a thing anyone could have done. It was nothing to do with her, she was to forget all about it. Then Mum and Dad disappeared for a few days and Colum said it was to be with Aunt Connie and for Claire's funeral.

There was more crashing, someone coming up the stairs. The emptiness left by Claire and that it could happen so suddenly. And it was all her fault. She was the one keeping an eye.

No one had said anything but that's what they'd thought. Now there was nothing of her cousin, just a space at the table. Not even clothes, not even a swimsuit thrown in with Rory's pile.

The bad feeling was still there. But not so much. Nell hugged the book, waiting to see if the noise would stop on the first landing. If someone wanted her, or had lost something, she was busy. Too early for breakfast. The house didn't smell of burning toast. More banging on the stairs then something exploded into the room. Aidan. Her brother waited at the end of her bed, panting, his chest wheezing in and out, mouth open. He didn't speak, stared at her. She'd seen a rabbit looking like that at night, eyes fixed in the car headlights.

Dad had said 'Shite', when they hit it.

Aidan, his cheeks flushed pink, mumbled something. Aidan was nearly seven, had a stammer and was always sent on errands which was silly and a waste of time. He'd forget and get caught up doing something quite different.

He smelt of salt and sea as if he had brought great gusts of outside into the room.

'I'm not going swimming before breakfast, Aidan.'

So that wasn't it.

'I'll be there in five minutes. I've things to do.'

Aidan nodded. She'd given him enough to satisfy whoever it was. He ran off, the door crashing shut behind him.

Nell turned back a page. The footsteps were getting nearer, a good feeling, that almost-fear. Marianne would not look but knew he was there. He would be smiling, waiting for her to stand up, take his outstretched hand.

She rolled on to her side, made herself small, pulling up her right heel. She pushed it against the bit that tingled.

She'd tell Father Rogers like last time. He only gave her three Hail Marys. Everything was quiet – the beady eyes of the seagull watching her through the window in the roof.

8

The phone rang at four am. Liam fumbled into his dressing gown, Mrs Drummond was in trouble. They hadn't wanted to disturb the doctor but the midwife was unhappy. He knew the evening before that labour might start early; should have called on the house rather than driving off to buy seedlings from the market garden near the new reservoir.

Elsie Drummond had five children already; they were all awake, clustered round the staircase, for once quiet. The midwife was typical of those from Queens, knowing well what she was about but wanting to make sure. Indeed the baby was in a little distress, needed forceps, so he pulled the sixth Drummond into the world and stitched the mother.

Liam stood with the husband on the front step and they watched another summer morning begin with the whir of the milk-float, crash of bottles. Mr Drummond was a grey, washed-out man who could have been any age. He delivered coal, black dust was etched into his skin. Both of them were too tired to chat but they exchanged necessary small talk about weather. Neither mentioned the robbery from a mail-train a few days before, which was of consuming interest to Mrs Lemon. She proclaimed her disbelief through the hatch from the dispensary to anyone in the waiting room as she collected urine samples, handed over the empty bottles or packets of pills. 'Bashing that poor man with an iron bar, leaving him for dead, how could they?'

Both men stared silently at the plants that were flourishing in the Drummond's tiny front garden.

Liam was trimming the grass edge around St James when Sister Anne crouched beside him, holding out a cup of stewed unsweetened tea. 'Sister Raphael is getting anxious, Doctor.'

'She can't manage on her own.'

'But it's all going.'

'That's not certain, Sister.'

'That is certain.'

He pushed himself to his feet. He'd forgotten his work-coat, tried to dust the soil from his good trousers. The nun walked with him as he took his tea up and down the paths. He didn't mind. She'd become an almost soothing companion.

The intensity of lilac merged into jasmine. He'd have to make his diagram clearer. Some grottoes had been built into semi-circles of rock like caves, a few were set high on ivy-covered mounds. Most were not visible until you fell over them; several hidden down steep steps. He liked the cool dark of those few so far below ground they were like crypts – one in particular, the simple statue of the Virgin hidden in the far corner.

Anne seemed in her own world.

'There is a plan,' he said.

'Does it matter? Now you've almost cleared the brambles, it's even more treacherous – children falling in holes. Thank goodness we're leaving.'

'It's a criminal waste of such beauty.'

'Yes, it is. But come and see the new school. We've playing fields, tennis courts, new labs, heating that works, a music centre.'

What would they do with the nuns' graveyard?

Once she'd left, Liam cleared the steps up to a grotto with a Child Jesus set into the wall. He ignored the chipped plaster doll with its pinked-up lips and cheeks. Some of these focuses of prayer had been neglected for years, with a sense of achievement he uncovered evidence – eventually each will make part of the whole.

It was hard work. He stretched himself flat on the grass, foxgloves and purple irises towering above his head, a heady smell from climbing roses. After a short rest he'd do some weeding. The sky instead of town-dusty was blue and deep. It was vibrating. Birdsong from the rowans circled his head, he felt light-headed and drowsy. Someone was close to him, breathing. A child's breath. He kept his eyes shut. It was the same too-hot noisy breath of a baby, a cheek a millimetre from his. Like Claire when she was tiny, and he'd rest his head beside her when she was sleeping.

Nothing. No one. How bloody stupid. He crouched again and examined the ground. Had his daughter during that first term, that term when she was just five, come down here – even though told not to – and slept?

Evening surgery was quiet. In a minute Mrs Lemon would bring in letters and prescriptions for signing. Liam needed a few more details for his latest map, collected crayons from Rory's bedroom to give his plans colour.

'It's all d. and v. and kaolin and morph. tonight, Doctor. You'll be glad when they're back for good, going down with flu.'

'You know about gardening, Mrs Lemon. What flower is closest to this?'

She took his scrap of paper with its splodges of purple, no doubt thinking of the unloved stretch of concrete, narrow border of tired bedding plants that surrounded the practice, a border that seemed to occupy all of a gardener's time for four hours a week.

'You want Arthur?'

'It's not for here.'

'I'll ask Mr Lemon.'

She brought in the list of visits the next morning without mentioning any purple plants and without repeating Mr Lemon's certain comment that heat was getting to that young doctor, better cure yourself before you start on others. Mrs M had been just as discouraging. There was a nursery out on the Fainsthorpe road that might be more helpful; Liam penned it in for the end of his rounds.

Mary Drummond was up and about, the baby feeding well and sleeping better than he and Connie had ever managed. She gave him some cuttings.

'It's a bit late for all this, Doctor,' said the man at the nursery, packing up the box of plants, ringing up the cheque. 'No benefit until next year.'

That would be fine.

'No one will thank you,' Sister Anne said as she brought over a mug of warmish tea. 'A waste of effort. Good money on the foundations of shops and building societies.'

'There's one thing, Sister.'

A couple of times, he'd found the back gate locked; had rung at the front of the school until some strange nun, emanating disapproval, followed him and his plants through the building and across the playground.

'We'll leave the gate open. You can't mean to do Sundays?'

'I'll come after Mass. And I'd like to have a bonfire.'

The gate was left open; Raphael, usually nowhere to be seen and no doubt still furious from the time he was her doctor, gave instructions to the convent kitchen about her sugar. His ban on sweets meant that her sole pleasure was sitting in one of the alcoves, eating biscuits borrowed from the pantry.

There were signs of progress. Now that he'd managed to burn the piles of rubbish, it was looking neater, annoying when Sister Anne appeared early one evening. 'Are you going to the family?'

'Soon,' said Liam.

'Your partner will take over our care?' Her thin face looked amused as if she knew this was a game. 'I'm not sentimental, Doctor. There's nothing in any of this when the spirit's moved on.'

'So you send these spirits on their way?'

'Claire is not here.'

The weekend before, he'd fought his way around the grottoes with Mr Drummond who had been a gardener before humping bags of coal; the man had good ideas on what could be saved and what cut away. They'd done a map of future planting. Raphael once muttered that she liked the Queen of Heaven high on a slope overlooking the old netball court. Liam would put in bulbs for next spring, and nicotinia, lemon verbena.

The statue's sanctimonious smile irritated him. What kept these women going, all these Catholic women, his dead mother, his aunts? Cover their heads, keep clear of the altar, off to moan to the Mother of all, the Virgin, their ally.

Gerry was nagging. 'You need a holiday, Liam.'

Liam had nodded, went back to his drawing.

When he arrived the next lunchtime, he could hear Sister Anne before seeing her. She was humming, a few straggling weeds in her hand, no apron; she must have wiped her hands on her habit, there were smears of mud.

He avoided her, went across to the box-hedge that circled Blessed Margaret, tucked in some lily of the valley. A plea to the convent's founder, let them flower next spring, defy the nuns. He'd put irises at the statue's feet, left the grass long so the ground quivered beneath her.

'Are you not needed at the surgery, Doctor?' Anne was behind him. Did they think he was neglecting his patients? 'Sister Jude would like to see you.'

Liam was packing up when the elderly nun appeared from the main building. He ran towards her. 'I would have come, Sister. How are you?'

'Fighting fit. I was in Lower Kindergarten while it's still a classroom. Claire was happy there.'

No point telling Jude what his daughter had said about standing in the corner for hours as punishment. He helped the old woman up the steps towards the hydrangea that edged the Pieta. He'd collected rusty nails and the petals were turning blue from the salmon-pink he loathed. 'Can you make it to Blessed Margaret? There's a comfortable seat.'

'Indeed, I can.'

The bench was looking out at rhododendrons. 'We'd come when those were in blossom,' she said. 'Sit and admire.'

She brushed her palm along a group of tiger lilies, collecting the orange pollen. 'I love these, but a sad flower, aren't they?'

Were they? They were so vivid.

'Now that Connie and Rory are away the house must be nothing,' Jude continued. 'We know that as teachers. Once the children are off, there's no school left. Just buildings.'

'This is not just buildings.'

'Whatever, Liam, isn't it peaceful? But it's enough now. Go to your family.'

9

Aidan hid himself in the hen-shed with the chickens. It was very dark. He liked dragging his fingers through the sticky straw on the wide shelves where the hens slept. He did it carefully, waiting for his hand to reach a smooth shell. He would hunt for eggs to help Mrs Pee. First he checked everywhere, without touching anything. Then he sifted through the straw. When he was lucky and found one still warm, he knew to be really, really gentle. There were none.

Everyone had gone for a swim. He didn't want to. The water was cold and full of salt and got in his mouth and up his nose. He'd slipped away and no one had seen him. Everyone in the house was in a bad mood. Except Mrs Pee. She never seemed to get cross like his mother and Aunt Connie.

This shed was the best place, the smell was sweet like Mrs Pee's compost. Not like the outside toilet, which was horrible. The hens made a soft clicking noise as they scrabbled around. The sun came through gaps in the wooden boards, dust bobbing around in the stripes of light.

'Same as the rest of this place, Jerry built,' his father had said.

Aidan wanted to ask what that meant but his father only stayed one day. 'Soon,' Dad promised. 'When I can get away from the boils and fevers.'

The light made yellow puddles on the wooden shelves, the piles of straw. It lit up the red and brown feathers of the hens as they strutted and pecked. It lit up their bald bottoms.

Mrs Pee had said something about shaving their bottoms. Some disease. Mum said that was a ridiculous thing to do. Aunt Connie had carried on smoking a cigarette, said nothing.

Aidan wasn't scared. Even when the hens got near, even when they did that clucking sound more loudly and pecked the ground around his sandals.

Someone was coming across the yard clanging a bucket. He tried not to breathe. 'So you are here, Aidan.'

Aunt Connie was smiling at him through the top-half of the door. She had pulled her long black hair into a pony tail. It made her face look tight.

'Will you come for a walk, darling?'

She had food in her pail and she tossed it around on the ground outside and the hens dived in.

'They've kidnapped Rory.'

Then why was she smiling?

'Don't look so shocked. Your mum took him with the others. He's been so grizzly.'

She dumped the empty bucket in the middle of the yard. He could hear his mother: 'Exactly placed for someone to trip over.'

Aunt Connie had borrowed Mrs Pee's Wellingtons and they were too big. She made a slopping noise as they walked up the path. Whenever he got stuck in the sand, Aunt Connie hauled him free. She smelt of strawberries, was walking very fast.

'Where are we going?'

'To visit a man about a dog.'

Dad told them that whenever he stopped the car, went into a pub. Colum always said Dad had gone to use the toilet. If Aunt Connie wanted the toilet she could have gone before they left.

He knew very well that they were not going to see any man. And not see any dog.

'Have you decided on your name for confirmation, Aidan?'

'I want Simeon. But Mum says pick someone simpler.'

'Simeon sounds pretty straightforward to me,' said Aunt Connie. 'Tell me about him.'

'He stood on a pillar and people came from miles away and prayed. He didn't eat. Ever.'

'That does seem extreme.'

Aidan didn't want to talk about his confirmation. He wanted to talk about Claire and why she was dead. But no one was allowed to say anything. Nell told him that he must not ever mention Claire's name. The grown-ups had forbidden it and would only get upset.

Last summer he and Claire had played together all the time, hiding, jumping out, giving everyone shocks. 'Little monkeys, I nearly had a heart attack,' Aunt Connie would groan. When they'd ambushed his mother, she'd smacked them both.

They had reached the road. Aunt Connie was striding out, still gripping his hand, he had to mix running with walking to keep up. His aunt had got fat since last summer. Her skirt was too tight and the zip didn't do up. Yet she still managed to go very fast. Aidan had tried very hard to avoid looking at her stomach. Nell said she was big like that because Claire had died. The baby was instead. He wasn't sure what Nell meant but knew it was rude to stare.

'What would you think, Aidan, if I came and stayed with you after the holiday?'

'That would be nice.'

'Good. I could come to your confirmation. I think anyway it's mandatory for a godmother. Make sure sponsors do a good job.'

He wasn't sure if he wanted her standing at the front of the church. The other children were not kind, they would stare at her and tell him how fat she was. They'd laugh and think they were very funny. 'Will Rory come as well?'

'Yes, of course.'

'And Uncle Liam?'

Aunt Connie was checking a piece of paper she'd taken from her smock pocket. 'Here we are.' She pushed open the gate. 'Not Uncle Liam. He has to see to his patients, otherwise who will look after them and make them better?'

The front door was opened by a really fat man. Much fatter than Aunt Connie.

'Sorry to bother you. This is Aidan Ryan, I'm Connie Dillon. Mrs Podrowski sent us.'

'Come in, come in. You're very welcome. We've our hands full.'

His aunt leant over and pulled off her boots. She had to put one hand on the wall for support. Aidan didn't know if he should help. She didn't expect him to take off his sandals, which was good because the buckles were stiff. She had no socks.

The man took them down a narrow passage to a scullery at the back. It was white-washed. It was important to keep away from the walls. The man had white all down the sleeves of his pullover. But his pullover was already filthy.

There was a dog – there were also five puppies.

'Go ahead, sonny,' said the fat man.

Aidan picked up one and cuddled it although it was wriggling. It was white and fluffy, kept trying to get away.

Aunt Connie was hugging another. Her bare feet were quite dirty. Her face was red. Mum went red like that when she was crying. The man had brought Aunt Connie a stool and she was balancing her bottom on it.

'It's not very practical is it, a dog, Aidan?' she said as she hiccoughed. He tried not to look. She made him feel prickly all over. Seeing her face all blotchy like that, Aidan couldn't breathe.

'I would love a puppy.'

'But your mum wouldn't.'

The man let them stay for ages, holding and admiring all five equally. It was important to make sure that none were left out. The mother dog watched. She didn't seem bothered.

'Do you think they have names?' he asked his aunt.

Aidan now knew for sure she was crying.

After a bit, she said: 'We'll ask.'

They didn't have names. The man said: 'That's up to whoever keeps them.'

They wouldn't be taking any home. They were just here to give the puppies a cuddle. After a while, the man brought tea and biscuits. They were nice ones with jam inside. Aunt Connie didn't notice he'd eaten them all. She didn't even seem hungry. The scullery had shelves and shelves of jams and jars with stuff inside them. It smelt of rotting apples and dog.

One really small puppy was very cuddly. It didn't seem to want any biscuit. Aidan put it back with the mother in the large wicker basket. The tiny dog looked at him with great brown eyes.

He wanted to cry too.

'Maybe we should go, Aidan,' said his aunt.

She half-carried him, gripping him round the waist, swinging him from side to side, back down the passage-way. She was holding him as if he were a puppy but he was much too heavy. He tried not to wriggle.

The man didn't seem surprised that they weren't taking any. 'Come back, whenever you like,' he shouted from the front door.

This time his aunt walked slowly. She was holding her back and dragging her feet. She was so slow he had to run ahead, back to her, then do circles. He made sure to kick into the ditch any of the rocks or pebbles in her way.

10

As he drove, Liam tried to remember the Yeats poem he'd read to Connie when they'd first met, *He Wishes for the Cloths of Heaven*. He had that second-hand or more likely eighth-hand MG, constantly needing work. The spare parts he'd bought with money made in summer jobs, coming over to the canning factories not far from where he was driving now. *Tread softly because you tread on my dreams*. He had walked all over hers.

He stopped for petrol near Kings Lynn, chatted to the man servicing a Jaguar. Their conversation drifted into silence. 'What are you waiting for, Sir? The jams'll be worse later.'

After driving through Cromer, he passed the Red Lion, could see the cluster of houses that made up Tottingford. Mrs P's bed and breakfast was top heavy with various extensions. The wood was weather stained, needed painting and patching.

All the doors and windows had been left open in the misguided hope that this would eradicate the smell of frying bacon. Connie's room he found easily – Connie had always been untidy, pyjamas, swim suits, T-shirts were rolled in a mess. The only relatively calm area was Rory's bed, white sheets folded over the pink blanket. Talcum powder had been spilt on the orange rag-rug, he shook it out of the window. A distress flare? The sun was shining but there was a sharp wind, his face was already gritty with sand. He disentangled sheets from blankets, made up the main bed with hospital corners. Did she let Rory sleep with her? He leant over, smelt Rory's sheets – no warm boy-body, just soap powder.

Why not lie in Connie's smell, roll in Connie's traces? Instead, he took off his tie, put it in his trouser pocket then shook out her red check dress, hung it in the wardrobe next to her raincoat; the coat buttons were stretched from Rory and Claire, a couple working loose. Everywhere now he could smell her black rose talc.

On the table was a pile of detective stories, a knife and plate smeared with butter. Mrs P hated it when things were taken from her dining room. He pulled up a chair to the window, lit a cigarette, could see the wide curve of the bay, a few fishing boats. He even thought he could hear Connie or Pat yelling. Birds wheeled over and around the house cawing and screaming.

'Anyone up there?' Mrs P raising her voice for once.

Taking one last look at the order he'd created, he ran down, carried the tray with tea into the garden.

'I saw the car,' she said.

Liam pulled out her chair. Mrs Podrowski was the sort of woman you pulled out chairs for. Not really elderly, still middle-aged, but frail and powdered, not the sort comfortable with frying bacon and eggs. The garden looked wonderful.

'The lavender's a weed, the only thing that flourishes. I hate it, so sickly. Have you been dreadfully busy, Liam?'

'What compost do you use? Do you make your own?'

She led him past the overshot salad patch to a heap of muck and potato peelings between two gnarled apple trees. Pat had been doing chips; Connie never bothered peeling potatoes. 'If boiling them in the jackets is good enough for Mamma, it's good enough for me.'

'Pee here, Liam, whenever you like.'

Connie must be wrong, hardly top drawer.

'I thought of suggesting it to the boys,' said Mrs P. 'I'm not sure if it works before puberty, might get them into bad habits.'

'I know you hate it but the lavender seems to thrive.'

'Take all the cuttings you like and welcome, but don't blame me. Why delay? They're down on the beach beyond the dunes.'

He walked along the path that led at an angle from the house past a few other families camped out by their wind-breaks. Connie and Pat always insisted that it was too public to dump their things right in front of the house – one thing, at least, the sisters agreed on. The air was salt and fresh. Why had he been pottering around in the centre of a town when he could be here? It was almost as good as being back on the cliffs in Howth, but this horizon could go out for miles, Pat's children would be looking for cockles.

The woman and boy were a hundred yards ahead. Connie was lying in the foetal position, her head in a book, fingers playing through her long black hair. When he'd first met her in Dublin, he'd gone home after each date and dreamt about that hair.

She had let it down, only the end was plaited; she looked like a tinker. She had on a bikini under an open shirt, an old shirt of his that barely covered the swell of her belly. She was being roasted by the sun, but the sun liked her and she was already brown.

A trickle of sweat ran from Liam's collar. Connie was no doubt reading some trashy novel, only occasionally looking over to check on Rory. The boy kept struggling up from the sea, both hands clutching a bucket, water slopping on the sand. Lips tense, he poured whatever remained into the hole he'd dug. He'd stare down intently, too soon was upright, distraught. Connie was pretending to be reading, no doubt fed-up waiting for the child to get the plot.

She could at least help Rory dig another hole nearer the water, let the tide do the work. But there was something concentrated about his efforts; maybe she was right, leave him to it. At least he had a sun-hat covering that red hair. Rory had Liam's colouring, with the merest suspicion of sun, that impossibly pale skin would go scarlet and blister.

Connie had rolled over to toss the boy a towel and gone back to the novel she'd probably dug out from Mrs P's excuse for a library. Exactly the thing Connie's mother would read. Marie relied on a good bloodthirsty escape in the few odd moments she found for herself. Oscar Wilde was right, he should have thought twice having met the mother. Marie was a hard-working woman who covered for Connie and Pat's father, an easy-going doctor who drank. Marie combined being a puritan with a daily consumption of lurid novels. Everything she read was banned by the priests, had to be smuggled into Ireland by Pat or Connie.

Easy to imagine what Connie was reading. The business of the floosie soaked in alcohol/petrol and burned/drowned in the basement of the Brooklyn church/factory would eventually be solved, and all the other odd deaths that would happen on the way, solved by either Albie Duggs or Lennie O'Brien, if only he could make the fat widow give back the wallet she'd stolen.

How much more lively that Brooklyn or Bronx must seem to Connie, that New York, rather than this dull country, its grey people, grey government, this flat grey beach, the grass that cut as soon as looked at. Better those Bowery boarding houses than this one with its grease-congealed eggs, stale bread, inedible marge. How much more lively than the grey Midlands town where they'd settled – better lose yourself in fiction than remember the misery of the last eight months.

Why had she said she'd have an abortion?

Connie had phoned the clinic for the result as soon as they'd finished the morning patients. Mrs Lemon had left for home, an assistant receptionist tidying the surgeries. She must have heard. When Connie told him a few weeks later that she'd changed her mind, Liam had gone to the park to bawl his eyes out with relief.

He wanted to walk down now and join her – but she couldn't stand him.

A Morris Minor skidded to a halt on the sandy track; Pat got out, polka-dot summer skirt, Jackie Kennedy sunglasses, a scarf over her hair covering her curlers. She'd be furious that he'd caught her unprepared. Pat hauled out a basket, slammed shut the door. She didn't notice him skulking like a spy.

'Why won't Rory play cricket?' Pat yelled before disappearing behind the wind-break.

She reappeared carrying packs of ice-cream and a knife; settled on the rug, started to slice and wafer. On cue her three children straggled across the dunes, Aidan within yards of Liam's hiding place, whining at being left behind.

There was a plea for Neapolitan and groans there was too much vanilla. Pat meant well, Connie must be enormously irritating. The children finished quickly and raced off, leaving Rory lying in the sand making engine noises. Getting to his feet while Connie and Pat were distracted, Liam made his way through the dunes.

*

When Connie looked up from failing to make something tidy with the ripped ice-cream packets, Liam was looming over her.

'Jesus Christ! Sneaking up on us like that.'

Was he about to kiss her? Connie ducked, Liam tapped her on the head, then nodded at Pat. He looked hot, uncomfortable and was thinner than ever. She should get up and hug him but that didn't seem what he wanted. Or, for that matter, what she wanted.

'Where's your crowd off to in such a hurry, Pat?'

'Cockling. Good journey?'

'Mad traffic.'

It was only a few weeks but his red hair was thinning; could he not remove that jacket?

'I've never seen you this tanned, Liam,' said Pat. 'You've never been absconding to the South of France?'

'Take my shirt off and like a navvy it stops at my collar.'

Pat collected the mess of wrappers and went back to the wind-break, a rare bout of tact. Liam squatted down, touched the novel.

'Is it good?'

So they would make small talk and Liam wouldn't mention why he'd needed to be away this long. Connie wiped her hands on her shirt then held the book so he could admire the stretched-out blonde, pool of crimson round the naked body, the enlarged silver beauty of the blood-stained knife.

His arms were indeed brown and the freckles on his face and neck stood out like some Van Gogh had gone wild with a brush in a deranged moment. He was as thin as his shadow, a bit more muscle, he could be a farmer.

Liam looked over at Rory. 'Did you put sun tan on him?'

'No, of course not, I let him burn.'

She mustn't be irritable. 'We could go and get fish and chips.'

Liam said nothing.

'The children are being delightful, include Rory in all their games.'

Nothing. Had the man forgotten how to talk?

'But there's over-zealousness about their enthusiasm, a kind of manic encouragement, then they give up and run off. And of course too much of an age gap.'

'Have you and Pat been rushed off your feet?'

He hadn't even been listening. 'As you can see.'

She'd been right to send that letter. Red heads were meant to be passionate, instead he was more and more the dead salmon. Pat always said he'd be too quiet for her. Pat was right.

Her final year. The great rush to get married once she knew – she'd been no better than a child herself.

Liam walked over to Rory, straightened his sunhat. The boy expressed no interest in seeing his father, carried on with his bucket filling. Nothing she could do to help. A relief Rory wasn't whining.

Her husband looked like one of those men who came into Westport from the country on a Saturday night, hung out outside the dance hall. They wanted to belong and didn't, their sharp butts and scrawny old-man necks, resignation they'd never find a woman.

And Liam couldn't bear to look at her belly. Connie rolled her palms all around and over it, so smooth. They thought she'd gone for it deliberately. All she'd wanted was for Liam to obliterate her, desperate to have her body taken over. But not by this. Oh, to abandon it this second, leave this great boat of a pregnancy.

Pat broke the silence by appearing with cups and a thermos. 'Milk and sugar in already.'

'That's grand.' Connie leant over and took one.

Liam had found her desire unseemly but isn't that what those so-called celibate bastards in Rome wanted: women surrounded by grasping fingers of newly-minted Catholic toddlers? Anne insisted it was all change in Mother Church, priests marrying any day, but Anne was too trusting – they'd not give an inch.

Rory tottered up with another bucket, ice-cream smeared all over his face.

'Is your son daft or what?' said Connie.

'Nearly three, that's all, and he's got patience.'

'Then the spit of you, Liam,' said Pat.

When Pat had left to join her children, Liam said: 'I'll take him and leave you in peace.'

But he didn't move.

Rory had thrown down his bucket, was squatting beside it, his shoulders shaking. Fuck this, Liam could sort it. Connie was not going to play this game. No guilt.

She pulled herself to her feet.

Rory was trying to wriggle away. 'What a big boy.' Why always a battle? He used to be such a grand cuddle – she'd even make excuses when he was sleeping, pluck him from the cot, let the weight onto her shoulder.

She wrestled her son, still trying to free himself, to the sea's edge, roughly smeared water over his cheeks, rubbing off some of the ice-cream and sand. Once released he allowed her to help dig. Two minutes later and Rory had lost interest in his newly efficient hole, was rolling around, playing trains.

Liam looked tired. It had been as bad for him; they'd shared the house like ghosts, unable to reach each other except with the lights off, their bodies unhooked from their brains. Anne, of all unlikely people, was the only one Connie could talk to. Liam had Gerry, but Gerry loathed Connie, considered her unstable: a failure as wife, mother, doctor, and he never forgot to make it clear. Well, Gerry was right, she had been deranged, was still deranged.

A relief to watch Liam swinging his still-ice-creamy son in the air. Rory looked away, not catching his father's eye, studied his own podgy fingers, was clearly relieved when restored to the ground. So it wasn't just her. Liam brushed-off sand from his son's shorts and T-shirt, raked it out of the boy's hair, replaced the sun-hat.

She put aside her book.

'Go ahead, Con, finish it. I'll sit here.'

'It's the denouement. Will they get the right one?'

'Probably not,' said Liam.

Well that was more his old self.

'You got my last letter?'

He reached over to touch her bump and Connie shifted away. 'You've sand everywhere, Con. Get your hair cut, it'd be easier.'

'Indeed I could and a nice perm from Monsieur Daniel in Cromer and look like everyone else.'

'I did read your letter.'

And as usual said nothing. The effort to describe her feelings: her suggestion they might separate for a bit, that she stay away until the baby was born then think again – all she got was silence.

'Don't you give a fecking damn, Liam?'

It was the same when she resigned from the practice. Gerry, of course, had been delighted, never wanted a woman doctor in the first place. Mrs Citric over the moon. At first Liam had kept her up-to-date with patients then he'd stopped, must have thought she couldn't care. But she did care, why had she not encouraged him?

Ah well, spilt milk now.

Liam took off his shoes, then tugged the reluctant Rory to his feet. 'Let's leave your mother in peace.'

Rory pulled himself free and ran back towards her, bashing into her stomach.

'Careful!' Connie pushed him off. 'Too rough.'

Her son stumbled away. Connie held out her arms but was too late, the boy was racing up the beach, kicking up sand. If only she could forget so quickly.

Liam half-jogged in pursuit, both running in exactly the same half-baked fashion. All Rory had wanted was a normal, loving cuddle. Claire would have leapt at her in a similar way, sinking in. Sitting on the floor sorting socks or darning and Claire would climb on her back, beg to be carried around.

The foetus was kicking. She picked up a few pebbles, skimmed them over the water; she'd lost her knack. If Liam couldn't even discuss this, she'd have to decide where to go and with what money? Stay here? Suffer the fried eggs and salt wind or – heaven help her – Newcastle with Pat? Fried eggs were too expensive an option, but to live with Pat and her family? They'd rip each other apart and Dermot would have none of it.

Her pebble skimming was getting better, one flat stone did three lifts before sinking. At least to get angry quickly, over with fast, was preferable to Pat's slow and lethal embers. Live with them? And Connie couldn't go alone, she'd have to take Rory. Or would she leave Rory with Liam to survive on Mrs McInerney's salads?

'So healthy, Mrs Dillon,' Mrs M would say, standing at the sink tearing a lettuce to shreds.

And after the baby, what then? Connie skimmed a last pebble

then lay back in the sand, watched the clouds drifting across. She could have taught Claire to skim stones, Liam was useless at it.

She'd have been better off with someone like Dermot. He might be pompous, but was physically there; he did take part in life. Pat and the children were happy. And none of them had died.

She could always go to Ireland. Go back to Westport, face the muttering and gossip? Out of the question, in that God-forsaken part of the world having a child die was a contagious disease.

'What dreadful wickedness were they up to?' Neighbours would keep well away. 'What was the Lord thinking?'

Last summer, the Bolands had thrown rotten spuds at Rory and Claire, Rory had been barely walking. They did the same when Pat brought her crowd over, but Pat's lot gave as good as they got. Rotten spuds for an English accent – what would they do now?

Oh, but the excitement there'd be: Mamma, in her Sunday outfit, standing at the window for hours, rolling rosary beads through her fingers, jumping every time she heard a car. She'd have spent days baking, ordering whatever benighted skivvy was helping in the kitchen to check again the beds were aired. The table already set with the gold-rimmed crockery waiting for sweet cake, scones, plates of ham. Papa brushed into his best suit, the pack of cigarettes removed from his pocket, tumbler from his hand.

Mamma would barely let them in the door while she'd listed all she'd prepared. After tea, Papa would take Liam to the sitting-room for a whiskey and monologue about horses, or patients. Papa never talked to Connie about work, she might as well be a farmer for all he ever mentioned medicine. No, the women and children stayed in the kitchen, the black kettle primed on the range.

And by the time Papa and Liam joined them, it would be intolerable. An incapacitating blend of claustrophobia and guilt after Mamma was released of the details of how she was flattened by the constant demands: patients not paying bills, petty-minded aunts and cousins, Papa drinking, gambling, or away fishing – the practice gone to pot.

'Will you hold the fort?' Papa would say. Mamma spent all her life either at Mass or holding the fort.

Connie would then let it out on Liam, who tried to be sympathetic. As they negotiated the bumps of the feather mattress, he'd listen and make reassuring sounds. But it was beyond his understanding. This was what women did, grumble, then get on with it. Liam was much happier talking medicine.

No surprise there'd been little enthusiasm for a visit. The last thing Mamma would relish was a deranged and pregnant daughter, Rory climbing all over the furniture, priests dropping in and neighbours keeping away – because of the misfortune.

Pat had said that Mamma was missing them but didn't want Pat turning up, leaving Connie behind.

'Easier that we all skip this year. Instead of two weeks we'll spend the whole summer with Mrs P.'

Connie tried to lick the salt off her knees. She missed her mother, Mamma would make her feel better.

11

A small child was racing across the strand in Liam's direction, bursting with the pleasure of running: dark curly hair, arms outstretched, hooting with glee. As it came closer, a woman from one of the families ran over to claim her. It was not Claire.

Pat jumped when he touched her shoulder. 'Would you call out first, Liam? I was miles away.'

'Sorry.' He looked at the empty sea. 'You drowned the children?'

They stared at each other then Pat laughed. Liam bent quickly, fussed over Rory, he was incapable of conversation.

'I tried to get your young man to join us, he'd have none of it. No to cricket. No to cockles.'

Nell came running over and gave Rory a spade, hauled him off to join the others.

'Have you been busy?' said Pat.

'The usual.'

She was waiting for more conversation.

'One patient since the beginning,' said Liam. 'A good man, five children, broke his back patching someone's roof as a favour. Otherwise a young girl, leukaemia, parents distraught. The usual seaside stomachs, some even needed to go to the General, a couple I thought we'd lose. What possessed us to be family doctors?'

'There's a sewage outlet a quarter a mile towards Cromer; we've told the children to keep well away. I wanted Connie to speak to the powers that be. She'd have none of it. I'd do it myself but Dermot has the right gravitas for those Norfolk clerks.'

Indeed, Dermot would not be dithering here, worrying about his children getting cold, he'd be kicking them under the waves. Yet they'd sent Colum away to prep school, sending him off as if distance would keep him alive.

'Is Colum alright?'

'Ah, she's much better, barely drinking. And you, Liam?'

'I meant Colum's new school.'

'Ah, he's loving it. What's going on? We expected you days ago.'

There was a sharp wind; the children only wearing shorts as they traced their nets over the wet strand. Rory was being very irritating, had wandered back.

'Come on, young man, let's join that load of ruffians.'

But Rory wanted Connie; Pat offered to take him to the house. Rory handed over his spade reluctantly as if expecting his father to wilfully throw it in the water or dump it in a rock pool.

The children greeted Liam with more enthusiasm than he deserved – he was always forgetting their names and they grew so fast. He narrowed his focus away from the disappearing figures of Pat and Rory, down to the glistening brown sand, the worm trails, dead crabs, shells. He started making holes to show he was serious.

Apart from Colum, who was twelve, there was Nell, aged ten, and Aidan, seven. The sort of family he'd assumed he wanted. A big detached house, dinner at the club, golf, bridge, summers spent hiking or fishing in Kerry, the occasional day of shooting. He could be their father: four intent figures sweeping the water line with the occasional whoop of success, and gritty, salty, inedible cockles for supper. How did other people do it?

Colum came to check if Liam needed a bucket. The boy stared through wire-framed spectacles at his uncle's naked feet settling into the foot-shaped pools of water as if expecting piles of booty.

'I'm sorry, Colum, I'm not very good at this.'

'That's ok. It's been an awful year for cockles. Mrs P says the fishing is down as well, boats coming back empty. Strange being here, isn't it, without Claire?'

It was that ice-wind, good that Liam had kept on his jacket. They both watched two trawlers set off on their apparently fruitless mission. 'Yes, it is strange.'

Whenever Claire fell out with Aidan, she'd follow Colum around, pushing in to make sure she sat next to him at the table. Colum listened patiently to her constant chatter. As soon as she and Aidan made it up, Colum was abandoned – last summer must seem an age.

Colum ran back, joined the others. There were a few arguments and fewer cockles, but it was more peaceful than anywhere else.

'We're going for a dip, Uncle Liam, will you come?' said Nell.

Aidan had thrown down his net, was looking furious.

*

Aidan was bored and he was cold.

'You not going in?' said Uncle Liam. Aidan shook his head.

'The boy won't risk being turned to ice.' His uncle was smiling, so it must be all right. 'Let's take their things, go back to the warm.'

Mrs Pee, Aunt Connie and his mum were on the veranda. They stopped talking, looked at Uncle Liam with his hands full of wet shorts – nets and spades tucked under his arm – as if they didn't know him.

'Don't you reckon, Aidan? That lot are staring as if we've some disease. Will they tell us the prognosis?'

They were drinking brown stuff in tiny glasses, even Mrs Pee.

'I'll put these on the washing machine,' said Uncle Liam.

Aunt Connie pulled Aidan on to her knee. There wasn't much room and her bump felt hard.

'You think we'll put the children back in wet things,' she said when Uncle Liam returned. He didn't answer, sat behind them holding out his arms as if they were still full of clothes.

'We know it's too early,' said his mother. 'Rory's having a nap. Aidan, run and get yourself some Tizer.'

Aidan didn't want Tizer. He slid down. His mother poured

another glass and Uncle Liam drank it very quickly and they all looked oddly at Aunt Connie who had reached for the bottle.

She was wearing the smock Aidan had seen his mother wear when she painted the bathroom. Mum was always angry when she had a paint-brush in her hand. It looked different on Aunt Connie but still ugly. Aunt Connie used to be pretty until she got fat.

'Right, Aidan,' said his uncle. 'Let's go for that walk you promised.' Aidan had never promised any walk. As they reached the road, his uncle asked: 'What are you thinking about?'

He'd been thinking about visiting the puppies. 'About that dress Aunt Connie was wearing.'

'Awful, isn't it? She's better off using my old shirts. She's not showing much so why rush into those ugly clothes?'

But his aunt had been showing lots. The smock didn't cover the skirt which came to above her knees and she had left the zip open. Aidan could see the inside of her thighs. Aunt Connie always spread out her legs, even though she could trip up people. He had to find somewhere else to look whenever she talked to him.

His uncle kept scuffing the gravel with his shoes. The shoes were brown leather. They looked like best and were already wet with sea water – they would be ruined. Aidan had lost his sandals again and his plimsolls were Nell's old ones, holes in the canvas over the big toes.

They were walking in the same direction as with Aunt Connie.

'I have to go back.' Uncle Liam had stopped suddenly. 'Your aunt sent me a list – clothes, linen, heaven knows what. Mrs M packed it. Do you remember Mrs M?'

There was a round woman who smelled of uncooked pastry.

'Will you come and help? No, forget I said that. Carry on with the walk; tell me later if you see anything surprising. Try and spot an adventure.'

His uncle walked back down the road, he was going quickly.

Aidan followed as far as the slope to the house and hid behind the wall. Uncle Liam took a big box from the boot. Why did Aunt Connie need those things? As his uncle carried it inside, there was laughter from the veranda.

What Aidan would have liked was to be swung on his mother's shoulders, or even Uncle Liam's, to be treated like they now spoilt Rory. Rory didn't even enjoy it. Would Aidan get into trouble if he visited the puppies? The man had been funny looking.

It was late in the afternoon, no one around. Only one bus a day and that came after lunch. Someone was mowing but that didn't count as an adventure. He should explore Mr Bronks's boatyard. Aunt Connie was always saying Mr Bronks was a smuggler.

Once Aidan turned the corner to the yard, he could hear the singing of the masts. Clank-clanking that never stopped. His father said they were sirens trapped in the wrecked hulls. They lured in lost souls. Aunt Connie said that was silly and not to scare the poor boy. They were only the tops of the masts for the sails. Nell said sirens were like fog-horns and meant an emergency.

There was an old concrete tower by the sheds where Aidan had climbed with Nell to look back at the house and the sea. It would be an adventure to do it alone. A boat upside down was half-painted but no one was around. The steps were crumbling and slippery but he was careful. And if he stretched, he could just see over the wall. No one was walking down the road from the ford. What day was it? Uncle Liam came, so it was Saturday, everyone was in town shopping.

Nell and Colum were trailing long ribbons of seaweed back to the house. They didn't know he was looking. Rory had woken up, was running to join them. Nell and Colum looped Rory between them. He was such a whingeing baby but now he was laughing. Up in the air and back they scooped him, time after time.

'You show an infinity of patience,' Mum had said to Aunt

Connie. His aunt had just arrived and was throwing Aidan in the air. Why did his parents no longer loop his arms and swing him?

He leant forward to see if a car was coming. Bam! Something sharp hit the side of his head – everything went dark and starry. It hurt.

Once he felt less like being sick, he touched his hair. His fingers were red. He was bleeding. This couldn't be Uncle Liam playing tricks. His heart was thumping. All he could see was moss on the concrete wall and slime and seaweed and shells all over the floor and a dead fish in the corner. There was giggling from below – he was trapped. This was a siege. He would die.

A long silence. Eventually Aidan made himself shuffle over, look down the stairs. He couldn't see anything. He waited a few moments then peeped over the bit of wall that was crumbling away. He felt sick again. Two older boys were searching the ground for stones. Who were they and where was Mr Bronks? If he told anyone about this, Nell would say he was making it up.

It was beginning to rain. If he stayed very still, kicked anyone who tried to get up the steps, he'd be all right. But they were so much bigger than him. If they did try to come up, he'd yell and scream and make a lot of noise. Maybe the rain would send them back to the council estate. They came from there because Mum said it was full of rough boys and to stay well away.

It was too quiet. Aidan tried to be patient but couldn't and took another look. Two big boys – looking straight at him.

12

Nell didn't want to get up. It was a Sunday. Like all Sundays with Mrs Podrowski, they had breakfast early. Everyone was sleepy and cross and no one ate anything except Aidan who was always hungry. Then Mrs P went to spend the day with her brother in Framlingham. No one had seen this brother. She'd overheard her mother and Aunt Connie giggling about him as if a brother was something funny.

Normally everyone went to eleven o'clock Mass in Cromer but Aidan claimed that his head hurt after being attacked yesterday. Uncle Liam said that he would wait with Aidan for Dermot.

'Dermot's a big boy. He'll find us.' Aunt Connie sounded sharp.

'I'm not feeling very well either,' said Nell.

They all stared. No one said anything. They were all in a mood. Normally it was Mum who said: 'Mass is compulsory, end of discussion'. No way would Mum let her. It would be a sin, an over-my-dead-body matter. Nell hated Mass – it went on for hours.

After rescuing Aidan from those hooligans, they knew she was in a strong position. 'My forehead is burning. And throbbing.'

'Mmm, Nell,' said Uncle Liam. 'Quite a rescue. When I mentioned adventures, I didn't think of Aidan being ambushed by a mob of gangsters.'

Uncle Liam was teasing, but Nell was saying nothing. She'd guessed Aidan would go to the boatyard. And the first person she'd seen was Alexander hopping around an obstacle course of stones with a friend of his she'd never seen before, the boy must be staying with the Lloyds. It was the perfect excuse to speak to Alex, but before she could say anything, he had flicked his head at the concrete tower. 'Your kid brother's up there. He won't join us.'

Success. The others had gone to Cromer, Mum looking very cross. Uncle Liam put Aidan in the back of the car. It was a treat to sit in the front – at last her uncle had come for his holiday. Mum said that because of him not turning up, Aunt Connie had been impossible.

'You're impossible, Connie,' Mum would say ten times a day.

Aidan still had a large plaster on his head, which was silly. He'd barely a scratch. He was attention-seeking but everyone cooed and oohed and Aunt Connie made a great fuss. It had been so embarrassing, climbing down from the tower pulling Aidan, bawling his eyes out. The boys had pretended not to look.

What a pity she hadn't known about Mass when she woke up, she could have enjoyed not going for longer. She'd heard Mum tell Dad that Uncle Liam always skipped it when he was alone, which was no example to set, having children and being the local doctor and patients expecting to see you.

They left the car at the end of the houses and walked to the ford. Nell was the first to spot their father's Jaguar coming down the narrow road.

'A welcome committee, how grand. Is it not passable?' Dad looked from the car window at the dried-out river bed.

'We're taking a walk,' said Uncle Liam. 'They're all at church.'

'Without these two? The children given up their faith already? And what's this young dandy sporting on his head?'

They looked at Aidan who blushed.

'Well, I'll join you in your perambulations.'

He parked so another car could only just squeeze through. Uncle Liam must want him to move but her father was already out and Aidan running over to hug his legs. Nell stayed where she was, she was too old for hugging. Her father pulled free and bounded ahead of them, banging his arms around his chest.

'He's a body released. That man is always on stage,' said her uncle. It wasn't clear what he meant but it sounded a good thing.

Her father picked up Aidan, who was beginning to whinge,

swirled him round. 'Look at your uncle, boyo. Thinner, I'm a deal fatter, a right dicey pair.'

'And you're red in the face and breathless,' Uncle Liam replied.

'Listen to the injustice, and I barely arrived from saving lives. Has Pat been nagging? Why didn't we get ourselves a couple of librarians, Liam? Nice quiet girls who'd never mention blood pressure, who'd tell us at decent intervals they loved us and we were all right – that's what we needed.'

He'd found a couple of dead branches, was showing Aidan how to swipe the hedge to shake out pheasants. They were following the narrow track that ran beside the river.

'That's a pale imitation of water. Uncle Liam and I should be sitting by the Moy or Shannon, fishing.'

One minute the two seemed cross with each other, then were best friends. Her mother said they'd known each other since school. Dad was in the Seniors and told to look after a new boy, Liam. When Nell asked why they were sent away, her mother had laughed. 'Why indeed? But we all were. Ah, it was thought necessary. And of course, your Uncle Liam had no mother, his father wanted the best.'

Nell ran up to be closer.

'Are you busy at work, Liam, or still skiving off gardening?'

'Who's been talking?'

Instead of answering, her father put his arm round Uncle Liam's shoulder. Uncle Liam was much taller so it looked funny.

'Doesn't medicine drive you mad, Dermot? The patients, the day-in-out routine, and the horrors that you've missed something.'

'Life and death, Liam – that's the bottom of it.'

Aidan made a face and tugged at Nell to come with him. He'd stuck his plaster in the pocket of his shorts. At least he looked less stupid. She pushed him away and he went to look for frogs.

'We were surprised that time we were down with you, that you'd gone for a baby so quickly.'

What did he mean? Went for a baby? As if it was in the grocers.

'Connie thought it might help. And then she didn't.'

'Hah, we're all good Catholics.'

'Connie is not that,' said Uncle Liam. 'She's nothing like Pat.'

What had that to do with babies? Her father was kicking stones along the road. They were like the ones Claire had wanted Nell to paint last summer. She'd been quite bossy, Claire, but you're not meant to criticise people who are dead.

'It's not hard. All we're asked is doze in a pew an hour a week.'

'Don't pretend to be the cynic, Dermot.'

'It's the God's truth. Pat counts her blessings I'm civil to the bishop, kiss his ring, pour whiskey into the clergy. Her children get to decent schools; we don't have to drill in the morals or whatever.'

Nell dropped back, grabbed Aidan's hand. Her father had forgotten she and Aidan were with them, had started to talk about patients. Aunt Connie said that after all this, Uncle Liam did nothing but grumble about work. 'He'd be better doing research in a laboratory locked away from people, talking to test-tubes.'

All this meant Claire's death. Aidan pulled away, went back to hunting in the ditch.

'I wouldn't mind a beer and I'm starving,' said her father. 'Let's find the girls, get some lunch.'

He left that evening, Uncle Liam, next day. Nobody explained why her uncle only stayed two days when he was meant to be coming for two weeks. It wasn't because it rained.

'Sun doesn't suit Uncle Liam,' Mum had said. 'Weak skin.'

Nell had to find her aunt, Rory had cut himself on the edge of an open drawer. She went to look round Mr Bronk's yard. Mr Bronks came out in his dirty overalls: 'How about you and your mum joining me on a trip? I need to try out this little one.' He pointed to an ancient rowing boat. They would drown in minutes, Mr Bronks was a murderer. Nell shook her head.

'No, thank you.' She made sure she said it nicely.

Even if hadn't been a wreck, she would have said no. She didn't like boats. The ones they took to Ireland were noisy and everyone got sick. Except she liked when they had a proper breakfast; the waiters were kind and there were thick white serviettes. But that wasn't every time. This year they were not going.

Colum had asked why.

'Because we're not,' Mum had said. 'And that's the end of it.'

Nell stood in front of the Lloyds's bungalow. Should she knock? But it didn't seem likely that Aunt Connie would be there. Aunt Connie never spoke to anyone. She just read books with pictures of dead women on the covers.

Aunt Connie even said: 'I know no one in this place.'

And she said it as if that were a good thing. Anyway, there wasn't anyone at home. Nell went further along the road as far as the bus-stop. There was one bus a day which Mum said was pathetic. The road was boring. Only two old ladies chatting by the post-box. Maybe she should go a bit further, as far as the sweet shop. But she had no money, was meant to be looking for her aunt.

More sensible to go towards the beach. As Nell turned the corner to the path, she saw Alexander. He was lying on the sand by a row of posts talking excitedly to someone on his far side where the sand had heaped at a lower level. Maybe it was one of the girls from the estate – they were always around.

It was not too late to escape, go back the way she'd come, or along the beach in the opposite direction. She stood on the spot.

'You need anything?' Alexander yelled.

'I'm looking for my aunt.' Nell walked towards him.

Alexander had turned to speak to someone hidden. They were laughing. There were two of them, they stood up and one waved. It was Colum. The other was the strange boy who'd upset Aidan.

Colum waited for her to get closer.

'Aunt Connie has a bolt-hole beyond the tents.'

'That's miles away.'

'I think you should leave her alone.'

'Rory has cut himself. He wants her.'

'He'll live,' said Alex, and the three boys looked at each other and laughed.

Nell stormed past, hopefully they felt thoroughly ashamed.

Colum called after her: 'You should try to leave her alone. It's her birthday. She's thirty.'

No one had said it was Aunt Connie's birthday. Thirty was very old. There had been no cards and no presents at breakfast. There might still be a cake. Mrs P had told Mum there was no icing sugar.

It was a long way past the tents when she heard noises on her right. In the distance a few children were playing with a ball, a man was swimming. But there was no one else. It was like a cat in pain, or a dog wailing. They didn't have a dog but that's what it sounded like. It came from the sand-hills between the beach and the road. She waited. The noises kept stopping and starting. After a few moments, Nell found a path that led up between the steepest slopes. Somebody was sitting among the highest dunes. A red headscarf bordered with white butterflies, like Aunt Connie's.

Nell ran back along the road – no one cared that she couldn't find her aunt. Rory was fine and his cut covered with a pink plaster. He was helping Mum make a cake.

The sad feeling returned. Nell found her book, told her mother she had a headache, was going to bed. She wasn't even sure anyone had heard. Mrs Podrowski was standing by the door peeling an orange, had stared at her as if she was a complete stranger.

'We'll call you, Nell, when supper is ready.'

People sometimes behaved so oddly. It was like those hushed

conversations between her mother and Aunt Connie when they first arrived. Even the night before, when Nell had forgotten to empty the bucket, went to collect it, she had to wait at the scullery door, the talk in the kitchen sounded private. Mrs Podrowski was drinking tea, listening to Aunt Connie who was making soda bread.

'That wretched course. My bloody diploma and we'd only been away two days. And we went out to catch a film. I drove like a maniac through the blizzard. Missed her by minutes.'

'There's nothing anyone could have done.' Mrs Podrowski was murmuring very softly.

'If I'd been there, I'd have known.'

'But surely.'

'Oh yes,' Aunt Connie had replied. 'I would have realised.'

13

A waste of time trying to write reports when the words kept blurring, if Anne took a break she could clear her head. Her desk and that of the school secretary were covered with lists and queries and potential disasters. The sun was shining – take the afternoon off, get away from the office and its bleak view of rubble. Two hours, she would steal two hours. Once again the convent garden could be a refuge. No one there, Raphael busy here, Liam away with his family.

Sister Jude stopped her to ask for a lift. 'I'd love another go with the books.'

'Isn't the work too heavy for you, Sister?' said Anne.

'If I did it properly but I'm having a read when I get puffed. Is Dr Dillon still away?'

'I sincerely hope so.'

Jude had disappeared into the library; Anne climbed up on the low wall by the bike sheds, looked out over the tennis courts, science labs, as far as the high wall that loomed down on the deep-red brick of the convent. The garden was an explosion of colour.

How were they getting on in Norfolk? Before going for the summer, Connie had come several times and they'd talked. Connie wanted to know about the children's home: Anne had described the freedom of it, gangs of them trailing off to spy through wire fencing at the men in the internment camps.

'And we safely at school in Ireland,' Connie had said. 'That bastard De Valera. When I came over, I kept telling people about relatives fighting in the first war, my uncle a navy doctor torpedoed in the second. But no one had asked; they seemed to not care. There was no judgement, or none I heard.'

'And Liam?'

'He can be over-sensitive, quick to hear an anti-Irish comment.'

That last time here, they'd climbed down to St Teresa, pushing their way through the brambles and overgrowth. So quiet you could hear the leaves breathing. Now, thanks to Liam, it could be reached by a path, had lost its magic.

She felt her way into the dark, knelt before the saint, recited her vows. She had told Connie too much about her own childhood, imagining it would help Connie talk. It had been indulgent.

It couldn't last. Anne was feeling her way up to ground level when she saw someone at the back gate. It was Liam, struggling with a box of plants, that familiar lost boy expression. The man was mad, he was meant to be away at least two weeks.

He was walking in her direction. She pushed her hands into the sleeves of her habit; a pity that he'd spot her so idle, not bent over digging up weeds. At least she was wearing a sacking apron, had been gardening. That would surprise him. Well, it was all ridiculous.

She walked out onto the path. 'We didn't expect you so soon, Doctor. How are the family, how is Connie?'

That was a mistake, she should have said Mrs Dillon. But why so formal? To call her Mrs Dillon was ridiculous.

Liam said nothing.

'You know,' Anne went on. 'This spot has always been a special place, even better now you've cleared the path.'

It was only a white lie.

'I hate magpies,' Liam said abruptly, putting down his box.

So the clatter and rattles in the trees were magpies.

'I was wondering whether to pull away the ivy,' Liam continued.

'The ivy keeps Teresa hidden.'

'So, she is your favourite, Sister?'

That didn't follow, Liam heard what he wanted to hear. Best would be to find Sister Jude, go back to the school. Only two weeks before the teachers arrived, then the girls would descend.

Maybe he didn't like Teresa. She'd indeed been an extravagant saint, beyond doubt a noisy and powerful one. Perhaps Connie's emotional extravagance was hard for him.

'You look pale, should have a blood test, Sister. Were you praying when I interrupted?'

None of his business. 'Faith is strange, or must be for doctors.'

'Maybe.' Liam gestured at the grotto. 'Roses, deep-red climbing roses by the steps, that's what Teresa needs.'

Anne wasn't going to indulge him by responding.

'Norfolk was fine,' he said. 'But I'm not keen on that coast.'

Five years of her life. The orphanage had been bearable, better than the one in London; the nuns tried to make up for what the children had lost. But what had been special were the walks on her own, an escape for hours and no one bothered. The sky, sea, land, as one with no horizon. That was when she'd glimpsed Teresa's joy.

They would soon be dodging bulldozers. 'It's the school that goes too, Doctor. Not only the garden.'

'No sentiment for chapels, classrooms?'

None at all.

She went to find Jude. All she could do was pray that they moved the spirit of the place to the new buildings, and they would, it would be carried over by the staff and the girls themselves.

14

Over the next few weeks it began to look more like autumn, Liam's garden was changing to golden-browns, reds, amber. The children were at the new school, the remaining nuns had been moved out. Raphael visited a few times and she even waved, was keeping an eye on him.

Anne probably believed beauty got in God's way, like music. A sin. She and her other nuns were no better than Calvinists to let this garden be concreted over, buildings demolished, wrecking even the chapels, shattering stained glass, smashing places of beauty.

He would not be budged.

One afternoon, Jude sat herself on a bench near where Liam was bedding in lavender. 'The girls would have loved this but aren't your seasons topsy turvy?'

If only she were more agile, he'd get her to see the design. 'The best view is from the back wall. There's a pattern.'

'Have me scrambling up a ladder, Liam?'

'I was thinking of you standing on the bench, me as support.'

'And providing me with a little imagination?'

'Ok, wait here.' He ran to his bag, brought back some sketches.

'Oh, they're beautiful.' She touched his arm. 'But I've seen it.'

'From the roof?'

Jude sighed. 'I wanted to live out my time here.' She twisted her fingers together. 'And maybe I did once climb up, or something similar? I'll draw you a picture.'

She looked more closely at the sketches. 'Or maybe not, Liam. I don't need to, you're the artist.'

*

Nell crouched behind the half-open kitchen door and listened. This was the second time since coming home from Tottingford she was going to get into trouble at school. And, as Mum said, this eleven-plus year was very important. But no one cared. She needed a book for homework, otherwise she would be given a black mark. And the book might not be on the kitchen sideboard.

She had heard her mother moaning to Mrs Billings that Connie coming with Rory 'had sent the whole house into uproar'. Rory had her room. It was horrible sharing with Aidan. All Nell had for clothes was a small cupboard. No wonder things disappeared.

She had crept down the stairs quietly because there was an evening surgery, a mumble of voices from the waiting-room. Aidan and Rory had gone to visit the neighbours. Aidan and the boy next door were meant to be writing a play about Guy Fawkes for the firework display. They would be wasting time with their Meccano instead. She needed that book. How else could she finish her test?

Her mother and Aunt Connie were talking softly, and it didn't sound as if they wanted anyone to hear.

'Aren't you pleased, Nell?' Her mother had said when they got back to Newcastle. 'A new cousin. Rory with a brother or sister.'

All she wanted was her bedroom back and everything normal. Fine for Colum, he was away at school. Why did Rory have to have her room, Aunt Connie all of Colum's? Couldn't they share like in Norfolk? 'Because there'll be a baby, Nell,' Mum had said.

Even more reason to be together. They'd soon be going home to Uncle Liam.

She might as well wait where she was. Her mother or Aunt Connie had to get up and boil the kettle or do something noisy. Nell made herself comfortable on the thick carpet.

'That floor's wasted on the patients,' Mum would say. 'They trail in mud and God knows what.'

Nell was hidden by the huge hall chest. She kept very still. The kitchen table partly blocked Aunt Connie. All she could see was her aunt's swollen belly down to puffy ankles and grubby pink slippers.

The flowery smock that Aunt Connie wore, Mum used to wear when painting the bathroom. Aunt Connie was sitting forward, leaning against the table. The edge pressed into her swelling. It looked painful, the way the enormous bulge strained against the cotton. The stitches of the seams were stretched so they must be about to pop. Every inch of the blue-flowered, paint-spattered material was pulled tight like skin.

If Nell had a pin she could reach across and pop it – blood, and goodness knows what, exploding all over the kitchen.

A feeling from sometime ages ago. A sick feeling in her stomach. Much worse than how she felt before confession. That belly was shameful. In there was a baby.

Her aunt was gripping her hands together so hard, the knuckles were red. She kept bending over then straightening up.

'Will she get her eleven-plus, Pat?'

'We're not even sure she'll need to, but she'd better, if they don't end it. We can't afford anything else. The boys will stretch us.'

So the boys go to expensive schools and she ends up in the secondary modern. Any moment Mum would start about how dreamy she was, always reading, always in a daze.

Aunt Connie was pushing her hand into the small of her back and rubbing it. 'Colum was managing fine, got his eleven-plus, and you send the poor boy to prep school. Then it'll be Aidan. The boys will be very posh, will look down on you.'

'They'll be neither of them posh.'

Colum said that the parents had to rethink schools after Claire died. Actually he had said *reset priorities*, whatever that meant.

Nell could remember now. She was about seven, sent to get

bread. A woman ahead in the queue holding a cracked jug, had come to buy beer. That woman was often there, getting paper twists of sugar or tea, and white sliced loaves. She lived with loads of children in the cobbled terrace below the shop.

The woman was beautiful. Mum wasn't beautiful like that, nor the teachers at school, nor Aunt Connie.

In the crowded queue for the grumpy man taking orders, Nell was pressed against the swelling that pushed out the woman's faded apron. She hadn't known quite what the feeling was. Somehow the swelling was shameful. The woman had looked down at her, a serious careful look, as if she knew.

One of the patients was leaving and Nell huddled further into the corner. She was well hidden. Eileen, her father's receptionist, closed the front door firmly on the still-talking man. Eileen, blonde hair brushed up in a beehive and sensible brown sandals, thick stockings, scuttled back to the surgery without noticing Nell.

There were coils of dust that Mrs Billings had left in the corners of the hall. Nell didn't want to hear about the eleven-plus. She wanted to know when her aunt was leaving then she could have her room back.

'Oh, Jaysus.'

A puddle was slowly spreading over the red kitchen tiles. Aunt Connie had stood up, was clutching the edge of the table, a damp patch over her bottom. How awful. She'd wet herself, her aunt had wet herself – meanwhile Mum was rushing around looking for towels, generally making a fuss.

'Wait there, Con. I'll get Dermot.'

Nell crawled away from the door, raced upstairs.

15

'Congratulations, Doctor,' said Mr Drummond as Liam met him at the gate. 'How is Mrs Dillon?'

'They are both fine.'

Liam didn't mention that Connie was still away as they walked over to the back of the convent garden, climbed up on the wall.

'You've done a fair job, Doctor.'

'Is there a pattern? I thought it might be more obvious now the trees are mostly bare. I'd imagined at first something like the Stations of the Cross.'

'Well, Doctor, it's tidier. I can see the statues more clearly, and the paths.' Mr Drummond seemed unsure. 'I'll get down now.'

'Those circles make no sense; the grottoes fit into those wedges but not quite. The centre's an oddity.'

'That's true,' said Mr Drummond, descending carefully to the ground. 'Only a heap of rocks and pebbles.'

'I didn't notice them before.' Liam jumped down to join him. 'Does any of it remind you of anything?'

'Well, it's ordered, I'd say that. The higher I was, I could see that. You'll give my best wishes to your wife and the new babbi?'

Liam had searched in the reference library for images. There seemed nothing near what he was looking for, he wasn't even sure what that was. He went through the Christian tradition making a detour into the Orthodox and to Constantinople, then tried more widely, helped by the librarian. She was a cheerful woman, a patient – he'd sorted her thyroid.

The nearest they found was a mandala: a multi-coloured design with squares containing circles, full of intricate patterns. The librarian had cut it out from some copy of an article about the exiled Dalai Lama.

Liam took it and his sketches to the surgery, showed them to

Gerry. 'You were in Asia doing National Service, did you ever see stuff like this?'

'What are you on about, Liam? How is Connie?'

'Fine, I'm driving up at the weekend. Tell me about this.'

'Look, there were pilgrimages and gods of all sorts everywhere, but I can't recall any like these. Are they coming home with you?'

'Isn't it meant to originate with the Hindus?'

'You've a new baby, the world in chaos, Kennedy shot in full view. All you care about is a doomed garden. Go see Connie and the children for pity's sake. We could at least wet the babe's head.'

Liam tried to get as often as he could to the garden, worried that the next time it would have gone.

Jessica. If that was what Connie wanted, he should stop thinking about this child as Shylock's errant daughter. She seemed healthy and had great lungs; Connie was polite whenever he called but distracted.

'I'll come back, Liam, in a few weeks. We'll talk then.'

Pat and Dermot were exasperated. And understandably. They lived over the practice and there was no room – no joy in being woken by a hungry baby. But Connie was not to be budged. Surely, she'd be home for Christmas.

One afternoon, Sister Anne appeared.

'I thought you'd gone for good, Sister.'

'A few things needed sorting. When the rain stopped, I thought why not, now?' She clearly included him. 'Here, I don't get interrupted, it's only a few minutes by car. How is little Jessica?'

He'd often seen the nun driving through town, muttering; no doubt saying the rosary to ward off accidents. No, not Sister Anne, she wasn't the rosary species of nun. She was probably making lists. Number one: Sort Liam. He'd wait a bit before asking about missing plants.

She paused to examine the new roses he'd put along the path to

St Teresa. They would be crimson next summer. But there wouldn't be any next summer, the bulldozers would have arrived. Was she already planning to steal them?

'We have those at home. I like them, just you wait till they flower.' He sounded as crazy to himself as he must do to her. What had he meant by home? The roses had been in his mother's garden, but that wasn't home. And it wasn't really his mother's garden, though he and Papa called it that. One day he'd take Rory and Jess over to his mother's grave. He and his father had planted these there.

'They won't get the chance. What about your own garden? And Connie? When are they coming home?'

'I go tomorrow, will bring them back.'

'Rory must miss you.'

Liam wasn't going to mention that Rory refused to come to the phone. Connie had needed these few months. In a day or so, she'd be home, Rory and the baby with her – they'd all return to normal.

He watched Anne walk away; all he ever saw was her pale face, anaemic skin, that expression of having just heard something rather funny. But her thin body in its concealing habit was agile enough as she climbed the wall by the bicycle sheds to rescue a stranded kite.

He'd bring Connie here, show her what he'd done before it was destroyed. And Rory too. Important for Rory to see this. Maybe, when the boy was older, he'd remember where Claire had played before it was all gone.

16

The super-efficient nun/secretary told Connie to wait in Anne's office. The school was completely new – corridors, stairs, offices painted a venerable cream and brown as if that could conceal how plastic and temporary it looked. The old convent had been built by Victorians who believed in permanence. Here, there were no Gothic spires, no flying buttresses – this was prefab architecture.

Nowhere was comfortable. Connie pulled up a chair to the desk, sat with her head in her arms. Just a few minutes.

Anne must have crept in, was watching her from the chair opposite.

'Jesus, Mary and Joseph! Anne, you gave me a heart attack.'

How long had the woman been there?

Anne reached across and took her hand. 'You look a sight.'

'From inside, believe me, it's a lot worse.'

'And the baby?'

'With Mrs M who swaddles her into silence, makes it look easy.'

Their clasped fingers, her own strong ones and Anne's delicate hands. But there was earth under the nails, had the nun being potting-up plants? There was no evidence. Outside the school was rubble and in here an already exhausted spider plant on the window ledge – Anne was no gardener.

'You'll be a constant, won't you, Anne? I can call on you?'

If only this woman could be her guardian angel, keep an eye on Liam, Rory, Jess.

'I've found a part-time job in London for after Easter. Liam and Mrs M will look after Jessica for those few days. A child that age is no trouble. I'll have her weaned, Mrs M manages to get her to sleep. I give out the wrong energy, Jessica looks at me and screams.'

'Are you tormenting the poor baby?'

'Probably.'

Anne would not understand. Jessica did indeed pick up everything Connie was feeling. The baby lay in her arms looking up warily – blue eyes guarded, assessing. That done, she'd scream with rage for hours, be impossible to soothe. Jessica knew what she could see and she didn't like it.

The best thing would be to lose herself dealing with patients, become competent at something again, let the black dog shift off her shoulders. Jessica would be happier, everyone would get some sleep.

'Isn't it easier now you have Liam to help?'

'He's even more anxious than me.'

Anne was playing with Connie's wedding ring. They looked at each other. Anne knew very well this part-time marriage wouldn't work. But what else was there? They would break up, that was it.

'So, Connie, what do you think of the new school?'

Should she say that it was ugly, a total failure of imagination?

'I hear the bulldozers will soon be at the lovely old one. You'll make sure not to lose Claire's treasure, won't you, Anne.'

Anne gripped Connie's hands more tightly. 'I've not forgotten.'

17

He would not come again. Connie was home with the children, the school soon be gone. His final afternoon, Liam spent sweeping up.

Before leaving, he went to check the hedge round the St Francis near the biology lab; Jude was sitting on the bench, running her beads through her fingers. He'd thought she'd left with the rest, without saying good-bye. Jude gestured that he should join her, made space among the books.

'Are you getting at all breathless, Sister?'

'I am not.' Jude nodded up at a robin perched on the statue. 'I was so happy to hear about little Jessica, Liam. We've kept her in our prayers. It's a mark of hope in sad times, isn't it?'

So, even the nuns were obsessed with Kennedy.

'I'd bring the little ones here, we called it our sanctuary. They all fitted comfortably, I'd tell them about Francis.'

The saint in his habit, brown paint chipped, looked impassively down, long fingers outstretched. 'Sister Anne showed this grotto to Connie,' said Jude. 'She was keen to see everywhere Claire loved.'

Connie had been brought here, not him. All the time he'd been pruning hedges, cutting back bramble, pulling out weeds, planting, he'd no idea Connie had been before, been here in his garden.

'You told me you saw the design.' Jude didn't reply. 'Intentional, isn't it? Not a maze, pretends to go somewhere, then not.'

If he'd done a better job it would be clearer.

'Oh, Liam, it's statues and paths. Call it a pattern if you like. We need those in our lives, don't we? You must let go.'

He hadn't found anyone willing to listen: Mr Drummond stared at the sketches and smiled politely, Liam had to rescue some from the salvage bag after Mrs M cleaned, Gerry had frowned, tapped his head knowingly at Mrs Lemon. They were happy to indulge him while he got done with the business of mourning.

This wasn't a random garden, it had been planned.

How quickly the hedge had got out of control. 'I'll sort this before heading home.'

'To be truthful, Liam, I liked it better wilder.'

'You agreed it's a pattern, Jude. But what exactly do you mean?'

She reached over and patted his hand. 'You should concentrate more on your sketching. This, Liam, is like a mandala.'

'I saw one in the library.'

'No, not the thing, the idea. Buddhists build them from various coloured powders. A form of prayer, and intricate – several monks give it weeks of intense work then all breathed away. A prayer. That's what I meant. All that work, then they break it up, carry it to some special place, a river, a cliff. And puff. All gone. And wouldn't that be a good idea.'

Once Jude had left, he crouched inside the grotto. With his eyes shut, he could feel a press of small girls watching, giggling. It was getting cold. Jude was right, it was enough; he should have told her this was his last time here – imagine this as dust, let it blow away.

Liam put on his jacket, took his cutters, started to work his way around the almost full circle of hedge. The day seemed to get even chillier; he shivered and paused.

Someone was on the other side.

How long had Sister Anne been there? He nodded, and pulled at a few escaped branches of box. She reached across and grabbed his arm. He held more tightly to the cutters, her fingers almost circled his wrist, were digging into the flesh. She was hurting him.

They were staring at each other, impossible not to look. She was almost smiling. He didn't feel angry, just determined, after all this was arm-wrestling. A game. Her eyes were a clear blue, he'd thought they were hazel.

Anne had gone mad, but despite her being so much shorter than him and so slight, he couldn't get free from her grip. She was taking the cutters, she'd not have them.

He tried not to catch her eye, concentrated instead on their hands wrenched together around the rusty metal. She was going to force him to release his grip. He wouldn't give in.

She was much stronger than he'd ever have imagined. His arms were turning to jelly, he might even lose. From the nun's breathing it was clear she was struggling too – both held in a grip that was impossible to break.

There was a yell from the playground. Raphael. Someone from the practice was on the phone. Liam let the cutters go.

PART TWO

1978

PART TWO

1978

18

It was dark in the grounds although the clock had only struck two. Connie was late – at least there were no other appointments, the girls were on their Christmas holidays.

Anne tucked her hands into the sleeves of her habit. Beyond the school wall, neon lit up two cranes, a new estate was being built beside the shopping complex. How naïve to have assumed it would remain as woods and green fields. On her desk another message from the police: the children had to be warned about taking shortcuts through any countryside that was left.

It was as dangerous when Anne started teaching. Anyway, the shopping centre was more inviting than trees and meadows; the moment school was over, the children would swarm off, drink milk-shakes from McDonald's, lounge around the broken fountain in the precinct. Pensioners from the new old people's home would jot down letters of disgust to the governors, and no matter how often her pupils were warned about expulsion, a few would hike up their skirts, roll up their hats to stuff in their satchels. And then, heaven help us, smoke.

Today was the beginning of a new year, and not likely to be easier than the last. Her superiors had hinted she needed a change, in other words she was making too many demands. And it wasn't just them. In the last clash, the governors refused to give her a physics teacher, claiming it wasn't a priority. How could she run a school with idiots in control?

She should have gone on retreat with the other sisters; Father Willis had suggested it, her superiors almost insisted. Her reply that she was busy would be a bad mark – another one.

Connie was bounding up the stairs, long black hair looped in a bun, tied round with a crimson scarf.

'The place is a desert, we can go dancing in the classrooms. Ah, Annie, don't frown. I know I'm late, the traffic was awful. And can't stop, I have to be in London by six but did want to see you.'

Better not mention Jess immediately, Connie would get irritable.

'Have you seen Jess?'

'For God's sake, I'm only in the door.' Connie threw her green coat on a chair, took a saucer from beneath the cup on Anne's desk and lit a cigarette. 'I phoned, they've gone to Stratford. Well, Maura and Jess have gone. I don't know how Maura manages. She got my daughter to go to a play.'

'Did you not warn them you were coming?'

Connie made a face. She was wandering round the room as she usually did, touching the books, straightening the crucifix. Anne liked Connie; their friendship was one of the few pleasures of the last fifteen years.

'We do need to talk seriously about your daughter.'

'No, we don't, I'm here to see you. It's not the summer holidays, Jess and Rory are Liam's responsibility.'

Which, of course, meant Maura.

It had been outrageous meddling, introducing the new English teacher to Liam – he'd only popped in to enrol Jess in the reception class. Maura was collecting sponsors for a parachute jump. Anne suggested Liam added his name, Maura liked him immediately.

Connie switched the kettle on. 'I can't help Jess; she snarls at me. But I do miss her.' She stood at the window peering out at the winter gloom. 'So, what's new?'

'I'm possibly moving on. I don't know what will happen or when. The mother-house suggest a change, I'll be able to get back to ordinary teaching.'

Connie looked horrified. 'Not as headmistress? Geography? Do you want that?'

How did she know? It might sort her increasing sense of frustration; maybe she'd become too used to having her own way.

'It will be unbearable, Anne, unless you're a total masochist. At least the hierarchy here in Moreton have been dealt with, you can do what you like.' She banged a mug of coffee onto Anne's desk. 'Of course, that's what they hate, a woman who thinks for herself.'

This was going to be another Connie tirade, the misogyny of the Church and Anne's collusion. A school devoted to educating more Catholic mothers should be shut down even if Jess would be set adrift. 'We have to talk about Jess.'

'Why?' said Connie. 'Why not ask why I'm going to London?'

'Because it will be for some man and that doesn't interest me.'

'Even if he's beautiful and French.'

'Especially if he's either of those. How is work?'

No point expecting Connie to help her decide what to do. The vows were not a problem, the challenge was faith itself. But Connie would deny that. She'd say that Anne's problem was obedience.

Connie had put her feet up on the desk, was staring into her coffee. She was most likely feeling remorse. 'If Liam and Maura can't cope, then of course I'll look after Jess.'

'You're such a child. And please put your legs down, this isn't your home.'

'My god, has any of your ferocity got through to the girls? Are you getting any more to Oxbridge?'

'There are a few possibles.'

'Oh, Annie, you say that, then they go for interview, see the gulf. You've witnessed that often enough.'

She had indeed: Oxford at the end of the forties was full of brilliant older men finishing their degrees having been interrupted by the war. And not just them, all the male students seemed so worldly, so much better educated. The girls in her college were clever, worked hard. They had more to offer than most male undergraduates but only a few had the confidence.

Connie was hunting in her bag. Did she feel a failure? By all reports she'd been a better GP than Liam. Now she was working all over the country as a locum, hadn't settled anywhere.

She'd pulled out some papers, dumped them on Anne's desk.

'You're giving me leaflets, Connie?'

Anxiety about failing at Oxford had almost stopped Anne doing anything but study, the hours she put in were not admired. Even her tutor told her to ease off, have some fun.

The Church had accepted her, it had been a refuge. 'These are about the Brook Advisory Service, contraception?'

'You've a school nurse, Annie? Can't she hand these out?'

'This is a Catholic school.'

'And they don't have sex?'

A few didn't just have sex, some girls got pregnant. But to condone it by giving around these? Out of the question.

Anne must check what the sister responsible for First Aid had as information.

'Great,' said Connie, stubbing out her cigarette. 'You'll arrange it. It's important.'

'The school doctor gives a talk to Fifth Form. That's enough.'

'I don't think so. What would be perfect is to have the girls taught not just contraception, but breast exams, and to nag their mums.'

That was ridiculous; the children would be embarrassed, the parents appalled, the teachers simply refuse. And the bishop would have Anne excommunicated.

'How is Nell?'

'In love with a Nigerian called Jerome and doing house jobs. I'll be seeing her in London. They're planning to live in Lagos.'

Connie's niece served only to remind Anne how she was failing her own pupils: no girl into medical school and only three to Oxford or Cambridge in the whole fifteen years. The numbers to other universities had steadily grown but that paltry Oxbridge number was seen as an achievement. And her anger at the injustice wasn't going to make a jot of difference. 'Is it my fault, Connie, that the height of ambition here is a teachers' training college and most girls only want to get a boyfriend?'

'Of course it's your fault.' Connie aimed a paper plane at a framed picture of the Pope. 'And those criminals.'

No point sending best wishes to Nell. Anne's name would not have happy associations – the only time they'd met was the night of Claire's death, the poor child had been shaking with distress.

'Oh, Anne, I'm sorry but I do have to dash.'

'And you'll leave Maura to deal with Jess? Is that fair?'

'Life is not fair and Maura loves it.'

Connie was maddening.

'You're so selfish, preach about other girls and their mothers, neglect your own daughter. She was almost impossible last term.'

'I know I know I know.' Connie was retrieving her coat.

The familiar sense of having missed something whenever they met. Connie was always rushing and Anne had never said all she wanted to say. 'What happened to that absurd blue fur?'

'My goodness, you remember. You are improving. It fell apart. Don't you like this green tweed? It suits me, doesn't it?'

'Nigeria will be tough for Nell. So much poverty.'

Connie came round the desk, gave Anne a hug. 'I won't tell her that.'

19

The downstairs bathroom was a veritable palace of fussy gold taps, two vast marble sinks, a toilet like a throne. The house belonged to the chair of trustees for Jerome's charity. 'Why do the wealthy, Nell, want to waste hours on endless committees?'

'No idea.'

Connie looped two green scarves round her head and glared into the bathroom's gilt-edged mirror. It wasn't the most flattering.

'Am I too ancient for long hair?'

It didn't matter, she was not going to cut it. Her niece was scrubbing her hands as if getting ready for brain surgery; Connie kissed the back of Nell's neck – you can always tell medics, they know about bugs.

'Are all three of you taller than Pat and Dermot?'

'Dad regrets feeding us vitamins. Your grey silk looks lovely.'

That was the least of Dermot's regrets, the man was impossible. Connie lit a cigarette, offered the pack. Nell shook her head.

'How was your day?'

'Ok. The last one was a six-year-old, her third operation. I could never do paediatrics.'

Nell was going to mention Claire.

'Let me sort your hair, darling.'

Nell had been there that night. Did Nell the doctor look back, realise that Liam had been negligent or that Connie should have recognised that Claire was ill before scooting off to London with Pat? Pat and Dermot certainly thought them guilty.

Connie searched her bag for her comb. Nell was now smoothing out her new linen dress. She looked wonderful; if not taken in hand, she would probably have turned up at Jerome's farewell party in jeans. 'I like the blue, Nell, we did an inspired shop. Have you organised any work?'

'I'll live off Jerome, catch up on sleep, do some reading. There's nothing available like his admin job here but he's been offered sort-of legal journalism work. I'll look for something eventually.'

'Get thousands of miles from Newcastle. They'll miss you like mad, beg forgiveness.'

Connie pulled her comb through Nell's hair.

'I wish my hair was as black as yours, Connie. I'm getting more and more mousey.'

'Then colour it.'

What a waste youth was on children. How stupid to be here. Daniel's last night in London before he went back to France and she somewhere else, pretending to be a good aunt. Insane.

'The trustees adore Jerome, aren't sure about me. It's my fault; Mum always said that if you make an effort, people like you.'

Pat was talking through the top of her head, mostly there was not much about people for anyone to like.

'What does the charity do?'

'Give support, legal advice. They've several emergency hostels. There's been a fire at one today, so he'll be late.'

Or Jerome might not turn up, and seeing him was the whole point of coming.

'Do you still like your friend Mr Marx?'

'I should've kept my mouth shut, not tried to convert everyone.'

'You were seventeen. I wish I'd come with you on that march, Pat said you glued diaphragms, dirty sanitary towels to banners.'

'Not dirty. And it was years ago. If I'd more energy when first in London, not struggling with exams, I'd have got really angry. Those public school boys waving their entitlement like flags.'

Had Nell forgotten her own brothers?

'Do your friends like Jerome?'

'Yes, yes, of course.' The poor child looked uneasy.

'Let's get on with it, Nell. Just imagine everyone as an animal.'

109

Connie steered her niece into the packed drawing room. A giraffe with expensive teeth approached them. Nell introduced Mrs Harvey, one of the trustees.

'Your aunt, how delightful and so glamorous.'

Connie slipped away to get Nell wine. She could hear Mrs H braying into Nell's ear. 'How long, dear, before you leave for Lagos?'

Did giraffes bray? Mrs Harvey pronounced Lagos as if she was getting her tongue around the word before eating it up. Poor Nell, the child had rushed here after hours in the operating theatre. The surgeon would have been a bully, dealt with any difficulty by yelling abuse, mainly at Nell. All house jobs were vile. Hers in Dublin while Claire was a baby had been a nightmare.

A young black man was working two trays of food through the crowded drawing room. The sausages were inedible. Another waiter gave her a glass of red wine and she took it back to Nell.

'Oh, Connie, tell her how lucky she is,' said the giraffe. 'Wonderful job. My life could depend on some baby like this.' The monster swirled her blonde page-boy hair to contradict any thought of age, then patted Nell's cheek. 'So romantic to be a doctor.'

She clearly hadn't worked a ten-hour day doing cervical smears.

'My aunt's a doctor too,' said Nell.

'Oh.' Mrs Harvey looked put out, then gathered more steam. 'But she's right, Connie, to get away from this country ruled by bungling communists.'

Clearly the woman would be canvassing for Mrs Thatcher and the Tories. Best to move on. 'Let's explore a bit, Nell.'

They plumped down on a sofa in an empty room, Nell rested her head on Connie's shoulder.

'Mrs Giraffe seems to think you only say the word, Jerome wouldn't go.'

'Of course Jerome wants to go. This country's impossible for a couple like us.'

Nell was right. Her father could give no justification for being incensed at the relationship, and Pat was a coward, said nothing. They preached charity, went to Mass, rejected their daughter.

'I drove up to see them on Boxing Day,' said Connie.

Nell muttered something, she was almost asleep. Colum had been there which stopped them obsessing about their daughter. He was joining the practice, yet once considered paediatrics. Colum would be good with children.

Aidan had already escaped back to London.

'Have you seen Aidan?'

'I'll phone his digs,' said Nell.

'I did my best, but you've goaded your father into a corner. Give him time, meanwhile do what you like. Though I'm beginning to think this man of yours an invention.'

Jerome wasn't an invention; he was tall, beautiful, clearly in love with Nell. 'You should take her home, Jerome. She needs her bed.'

Nell was dozing. Her dress was crumpled, her dark hair a mess, and she seemed very peaceful.

'I will soon but ought to circulate first.'

Connie pulled up a chair, pointed to a space on the sofa. 'Hide for a moment. Doesn't she look regal?'

'Ready to spring into action the minute the pager goes.'

Jerome settled back, put his arm around the sleeping Nell.

'Did she admit her real name was Eleanor?'

'Yes, and I told her mine was Nonso.'

He looked more like a Nonso than a whiskered Saint Jerome and he looked tired. How old was he, about 30? Nell had said that Jerome was fifteen when he came to London to stay with an uncle. Something vulnerable about him, was her Nell too tough? Jerome had shut his eyes – don't let him fall asleep too.

'So, you're going back,' said Connie. 'I must say I've never wanted to. I was Nell's age when I got off the boat in Liverpool, Liam already here, working all hours. The late fifties, England such a quiet country. Ireland might have been poor, feudal, run by priests and De Valera, but people did like to talk. Even so, I couldn't imagine returning.'

'I arrived Christmas '63. I imagined people out celebrating but everything was shut. I wanted to buy presents, there wasn't even a place to buy food.'

The same year Claire died – while she and Liam pretended for Rory's benefit that it was a normal Christmas, two parents who couldn't speak to each other, a baby screaming in the cot – Jerome was a young teenager walking through an abandoned London.

'Were you tempted to go back?'

'I'm not that tempted now.'

Jerome stroked Nell's hair. Was Nell using him to escape her parents? No, an absurd thought. The girl wanted to help save lives, and whose fault was that, witnessing death when so young?

Should Connie apologise for her sister and brother-in-law?

Jerome lay back and closed his eyes. 'So many here are lonely, disconnected from their family.'

He was speaking so gently it was hard to hear.

'Who would try to burn down a hostel full of homeless?'

Lots of people.

'At least Nell has a family.' He looked directly at Connie. 'I should have gone back ten years ago.'

The Biafran war? Why hadn't he?

'I was a coward,' said Jerome, as if Connie had spoken out loud.

He stood up: 'I'll circulate while Nell naps, then take her home.'

The chairman of the charity made an incredibly boring speech. They gave Jerome an expensive suitcase and he thanked everyone including Nell who was in the next room fast asleep, heard nothing.

For her sins, Connie was stuck again with the giraffe. After a brief exchange about Northern Ireland and Callaghan, she heard all about Mrs Harvey's children, arthritis, and delightful farmhouse near Toulouse.

'Nell once told me,' said Mrs Harvey. 'She and Jerome were walking down Regent Street, someone spat at them! In Central London.'

They might be happier in Nigeria.

20

There were lights on downstairs. Liam closed the garage doors, let himself quietly into the house. He left his medical bag by the table, picked up a message, tiptoed across the hall to the sitting room.

Maura opened her eyes. 'I thought you were Jess.'

'She's not back?'

'No, I'm sorry.'

It was hardly Maura's fault, his daughter was impossible. Two a.m. and she'd just been expelled, swore she'd change her ways.

'It's pouring out there.'

Maura got up from the sofa, brushed down her nightie.

'Was it Alec Bellows?'

Liam tucked a cardigan over his wife's shoulders, kissed the crown of her blonde hair where the roots were showing. He liked the practical way Maura did certain things. He wanted her to pat him down, put him to bed, climb in beside him. A glug of joy went through his body – with Maura it was often very good to be alive.

'He died an hour ago.'

'Well, thank goodness,' Maura said briskly. 'He's had such a drawn-out death.'

It had gone on too long, Mrs Bellows begging Liam to make it easier. Liam had been there earlier, then the nurse had called for him after midnight when it was almost over. He had only to sign the papers.

'Is Rory asleep?'

Maura nodded.

Liam crumpled up the phone message, stuffed it in his pocket. 'Why did Connie ring?'

'She's hoping you might talk to Pat and Dermot. They refuse to see Nell, let alone the boyfriend.'

There was no point. He steered Maura towards the stairs. 'You go up. I'll wait for Jess, make myself a cup of tea.'

'He was a good man,' said Maura.

'Ellen Bellows is devastated.'

'Well, nearly seventy.'

Maura thought that was old? Sometimes the gap between his forty-five and her thirty-eight seemed more than seven years.

'Ok, darling,' said Maura. 'I've a meeting before Assembly. You'll say something when Jess comes?'

'I'll sit up for half an hour then join you.'

Liam must have fallen asleep on the sofa, Jess was standing over him, peering at his face as if making sure he was dead. He jumped to his feet – she stepped back, startled. She looked a mess, her curly red hair wild and tangled. But at least she was in one piece.

There was a cup of cold tea on the side-table, the image of Alec Bellows still in Liam's mind. But he had to deal with this, remember how furious he'd been. For Jess to behave so badly after what had happened yesterday. Did she want them giving up on her? He was not going to sit in front of any headmistress, ever again.

Three years since Jess had moved back after a few months with Connie in London. Recently, either he or Maura had been waiting up in the early hours for her footsteps to clatter down the road or the slam of a taxi door. And where did she get the money?

'I'm off to bed, Dad.'

'No, you are not. We're going to talk.'

'I'm dead beat,' she whined.

'That's your fault. Sit down.'

Jess clumped down into an armchair. Mascara all over her face. Fourteen and she looked like a hooker. His daughter.

Alec Bellows had been sixty-six. Maura reckoned seventy was old enough to die. Life was going much too quickly, he needed to slow it down.

115

What could he say to this child collapsed in the chair opposite? A whole hour yesterday with her headmistress, he the one being told off. Summoned to Jess's school as if he were the naughty pupil. Normally, school stuff could be handed to Maura. There were no nuns left as his patients, Gerry saw to all of them. An hour with nothing to do but look at Anne's concerned but determined face – Maura had refused to go.

Anne had witnessed those months before Jess was born, him wasting time over a garden now buried under offices, and building societies. All these years later, trying to decide the appropriate expression, while his daughter was outside chewing gum, her skirt hitched through her belt so it barely covered anything.

Anne was as pale as ever, and she seemed genuinely upset: 'This is no longer the right place for Jess. I'm so sorry.'

No one could say the school hadn't done their best. Jess had already been expelled once, aged ten. She'd been suspended twice. Sending her briefly to Connie hadn't helped.

Anne had read out a list of Jess's latest misdemeanours.

'I'm afraid you need to arrange something else.'

Something else was Connie. Connie would not thank them.

Jess had been waiting, slouched against the wall outside the office, smirking. Thank goodness no one was around as he hauled her along the corridor.

'This isn't remotely funny, it's appalling. Back less than a week, smoking's the least of it. Playing truant. Punching your chemistry mistress. Kicking another girl in the playground, scratching her.'

'Ow! You're hurting me.'

Jess had pulled away, rolled up the sleeves of her pullover; she was examining her freckled arms for bruises. Next she'd accuse him of child abuse. Infuriating. No point saying she must change her behaviour, she'd only reply, 'Make me'.

'We need to get home and talk.' All he'd been able to manage.

And there she was, half-asleep in the armchair, his hopeless, sullen daughter. Was it his fault? There was something wrong with him. He should never have had children – but Rory was ok.

'You promised me, Jess. You promised.'

One minute he wanted to hug her, the next slap the child. Five minutes after they'd driven away from the school, Jess was in tears, sobbing and choking, saying she was sorry. Heart-breaking and he had believed her. Then this.

'Instead of staying home, off you go somewhere you never say where. Was it that disco?'

'I weren't at any disco.' Her voice trailed off, she was exhausted. 'I wasn't.'

'I were not, I was with friends.'

It was impossible. Maura had tried. Hopefully he'd tried.

'Ok. Tomorrow, or in fact today, Jess, you pack your stuff. You're going to your mother. I'll drive you to Derby.'

'Mum's squatting in a grotty bedsit, there's no room. Anyways she's going back to France.'

'Not till Easter. She has a floor. So find Rory's sleeping bag, I'll buy him another. You can catch up on school when eventually you stop bullying us, wasting everyone's time.'

It was shamefully gratifying to see the shock on his daughter's face.

21

Jerome was already at the hospital gate, Nell handed him an unopened airmail letter. 'After months, our first communication.'

They kissed, to the amusement of two small girls squatting on the edge of the ditch near where the minibus would stop. Just before sunset, warm, no breeze, a smell of rotting fruit. They'd do the long journey home, repeat it early in the morning. Soon, once his job came through, she'd have to face it on her own. Six months, no letters. At last this.

'Why didn't you open it?' Jerome checked the back of the flimsy blue envelope. 'How come Connie sends it to the hospital? We have a flat, our own address.'

Exasperating, Jerome's stubborn optimism that next time he opened the letter box nailed to the front of their building-site, there'd be something there.

'I bet there's a pile of post in some bucket of builder's waste.'

'It will happen, Nell. My job will happen.'

A tiny boy shook his basket inches from her face, a pitiful pile of something Nell couldn't even see. 'I sent Colum the hospital address when they offered work. He must have given it to Connie.'

She took back the letter, tore it open. Connie's hurried scrawl, how were they getting on? Not much news, nothing about her parents. 'Cousin Jess is with her in Derby.' Jess must be thirteen, fourteen? A horrible age. 'It's a letter. Isn't that good?'

'Are you homesick?'

'Of course not.'

He kissed the top of her head, the small girls giggled again. The boy with the basket seemed to be selling peanuts, She had a few kobos in her pocket, bought a paper twist. The child looked desperate. Not that they must appear so impressive, Jerome was sweating as much as her in the evening heat. They were both scarecrows, both beginning to look shabby. Thank goodness she had a white coat for work. Jerome was thinner than in London. His tunic was patched and his trousers too heavy for the humid day. Her cotton skirt and T-shirt – unlike Connie's other purchases of two linen dresses – were the most useful thing she had.

'Did you meet up with that friend, Ifechi?'

'I saw his smart new office,' said Jerome.

Ifechi had come back a few years before, but like Jerome's other contacts from London, had proved elusive.

'He has some suggestions, doesn't think there's anything surprising about my experience. It's typical of Lagos.'

'But he didn't offer anything?'

When they'd first arrived, people had confirmed Jerome's job, given him appointments for the final paper work – just wait a few days. Slowly, hideously, the job melted away. Whoever promised it, disappeared; suddenly no one knew anything. At least the hospital had offered Nell a few sessions so they could pay the rent. The flat had been hard to find; they were lucky, but it was miles away.

'He got married as soon as he arrived, has a couple of children.'

Jerome didn't sound envious, just resigned. Thank goodness they didn't have a baby, how would they manage? The boy tilted the basket to show Jerome a few nuts but Jerome was tougher than Nell, brushed the child away.

They crammed into a space by the door of the packed minibus, its sign *In God We Trust*. Jerome took her hands in his. 'Wasn't it Connie who asked whether you'd thought things through?'

'Then said you'll never do anything in life if you do.'

The road was blocked, nothing moving. The hospital was the opposite side of the city from their flat, after a while they'd have to change buses.

Connie had also asked if Nell might have pressured Jerome to return to Nigeria. She wouldn't mention that. 'Let's get out.'

At first it was a relief. The buses were always packed, the other passengers checking her like some pathology specimen. 'They stare as if I've got horns.' Now she'd stopped noticing.

A crazy idea to walk, there was no path for pedestrians; on one side was a stream with sewage and rubbish, on the other the kamikaze drivers: lorries, buses, vans, revving up to the next jam. Everyone used the centre of the road because the potholes at the edge were lethal. The din, as drivers sat on their horns, the screeching brakes and tyres, was deafening.

Jerome was walking too fast. A motorcycle missed her by inches as she avoided a couple of emaciated cows being cajoled to the slaughter-house. It was clear from the beginning that they should stay this side of the ditch; the shacks, kitchens, and stalls beyond were the same as the miles of living space they'd seen on the journey from the airport. Not their land, they'd be trespassing. Each square foot accounted for: huts, tea-chests, boxes, tarpaulin hooked over ropes, shells of abandoned cars. Villas for the less affluent – old suitcases, tin cans, marked the boundary of each bathroom, kitchen.

'Jerome,' she yelled. 'Slow down.'

The women standing over stoves had been there since first light. It was mostly children who carried water; tiny children tottering miles balancing rusty pails on their heads. One boy they passed couldn't have been more than three, water from a chipped enamel basin spilling down his back on to the red dust.

At last Jerome was jogging back. A couple of children screamed out 'Oyinbos'. Being called a foreigner infuriated him.

'Let's celebrate,' she said. 'We've at last had a letter. It's like a message in a bottle; let's wander around Kingsway, admire the clothes, buy a drink.'

A blind child was begging outside the department store, an ill woman with a toddler swaddled to her back, kept to the shadow of the building.

Nell breathed in deeply the stale, cooled air.

'It's as quiet as a church,' said Jerome, joining her.

'Did you give them money?'

'What do you think? I wrote them a cheque.'

They went up the escalator, wandered through the clothes section: neat rows of shirts, carefully arranged scarves, racks of jackets; everything looked so irrelevant and grey compared to the colour and chaos of the street markets. The cool musty air might be comforting after the heat but this was dull compared to where they normally shopped. There, the stalls were packed together: tinned milk next to maize; meat beside plantain then a few rolls of material. On a tiny piece of land by a stall of yams, someone would have set out shoe-laces or a couple of tin plates on a rag. The only space to walk was often the channels of contaminated water trickling into the ditch.

Two nuns stood at a counter in animated discussion over a pair of socks. They must be baking in their heavy habits, and they were both fat.

'Let's share a Coke,' said Jerome.

'This place is unreal.'

Jerome took her arm. 'And you love it.'

22

It was gloriously hot, water slapping gently against the side of the pool. Nell shut her eyes. Wafts of jasmine. August. In England it was probably raining. Blissful to be here. A midday African sun hit the blue, the reflections puddling the tiles.

'Why not get in, Nell?' said Ifechi.

Her swimsuit was tatty, and, anyway, it was heaven to stay in the shade of the umbrella, admire Jerome doing front-crawl, ploughing his way through more relaxed swimmers. Ifechi poured her a cola slowly, letting it drip into the spaces between ice cubes.

Nell took the drink, shook her head.

'No, you're too clever. I don't swim either. Never have.' Ifechi shuddered as if swimming were a perversion.

An overweight, unfit, middle-aged man, this old friend from London, from before, was meant to be Jerome's most important contact. But Ifechi was unsettling, Jerome insisted he had nothing to do with the vanished job but he looked shifty, and he flirted.

'Are you homesick, Nell?' said a beautiful young woman. She'd arrived with Ifechi and another woman, and a gang of children.

Had Nell heard correctly? She must be coming over as some kind of misery. 'No, no, really. I love it here.'

The two women were fascinating; chatted easily to each other or to Nell but when addressed by Ifechi, refused to answer. Instead they sat back and mockingly admired him. Ifechi clearly found this infuriating. Better not to notice how charmed Jerome seemed.

'Ifechi is publishing a few more magazines,' Jerome had muttered when they arrived. Well, that might be helpful. A couple of the tiny children splashed out of the pool, landed themselves in Ifechi's lap. He hauled one up, swung it in the air. One of the women frowned, brushed water from her swimsuit.

'Are they all his children?' said Nell.

'I guess,' said the younger woman. 'Ifechi has several.'

'Really? Which of you is their mum?'

The girl smiled, patted her on the leg. 'Oh no, she's not here.'

Nell winced, what an idiot saying that.

Jerome pulled himself out and dived again into the water, a clean and perfect arrow that just missed two men.

'Foolish boy,' said Ifechi. He wiped the moisture from a glass of cold beer. 'Well, Nell, that's good that you feel at home. Mmm, Star beer. Not your American rubbish.'

'Not my American.'

'Don't get cross. I love Jerome, truly I do.'

She must try harder to appear agreeable. 'I like the Star ads.'

'Ah, been to the movies again? I love the movies.' Ifechi made a gun with his fingers and took pot shots at the sunbathers.

'This is a film-set.' Nell gestured to the heavy pots overflowing with flowers, the poolside bar. 'Or an advert.'

Going to movies had become her treat, though Jerome said they couldn't afford it. They were usually American gangsters, the ads mostly done locally – Lagos a set where beautiful couples drank beer, smoked, drove sports cars and wore expensive Western or Nigerian clothes. The roads were empty. The water lapping the shores of the harbour uncontaminated with rubbish, oil, sewage, dead dogs. Colours were vivid, sharp, making up a world which could be day-dreamed into, and it was here. The other doctors chatted about nightclubs and highlife music. It was a world she and Jerome couldn't quite get to. No sitting drinking beer as the sun went down, the right camera angle, lazy long shot.

Jerome was doing a perfect crawl with speed and ease down the length of the pool. He swam so beautifully. Ifechi caught Nell's eye. He was going to be no help to Jerome at all.

23

Maura came rushing out of the front door, pushed several bags into Liam's arms as he stood blankly examining the drainpipes. The house looked solid enough but he'd have to get those elms pruned. Leaves from last autumn were blocking the gutters.

'Stop standing looking cross just because I've dragged you out of your precious bolthole. You were next to me when I told the Lipcotts we'd take the twins; so far I've done all the work. My summer holiday too. I want an afternoon off.'

'I was standing next to you but not necessarily complicit.'

'Complicit, Liam! You weasel individual.'

'Keep your voice down, the children will hear.'

'They're making too much noise. Oh, you liked it when that lot moved in next door.' She was steering him towards the Rover parked in the drive. 'Loved it whenever children turned up. Well this is what it means, and by this evening Rory will have finished studying, I won't see either of you for dust.'

'I can't manage tiny children on my own.'

And he was relying on having a free day.

'They're six, Liam. Not so tiny.'

Maura took the bag from him, threw it in the boot.

'You like small children, Maura, you liked looking after Jess.'

She linked her arm through his. 'I was daft enough to think it part of being with you.'

The twins appeared looking apprehensive, and Maura helped them into the back of the car. As she leant over to fix their seat-belts, Liam slipped down the zip at the back of her skirt.

'Stop that,' Maura smacked him away. 'Now disappear, Anne's coming round, something she wants to talk through. She did say both of us.'

'Don't her superiors have an opinion on her frantic social life?'

'Off you go.' Then she added quietly: 'Just keep Poppy and Robin happy.'

What could Maura possibly gain from an afternoon chatting to some nun? Maura seemed to even like the woman. What did Anne offer a contented atheist with no perceivable baggage like Maura?

They were both childless. Maura said she didn't want children. Not yet forty, she could still have a baby. She seemed to make more sense of his daughter and son than he'd ever done and she wasn't terrified, like he was, of missing something. But now apparently she found small children a chore. Well, at least Rory had become a pleasure and Jess had gone to Connie.

'You two ok?'

No reply. The children were already dozing. It was hot, the car suffocating, the steering wheel burning, the twins would be happier with an afternoon in the garden with a hose-pipe. They could have helped Maura weed, done a bit to the plots she'd set apart for Jess when Jess was small, plots the child claimed to love then neglected.

A whole day lost. He could have finished that landscape. Nobody took him seriously; he should have rented that room in town, got into the car this morning as if going to work. He could disappear there after surgery without any interrogation.

They were right. It was an escape, any peeping toms would see a man holding a paint brush, gazing vacantly out of a window.

He owed Nell a letter.

'I've not an iota of sympathy for her,' Maura had announced. 'She should have persuaded the man to stay here. Taking off like that when she could have gone on with her career.'

Once he had these twins happily playing, he'd work out what to write. 'I'll help with them later,' Rory had said before disappearing to his room to study.

Rory didn't mind playing silly games, reading the same story again and again, endlessly tedious hide and seek.

The car park by the lake was packed; Liam left the Rover at an angle on a slope. 'Shall we change here?' he asked brightly but Robin was already running ahead. 'Right Pops, this is for you to carry, the rest for me.' He passed Poppy a towel and they followed Robin. 'Isn't it lovely?'

The three of them stared at the greenish swamp, Robin jumping up and down. Children squealing at maximum decibel hurled themselves into the water, outrage, hoots of protest. Some of the older ones were swimming around a small island of weeping willows and birches – idyllic, if you got rid of the crowds.

'Ok, let's find a good place for our things.'

Liam had once known it as idyllic; whole days spent here with Connie under the oak trees – Connie, Claire, baby Rory dappled by sunlight, skin glistening gold from the water.

A woman drying a small boy with an enormous orange towel seemed familiar. 'Hello Doctor, you going in?'

On his own he would, but with these two? Neither were competent swimmers despite their mother Angelica saying they were water sprites. Robin would be happy to go ahead, Poppy clung to her brother. 'They're a bit young.'

Six, seven? How old were they? 'How old are you, Robin?'

'Five and three-quarters.'

The woman looked doubtful, carried on drying her son; another glanced over suspiciously, he was nearly fifty, too old to be here with this age of child.

This wasn't a beach, it was an overcrowded semi-circle of grass, a stagnant pond full of disease.

Those five years before Connie left, after the births of Claire and Rory, he and Connie had been happy, hadn't they? 'We should have been warned,' he had said to Connie during one awful session.

She'd just arrived from Newcastle with Rory and baby Jess. He thought she was home for good, then Connie went to the convent, he'd no idea why. She announced as soon as she got back to the house that she was leaving. Had Anne been interfering? Connie claimed Anne had tried to dissuade her.

Robin was bobbing up and down, shaking himself. Poppy, her shoulders drooping, waited patiently for someone to do something; how long was she going to stand there? He'd left the thermos with cold lemonade in the car.

Liam pulled off Robin's shirt and helped Poppy, who had got stuck with one arm in her dress.

'Wake up for goodness sake, Pops, you're half asleep.'

Why so dopey? Almost the same age as Claire: tired and irritable. He put his palm on Poppy's forehead. Normal.

It wasn't their fault they were stuck with him for the afternoon. The orange towel woman had settled with a bag of food only inches from where Liam had put the rug. He closed his eyes – the arguments, laughter, splashes of water, screams, faded into a background of just acceptable noise.

What was her name? Her son was lying against her, dozing and chewing on a sausage. Wasn't he asthmatic? He was a mouth-breather, but so were many children that age. Robin on the other hand was a perfectly healthy five-year old, now paddling cheerfully, chatting vigorously to the child splashing next to him. No tears from either when a group of older children knocked them over.

Liam squinted at the view, at the light on the water, and pulled a sketch book from the picnic bag; packing it was Maura's concession to what she called 'his hobby'. But first Nell. The flimsy airmail letter had been in his pocket for days. Her tight cramped writing was getting more illegible: children in the hospital dying needlessly, mothers sacrificing themselves. When he'd shown this to Maura, she'd sent a cheque to Oxfam. He would write Nell a letter that was long, newsy, encouraging. She'd added something about Dermot before posting hers so must have heard her father had that heart scare on his birthday. Almost fifty. Dermot insisting vigorously that Nell was to blame, giving him all that strife. Ridiculous. At least he'd given up cigars and lost weight.

Liam's notes soon turned into ideas for a drawing; it was increasingly as if he were trying to reach something, never enough time. Medicine was occasionally rewarding but mostly tedious and stressful; it took him away from what seemed more real. Which was absurd. Maura said he was only posing, one day he'd be found out.

How to respond to the unfairness Nell was witnessing? Maybe it would be better if she gave up that man, came home, found herself a dull life too.

There was a yelp of indignation from Robin who seemed to have fallen out with his new friend; they were fighting over a ball which most likely belonged to some other child altogether.

Where was Poppy?

Liam's heart started to race – one minute looking away, and she'd gone.

He dragged Robin out of the water, pushed him on to the rug. 'Stay there, don't move or else. The girl, Poppy," he yelled at the woman near him. She looked confused. 'The girl, Poppy!'

What a stupid name, he ran round the edge of the pond, checked the ice-cream queue. The child had no money. No policemen when you wanted them. After several fruitless dashes round the clumps of families, a few people recognised what was happening; he eventually had a search party going.

'Red swimsuit, yellow hair. Five years old.'

Oh God, how had this happened? Those scruffs fighting, they'd distracted him. Last thing was pulling on Poppy's swimsuit. Did she go in the water? Unlikely. She was much more timid than Robin.

Several teenagers volunteered to swim to the island, were striking off with amateur crawls. A couple had snorkels and said they would search the water; an image of the pond draining in

Women in Love, the helplessness of the observers.

Poppy had just wandered off for God's sake, no reason to imagine drowning. And hadn't she insisted as they stared at the pond that it looked much too dirty and full of green stuff?

There must be a phone box. He started hunting around the cars, the hot and ticking metal, peering through the windows – interesting how many people left food, bottles of pop, in the oven-like interiors to go to ruin. He caught his reflection, red, sweaty, mouth gaping, a Munch scream.

Wherever he looked, he could only see Claire, her bouncy black curls, her grin. Claire racing off into the trees. No, no one. How long had it been? He couldn't drive to get help, couldn't return to Robin, the rug, the pile of clothes. Ten minutes, half an hour, ten hours? How to tell Maura? Perhaps by now Robin had done a runner. Why not lose the lot of them, but Robin's blonde head was just visible behind a family having an argument. How dare they get on with happy normal life? The man was hurling a doughnut at a fat, spotty child, and it wasn't peacefully.

The woods? A few women had said they'd check but they had appeared pretty half-hearted.

He waved at Robin but the poor little mite didn't notice, was constantly scanning people. Poppy would surely have been seen if she went swimming – the lake was the dangerous place. Forget anything else, look there. He started taking off his clothes.

'Doctor?' That patient again. 'Betty has gone for a policeman.'

Who was Betty? Liam pulled on his shirt, jogged over to Robin.

'You ok?' Robin nodded, said nothing. He didn't look ok.

'Poppy just wandered off somewhere.' Important to hit the right note. 'You know what Poppy's like.'

Robin sprung to his feet as if released from some spell, started jiggling around. So annoying. 'She didn't say anything, Liam.'

'I know. I would remember.'

That was a lie. He hadn't been paying attention, been making notes for his letter to Nell, irritated by that woman patient, making plans to move to a more private patch of grass.

'Are you sure, Robin? I mean not just now but earlier.'

'She had the towel, Liam, she wouldn't let go of the towel.'

Did he expect Poppy to have announced to her brother: 'Today I must go for a long, deep, swim.'

One minute Poppy was struggling with that wretched dress, then this absence. Robin was jiggling again.

'Keep still, for goodness sake.'

'Sorry, Liam.'

Liam started to jog round the edge of the pond, Robin swore he'd not move an inch. People kept asking if there was any news. How bloody stupid. Would he be looking this demented? The swimmers in the middle of the pond had given up, were pretending to be exhausted. If Connie had been here she'd be down on her knees offering a pirate's ransom to St Jude or Anthony or whoever was responsible for lost children. He ran up to the women emerging from the woods. They shook their heads.

'The police are on their way,' one of them said. 'No one saw anything.'

No dirty old men in raincoats lurking around, but it might as easily be older children, psychopaths everywhere.

Before the police turned up it was Maura.

'Sit down, both of you. Stop twitching, Robin.'

Maura pushed the boy on to the grass.

'How did you know?'

'Betty rang from a call-box.'

He hadn't even managed to do that. Liam squatted beside Robin, dug out a handkerchief to clean the boy's nose.

'Anne came too. How long has it been, Liam?'

'An hour. Maybe.'

Anne was walking between the families, talking to everyone; many seemed to know her, were trying to be helpful. She looked absurd, covered head to ankle in black, so unlike the sloppy half-naked bodies spread over the grass. But they took her seriously, people got to their feet, gathered around, answered questions.

Maura found a bottle of juice in the orange-towel woman's abandoned picnic. The woman was standing near Anne, the boy clutching his mother's leg. Maura handed the drink to Liam, pointing impatiently at Robin. Robin gulped it down.

'I should never have trusted you on your own. Should have come too, helped Poppy practise her swimming.'

'The water's toxic,' Liam said, opening his eyes slowly. The world was swirling.

'Don't be ridiculous.'

Anne was giving instructions. One minute no one cared, then they all had this expression of self-importance. Anne didn't somehow, she looked serious and severe. And capable.

Maura got to her feet. 'There's the police. Don't let Robin go anywhere.'

There was nothing Liam could do. By now most of the families had spoken to Anne, the adults had joined her search after settling children on rugs with the remains of picnics. Everyone suddenly seemed bothered, everything was muted, conversations quieter. The teenagers who had apologetically raced off to play with a Frisbee were back and joining in.

'I suppose you were dreaming, not paying attention,' said Maura, returning from talking to the two policemen. 'Oh, Liam, they think someone might... are trying to contact the Lipcotts.'

Her distress was unbearable. How dare the sun shine as if nothing has happened?

'Betty's talking to them.' Maura began to scratch the back of her hand, Robin watched fascinated. 'She's friendly with the Lipcotts.'

'Who is Betty?'

'You know her well, she teaches with us. Thank goodness, people do what Anne says. The police are useless.'

Maura was staring across at the trees. Oaks and birch circled the grass. They should have given protection, instead the trees were menacing.

'I told Anne these woods go as far as the road. They do, don't they, Liam? Barely three hundred yards.'

'There's a high wall. Too high.'

'Poppy's not adventurous, unless…' Maura pointed at Anne who had stopped by a low wall of logs in a circle on the far edge from the path to the car park. She was waving.

Maura jumped to her feet, was off, running. There was a blank moment as she stormed straight through people's picnics, plastic plates, cups, thermoses, wrinkled remains of sandwiches, ice-cream wrappers, rejected tips of 99 cones. The van was doing a good business.

Someone was calling him. It was the woman with the orange towel. 'She fell asleep, Doctor, that's all, went somewhere cool. She was hidden by a pile of wood.'

Anne and several others were waiting for Maura. It was Maura who came back with a sleepy Poppy in her arms.

24

When Nell's colleague, Femi, heard that she and Jerome planned to spend Saturday evening at the Federal Palace Hotel, he'd laughed. 'Hardly highlife.'

Better not say that it was her idea: the marble ceilings, deep settees, bustle of waiters, made everything outside less fragile.

As the waiter reached for their almost-empty beer glass, Jerome covered it and the man walked away, flapping out his white serviette. 'What's bothering you?' said Jerome.

'A young boy this afternoon, he'd been knifed.'

The porter had told her the child was Igbo and it was unprovoked. She'd been stitching back the hand of a man who'd been using a home-made butcher's mincer when called to help. It was a mess. Nothing they did made any difference. She'd gone back to suturing her patient.

The band started to play *Seventy-six Trombones*.

'We must find better places, Jerome, better music.'

'We tried, you got bored.'

Jerome had taken her to a shack just off the abattoir road – it had been packed, people dancing, the music loud. After several hours, they'd left. Despite practising for hours in front of the mirror in the flat, Nell couldn't dance like that.

'I talked again to Ifechi,' said Jerome. 'He suggested that if I want to set up a charity, I should find religion.'

'He is religious?'

'No, or no more than necessary, but that's where I'll get the naira to set up what I plan. He says don't waste time waiting for people, try some other way. Anything.'

Jerome finished the beer and stood up. 'Did the boy die?'

'Yes.'

'I need some air, I'm going to walk around.'

After waiting half an hour, Nell left her scarf on the chair, went out through the side of the hotel into the enclosing warmth of the evening. It was so dark she could barely make out the edge of the path – silent except for cicadas, occasional rustling in the bushes. After the control of inside, the garden felt unleashed and intoxicating. Flowers she couldn't see saturated the air with perfume, lush freshness of pampered greenery. Oleander, hibiscus, bougainvillea. This was the Nigeria she'd dreamed about.

Having nearly walked into a parked car, she could now make out others. A rosary was hanging from a driving mirror. Her family kneeling, hunched over the chairs and sofas on a Sunday evening, droning out prayers. More rustles. She was being monitored by two boys; they seemed anxious, were there to keep the hotel protected from the outside world.

Jerome came back not long after her, his eyes inflamed. Had he been crying? She'd been ready to moan about him disappearing.

'Are you alright?'

'Fine. Come on, let's boogie.' He took her hand and they went on the dance-floor. Everyone around them was beautifully dressed, Jerome had ink stains on his shirt, her skirt was creased. They'd never fit in, would always be poor.

How could she think that, then remember the real poverty?

Jerome stretched out next to her on the iron-frame bed, the only furniture in their bedroom. 'My shoulders feel so stiff.'

Nell pushed him on his front, started kneading his back. 'We must buy more oil.' She worked hard on the knotted muscles, smoothing them until they felt silkier.

Then she curled herself around him.

'Are you cold?' Jerome pulled up the sheet. 'I'll move the fan.'

'It's perfect.'

The fan was their latest acquisition; it didn't keep away

mosquitoes but kept them, or parts of them, cool. For at least an hour each evening the power would be on and she could enjoy it.

Nell had suggested a mosquito net, Jerome was not keen.

'You'll get used to mosquitoes, they'll leave you alone.'

'Never. They love me. I'll take you on a tour of the wards with people dying from malaria.'

The dreaded whine, in, out, then the ominous silence. Jerome would pursue any that were persistent, leaving a palm print on the wall over the corpse.

She'd get a net from Supplies. She rolled on to her back, waited for the fan to revolve, was drifting into sleep when Jerome began stroking her nipples; he pulled her on top.

'I was dreaming of orange juice,' she said.

'I know, you were puckering your lips and slurping.'

'Liar. And please slow down.'

'Stop criticising.'

In England she'd been the one in a hurry: the fear that Jerome wouldn't come, that she wouldn't, that they'd be interrupted. He'd managed to stop her listening for the on-call bleep. Jerome had taught her to enjoy sex. Here, where she could stretch and luxuriate, relax into his body, her own body, he'd changed. If only he would be more patient, give her time like he used to.

The warmth, the humidity, had softened her. Eventually she might glide along the road as smoothly as those women sauntering between cars with loaded baskets on their head, move her body as easily as those young girls dancing. Fluid and lyrical.

Jerome pushed even harder, was speeding up rather than slowing down. He didn't wait for her, but came quickly, then rolled away. She spooned her body around his. Held him tightly, willing him to relax, willing him to turn back and pleasure her.

25

Connie gave the patient a few moments to check her Filofax, reach some kind of decision. At least this one, unlike two earlier, hadn't presented with an obscure sexual disease picked up on holiday. The beginning of September, instead of sunning herself in France, she was marooned in Derby ensuring her disaster of a daughter attended school. She examined her nails. Pure hypocrisy to be still wearing Liam's rings but people liked to see the diamond next to the shiny gold, it made Connie less intimidating. Patients thought unmarried women doctors more terrifying than any others.

'It's not a criticism of you, Doctor, I'd prefer to wait till Dr E gets back. He knows me and knows what's best.'

'That's absolutely fine.'

It wasn't life or death, so John Edwards could deal with the patient, but the woman would never get her mood swings treated. John didn't believe in mood swings. If he'd picked up on his wife's depression he might not be stuck on his own with two boys while she sunned herself in Florida. Connie slipped the rings into the desk drawer, went over to the sink.

There was a crash. Someone burst in. Jess, slamming the door behind her, then flinging herself against it. Arms stretched wide. What a drama star. 'You won't believe what's outside.'

'What I don't believe, is you here and not at school.'

Pointless. A miracle if Jess was ever at school. She must want money. 'I left all you needed to make sandwiches.'

'Couldn't we have something together? I never see you, but we can't go back through the waiting room.'

Jess really wanted them to have lunch? What would they talk about? Oh, don't start feeling guilty, the child looked healthy enough. Remember how devious she could be.

'Anyway, it's not what's outside, it's who. I'm expecting Anne.'

'Don't I know. Like a horror movie when I saw her. I couldn't breathe.'

'Did you say hello?' Connie dug in her bag, took out a fiver.

'You joking? And don't ask me to. Anyway she's filling out forms, isn't she? Why is she here?'

'To talk.'

'To you! Then swear you don't mention me.'

Connie waved the note, Jess leant across and took it. 'I'd better go while she's busy writing an essay about why she's such a bad person. You can't possibly want to see her, she's not human.'

Her daughter blew a kiss and was gone.

Jess would soon be fifteen. Had it been another of those innumerable lost opportunities? Fifteen years since those nightmare months after her birth – at least patients with post-natal depression were more understandable. Another condition that John Edwards doubted existed. Leave Jess behind next spring, ask John to help, then spend longer in France. September was brutally early to be back at work, away from Daniel.

It should have been good having Jess in the flat – a break from the boredom of life in England, no church, no golf, no friends, almost no alcohol. Minimal contact with Pat, none with Mamma or the Westport aunts. She had no one. Except Anne.

Could her only friend be a nun?

Connie stood by the window while she waited for the buzzer. Jess was rushing up the road to the bus-stop in the opposite direction from school, her bag slung over her shoulder, pulling her body to the side.

She couldn't be? She was. Jess was dragging on a cigarette.

Reception called through that Anne was ready.

26

Nell stroked her belly and the dream slipped away – something about the child they'd seen that morning. The power was off so it was warm, quiet; she leant over, traced the outline of Jerome's profile. His long eyelashes flickered as she kissed him. He always slept flat on his back, not curled over like her, hiding away.

The power had been out most evenings but suddenly the light clicked back on, the fan started to revolve. Her book was somewhere under the bed. Since they'd no radio or TV, they were getting through novels, both making up for lost time. She'd started dipping in and out of a battered copy of *Ulysses*, was trying to like it. Why did Molly get talked about as such a great character? Why did everyone want to be Stephen? No, Nell was definitely more sad Leopold Bloom, the cuckold and outsider and ever-obliging.

Next to the books were three letters. Colum said their father was fine, had given up smoking. 'I know GP is not imaginative, but it suits me. Dad leaves me to get on with things.'

Dad must adore having Colum at his beck and call.

Liam's letter described losing one of the neighbour's children. 'Do you remember, Nell, the night Claire was ill? I didn't talk about it to you. I'm sorry. No use whatsoever. I hope we learn, I learn.'

Liam thought she was responsible; he'd never said but he blamed her. Why had she messed around admiring the Christmas tree? Not gone up and checked how Claire was?

The last was Connie's. Nell hadn't answered any, they'd arrived ages ago. Connie would understand what Nell meant about two Lagoses, the seduction of one, impossibility of the other. It had seemed important to do something that made a difference, instead she was useless. Connie once said that was the hardest thing, the impotence, having to stand back and watch.

Her parents never talked about medicine in the way her aunt

did. What would Connie have done about the child that morning? Would Nell's paralysis have disappointed her?

The tiny girl had been squatting in the dust a few yards from where they usually picked up the minibus. She was folded against an oil drum, her eyes open but without seeing. Her breathing was laboured, features wizened. She could have been about six, but it was difficult to say. Jerome had told Nell to keep away.

'And let her die? Ignore her like they're ignoring her.'

The people near the shacks had been watching, but they'd seemed hostile and wary.

'No one is ignoring her, she's maybe not their child, Nell, not their business. They know more about this than we do.'

'We can't leave her.'

Jerome had jumped over the ditch, run across to the onlookers. As he approached, each person moved away except for one small boy who shrugged, giggled and, after a shout from one of the huts, had run off.

'Don't touch her, Nell,' Jerome had said as he joined her again. 'They might think you're dangerous.'

'Dangerous? We have to get her to hospital.'

'Have her die in our arms? We'll get lynched. They're used to seeing children shitting themselves to death. That doesn't mean we can kidnap any, even dying ones – and if it survived today, what can the hospital really do?'

There was nothing like a phone box, no way to summon an ambulance. No ambulance to be summoned.

They could all die here.

'Let's go, Nell, leave her to these people. Once we've gone, they'll help. I'll fetch some water.'

As Jerome jogged off to a stall a few hundred yards along the track, she'd crouched down, examined the child, using her book to fan away flies. It was early in the morning but already hot. The small girl was feverish. A taboo against touching? But the child was frightening, letting go in front of them. It was as if Claire was in front of her, Claire's scared brown eyes the morning she was ill.

Jerome had eventually stuck out his hand for the minibus. The girl hadn't stirred so he'd left the water for others to give. They'd managed to find two seats. 'If we'd taken her to hospital she could have had an infusion. Children are tough. Why did we leave her?'

'Take her for what? She's surrounded by her own people. It's their right. They wouldn't have let you.'

'Or they might want us to.' That was it, they might have wanted her to, and Nell had done nothing. She'd left the child in the heat of the morning to die unprotected.

They'd passed the market and were picking up speed on the wider section normally blocked by cattle. A coach on the far side was in flames. Seeing the fire was the last straw for their driver; after a few more yards, he pulled to the side of the road, ordered everyone out. Passengers started to argue. Jerome had grabbed her arm. 'Come on, before it gets nasty.'

They had slipped past the crowd, started the last few miles to the hospital.

'If we'd brought the child, Jerome, he wouldn't have stopped.'

'Please don't tell me you believe that. Not after all you've seen.'

When they had returned in the evening, the girl had gone.

Jerome sat up and flicked at her notepaper. 'You don't know what to say to your aunt, do you?'

He was right. Yet children were dying in this city every minute. They came to the hospital with their desperate parents and nothing could be done. She was not responsible, why did she feel she was?

Jerome would say it was because she was responsible. They all were, were all guilty, and had to somehow live with it.

Connie could see Anne by the bike sheds – the nun was brushing up leaves. What was it made a playground so bloody depressing? It needed loads of trees and grass to get rid of the ghosts of bullying.

'Searching for butts, Annie. Or a quiet smoke while the girls are in class?'

Anne looked flurried. 'You made me jump.'

Connie had promised to drop in Anne's test results.

'As I said on the phone you're not about to meet your maker. In fact, despite the fact you're too thin, you are incredibly healthy. Blood and urine perfect, no suspicious growths.'

She should have posted them, but unthinkable to be in Moreton, not come here.

Anne ripped open the envelope, started reading the report.

There was no time for this. 'I included the details of a local doctor, she's gentle and will do your smear.'

Anne shook her head and smiled. 'No, thank you.'

'Take the other sisters. I've used her several times – the most darling variety of speculums, all shapes, some very small.'

'Please come up, Connie. Have a coffee.'

She'd be late for Rory, who was worried about something. He'd get anxious waiting, then late arriving home to Jess who might be out. God knows where. 'I can't. I've Rory, the journey back and an early start tomorrow.'

'You're always in a hurry.'

No one believed she did three half-time jobs, and not much of a summer break, thanks to this woman expelling her daughter.

'Five minutes?'

Connie followed Anne up to her office: a grim room with a forbidding crucifix over the desk and a picture of the order's founder whose name Connie had never known. It was too familiar.

For fifteen years the cream walls had absorbed her misery – being here felt so deeply sad. Anne made another of her undrinkable teas while Connie checked the bookcase, nothing exciting. Five minutes, she could spare five minutes.

'Connie, they think I'm not up to this anymore. I almost believe them. I hear myself talking to the girls and it makes no sense.'

It was not the time to be flippant. But Anne should get away, the religion which Connie had once blindly accepted with its virgin mothers, flesh-eating communicants, now seemed absurd. Anne would be better free of the convent.

'Then stop. You're young enough to build an independent life.'

'Too old, far too fearful, and I made a vow just as you did.'

'And you saw how easy to get out of that.'

'But it wasn't easy, Connie, as you well know.'

They were getting nowhere, Rory would be waiting. What did Anne need? A physical check-up was easy, Anne's state of mind more challenging. And Connie didn't truthfully care, nuns were not a species she wanted to preserve. Anne as an individual, when less dithering, fine, more than fine. It was usually possible to forget Anne was religious if you ignored her clothes and the chunky rosary beads round her waist. There was no sanctimonious twaddle. But how good if Anne could dump all this.

'It's beyond me how you've managed to be tolerant this long with the whole cabal – the pompous priests, misogynist pope.'

'We expected too much.'

If Anne's big boss nuns had plans then maybe they were in her interest. Anne sounded bereft but there was no time, nothing helpful to say. 'I'll phone in a week, see how you are.' Connie came round the desk, kissed the top of Anne's veiled head.

'You don't have to face this alone. If you want disrespectful and ungodly advice, then ring me.'

Connie hesitated at the bar before picking up her tomato juice and Rory's beer, looked over at her son. He was even paler than normal, the neon light of the pub doing him no favours. The poor boy had inherited Liam's hair, why had neither child got her colouring? Only Claire. Something had grabbed the top of Rory's head, he'd grown a foot in the last year. His face hadn't caught up, his cheekbones too big, shoulders too wide, and he was so clumsy.

It was unbearable. Connie wanted to go over and hug the breath out of the boy, had to hold off; he'd find that excess of affection mortifying. But his red hair was almost Pre-Raphaelite – the girls would love it. 'Don't dare let anyone trim those locks of yours,' Connie said as she handed him his beer.

'Maura is threatening to come in one night, cut it off.'

Poor Maura, not here to defend herself – Samson fantasy or penis anxiety? – whatever, Connie was to blame.

'What are you grinning at, Mum?'

'Have you told Liam and Maura about whatever this is?'

Rory shook his head, looking even more bereft. 'It's Ondine.'

He must mean that girl at the school in Dorking with incredibly rich parents. Whenever Connie visited Rory, she'd tag along for lunch at the Red Lion.

'She wants us to go away together, to India.'

You bet she did, the spoilt little madam. 'That's interesting.'

'I don't want to go to uni. Ondi agrees, says it's a waste of time.'

Of course it was. After all Ondine had managed to fail every one of her exams. What to say to this absurdly innocent boy?

'India's a wonderful idea. Money? What do you plan as money?'

'I'll have my grant.'

Ondine would eat him for breakfast. 'I suspect the authorities will want it back if you don't use it, Rory. Why not invite Ondine to meet Liam and Maura?'

'You joking? They haven't a clue so don't blab. Anyway Maura is always at meetings, Dad hides away in his room with his canvases, splashing paint around. He's banned Mrs M from cleaning, boasts that every few months someone leaves the hoover by the door and he shifts it slightly.'

Was Liam serious about his painting, or only escaping? So the tortured artist had to fight off those pesky women plotting to keep him from being Picasso.

'Do you really not want to go to university, Rory?'

'I dunno.'

Of course he wanted to go, and probably wanted to escape Ondine. Had he been over-protected? It was an eventful enough childhood – a hopelessly neglectful mother – hardly sheltered.

'All I can offer is that life does get better as you get control.'

'That's what you and Dad said before sending me to Dorking.' Rory helped himself to one of Connie's cigarettes.

What a mistake that had been. Liam had insisted that Rory get away from London, Rory had rejected Moreton. She'd paid half the fees. The school cost a fortune, Rory was taught nothing but how to roll a joint.

'Your dad thought you needed an easy-going place where you'd feel at home. He had such a bad experience.'

'He said Uncle Dermot saved him. The comp in Tottenham was better, it was getting home to your flat without being knifed. The jerks assume I'm Irish, therefore IRA.'

'How daft. Anyway there might be a few jerks at uni, Rory, but you'll find more students support the IRA and Troops Out. Plus you don't sound Irish.'

But he did look it. His red hair must have been problem at school and he'd never said. Then there was his name.

Nell stopped, goose-bumps all over her body. Something was disturbing the packed clinic. Nneka had scooped up the used syringe and disappeared, dragged into an argument with a patient. It was late, a queue stretched the length of the room. A man was staring at her, his gaze like ice slipping down her back. No question what he was feeling. He hated her.

Nneka returned, eye-brows lifted in a question.

'He's putting me off. Who is he?'

'Waiting for a woman having the free vaccination.'

'Can you ask him to leave?'

Nneka laughed. 'How? You made as much fuss when my friend was here. That poisonous nun, you called her.'

Nneka didn't budge. Normally she wouldn't hesitate to eject people. 'I can't, his sort argue. That man's been to Europe.'

Nell was on her way to the Paediatric Ward when she saw Femi picking at the bark of one of the enormous trees that separated the hostels for the male and female nurses.

'You've been to England, haven't you?'

'I have.'

'Do you hate the English?'

'I do.'

Should she say she wasn't English, she was Irish. But she felt English, whatever that meant. She took the bark from him, pushed the pieces back on the trunk.

'Do you hate enough to kill them?'

'Not quite that extreme.' He pulled away more bark, threw it on the ground.

Outside the morgue, people were sitting beneath the trees.

'Why do they wait, Femi? Queues in Pharmacy or Out-patients

make sense but people over there stay days, nothing ever happens.'

'They do wait for days. They have to queue for the right body, to make the right negotiations.'

As they walked back to the clinic, he told her a story about a three-day-old corpse that had come back to life, then was run over by a car.

He'd heard her talk about Mass to Nneka, was he mocking her with the resurrection?

Nneka greeted her at the entrance to the clinic.

'You look worried.'

'Femi was describing the fate of a revived corpse.'

'He's flirting, noticed how daft you can be. I've a better one from my auntie: a whole crowd after this robber, and he disappears into thin air. Instead there's this donkey, so they arrest it, take it to the police station.'

'Well at least you don't believe it.'

Nneka winked before rushing off.

Jerome was waiting for her that evening in their usual place outside the hospital. Nell told him about Nneka's thief.

'We live on the main road to Kirikiri prison,' said Jerome. 'Why else do donkeys end up hiding behind our block?'

It took a second before she realised he was joking.

As the k-k bus came swerving towards them, she spotted the man from the clinic.

'He looked earlier as if he'd kill me. Nneka says he's a Been-to.'

'But so am I,' said Jerome.

29

Liam used the windscreen cloth to polish his shoes. He went round the car checking the tyres.

'Sorry, Dad,' Rory called out. 'Seen my spare glasses?'

Maura would be helping Rory search. Liam straightened the cases in the boot, tucked in the squash racquets more carefully than Rory's effort, made sure Maura's food parcel was safely upright. When he came back to Moreton, Rory had learnt to study. And now, if he ever found everything he needed, was leaving home. Biochemistry, but he might switch to medicine.

'No patients though. I'm not cut out for watching people die.'

Whatever. It depended on whether Rory could organise himself sufficiently, at the moment he was much too scattered. Maura had been worried he'd decide not to go, some girlfriend. That wasn't likely, knowing Rory. Liam wandered over to the hedge, pinched out the centre of a cobweb resting like the softest muslin on the privet. Webs were everywhere: some garden spirit had flown in overnight, spread them to dry.

He'd untied the L plates, Rory was not showing any enthusiasm for learning. Think of advice, say something fatherly. Best to resist the temptation to go back inside, ask Maura what that might be.

'You don't mind about Pat?' said Rory, once they'd reached the M1. 'I want to settle in.'

At least Rory had the wit to avoid his aunt. Liam had been too dutiful at his age, tedious visits to decrepit relations.

'Did you read that introductory stuff? Was it any use?'

No reply.

'University is a chance to think, Rory. I found I could step back, look at Ireland, at myself, at the church, get perspective. There'll be various societies for students.'

'I know, Dad.'

'Maybe some debating thing?'

Again no reply.

What about the practical business with girls and having protection that fathers were meant to prepare a son for? A shudder of embarrassment: the cloying smell of hay and cow in the old Ford, his father's broad right hand gripping the steering wheel, the other, tobacco-stained, stabbing the air as he spoke.

He didn't have his father's square calloused fingers but the same red hair had bristled from the knuckles. 'Keep clear of women, Liam. Nothing but trouble. And always have a rubber to hand.'

'One important thing, Rory.'

His son looked across and grinned. The little devil knew exactly what was coming.

'It's not the Dark Ages, Dad. Think of the school you sent me to that year, that's all we were taught.'

So it wasn't only building model Tiger Moths.

The Dark Ages had probably been a lot easier than life for him and Connie in Dublin in the nineteen fifties.

'You be careful, your mother and I weren't. Blighted us both.'

'Well, thanks very much.'

Liam dropped Rory off, and drove to the tree-lined suburb where Pat and Dermot had moved after years living over the surgery. It would be marginally easier if Dermot was at home but he'd gone to Northern Ireland to play golf. 'I'm not allowing bombs and those murdering bastards to put me off.'

Perhaps it was as well. Conversations with Dermot usually ended up in an argument. Pat was little better; she and Maura could barely be civil with each other.

Pat took several minutes to answer the door. Sunday at this time, Maura would be in her dressing gown. Pat looked impeccable, full make-up, a pink linen suit, a carefully arranged Hermes scarf.

'You look dressed to go out, Pat.'

'This old thing? I was at eleven o'clock, that's all.'

'High Mass?'

Pat nodded and hung Liam's jacket on the hall-stand, steered him into the dining room. 'You needn't go on about it, I know you're a heathen.'

The long polished table was set for three. He picked up one of the Waterford wine glasses.

'And don't go on about those either. Mammie was clearing out and Connie is never settled anywhere enough to care after anything. Help yourself to a drink.'

She disappeared in the direction of the kitchen. Over the fireplace was one of his pictures. Had Pat quickly hung it, knowing he was coming? Its wispy blues, faded sky and sea, filled him immediately with the same yearning as when it was painted years before. He would never again do anything like that. There'd been a small exhibition at the gallery in Moreton; he'd overheard Mrs Lemon whispering to a patient about 'Doctor's little hobby'. Maura summoned everyone, a quarter of everyone dutifully turned up. Excruciating. Dermot had driven down, bought this.

It couldn't look more out of place, yet should have fitted in. Pat had prints of Jack Yeats's Connemara landscapes above the book cases. But it wasn't nostalgic – it was sad.

Rory was gone, Jess gone. Could he give up work and paint?

Where was Pat? He found her in a transformed kitchen: on a central work station you could boil twelve saucepans at once, overhead was a giant extractor fan. Vulgar or enviable? She was standing by one of the double-sinks, holding in each hand a bowl with half a grapefruit. She was flushed, had been crying.

'We first decided after Aidan left. It's taken all this time.'

He removed the dishes, took Pat by the shoulders manoeuvred her into a chair by the breakfast bar. He was hungry. Could smell roast lamb.

'Will Nell ever come home, Liam? How did we manage to mess up so, Connie and me?'

'Three lovely children and you've a grand job.'

'I loathe public health, no respect if you're not your own boss. Colum does Dermot's night calls. Both earn far more than me and no one telling them how to run their clinics.'

Liam hated grapefruit. 'Could we skip these, go to the roast?'

'I thought Rory was coming. He'd need feeding up.'

They both looked at the inadequate first course. Pat snatched it away, began to carve the lamb. 'Rory off into the world. Will it make any difference? It did to us. Dermot misses them. Jessica seems fine staying with Connie, you must feel freer.'

Pat was right but where was the courage to make the change? Once he announced painting as more than a hobby, the vultures would be on him.

When he'd finished a second bowl of trifle and plate of cheese, Liam wandered into the sitting room. Pat came in with coffee and he held out a silver-framed picture of Colum getting his degree.

'Dermot said he was happy doing GP, but I thought the boy more ambitious. Last time, he mentioned paediatrics, a while ago he'd be a classicist, no thought of medicine?'

'Nothing wrong with GP,' said Pat. 'He got hit on the head with common sense. What good is ancient greek? He said he'd pop in.'

Colum had found classics so absorbing. No photographs of Nell's conferring, she probably hadn't gone herself.

'Aidan's studying hard, only Nell to worry about.'

A relief to hear Nell's name. 'Why is Dermot not budging?'

'She's ruined her life.'

'For goodness sake – she's qualified, working and happy.'

'Happy!' Pat took out a handkerchief and flicked imaginary dust from a statue of the Child Jesus of Prague.

'We were steam-rollered into careers, Pat. Too early.'

She had sunk into an armchair, was stirring her coffee as if whisking cream. 'Do you know anything of her?'

'It sounds a tremendous experience.'

'I'd love to get a letter, I don't care if Dermot goes wild. Will you leave her address?' Pat was like Marie, her mother, who attributed any of her grievances to her husband.

After Claire died, Connie and Pat's father a year or so later, Connie had refused to visit: 'Mammy has lost focus for her bile, hates everyone except the fecking clergy.'

Liam had taken Jess and Rory over for a week most summers when the children were younger; Maura had no problem leaving him to do it alone. A thankless business, they'd to pretend they went to Mass every Sunday in Moreton. He coached them before they ventured out to the granite church.

'You took communion. The hypocrisy of it,' Connie would say, when Rory described kneeling down each evening in the over-upholstered sitting room, in the dark draughty house, saying the interminable rosary and doing the responses to the interminable litany. He even liaised with Dermot so they didn't overlap. 'If that happened,' Dermot had said. 'The mother-in-law would have the bejasus and kill Pat with talk of the hard labour of it all.'

Duty, he had thought it his duty. Crazy. Fortunately, by the time Jess was eight and Rory eleven, both refused to go.

After more coffee, chat about work, the Polish pope, Dermot's health, the virtues of absent Colum – a reasonable time to get away.

A red MG scraped to an emergency stop on the gravel drive.

'Good to see you, Liam.'

No more being called Uncle. They shook hands.. Colum was handsome, a couple of years and the boy had filled out. Twenty-six -seven? Taller than his father, black hair short. He looked confident and content – contact lenses, thick horn-rims had gone. Starting out on life, and Liam wouldn't swap his future for a second.

'Pat, do you have a pen? I'll write down Nell's address.'

She disappeared into the house.

'I could have given it to Mum. She's never asked.'

'How is it with your father?'

'Pretends he's not smoking, won't let me take his blood pressure.' It must be difficult for Dermot, slipping off for a smoke with his son around.

Colum ran his hand over his car. 'Isn't it beautiful?'

Was this it for Colum? 'You still doing those Latin translations?'

'Am I heck, Dad has me run off my feet. I haven't had a moment since leaving school. Rugger kept me sane not Horace. How is Jess?'

'Living with Connie, driving her mad.'

Pat returned, grabbed her son's arm. 'Come in for a moment.'

'I can't, Mum. Didn't want to miss you, Liam.'

As he handed over Nell's address, Liam wondered from Pat's reluctance if she'd already changed her mind.

30

As soon as her mother had driven off to work, Jess abandoned her hiding place behind the hedge. It stunk having a birthday in November. It was usually freezing, almost always raining. She tiptoed back upstairs, let herself into the flat. Creepy 'you can call me John' and his creepier sons from the flat next door had already left – but she couldn't be too careful.

The hall was full of coats and shoes, the kitchen full of dirty dishes. Why could her mother never make anywhere homely like Maura or Aunt Pat?

No way today was she going near that school. Fifteen. Ancient. She poured herself some of the sherry that Connie used for cooking. Disgusting. She found cigarettes in her mother's dressing gown pocket. Connie had made an effort over breakfast, scrambled some eggs. She'd even wrapped up a Body Shop box of soap and talc and bubble bath, or more likely the shop assistant had done it. Most impressive was the cassette player from Liam and Maura, small enough to put in her school bag.

First, Jess had to organise her alibi. The plan was to doll herself up, go and see *Grease* at the Odeon. Connie had given her money, so she could shop, buy tapes. After that she'd watch the fireworks.

'Is there anyone from school you can invite back, Jess?'

'I'm having tea with a couple of friends.'

'Who are they?'

'Friends.'

Perhaps she should have invented their names, and some heart-warming back stories. However from experience she knew the best tactic was to say as little as possible.

'Do you want something special for when you get home?'

Something special? Connie had abandoned any ambition to provide a decent meal ever. Jess being a vegetarian was beyond her so Jess lived on chips and cheese and bananas and peanut butter.

'Anything special in mind, Mother? Maybe Heinz beans on toast rather than the Price-rite version?'

'Don't be snarky.'

Connie had then discovered she was late, and Jess was late. While her mother raced off to get ready, Jess had grabbed her school bag and made her way to the hedge; after first slamming the door as noisily as she could, and yelling good-bye.

One of the boxes in Connie's bedroom was full of papers including blank appointment cards from former jobs. Jess found a favourite, carefully wrote in her name and the time of the appointment, making it half-way through the day for flexibility. Once the school secretary saw the words Brook Advisory Service she would stop reading, flush pink and wave Jess out of the door. For good measure there was an additional note in Connie's writing and Connie's signature which she'd got down to a work of art.

The phone was ringing. Panic.

It could be the school in which case the best thing was to answer it, say she was off soon to the doctor. It couldn't be Connie or Dreadful John. She knew no one else. Jess had been in this town since January and had not one friend. Well, if they hadn't all been gross and in gangs and spiteful, it might have been better. They called her names, nicked her bag, pinched her arms, until eventually she took revenge on the biggest one by punching her in the face, and kicking another in the stomach. Since then they'd kept away, and Connie had managed to calm down the head-teacher.

Connie had nursed hopes that Jess would become bosom pals with Dreadful John's two sons. Say that again, Mother? Are we all on planet earth here? Those spotty smelly morons?

Jess stubbed out the cigarette and answered the phone.

It was Rory. 'I knew you'd be bunking off. Happy birthday, skiver. I left something in the bottom of your France bag.'

Rory knew that she never unpacked that bag until she needed to find things before the next holiday.

'Rory, what happened with Ondi? I thought you were about to be wedded and blissful?'

'A mutual agreement to split.'

So Ondine had dumped him. Well – exceedingly good news. That princess had been more evil than Snow White's stepmother.

'Are you truanting all the time, Jess?'

Jess said nothing. You could never be quite sure with Rory.

'Can't blame you, it's the same here. Uni is tedious, the lectures rubbish and tutorials worse. It might get better when I can stick to pure biochemistry, give up what they think's essential background.'

'This time next year I can get a job,' said Jess. 'Stop this school rubbish.'

'A job might bore you to tears.'

The flat seemed very empty once he'd rung off. Jess took ten more pounds from the emergency fund in the Jasmine tea caddy. In the bottom corner of the France bag, below some mouldy T-shirts, was a tiny pack of cellophane. Inside was a small brown lump of what looked like clay.

Rory was infuriating. She hadn't a clue what to do with the stuff and knew no one who could help. She put it back. Fine for him, going to those fancy schools.

'You hate the convent,' Connie had said. 'Why not go to Rory's school? He loves it. Why not?'

Because even if Dad and Maura's house was hideously suburban, she hadn't wanted to be so far from home.

31

It wasn't the intensity of the blue sky, pale yellow sand, it was the water. Breakers twice their height crashed to a beach that stretched miles. The roar made it impossible to hear anything else.

Nell and Jerome changed behind the dunes, chased each other into the breakers, able to scream at full strength. They splashed, wrestled. They were seals – slimy, slippery.

Several blue-robed evangelists were praying further along the beach: 'It's Christmas. Baptise me, Jerome.'

Nell's voice was swallowed as if she'd made no sound.

An enormous breaker and she was under water, Jerome holding her down. After a panicked few seconds, she managed to shove him away, gasp in oxygen, splutter out sea-water.

'Are you ok?' Jerome helped her back up the beach.

'What possessed you?'

Jerome shrugged. 'You asked.'

She followed him to their haven behind the ridge. What had actually happened?

He'd never before been rough. Was he angry? He was so quiet lately, much more than usual. He'd been fed up with her going to church with Nneka. More than fed up.

'It's hypocrisy, Nell.'

No. It had been curiosity.

She threw herself down beside him. 'Is this about Mass?'

'Don't be daft. I thought you wanted baptising. Or are you after absolution because you and Nneke were up to something else?'

What did he imagine? They were partying on Sunday morning?

She lay back and looked up at the deep blue of the sky.

It was Christmas Day. They were having a traditional family row. But where was the turkey, stuffing, the bread sauce?

It had been shocking, the familiarity of the church. There was even a tatty crib, an off-white Holy Family with lumpy lambs, straw, cotton-wool snow. Except the congregation were dressed for a party – no huddled shapes keeping their eyes down, thoughts muffled.

Jerome had asked if she'd expected everyone to whirl around, dance up and down the aisle, then fall in a faint. No. But a black Jesus in the crib would have helped.

Had it been an accident, he'd misunderstood? It was terrifying to have the water in such control.

Exactly what the man in the tent in Norfolk had described: a wall of water taking you from your feet, throwing you around, drowning you – nothing you can do.

1979

32

Connie's gift, Anne put away in a drawer, then began copying appointments into a new diary. Connie was impossible; she'd sent a calendar of churches: Protestant, Catholic, Presbyterian, all grey-stone and austere from various parts of Ireland. July in Armagh was as severe and unlovely as January in Cork. On the back were small pictures of each, at the bottom Connie had scrawled 'Spot the odd one'. It was a joke, but Anne was feeling too dense to get it. Better to hide the thing away.

Many of the sisters were Irish, would anxiously gather around the wireless for news of the latest atrocity. What a mess over there in the North. All these churches were complicit, especially the Catholic ones. A one true faith, and she was head of a school that promoted it – bombs had been exported to England, so had the ideology fostering them.

She snapped the pencil she was holding, now both halves were useless.

Phone Connie. It was an acceptable time to offer greetings, the whole convent had benefited from the women doctors at the clinic. To call and thank her was not a waste of money.

Connie was delighted.

'You never do this, Annie, it's always me. What a breakthrough, the warders must have taken the day off. Are you ok?'

'I'm fine, thank you.'

'Well, I'm not. No idea why I let myself in for slave-labour in this middle of nowhere. Four months before parole, I even feel sorry for Jess. Are you sure? No fatigue? No mid-life crisis?'

'No. Tell me about your daughter.'

'The little menace was with Liam and Maura for Christmas. She came back so downtrodden I'm indulging her, allowing her out one night a week. Not that I've a clue what I'd do if she disappeared all seven. Alcatraz? Talking of which are they demoting you yet?'

'If you mean transferring me, they haven't decided.'

'Ah, clever, they will when you least expect it.'

'You know, Connie, I miss your daughter.'

'I'll send her non-recorded delivery.'

Jess had been a nuisance during RI but an interesting one. Those hazel-green eyes, unruly red hair – the child glaring at Anne, demanding to know how she could possibly be responsible if God knew everything first. Jess was not convinced by free will. No matter how much Anne argued, or indeed obfuscated, Jess was outraged at the absence of logic. No easier when she stood in Anne's office, asked why she was being punished for thumping Mary Peters? First, God planned it, and second, Mary was a bully.

'What did you expect me to do with the calendar, Connie?'

'Did you discover the odd one out?'

There hadn't been an obvious one. 'They're all as architecturally challenged as each other.'

'Ah, you're not rooted in that unforgiving bog. Too many Italian spires and domes, gorgeous frescos in your version. Well, Castlebar was the only church that had a side door open.'

She hadn't checked the doors. Did Connie mean open for Anne to leave, or for someone else to enter? That someone certainly wouldn't be Connie.

'Oh, Annie, come to France and let's go to Chartres. You fixed us up with Madame Martin, I'm eternally grateful. And I want you to meet Daniel. He's so perfectly uncomplicated, absurdly young, and no doubt will abandon me soonish, but while he's around I'll make the most of him.'

Connie would exploit him.

'You could use your friend at the presbytery as an excuse.'

The nun was a remote acquaintance; under no circumstances was Anne holidaying with Connie and some boy in France.

It had felt right when she'd decided to phone, but now she wanted to put the handset down.

'And you'll take Jess out of school.'

'Don't worry, she'll get some education. I've a friend who'll look out for her until the end of the summer term. John Edwards is a doctor at the clinic, has two children and lives in the flat next door, so you have to approve.'

'She needs her mother, Connie.'

'We are talking about Jess, that fifteen-year-old going on fifty-five? Plus she has more sense than you. You're letting them grind you down. And compared to Pat, I'm an excellent mother.'

Well, that was debatable. Anne pulled over her diary, opened the first page. What had she expected from any of this? Connie was not going to change.

'No softening of attitudes in Newcastle?'

'They don't want to know. Nell writes occasionally but doesn't say much – at first it was about work, now it's more superficial. It's as if she's given up noticing. I'd like to be a fly, or mosquito on the wall. Don't you have colleagues there to do some snooping?'

There was no one to ask. And no point. Nell was an adult and all Anne could do was include her in her prayers. Connie must imagine some network of sisters scattered throughout the globe, taking notes.

'Pat and Dermot need reminding of the Good Samaritan, but they were always hopeless. Pat studiously ignored our collection box when I was with Liam.'

It was on the mantelpiece the night Claire died.

There was a pause before Connie said: 'Do you think Maura or Liam dumped it when they moved? It was always there, wasn't it?'

Anne had no answer for that.

After a moment, Connie said: 'Look, ring me again. And don't wait months.'

And she had gone. Anne slowly put down the phone. What had she expected? There was no one she could talk to. The only people she felt close to, apart from Father Willis, were Connie and Maura. Both non-believers. And they'd advise her to leave the convent.

'Of course, it will be difficult,' Maura had once said when Anne tentatively raised the possibility. 'You've been in some kind of institution all your life.'

Change was not possible. She'd been certain of her future the night Connie's daughter had died. Exactly sixteen years. Had Connie realised?

Of course, that's why she'd rung off so abruptly. Connie didn't want to go back to then, to the box for the African missions on the mantelpiece. The pictures of smiling children.

As for the behaviour of Nell's parents, hadn't Maura once said Pat was on the Cafod committee, raised money? They probably went to the annual ball.

Anne had scratched a hole in the first page of her new diary with the stub of the pencil – a hole that would be there all year.

33

Nell picked up the next file. The child was sitting in a corner of the clinic resting his hand lightly on a woman's knee, making no demands. He had his back to the room. He was probably about three. His head was slightly tilted as if he were tired, soft black curls resting against the creamy skin of his neck.

Nell must delay this. She could run her fingers up his spine, tickle his hair, but she made herself crouch in front of the boy, read his notes. His mother's expression was blank – she was staring at the wall, not seeing anyone.

The patient looked at Nell, his huge eyes cautious. She smiled back. His nose was snub and smooth. His lower lip trembled slightly. Where his left cheek should be was nothing, a cavity with no skin or flesh; it exposed the inside of his mouth, his teeth, his pharynx.

The mother knew the loss was irreversible, its progress inevitable, triggered by malnutrition. He would be given a pointless injection of penicillin, sent home. The mother would probably carry him for miles. A new year, no hope.

How could any mother do that, watch her child die day by day? Nell would never have children.

*

Mrs Hargreaves thanked Liam profusely, even though he'd refused her plea for Valium. An awful time of the year, trying and failing to be spring. He should have relented.

Still muttering thanks, she shuffled back with the screaming baby to the pram in the waiting room. What more could he do but sympathise, and arrange to see her again?

Mrs Lemon put her head round the door. 'Dr Ryan was on the phone. Not urgent.'

'Dermot?'

She nodded. 'He'll call you later.'

The car was in for repair, he had to walk. What did Dermot want? On the rare occasions he phoned, it was usually to ask for something.

Once home, Liam poured himself a whiskey. Phone calls with his brother-in-law were not a favourite way to spend an evening. The main thing was not to get irritated. Maura was at some meeting at another school – sandwiches under a cover on the kitchen table.

Dermot said he'd rung to talk about the latest IRA bomb.

'What do those bastards want with a man like Airey Neave? Gets out of Colditz. The man a hero. The cowards slaughter him.'

Because they were maniacs.

'All these years of mayhem, Liam,' Dermot continued. 'I haven't had one single patient berate me.'

'A few commented.' Liam unpicked a sandwich, took out the tomato. 'Especially after Birmingham.'

But that had been more mystification. People wanted an explanation. And he'd failed to provide it. Connie would have ranted on to anyone curious about the fanaticism of the priests. Maura would have mentioned the poison of nationalism and given a history lecture. He'd offered nothing.

He took an apple from the fruit bowl. Like many of the other boys at school, he'd supported the IRA. He'd even imagined himself a sympathiser while studying in Dublin. When Dermot found out, he'd told Liam to stop being a bloody idiot. But that was before the 'Troubles' kicked off in '69.

Where had his certainty gone? They were all, the various splits of the IRA, the Ulster Unionist lot, the whole British Army, all no more than a bunch of thugs.

He took the kitchen phone as far as it would stretch to see if Maura had chutney in the cupboard. None. He threw the rest of the sandwiches into the bin.

'I suppose your good lady is still for this protest they're at in the Maze? Spreading their faeces on walls.'

'I agree with Maura, Dermot. They're boys and being bullied.'

They were no more than children. Some mothers' sons. Oh, to feel that certainty himself. What would he have done at Surgeons if it had been like now, and he was approached to help? Liam pitched his apple core at the bin. He missed.

'How are the children?'

So Dermot had phoned because he wanted to talk about Nell. Liam retrieved the apple core, tried again. Success.

'Neither of them interested in politics. I don't think Rory even reads a newspaper. And Jess doesn't read, full stop.'

'You should have given them a decent Catholic education.'

This was getting close to familiar and annoying territory.

'Have you written to Nell yet, Dermot?'

'Is Connie still drinking?'

That was a bit uncalled for, Liam should make a list of all subjects not to be mentioned. Whenever he slipped up, Dermot would retaliate, become vicious. Nell was out of bounds, Catholic observance a risky subject, but that might be because Pat was getting more and more devout. And the longer the silence between Nell and her parents, the worse Pat would get. Any comments about private education were also tricky. Dorking, fortunately, was never counted as private. Far too wacky, and too brief a stay for Rory, to be taken seriously. Liam and Connie and Maura were consigned to the world of deluded socialists.

'Write to Nell, or you'll regret it.'

'Stick your nose in someone else's business, Liam. Not mine.'

'But that's the same rigidity that keeps these bastards building their bombs.'

'You've the fecking cheek to say I'm no better than them?'

The front door slammed. Maura appeared at the kitchen hatch, gesturing over her shoulder. Liam caught sight of Anne. Weren't nuns meant to be in their convents praying for the salvation of souls, not making unannounced visits?

And someone would have to drive the woman home.

'Maura has just arrived. Do you want a word with her, Dermot? She's brought Sister Anne.'

That should calm Dermot down. He might even pass on to Pat, they were socialising with nuns.

The first time he'd seen Anne since the afternoon Poppy hid, then fell asleep. Anne had saved him. That image of her organising people at the pond was engraved on his mind like a luminous circle dissolving the horrors of the surrounding afternoon; he'd even tried to paint it.

'I don't give a tinker's curse who you have there, Liam, I did not ring to be insulted.'

This was taking a familiar route. Maura was hunting in the fridge, should he rescue the sandwiches? But then there were the tea-leaves, apple cores. Perhaps not.

'I'm not insulting anyone. You've a lovely daughter, she'd like to hear from you.'

Maura took the receiver. 'Everything alright, Dermot?'

Anne was examining a sketch he'd done of Rory that Maura had pinned to the wall. She was wearing a cardigan over her habit, half buttoned; she looked untidy for once.

He'd an urge to straighten her up.

Odd to see a nun in his kitchen. He had no link to his religion apart from the occasional attendance at Mass; since the divorce and moving here with Maura, no priests had visited – he'd been dropped from the list of Catholic families.

Papa said faith had helped after Mamma's death. Papa actually said that it had saved him, but religion became his straitjacket. If his son was to reject the church, they'd nothing to say to each other. 'Don't waste your time looking for logic, Liam. You either have faith, or you don't.'

'It's like a hand-knitted sweater, Papa. If you pull at a bit of wool, the whole thing comes apart.'

Maura was making faces, Dermot must be in full spate.

She handed him back the receiver. 'You pissed him off, Liam.'

Dermot sounded breathless.

'I didn't ring for a lecture. And to be insulted.'

'Come on now,' said Liam.

But Dermot had slammed down the phone.

34

Jess lay in the long grass by the lavender beds and waited, a typical dozy summer morning in France. In the distance, Madame Martin was screeching at her hundreds of children. No sounds from the summer-house. Hide here and tick off her wants. The Martin children must go straight to the river, not anywhere near this field. Her mother must come out of the summer-house alone. They could sit together on the porch, drink lemonade freshly made this morning. There were other wants, nastier ones about the midget Daniel. But it was too hot, the jasmine and lavender too dizzying.

The sun was moving up the hill in and out from behind the branches of beech and apple and it flashed across her eyelids, the same warm pink as the roses her mother had planted by the barn. She must not fall asleep.

There was a clatter, Daniel leaving the summer-house. He looked like a child, small and neat but so noisy. Connie said he was almost forty. No way. He'd be looking smug. The muttered shush that followed was her mother – slow giggling steps to the cottage.

When her earth was restored to quiet, Jess stood up and flicked away grass. Everywhere was silent, the children had vanished, the Martin house beyond the fence, deserted. The Martin's washing, impossible numbers of shorts, blue work trousers, T-shirts, aprons, vests, hanging inertly.

The summer-house smelt of wood, of heat and glue and Daniel's aftershave. Her mother's pink cotton wrap was slung over a canvas chair – Jess tucked it around her waist.

Daniel had gone and Connie was in the kitchen smoking and reading a letter, her black hair falling loose to her waist. Ridiculous at her age.

Connie jumped, startled. 'Can't you make a noise when you come in, not scare me to death?'

'Who's been writing?'

'Nell. I'm not sure she was told that Dermot had an angiogram. Well, he's fine. More gloom and doom and despair from her at unnecessary deaths. Poor kid.'

Nell was such a saint. 'I made lemonade,' said Jess.

'It was delicious. I had lots but desperately need coffee.'

There was no coffee. Her mother threw the airmail to one side, picked up a three-day-old copy of *Le Monde*. 'I thought you were in bed.'

Connie was the one who could sleep all day.

'You'll have to get your act together, Jess, can't laze around all summer.'

Connie stubbed out a Gitane on the earth floor.

'I should have been more resolved, forced you on that train. Liam was all set.' She pulled out her purse, tossed it on the table. It looked fairly empty. 'I'm running out of money. Almost August. For God's sake, go to your dad and Maura. Start studying.'

They glared at each other. Her mother sounded unhinged – it must be the menopause. So, Jess should give in, slink back just because it was convenient.

Anyway, Maura wouldn't have her, nor that headmistress. Connie should face her responsibilities, not let a parasite like Daniel stop her looking after her own daughter. Her only daughter.

Rory once asked if Jess minded Granny insisting that Claire lived on in her. 'Only I've stupid red hair like Dad, not Claire's black curls. And I'm not sweet.'

It was as if she'd been born into a great sadness that no one but Granny would talk about, and all Granny ever did was hold her too tightly and cry.

No, her mother couldn't wait to send her back to Grimsville.

Connie pulled herself up with a groan, started opening cupboards. 'I'm starving. What I would give for coffee, eggs, a brioche. You'll have to help me here, I can't pay the rent. We've a week to sort it. All I can think of is that Daniel and I head south with a tent, camp for free on the beach in the Camargue.' Connie waved an empty tin. 'Look at this. Not even a lousy tea-bag – Daniel and his mates, thieving gannets.'

'I want to stay here, I want you to stay.'

'On fresh air?'

Jess felt sick. Even with Daniel sleazy in the background it had been good lazing about, cooking food with her mother.

This couldn't happen.

'Let's both go to England. You could find another job.'

'Give me patience. Be in Derby in the rain when I could be lying on a beach. I'll be back soon enough in the autumn.' Connie came over to the window and hugged her. 'I'm at the end of my tether with you, Jess. '

So now it was her fault. Her fault that her mother didn't love her, had no intention of looking after her. To decide to leave now when they were happy and all together and everything was fine.

She could always try and be nicer to dreadful Daniel.

Nneka watched Nell hang her white coat on the hook outside the changing room. 'How are things with you and Jerome?'

'Fine. Why?'

'He used to chat when he picked you up, lately he's in his own world. Sometimes he looks very miserable. Do you think he wants to go home to England?'

This was home. If Jerome was miserable, it was hardly surprising. But what could she do? She'd been busy working, while he was queuing to see people who, more often than not, never turned up. And he was probably being hassled, an Igbo without job or connections.

Nell had a few times come across Been-tos who glared as if they wanted to kill her, but that was nothing compared to the hostility that Jerome described facing almost every day. Most people she came across were like the patient this morning who had asked where she was from; the man had been friendly and curious.

Even so, Jerome couldn't possibly think of London as home.

Was Nneka right?

'My home's wherever Jerome is. Certainly not Newcastle. Where's yours?'

'With my mother,' said Nneka.

Could Pat be placed in one of the doorways? She could easily be that woman, wearing dark glasses, leaving the finance office with a box of papers. Or maybe the one over there in the oasis of dusty trees, sheltering under a giant palm.

She didn't miss her mother. What a thing to admit.

'What is Jerome's African name, Nell?'

'Nonso.'

'And he never uses it? He must feel so cut off from his family.'

'Have you any intention of cutting off from yours?'

Nneka didn't reply and Nell was about to ask her again when Femi appeared. Nneka shook her head at both of them and left.

'The ward round starts imminently. Stop dawdling, Nell.'

Pointless tagging along with Femi. She'd no role except to trail behind the others, one more of the seemingly enormous people all wearing white coats.

The child in the first cot was just hanging to life. Eleuwa, the consultant, refused to notice his small patient barely held from crying. He spoke a few seconds too long and the child collapsed, burying his bald head in the pillow.

A nurse pushed the boy back to face them.

'Where is he from?'

'Somewhere remote,' muttered Femi. 'His father had to go home, left him for us to heal with your Western medicine.'

'You're a magician. Give him both.'

'I'm not his magician.'

Eleuwa's ward rounds were usually easy but lengthy. He took control, occasionally throwing a question at Femi. It was the nurses who knew everything, the ward sister who kept Eleuwa briefed.

Femi took her arm. 'When we've done here, let's have lunch.'

Nell picked a corned beef roll from the glassed-in display in the Common Room, Femi bit into a mango. Talking to Femi managed to make all this more bearable: the children on the wards with only a few days to live, all the other incurable patients, the mother that morning with elephantiasis who tried to keep the evidence hidden while they treated her toddler, because she had no money. She'd objected angrily when they'd stamped Pauper on her files. Why? When it meant she could have free treatment?

'Do people in this hospital make you feel a stranger, Femi?'

'Of course, how about you?'

'I'm so obviously strange, it's as if I'm in the right place at last.'

Was that as true for Jerome?

Femi wiped his fingers on an impeccably ironed handkerchief, looked round the room. There were a few other doctors, all male. All had their heads in newspapers.

'You are full of questions. Well, Lagos is not my home, my people are from the North, very different. If stuck, we address each other here in your language, thank you, but don't rush to chat.'

'You sound like Jerome, you all hate us.'

Why had she said that about Jerome? It wasn't fair, or true.

'Well, for some reason,' said Femi. 'You English don't like us either, don't like letting us in. You write about us, visit us, don't let us return the compliment.'

Should she disown England? Was that racist place actually part of her, even the toffs? No, never the toffs, nor the National Front, nor the Queen for that matter.

Nneka was by the line of wash-basins in the children's ward chatting to one of the porters.

'You shouldn't be friendly to that man,' she said, passing Nell a towel. 'He's no good.'

Femi had pulled up a chair by the bed of a ten-year old girl in kidney failure.

'I'd like him as my doctor, Nneka, if I were that sick.'

'He has no soul.'

'Just because he's not Christian?'

'Some people are dangerous. And you know he has thousands of girlfriends.'

Jess had to stretch it out so Connie could make it from the post office to the bank and, if that failed, track down Daniel. He'd be either in the vineyards beyond the old mill or the back room of Duval's bar by the brickworks. If the vineyard, Daniel would be delighted, he was only pretending to help his brother before escaping Pontissy – but he wouldn't have any money.

She sipped her grenadine. This couldn't end. Summers were France. A few times, they'd also gone to Westport with Dad, to visit Granny. But summers were France with Connie.

Connie refused to come to Ireland, even though they were visiting her mother who was on her own after Grandad had died. A completely embarrassing experience, having to go to church and pretend holiness. All the cousins and seriously weird great-aunts. Dad was super-polite but she and Rory could tell they hated him, blamed him for the divorce, blamed him for their mother never visiting. They definitely blamed Jess for looking like him and not like Mum. Probably, even blamed her for Claire's death.

Jess always came out in spots when she was at Granny's, which Dad said was from drinking milk fresh from the cow, but no one stopped her drinking it. So they wanted her to die too.

It was hot, even under the shade of the chestnut trees. She licked the drips of grenadine from the outside of the glass. Slow down, Connie might be ages. When they first came to Pontissy, they'd cycle here, hang around in the square. Rory would join in with boule and Jess tried to play and always some locals would chat. Today two old men in shiny black suits were hunched over a chessboard. Mainly men like that used to sit around and they'd whisper secrets to Rory – he'd refuse to say what.

Connie had said they were probably smutty jokes.

Rory had been learning French since he was seven. Apart from the couple of years with Connie in London, at the local comp, he'd been to all sorts of schools. All loads better than her convent.

Liam had claimed to be powerless. 'Sorry, Jess. Best do what Maura recommends.'

Pathetic. Her French picked up listening to Daniel and his friends, some use that. Once Rory stopped coming, Connie became even more glued to Daniel. He'd turn up like a bad smell each morning. They'd waltz off, often for the whole day.

But it was ok to stay alone at the cottage, she could practise her songs. The best thing though was to doze in the field or by the pond, the dusty perfume of the valley drifting up through the fruit trees. It must not stop, not any of it: chopping vegetables on the front step, setting the table under the old walnut with bowls of milky coffee, fresh bread after one of them had collected it from the boulangerie.

An old man tottered past talking to himself. Jess took two sips.

No one cared. 'You brought it on yourself, Jess,' Dad had said when he put her on the boat train in June.

He didn't seem at all guilty that he'd banished her to Derby of all places, after that monster nun, that twisted wreck of a person, that shrivelled ghost had expelled her. And then Connie had signed her into that dreadful school full of enormous thug-like girls.

Jess put down her glass. Somehow she'd nearly finished and Connie was nowhere in sight. She should report her parents to the NSPCC. Left on her own with creepy John and his Neanderthal sons. Once Connie had swanned off, she had to join them for supper and meals at the weekend but the food was disgusting. The boys smelled of dirty socks and talked of nothing but rugger. She tried to be as rude as possible but they were all in their own boring worlds, and didn't notice.

One morning at the school without Connie to check was enough. She hadn't meant to bash that girl so hard but the kid was asking for it. She'd typed a note from Connie on John's machine, signed it with a perfect Connie signature, said how terribly sorry Jess was and how she, Connie, was taking her away pronto.

Apart from an hour dragged out over a milky coffee in a café, she spent all day, every day, in the local library. It was warm and free, Connie had given her a feeble allowance. After three weeks, she'd cried into the phone so hard, Dad couldn't understand a thing and drove immediately to Derby. 'What do we do with you Jess?'

He had given her the fare for France, put her on the train.

Only a few weeks later, and Connie had started to nag.

On the opposite side of the square, with its verdigris covered fountain and benches under poplars, were shops between the alleyways and cream houses. Most of them were shut for August. Several dark-suited old men were deep in conversation; a few ambled around waving their sticks at no one in particular, or at cross-faced old women with shopping bags. The women didn't have to stoop like Jess and Connie to avoid the dried herbs and packed baskets hanging from the grocery ceiling. Next to the closed chemist was a closed patisserie: no more glazed-fruit tarts, strawberry and blackcurrant and cream. Jess was starving. Three doorways further down, a dark window, a striped blind and a notice saying Open. But it also seemed shut, the few who sidled into the darkness looked furtive.

Robert emerged from the hotel. 'Jessie!' He was beaming as he adjusted his trousers. 'How good to see you, such a stranger. I keep hoping you and your mother would turn up at Mass. The Martins are always at eight o'clock.'

Robert was the local curate. The nun who housekeeped for the presbytery was their introduction to the village and knew the terrifying Sister Anne. She had found Madame Martin's cottage for Connie; Robert had been a regular visitor in Rory's time. Even though he was old, at least in his thirties, he and Rory got on. But

Connie said Robert made her uneasy, he looked so unhealthy, so fat. When Rory stopped coming, Connie made it clear Robert wasn't the most welcome local. The good sister they never met.

'Can I join you?' His too-wide smile broke up the otherwise vacancy of his pastry features; he settled himself opposite, folding his flesh into the wicker chair. 'You look sad, Jessie; they haven't gone, have they?'

It was common knowledge.

'She always stays to the end of September, no matter how broke. She wants me to disappear, but I won't. It's my place too.'

Robert leant over, patted her hand. 'Calm down.'

She played with her glass until the cramp in her chest had gone.

'Do you want another?' Robert called over the waiter.

'I hate grenadine.' It was the cheapest thing on the menu. 'I'd love a cafe crème.'

'Anything else?'

She had no idea how much curates earned but definitely more than she had, enough to buy a snack. 'A sandwich, salad and gruyere?' After all, he used to come to them for loads of meals.

'A rich daddy, that's what you need,' said Robert.

How could she convince her father to send money?

'Do you know, Jess, as you get older you look more like Rory.'

Oh, great. Freckled Rory with his lank, shoulder-length hair. 'Thanks so much, Robert. Actually we both look like Dad.'

People would say that as if it was a good thing. Well, it wasn't at all flattering, her father's beaky face, long body. 'You're both so badly strung!' her mother would laugh. Connie could mock – her perfect figure like those dancers on TV and absolutely no exercise, it wasn't fair. 'A fine looking woman, your mother,' Monsieur Martin would say. He was definitely thinking of Connie's breasts, which had not been inherited, Jess's were like fried eggs.

She missed her father, his long silences, then his urgency trying to explain something. Always managing to make it more obscure. She missed him even if he spent most of his time hidden away painting. But not Moreton, nor Maura and that teacher's voice, on and on and on. Though Maura wasn't really that bad.

Connie was coming out of the bank. She'd clocked Robert, would be torn between sitting with that creep and the chance of a free breakfast. Connie's stomach won. 'Lovely! It's been ages.'

Once Connie had arrived, Robert seemed to shrink. How was it that people could change so quickly? Connie had an espresso and croissant, shaking her head at the mention of anything more substantial. She must be starving but, even so, her mother seemed exhilarated. That was worrying.

'We have to leave today or I'm due another month's rent with the cottage. Madame has people who want to move in immediately. We'll follow the sun, when the car gives up, we'll hitch.'

Hitch, how cringe-making. Nearly fifty, impossibly ancient. And not a word about her daughter.

'I worked like an idiot last winter, thought I'd saved enough but it's nearly run out. Daniel can pick up some work.'

Daniel pick up some work? That was so likely. It was Daniel and his friends eating the savings that meant Jess would be homeless.

'And Jess?' said Robert.

'At last she can do those exams she keeps avoiding, can't you darling?'

'No, Mother.'

'Yes, darling. You keep changing, what is it now? French would have been useful.'

Her French was ok.

'Your French is excellent, Jessie.' Robert took a chunk of brioche and dunked it in his coffee. Soggy bits fell on to his black shirt, leaving splodges of brown. Disgusting.

'When do you plan to leave, Con?'

'Now, or rather, tonight. Anyway, as soon as possible.'

Tonight? They drove back in silence. Her mother was an awful driver, went too fast yet gripped the wheel as if terrified. Although, a crash would be perfect, they'd both die.

'Stop the car.'

'It's a couple of months.' Connie reached across and squeezed her hand. 'There's not much choice.'

Jess forced opened the door, the car still moving. Connie swerved to a halt, screaming as Jess half-fell out. 'You want to kill yourself!'

'You don't give a shit, as long as you and fucking Daniel are ok.'

'Idiot.' Connie slammed the door, followed her up the road. 'Stop and bloody talk about it, don't go storming off.'

Jess began to run towards town.

'It's only a couple of months.' Connie stalked back to the car.

Her mother was clearly not about to come after her. There was a series of bangs from the exhaust as Connie accelerated away.

Eventually Jess turned and headed for the cottage. It wasn't just a couple of months, was it? This talking of leaving that her mother badly wanted had been all of Jess's life, ever since she could remember. There hadn't been one house with Connie ever. The two winters in Derby had been so boring – that dreadful school with stupid girls plastered in make-up who, once they'd given up physically bullying, walked away when Jess said anything. Those pathetic performances in class when they sat as far from her as possible. 'But she smells, Miss.' The equally pathetic teacher would go pink, ask them to settle down. All Jess could do was nip as hard as she could anyone who came near; the victim traipsing off to the Head who added it to the Jess crime-list.

'How come everyone hates her?' said Mary Wight one morning as Jess got off the bus. Beating up Mary outside the main gate till she screamed for mercy had been excellent. Jess's last visit to the school but she'd left in triumph. Then weeks sitting over a cold coffee in the Moo Cow all morning, the library all afternoon.

She wanted to be with Connie, but her mother would have to be ok with her tagging along on her sad holiday, which obviously she wasn't. Was the only alternative returning to Liam and Maura's five-bed detached, fake Tudor with garden, double garage, an hour wait for the bus to town? That was inconceivable. A no-brainer.

The cottage was still miles away, a relief to see the car puffing towards her. 'I know it's lousy,' said Connie. 'But I can't think what else except Derby, which you hate.'

Had her mother been crying? Her face looked blotchy, her voice was wobbly. 'I want to take off tonight, miss the August traffic.'

Connie turned too swiftly from the main road; the car gasped its way up the rutted lane.

'Oh, great.' Try not to whine.

'Let's have a special supper. I've no money, you know that? Go back to Liam and Maura. You like them.' Connie paused to negotiate a horse watching them from the middle of the lane, refusing to move. Jess got out, steered the mare through a gate.

'If, however, you promise to be an angel with Madame Martin and want to stay a bit, Dermot and Pat will be in Quimper. They're there for several weeks, know you're at a loose end, be pleased to see you. I can find the train fare and a little to keep you going, can manage a week or so with Madame but can't afford the cottage.'

Connie skidded through the mud and braked with a horrible screech. 'Can you consider going home to Moreton?'

'No.'

Daniel had been given steaks, and enough cheese to keep vegetarians happy, Connie borrowed vegetables from Madame Martin's garden. They took photos of Jess's efforts at gardening – five potatoes and one runner bean – then boiled them. Jess decided to be civil, Connie might leave her more money. She found loads of wild rocket and picked out some young dandelion leaves. One of these days she'd try the young nettles.

Daniel stacked the fire with wood despite complaints that a fire was a waste, then handed over her guitar. 'Play your songs, Jess.'

No way.

Daniel started plucking at the untuned strings, crooning some mushy French thing. The smell of herbs and bay leaves from Connie's soup. How could they want to leave?

'I absolutely cannot wait to get to the sea.' Connie stretched and bashed Daniel on the shoulder. 'You could do some fishing.'

Jess leant out of the window. She wanted to vomit – too much Roquefort, she adored Roquefort. No moon, a faint reflection from the Martin's hall light on the hedge surrounding their yard.

She heard them leave in the middle of the night. Connie had tiptoed in and kissed her, Jess pretending to be asleep. When the car had sputtered into the distance, she went into the kitchen. A note was on the table with an open return to Victoria, and a bundle of francs clipped to a sprig of lavender.

'You know I hate good-byes. That sweet monster Madame Martin says she can put you up at hers for a few weeks. Ask her if you need anything. Dermot and Pat are expecting a visit. Some people plan to collect keys for here tomorrow. Be nice to yourself, remember I love you. Miss you already xxxx.'

Jess went through the pitch-black of the yard to the toilet and threw up.

37

The miles of interweaving lanes were unlit, no moon. Nell and Jerome were lost. They clutched on to each other, could barely see their feet.

'I never thought of bringing a torch,' said Jerome. 'It shows how unsociable we've been, not venturing out at night.'

Nell had been as content as he was to stay in the flat. Apart from Ifechu, Jerome's friends had remained as names, people he had lunch with. There had been only one invitation to meet another couple – the man was Hausa and intimidating. His German wife had looked washed out, exhausted, and as they walked around admiring the house, unruly children, she'd seemed uncomfortable with Nell's questions about life in Lagos.

Nneka had slipped the invite into Nell's pocket several days before.

At last, by following traces of music, they found a gate set into a wall; people milled around a central pool of light in a large space circled by small huts with low entrances. Nneka looked luminous. Gold earrings, necklaces, bracelets, gold threads studded with gold beads braiding her hair; chains of gold circled her wrists, ankles, neck. She wore a lemon brocade waistcoat over a lemon satin dress, carried a small chest already overflowing with naira. As she greeted each guest, notes were stuffed among the others.

'You should have warned me about the money, Jerome.'

'She's your friend. Is it only her birthday?'

After handing over their gift – a scarf from Kingsway – shaking hands with numerous strangers, they sat on one of the benches. Young children ran around handing out cans of cold beer and soft drinks. One of the tiny ones stopped, held tightly to Nell's leg. Nell hauled the child up to her lap. How good, the girl using her like an armchair, letting herself be cuddled.

'That toddler suits you,' said Jerome.

Was that what might happen? She'd end up exhausted and drained like the German woman, have several rough children, and Jerome away enjoying himself with Ifechi? And if the children got ill? No, the thought was inconceivable.

Oil lamps had been strung along wires between posts. Nneka and her family walked among the guests, in and out of the light. People had started to dance. Reflections spat and shimmered, not just from Nneka's gold, most people were wearing lavish jewellery.

'We're so drab, Jerome.'

'Rubbish, you look beautiful.'

Thank goodness for Connie's linen dresses. Nell kissed the top of the child's elaborately plaited hair, the girl smelt of rose-water. The women wore expensively designed wrappers and the men, Jerome the only exception, were in embroidered agbadas, mostly full length with matching pants. Guests were still arriving, picking their way along the same mud tracks.

Dishes started to appear, Nneka brought over chicken and rice.

'You look wonderful, and such a wealth of presents,' said Nell.

'I'm so old it's like a dowry.' Nneka shooed away the small girl.

'Oh, no, Nneka, don't.' Too late to stop her.

Jerome finished his food quickly, handed Nell the empty plate. 'How about more? Quick as you can.'

'And? If I don't?' said Nell.

He was showing off in front of Nneka. All of this, the extended family, the party, the glamour, this crowd of people enjoying themselves, was upsetting him. But Nell could do nothing. She couldn't conjure up any relatives; neither apparently could he.

Nneka grabbed her arm. 'Come, let's get the man more chop.'

As they reached the cooking area, Nneka said, 'You shouldn't talk to Jerome like that.'

'He shouldn't to me.'

Everyone pushing her around. Why had Nneka sent away that child?

An elderly man joined them, Nneka introducing him as her uncle; he asked Nell for a dance while Nneka took more food back to Jerome.

When Nell left the dance-floor, tired but slightly happier, Jerome was gone. He wasn't at any of the tables where people were slicing cake, carving up chickens, wasn't collecting beer. Where could he go? He'd disappeared. He'd been as lost as she had.

There was a dark corner where she could make herself comfortable, see the entrance and bench where they'd been sitting.

Nneka was having a subdued row with a large older woman in red silk; the woman tugging at an ornate silver necklace whenever she paused to listen. At one point, Nneka reached across, gently touched it.

As the hours passed, people drifted off. A few dancers stayed with the music, a couple giggled in the shadows on the left. Nneka was now chatting to a lean-faced woman in a drab-blue suit, no gold or glitter. The woman looked familiar.

Wait till dawn, find her own way home, but the night was never-ending. She must not cry.

Nneka didn't seem surprised to see Nell appear, didn't mention the absent Jerome. 'Come and meet my mother.'

The woman in red who'd been arguing with Nneka was boiling water on a stove in one of the huts; she beamed a welcome. The room smelt wonderfully of coffee. Nneka filled a few mugs and her mother added dollops of condensed milk. 'Mary, give out the cake, I'll be back.' The mother was gone.

'Mary?'

'My given name.' Nneka handed Nell an enormous slice of date sponge.

'She was giving you an earful earlier.'

183

The coffee was very sweet.

'She thinks I'm wrong to walk out on this.'

Nneka made a circular gesture that could mean the people in the compound or all of Lagos.

'Why would you? Are you?'

Nneka had once told her that her mother had come with them to Lagos to find Nneka's father who'd left their village during the Biafran war. By the time they'd got here, he was dead. No money. No support. Three young children. 'The nuns helped us.'

The sweet drink and rich sponge were too much; it was so warm inside the room, some lilac perfume mixed with the smell of coffee. Nell could barely make out Nneka's face, it would be wonderful to sleep. Then she remembered why she felt miserable. Jerome had vanished.

Nell woke to the sound of muttered voices. It was still dark. To her relief, Jerome was back. He was standing under a lantern by the door, arguing with Nneka and the lean woman in the blue suit. At first it was good to see him, but he seemed agitated. Jerome liked to debate but this was more heated.

Interrupt them? Two toddlers were lying on her legs. The blanket felt comforting, the children fast asleep, there was gentle snoring from the far corner.

'You're bitter,' Nneka said. 'I'm happy. Love my neighbour. Your bitterness doesn't help me.'

'Love God and let be,' murmured the strange woman. Definitely a nun, definitely familiar from the hospital.

'But you don't let be,' said Jerome to the nun. 'Leave Nneka alone, leave all of us alone. You'll make Nneka a dry old woman.'

There was laughter from beyond the entrance. A bright light blinded Nell as it flashed through the open door; one of Nneka's cousins burst in holding a lamp.

'You is an old woman, Nneka,' said the cousin, tossing her shoe into the corner.

The snoring shape grunted; Nneka's mother lifted her head from the mound of blankets, threw the shoe back. The cousin clutched Nneka, both shook with laughter. Nneka's gold braided hair flashed in the light, some of the strands were coming undone. Their hug turned into a dance. They looked glorious.

Nell pushed the children away gently and got up. She'd try to sound calm. 'Where were you?'

'I met some relatives,' said Jerome.

He had never mentioned relatives.

38

Jess couldn't sleep. Admit defeat? Spend time with her aunt and uncle, the last people on earth she wanted to be with? If her father found out that Connie had swanned off like that, he'd assume this is what Jess would do. And Maura would agree. Although Maura might get heavy, insist she came back to England, take life seriously. The cottage creaked and shuddered. It was so utterly dark she kept her light on. As soon as seemed decent, she carried her bag and guitar across the field.

'But we've already finished breakfast,' said Madame Martin, giving her a bowl of milky coffee and baguette, before showing her the tiny attic room. Should she pay and how much? Her money wouldn't be nearly enough.

During the next ten days, Jess went into Pontissy several times. The farm was noisy and distracting, she couldn't concentrate on Rory's half-read copy of *The Idiot*. But cycling around the square, not stopping for something to eat, was miserable.

She phoned the number that Connie had left; the people in Quimper said the English doctors had changed their dates to the middle of September. Five weeks. It was a muddle and typical of her mother. Be decisive. Going to England was not an option.

The following day, Jess got up before anyone else, washed her hair, brushed it with the same effort Maura used to use, tied it in two plaits on the top of her head. She was now employable. She cycled to the presbytery; a blank-faced nun, round wire spectacles, eyes looking only at the ground, answered the door. Jess made herself smile hugely at the top of the woman's veiled head while she asked to see Robert – there was not going to be a flicker back.

Hands tucked into the roomy sleeves of her habit, the nun swished across the hall having twitched her head for Jess to follow, taking for granted she'd scuttle behind. A heavy oak door was swung open; Jess was ushered into a large room.

'Well, hello.' Robert got up from an enormous armchair by an empty fireplace. He looked less substantial, almost tiny among the huge cupboards and dressers, dark brown polished table, high-backed uncomfortable chairs. Battered green filing cabinets, drawers half-open with papers sticking out, lined one wall.

'Where have you been, Robert?'

'Here, Jessie, where else? Have they gone?'

He must know they had. 'That nun who answered the door is not exactly welcoming.'

'Did Sister not chat?'

Chat! Hardly. Why did Robert need some slave opening the door? Couldn't he do it himself?

'Sister St Paul has been to Moreton, speaks excellent English. She met your father.'

'What?'

'A job,' Robert said. 'I have found you a job. Or at least Sister has found you a job. Difficult during the summer, we were lucky.'

'I thought I could be your secretary, Robert.' The mess in the room was inspiring. It needed clearing up. 'Could tidy your papers.'

'The sisters do that. Look, sit down, I'll get us tea.'

The nun brought in weak instant coffee, and Robert described his plan. Maybe he didn't mean what Jess thought he meant – it was impossible, couldn't be worse, he was crazy.

'You're no better than Mum, what species of monster do you think I am.'

'Calm yourself. Let's take a walk.' Robert ushered her out past the holy sister who was now down on her knees polishing the hall parquet. 'It'll be part-time and cash. This way you can get to your field, afternoons, weekends, evenings. You only need to take the customer's money. Nothing hands on, I knew you'd hate that. I've explained it to René.'

'Is there nothing else?' He was a priest, wasn't meant to lie.

'Maybe in a few months. This will be good for your French.'

Jess hesitated at the shop door then followed Robert in. It was cool after the square – the smell hit her immediately, chilled and faintly sweet and not unpleasant. At first she thought the place was empty, then saw the boy behind the counter. She backed away from the carefully arranged squares of flesh on the white slab. There was sawdust on the floor and a glass booth by the door with steps up to a wooden stool and ancient brass till. The sort-of strange odour beneath the cold penetrated the whole room yet it was all very clean; the boy was wearing a spotless white shirt and white trousers.

He was called Jacques, his French fast and difficult but he had a sweet face.

'You might as well start,' said Robert. 'Jacky will explain and he needs help. Apparently, René Lorent won't be in until tomorrow. You'll be in your glass booth taking money, need do nothing else.'

This or going back to Moreton, begging Liam and Maura to forgive her. She would try it for an hour.

Jess climbed up into the box and settled herself by the till. No point dithering. If she stopped to think she'd be back on her bike, cycling up the hill, having to face Madame Martin and the ugly vulgar strangers in her cottage. To the side of the desk was a pile of accounts. The writing was mostly the same, neat but illegible; she could at least make out the figures. A few had thumb prints, the shadow of blood prints on the corners.

Jacques had put on a dark blue apron with one strap over a shoulder, was placing joints of meat on a glass slab, lamb joints he told her.

'I'm vegetarian.'

He nodded and looked blank, as if she had said good morning.

Her glass box felt comfortable. The morning passed quickly, a steady flow of women with well-worn shopping bags or baskets.

Jess thought she'd feel exposed but it was as if she were invisible. They passed up their chits and their money, she handed down change. It felt quite calming. She had never been in a butcher's before. Connie, who was no vegetarian, would have shopped here, leaving her on the bench outside the hotel. The hardware shop in the next town had a similar glass booth; there was no chat there between the woman and the customers, and it was always a woman taking the cash. The bluff talkative men behind the counters seemed delighted at having to solve Connie's problems with a leaking tap or broken hinge. They'd disappear into the back, emerge with sprockets and nails and more advice. Then the cashier would take Connie's money, grumpily hand down change.

Madame Martin appeared with a couple of small boys in tow.

'How did you know I was here, Madame?'

She didn't bother to answer, was already looking suspiciously at the kidneys Jacques was offering. This town was a mystery; everyone knew everyone's business yet mostly passed each other in silence, just the nod of a Good Day.

'Supper? Still those vegetables? I'll cook you rice, Jessie, but if you change your mind, want beef, you see there'll be plenty. Or I'll make you chicken.'

Thank God she was here, not in her field listening to the panic and squawks, crashing of flesh and feathers against the hedge that surrounded Madame Martin's hen house. One afternoon a hen had flown into their garden. By the time she got Connie to rescue it, Grandfather Martin had trotted over, wrung its neck.

Jess took the chit from one of the Martin boys. Jacques' writing was clear – and there were no prints.

After supper, she went to her field. The summer-house was empty. No sign of life from her cottage. She lay down on the grass but it all seemed less safe. There was wood smoke from the farms below, a syrupy sickliness in the air which was abuzz with wasps and hornets feeding on rotting cherries. Gross of Robert to find her such a job. Survive the week, then decide.

Next morning she could see the butcher's van at the end of the alley beside the shop when she parked her bicycle. He was sitting in her glass box and it was too small for him; he was a stocky man, older than she'd expected, probably in his thirties, like Daniel.

'Good morning,' Jess said, her heart thumping.

He nodded, without looking. His T-shirt was too tight on his hairy arms; he had pock-marked skin, brown eyes, and thick dark eyebrows that almost met in the middle. A murderer, a classic criminal's face.

'You appear very young,' the butcher said, looking suspicious.

'I'm sorry.'

'Do you want coffee?'

That meant going with him into the back of the shop, Jacques was away delivering orders. Was it Sweeney Todd who chopped up people? She hesitated, then followed. It was a long cool room smelling of soap, with high ceilings and stable half-doors at the end that opened on a yard: a motor-bike leant against the back gate, a couple of sheds, several bins, three pots of red geraniums.

Two well-scrubbed wooden tables stretched the full length. What seemed like hundreds of saws, chisels, knives hung from one of the rafters, from another, pans, saucepans, jugs. It was difficult to breathe. On one side there were two padded, insulated doors – better to forget the dead animals hanging in rows.

One end of the table had no barbarous instruments lined up ready for action, so she waited there. The butcher stood over the small sink next to the cooker, grinding beans, measuring them out. He slowly filled the pot with water. It was a ceremony. Did he ever speak? She could be another lump of meat. He unhooked two small cups – he was used to being watched.

The coffee was delicious.

All morning Jess sat on her stool taking chits and cash, handing down change. Jacques came back and dealt with the customers, chatting to them while the butcher moved silently in and out. She didn't leave her box until twelve. Today, they'd work the afternoon.

She went with Jacques to sit under the chestnuts. Madame Martin had put cheese and tomato sandwiches into her bicycle basket; Jess refused to exchange them for Jacques's ham. She was getting used to his accent, he was being patient with her French.

'You children happy?' Robert settled himself on a bench beside them. 'How is the meat trade? Well, this is a turn-up, Jessie, we didn't think you'd last ten minutes.'

'We?'

'I mean me,' said Robert.

'Good at her sums?' Robert asked Jacques.

'Very good, of course.'

She could hardly blame Robert. She'd always gone on about everyone else eating meat and the hideous cruelty that involved. She hadn't much choice, would stick it for a couple of weeks – it was interesting in a weird way, would definitely shock the lot of them.

39

The days at the shop passed quickly: a week, then two weeks, a month. Each Friday morning, an envelope with cash would be left by the till; her name in a script that was not René's, not Jacques's. Jess gave most to Madame Martin, who at first seemed surprised, thanked her effusively, then quickly accepted it as routine. Maybe it was too much. Connie never said what she paid for the cottage but Madame M was giving her full board – anyway she had hundreds of children and not much money.

At first Jess would strip and wash as soon as she got home, scour her whole body using Connie's Pears soap, scrub her clothes in the bathroom sink. After a few weeks she left her dirty things in a pile with everyone else's; they'd reappear on her bed a few days later, folded and ironed. No one had ironed her clothes before. In fact she'd never seen either Connie or Maura using an iron, a vague memory of Liam struggling with a pile of shirts when Mrs M was on holiday.

At work she had a system and the accounts were soon filed, her desk clear. The butcher would disappear leaving Jacques to serve the customers, clean and sweep. Jess started to help, wiping down the counter, brushing the floor, but that was it and she left the back room to Jacques.

It was peaceful when René was out. Once he returned, the air became urgent, customers demanding – as if he charged the place.

One morning he called her into the back room; it was like being called in to see Sister Monster Anne. He was separating fat from sheep's kidneys, the far end of the table covered by white lardy blobs. He nestled the soft pink globes in his palm, rubbed off the yellow skin. The door to the chill cabinet was open, rows of carcasses hanging from steel hooks.

'Would you serve next week, Yessie, when Jacques is away?'

It would mean touching the meat. She hesitated – he was now slicing mounds of sweetbreads. There was a sweet cloying smell of offal. Would she get the sack for saying no? Was it such a big deal? In fact it was rather impressive. She'd been promoted. She still didn't have to eat the stuff. 'I suppose.'

An urge to giggle had to be suppressed. She could hear Rory. 'All that fuss when you gave up meat. You were what, eight, nine? Cauliflower cheese ever since. Maura full-on at the allotment, hunting for recipes to please the little madam. At least Connie brought home chips, let you get on with it.'

That's exactly what he would say, what they'd all say. But this didn't mean she had to do anything. Just pick up the meat ordered, wrap it and take the money. René would do the other stuff. It would be good for her French. She'd have to increase her knowledge of parts of animals pretty quickly. Since Mum had left, her vocabulary was getting quite impressive, but knowing the difference between rump, ribs, flank, had never been necessary.

Jacques appeared with his empty basket, set it down by the sink.

'Start showing Yessie how everything works.'

Jacques didn't even look surprised.

A few days later, René was packing up knives, wrapping them in sacking. He saw her hovering. 'I thought you'd left, Yessie.'

She liked the way he said her name. 'I promised I'd lock up.'

'No, Jacques will do it.' He looked at her. 'Do you want to come? It might be of interest.'

She didn't completely know what he meant but followed him to the van. They were silent as they drove but the engine was making such a racket she wouldn't have heard if he had said anything. Jess tried to forget the bag that he'd thrown in the back until they bumped up the track to a farm several kilometres out of town.

'It's a favour,' he said. 'For a friend.'

She went with him and a couple of children, who had come running up to the van, to the back of the house. A pig was tied in a corner, snuffling gently through cabbage leaves. An elderly man with an enormous grey moustache and a young plump woman came over from a long wooden table set up in the middle of the yard, kissed the butcher three times. They examined her with nods of cautious welcome as they shook her hand. It was a late summer evening, the air sweet with wood smoke and rotting plums – everything was in too golden a haze for murder.

The woman handed round small glasses of a white liquid which made Jess's nose pop and clean aprons which she refused. As soon as the butcher began to un-wrap his knives, she walked over to the far wall, turned her back, stared away over the ploughed fields.

What had she been thinking? She tried to block out the noise – the heavings, grunts, extended screams. Unlike any noise she'd ever heard, it filled her head and the world, and went on and on and left her visualising everyone in the yard panting and screeching.

There were ripe plums above her head. She reached for one, the gold flesh was syrup. Delicious. A small boy tapped her elbow, thrust a glass of brandy into her hand, ran off giggling before she could thank him. She wandered round the vegetable plots, sniffed at the cabbages, waited for what seemed hours, got bored and returned to watch.

Now that the noise had stopped, it was if that horror had never happened.

'I'm sorry,' she said as they drove back. 'For not helping.'

He smiled. 'You were there to help?'

She stared at his white jeans. There were tiny spots of blood. At her feet was a neatly tied parcel for Madame Martin.

40

Nell sat on a stool with her back against the concrete wall in the kitchen watching Jerome negotiate. It was early but already hot; all the doors and windows of the flat were open but no hint of a draught.

'Three pairs of white shorts,' said Jerome. 'Have you bought the material? Was the money I gave you enough?'

The two boys nodded. They were both about ten although she always found ages tricky to estimate. They watched intently as Jerome took a piece of string, cut off his waist size.

He was too thin.

'Don't nag, Nell, I'm eating. Look at yourself; you've lost too much weight.'

The older boy was squatting on the ground, his arms round an ancient Singer sewing machine. 'How many, sir? We do it quick, very quick. Tomorrow?'

Jerome was haggling. 'Is it your machine?'

The boys looked at each other as if the question was incomprehensible. Then the spokesman said: 'We rent it each day.'

How could Jerome not offer all the money they had? He was the one in London who gave to people begging.

Her back was dragging cold from the wall; it immediately turned to sweat. She was sitting in a warm puddle.

Jerome would be furious if she interrupted.

'Do your family help you?'

The boy turned as if only then aware Nell was in the room.

'No family missus. We come to Lagos to work.'

She had often seen these children at the side of the road. They were usually in pairs, one with a sewing machine. It hadn't occurred to her to imagine what kind of life they had. Was she becoming cut off from the other lives existing in this city?

'But there isn't any work.'

Or there wasn't if you didn't have family or connections.

Jerome frowned, the boy shrugged. His companion was absorbing everything. He'd already examined the bare rooms, the cracked mirror in the bedroom, the two suitcases in the corner, the neat piles of clothes.

Now he could turn his attention to her, study her as if she were a weird piece of furniture.

'Make these and bring them first thing,' said Jerome. 'I have to go out early on business.'

Who was he kidding?

The companion had spotted the new but tiny fridge in the corner of the kitchen. They both gazed as if it was magical. Nell got to her feet, Jerome held up his hand to stop her. She hesitated. She should ignore him, give them a Coke.

'Why didn't you offer them something cold?' she asked, once the boys had backed away and left, the heavy machine weighing down the older one.

'Have the whole neighbourhood think us an open house? There'd be queues.'

'That's crazy. No one knows us.'

'Of course they do,' said Jerome.

'You cheated those boys.'

It wasn't even Jerome's money. 'They're starving.'

'You believe them?'

Of course she believed them. A year ago Jerome would have too. He was angry, and she was angry.

She left him to bash dishes in the sink, went and stood on the balcony. She must try to calm down.

Was she being unfair? Love, survival, ordinary existence, they were all more fragile here. If anything happened to either of them in this building site, no one would know.

When they'd first moved in, there was a half-finished wall around the building. Each day, bricks would disappear. Now, there was nothing left.

How to get things back to normal, Jerome his usual self? How to get herself back to normal? They were cut off here. Everything was too hard, all the travelling each day through the crazy city. Now that her job was more secure with longer hours, they needed a permanent place at the hospital.

The housing officer had sent them to look at a flat, promised it would soon be available. It was such luxury: everything newly finished, double bed, cupboards, fitted kitchen, bathroom. No travelling.

They'd heard nothing.

'Dash,' Jerome had said. 'You have to find out who gets the dash.'

Who was she meant to ask? What should she say? The various clerks and officials looked at her as if beneath consideration.

They barely talked that evening, then slept as far from each other as was possible in such a narrow bed.

Early the next morning, Nell woke to hear Jerome chatting in the yard to the two boys.

She pulled on a wrap and joined them.

'That was quick work. The shorts look great.'

Jerome was still paying. He ignored her.

'Ok, you two,' he said. 'Go now.'

The boys waited. 'You want anything, Missus? We do it cheap.'

The sewing machine was nowhere to be seen.

'Not now,' said Jerome. 'Another time.'

'We come back tomorrow?'

'No, no. Next month. Maybe.'

The boys looked desperate, Nell felt nauseous. Even Jerome

sounded strangled, as if he couldn't breathe properly.

'Go, quick,' said Jerome, sharply. 'I've things to do.'

The boys turned and ran. They hadn't even looked at the fridge.

She followed Jerome into the kitchen. If she could try and make this better, get it so they could at least talk. Jerome had faced the wall, was pulling off his jeans.

'You have great legs.'

No, it was the wrong thing to say.

'There's nothing for those children. No work.'

Jerome had spoken without turning round.

Why not face her? Why this sudden modesty?

The boys had looked so undernourished. 'You gave too little.'

'They're smart, but what they need is a co-operative. Own the machines between them, cut the middle man.'

He couldn't be getting like Ifechi. This wasn't the same Jerome. 'You exploited them.'

He turned quickly. 'What? What was that?'

Jerome had looked so sure of himself with the boys. The big man. She'd better keep quiet.

'You're no different than the fat-cat renting them the machine, Jerome. You could have given more.'

'Stop it, Nell.' He held up his hand.

Back off, leave him to calm down, leave herself to calm down.

'At least give them a cold drink.'

'You know so much, Doctor?' Jerome came closer: 'The white lady with a job.'

She wanted to jeer: oh yes, yes, the one with a job.

'Don't be stupid.'

He grabbed her shoulders. 'Yes, I've been really stupid. You and your boyfriend.'

Nell pushed him away.

'What right? What right do you think you have, Nell? From the beginning, you've been judgemental. Always, always negative. You imagine I'm an idiot – see nothing, hear nothing.'

She shoved past him. 'Watching you cheat starving children.'

'Cheating? Who exactly is cheating, Nell?'

'You could have given them more money.'

'Cheating! And I'm the last to find out. Everyone at your precious hospital laughing behind my back. The poor man, doesn't know a thing – the fool must be blind.'

What was Jerome saying?

'You fuck around like a whore and think I don't know.'

His words made no sense. Nell ducked his blow and kicked back. Everything slowed as Jerome's fist slammed the side of her head. For a second she was stunned.

She ran to the bedroom, locked herself in, crouched down on the floor. What had he meant? Cheating?

41

When there were no customers, Jess began to stay in the back and watch the butcher. She'd soon be in England with its supermarkets, its plastic-sealed meat. No hint where any of it came from. This was too interesting. She'd stand at the door to the back room, watch René reach for saws and axes from the ceiling hooks and chop, flatten, slice. He'd peel off blankets of fat, render it down in pans on the stove – he rarely spoke.

The first time she'd held the lump of cow muscle, the solid cool bulk of it between her hands was a shock. Impossible now not to imagine the animal warm and alive. Repulsive, yet fascinating: she could never, ever eat meat.

One evening René looked at her with a more focused expression than usual. The butcher wasn't someone who seemed much at ease with anyone. She'd changed into her shorts and T-shirt ready for the bike ride home. He walked over slowly and touched the plaits of red hair coiled round her ears, lightly stroked her freckled arms. He stooped and stroked the inside of her legs, then he went back to his work.

One Wednesday, a pale young woman came in with a rather ugly toddler. René swung it in the air and gave it several kisses. The woman had forms for René to sign, a box of patisserie. She nodded greetings at Jacques and Jess, collected the child and left.

'His wife,' Jacques said, his mouth full of choux pastry. 'She's been away with her family for the summer, but doesn't like the shop, doesn't come often. She teaches in the infant school in the next village. She is very busy.'

Of course the butcher must be married. All men of his age in the town were married.

42

There was a knock on the door; no one ever knocked this late, Nell opened it an inch. There was a profound darkness outside. Her cabin was separate from the other hospital buildings. No reason to feel spooked, but she did feel spooked. One of the secretaries from the main administration block was standing under the porch light.

'Phone call, Doctor.'

He looked anxious. She followed him across the compound to his office. At least he had a torch. She kept as close as possible. Whenever she stumbled, he stopped. It was almost eleven, the isolated lights over the various entrances to the wards didn't reach more than a few feet.

It was Ifechi.

'Meet me at the Federal Palace. Don't go back to your room. Don't speak to anyone.'

The secretary was busy stacking letters, pretending not to listen. He looked nervous, was avoiding catching her eye. But Nell needed money for the taxi and she grabbed the torch.

Getting back to her room took forever, everywhere was now unrecognisable and threatening. She kept telling herself that all she needed to do was walk into one of the wards and it would be familiar. Eventually, she saw the cabin and its lit window. It had been left unlocked. It was empty. No one.

Ifechi had said come immediately. Better not to even pause. Nell grabbed her purse, raced through the silent dark to the gate.

There was a taxi, the driver chatting the secretary and a security man. Nell returned the torch; the taxi was at the hotel in thirty minutes.

People were leaving, cars driving off; the staff getting ready for the night. She waited inside the foyer while the main reception areas emptied of visitors, two men started hoovering. Nell was clearly not welcome; the three men behind the reception desk kept glaring, guests passing her were suspicious, no other solitary women waiting around. Jerome called them good-time girls – she was much too scruffy to be seen as a good-time girl.

Ifechi had sounded urgent. Why was he not here?

She went out the back doors to the swimming pool. It was still fully lit, the blue water soothing. Nell walked round and round it for two hours.

She felt sick. How had this happened? They'd had a row and then another, Jerome convinced she'd been cheating on him. After the third fight, Nell had waited until Jerome went out then packed a bag, taken the mini-bus. She'd expected him to turn up and stop her but he'd vanished.

Nneke knew someone who wasn't using his cabin, Nell could borrow it.

It was several days before Jerome appeared at the hospital, asked her to come back. But by then Nell knew for sure she couldn't, or at least not yet.

They should never have left London. She went obsessively through their years together: the first meeting at a party in Hackney, she couldn't even remember whose flat. The holidays, the day trips, the protests. She missed him.

But now was different and she didn't want to get trapped. She'd enough money for a flight to London. Aidan or Connie would help, then she'd come back and decide about Jerome.

'Sorry,' said Ifechi, puffing out of the pool entrance from the hotel. 'I couldn't see you.'

'I thought I'd misunderstood, was about to leave.'

'You can't return to the hospital.' He led her into the shadows. 'I spoke to Jerome. He's not recognisable.'

'He came in to work and we talked. I thought he'd calmed down.'

Ifechi pulled out a handkerchief, mopped his bald head. 'You can't go back. You mustn't.'

'He imagined I had someone else, but it's rubbish. How can he think I'd do such a thing?'

'Somebody told him.'

'But who? And why? He really believes I've betrayed him?'

But Jerome now thought everyone, including Ifechi, had betrayed him. It had taken all her patience to convince him there was no cause for jealousy. A few days before, they'd sat for hours in the corner of the clinic while cleaners put their heads round the door then disappeared. He'd seemed to believe her.

'He eventually accepted none of it was true.'

'We spoke this morning – he's angry, and dangerous.' Ifechi looked around. 'Certain friends he's picked up are a nasty lot. It's impossible for him, he'll lose face if you leave him. He wants to know who your boyfriend is.'

'But he's realised there isn't one.'

There was rustling in the palm trees, a parrot flew out with a clatter. Ifechi shivered. 'If he knew I was here, talking to you. You can't just walk out on him, the man has nothing else.'

'You're telling me to go back?'

'No, definitely no.'

How could she trust Ifechi? She'd always loathed him. Even Jerome had to agree that Ifechi was deceitful, not to be trusted.

Yet, it was true. When Jerome had come to the hospital he was one minute as gentle as usual, the next threatening.

'Is there anywhere safe you can stay? I don't want Jerome suspecting I'm involved.'

She had Femi's phone number, Femi had contacts all over the city. And he would still be awake.

'I can call someone.'

43

Aidan rewound the tape, got back into bed, pulled up the blanket – a Schubert piano trio filled the tiny room. He started to cry. He should have kept up the piano. That would be something, some world to be part of. The room was filthy. He wasn't responsible for the squalor in the shared kitchen but could do something about here. The blanket was rank, almost slimy. He'd long abandoned sheets and pyjamas, his T-shirt a surgical top from the hospital.

What could he say? This was clearly a special trip since Dermot was meant to be on holiday in France with Mum; Aidan's tutor had written and the letter sent on.

They hadn't spoken since last Christmas. His mother was sulking, Colum about to go off for a few days with the girlfriend's family. A nice Catholic girl, a vet. Ideal. Usually Mum left him alone, a letter once a month to say how busy she was, instructing him to call. Which he didn't. But he must have said something that had annoyed her. Or they were preoccupied with absent Nell and her relationship with unsuitable Jerome, and it was nothing to do with him. Colum was consumed with passion for the new lady love, while he was the sad son. Soon, another Christmas – bugger.

What a mess. He and Colum sent to boarding school to get even more screwed up. Aidan hadn't wanted to go; Colum said it was full of bullies and lonely but the parents decided to make a sacrifice, send them both. It would make them safe. What did that mean? Aidan had asked his mother and she said it was better no one mentioned Claire, as if that was the logical connection. Great.

He could escape before his father turned up. The tape finished, the room returned to silence; only the drip of the tap in the shared and utterly disgusting bathroom, the rattle of traffic along the North Circular, the relentless rain.

No one was going to answer that door-bell. That wouldn't stop

Dermot and the door was never locked properly. A blast of fresh air and Old Spice. 'Great security, you have here, boyo.'

His father pulled up a chair to the side of the bed, straddled it. His belly pushed against the vertical wooden slats, his short fat legs straining in too-tight trousers.

The routine was familiar. Dad would take his wrist, pause for a couple of minutes, look at his watch.

Next thing, check for anaemia. 'Let's have a gander.' Sure enough, his father leant over, yanked down his lower eye-lid. 'Pale, too thin, heart racing. Open up, say Ahh.'

'Ahh'.

'The boy will live. When did you last eat?' Dermot tossed the wooden spatula at the overflowing bin, didn't miss. Amazing, whatever Aidan was throwing, he always missed.

They went to Bertorelli's. Dermot had gone into the next bedroom and taken clean clothes from the superior-looking Frenchman who had moved in the week before. The man would be furious. Dermot left a tenner on the bed.

'For his trouble,' Dermot said, then he winked. 'And the laundry, there might be lice you know.'

He made Aidan shower, wash his hair. 'You've your mother's good looks and dark curls, make the most of it.'

Dermot helped him dress as if he were a child again.

'I'll have the chicken cordon bleu,' Dermot told the waiter, then added. 'Twice.' Well at least he didn't say Gordon Blue or ask for a really good steak 'for the boy'.

'I've had a word with the dean, Aidan. They'll give you six months off. It'll be a breathing space. I was going to suggest a bit of travelling? Get out of London.'

Where? Did his father mean for him to visit the grandparents? He couldn't possibly. His father's parents were incredibly boring and Granny in Westport quite mad. Even Mum had to admit her mother had a dose of religious mania. Where then? He'd only been abroad twice, Sweden with the Sixth Form and that week with Camille in Paris. Camille had dumped him shortly afterwards. And then she'd dumped the exam grind and married a man who sold cars and always had wads of notes in his back pocket. A relief. Aidan had never known why he stuck with Camille. He'd never fancied her. She had big hips.

He had never spent summers with Uncle Liam like Nell, the never-to-be-mentioned Nell. Travel was fishing with Dad on the Shannon, or sailing with Colum and Colum's friends. What an unimaginative life.

'Look,' Dermot said reaching into his pocket for a cigarette. 'I'll give you a cheque.'

'You're not meant to be smoking, Dad.'

'Gobshite to that. Go away and think. No one said you have to be a doctor but you might regret chucking it at this late stage, fine to do once the letters are under your belt. You don't always need to be repairing sick people; do research or something like. Just keep a grip on the options.'

Thank goodness Dad hadn't gone on about this being the worst moment to stop, when of course the strain was more than at any time, everyone had doubts. That's what his tutor had written.

'Your mother will back you to the hilt. Whatever you do. Tell him to become a mechanic. Stick to cars if he hates those smelly bodies.'

Hard to imagine his mother saying that.

'Engines are pretty smelly too, Dad.'

44

The wind was getting stronger and the walls of Connie's tent collapsing then buffeting until almost adrift from the few remaining pegs. The sea attacking the edge of the rubbish-strewn waste-ground was wild and unwelcoming. It was gloomy, crazy weather, but peaceful without Daniel's sulks. He had found himself a lift back towards Pontissy.

'You're in such a bad mood all the time, Connie.'

The end of October, almost as cold as Norfolk – the same sand in the mouth, face, ears. She was bored, had to get back to work, snap out of this. But this was a special kind of boredom, an addictive one. John Edwards had sent the final remnants of money that had dribbled into her account; no more was due. At least there was a job waiting.

She pulled on a sweater, walked down to the beach. Claire was making mud pies, getting covered with wet sand, giggling and pushing lumps of it into her mouth. She was watching Connie, watching for her mother to protest.

This was not healthy, she was being self-indulgent. Oh god, how she missed the child, a child who had never grown up.

It was too cold here, only a few hardy people. Working again would keep her mind distracted, but the thought of going home, facing Liam, Derby, made her feel sick. Best to be far from people as possible, away from Rory, Jess.

She missed Jess. Sulky rude belligerent Jess. Was she all right? What had possessed her to leave the child in France, not force her to go back to Moreton? Force Jess? Well she had an income now, the Martins would look after her better than her own mother.

Of course there was the option to never return, disappear, fall off a cliff. Who would care? Anne would care, and be furious that Connie hadn't kept to the deal. Did Anne count?

Too rough to swim, by now the shop would be open. Connie went back to the tent, found a second sweater, walked across the almost-empty camp-site. She'd buy wine, a rubbish selection but beggars can't be fussy; despite asking, there were no end-of-season reductions. At least the cost meant she'd only get one bottle.

While Connie dithered, the man at Reception yelled her name, waving the telephone. The last call, a few days before, had been from Pat asking Connie to get in touch with Aidan, give him a pep-talk; Connie had declined, suggested that Aidan might be happier fixing cars.

The man liked saying Madame le médecin; he said it as often as he could, as if the absurdity of her tent, her vanished lover and poverty could only be put down to her being out-of-work and not French. But she was practically his only customer. The sensible others had taken their tents and camper-vans home.

Pat had got Connie's campsite number from John. Despite the poor man agreeing to feed and keep an eye on Jess for those few weeks when Jess was on her own, saying he'd never do it again, he still organised Connie's post. It was him.

'Hello Mission Control,' said Connie.

'You've a letter marked urgent from Lagos so I opened it.'

Oh, God, what had happened? You worried about one person, then it was someone else.

'It's from a doctor who says he knows Nell and that somebody has to find out how she is. She's abandoned Jerome, given up work, has cut herself off.'

'What?'

'There's an address of a friend of his. Nell is staying there but this Femi hasn't given any phone number. He's gone for six months to Ghana, will be out of contact.'

Nell had abandoned Jerome? 'How on earth can I help?'

That was the last thing to want happening, a crisis in Lagos and

Nell's parents worse than redundant and to be stuck here with a wreck of a car and no money.

'Any plans to come back to Derby, Connie?' said John. 'We could do with some help.'

'Is that really all it said?'

It was. Connie borrowed a pen and wrote down the details. No phone number. How was she going to find out anything? Poor bloody Nell.

Connie picked out a less expensive Shiraz, counted her change. No point calling Pat and Dermot. Could she rely on Colum? Aidan was useless, he'd probably be a desperate mechanic. If not Colum, then who? Maybe both Colum and Aidan together; Aidan had that Nigerian friend and Colum would organise Aidan. They could find someone in Lagos who'd go and see Nell. Would Anne know anybody? Meanwhile Connie was stuck here in the middle of nowhere.

What had happened? Jerome was a bright and ambitious man, ideal for Nell. He'd seemed kind, clearly loved her. Anne had said something about the unfairness in Africa being tough to live with. Was that it? Nell's letters had mentioned poverty and lack of drugs; she'd always sounded happy with Jerome.

To become so suddenly out of touch, how quickly it could happen. But Connie hadn't written to anyone for an age, she'd have to make some phone-calls. She put back the bottle, recovered the money. The assistant looked at her as if she were totally mad, then returned to her magazine.

*

As far as Aidan was concerned it was minutes since his father had visited but it was more than a week later when the French flatmate answered the phone, yelling through Aidan's door that his brother was on his way. Had Dad sent Colum to check? The French man already knew not to expect Aidan to appear. No one came near him, or, to be more accurate, came near his room. Aidan only went to the toilet or occasionally to the kitchen when they were all out, to eat their cornflakes or someone's tin of baked beans.

An hour later, the bell rang and Aidan roused himself. Colum was glowing with health and contentment. Aidan huddled again under the blanket. 'You're thinning on top, Col.'

'I won't even start to describe you and this swine-sty. I was going to give you a hug but frankly you look contagious.'

'Did Dad send you?'

'Should he? No, they're away in France. I'm on a mission from Connie.'

'Connie? Does she want to nag too?'

'My God,' said Colum. 'Self-centred as ever. It's about Nell.' He pulled up a chair, straddled it in exactly the same way as Dermot. Fortunately Colum had, like all three of them, inherited his mother's longer legs.

'Connie called me from Spain. She had a message saying Nell had left Jerome and things don't seem ok; you know how she adores Nell. She made me swear not to tell Mum or Dad. She needs us to help, mentioned you having a Nigerian friend.'

Colum meant Sam. Someone else to feel guilty about.

'The letter went to Derby from Lagos, marked urgent. One of Connie's numerous lovers rang her with the gist. Here's my notes.'

Aidan closed his eyes, tried to pretend nothing was happening. He was so tired.

'I haven't managed to contact this Femi. If your friend can't help then either you or me, Aidan, has to play Sir Galahad, go to Nigeria. Tricky for me as Dad might notice my absence.'

Colum always imagined that irony was cool.

'Help yourself to coffee, Col. There's some in the kitchen.'

A bad idea. Somewhere else for Colum to be operatic about.

According to the notes, Nell was not with Jerome. She was not well, needed someone to come. How had this Femi got Connie's Derby address?

Colum returned with two cups. He'd found sugar and milk. A miracle.

'How about that girlfriend of yours, Phillipa? Can she go?'

'Fiona.' Colum gave another of his ironic looks. 'You want me to ask Fiona to stop being a vet for a week, and travel to Lagos.'

Aidan lay back on the pillow. 'Mmm, well, I think I can sort it.' It might be quite interesting. 'I could fly there.'

He sat up and reached for his coffee.

Seeing Aidan look more energetic, Colum became keen to dump responsibility. 'I'll leave you money.' He took a pile of clothes from the armchair, put them on the floor, and sat down.

'Connie said she'd pitch in when she earns some. I've no idea what it might cost.'

Best to own up, and Dermot was bound to say something. 'Dad was here. Told me to take a holiday, he left me a cheque.'

'You're joking?'

Colum paused as if processing this, then stood up.

'Right. You can start now.'

45

There was a letter from Liam that Jess took to her field. He started with a plea to come home, then launched into an extended grumble about Thatcher and what would happen to the country. Jess had only the vaguest idea who this Mrs Thatcher was.

Liam included the usual lecture to behave sensibly: this birthday was an important one. A postscript from Maura asked if she was having some wild romance. If not, Christmas next month – please, please, come home.

Her aunt's voice could be heard from the lane. Pat's French was appalling, she'd gone to classes but the accent defeated her. Jess could turn back, return to the shop. But that would be stupid, the place was locked for the weekend. Jacques would be having tea with his family, the keys on the usual hook in his hall. His shrew of a mother considered Jess quite mad. She'd already told Jacques that Jess was a pervert, a vegetarian working in a butcher's. Probably Maman thought she'd poison the meat.

Anyway, nearly sixteen. She had a job, needn't run away.

Pat came over to hug her. 'Jessica, darling!'

Madame Martin beamed from her permanent position doing something important with saucepans on the black ancient range.

'What a beauty you are! Why didn't you visit? And don't tell me it was that job of yours. We've been in France ages. Dermot has even popped back to London to see Aidan.'

Jess squeezed herself next to her aunt. The long wooden table was loaded with food, each inch of the benches occupied. She had stopped asking for the names of the Martin children; more seemed to turn up every day. And more elderly relatives. She helped herself to a bowl of lentil soup. 'Is Aidan ok? How are they all?'

She knew from Connie's explosions each time she got a letter from Pat that Colum and Aidan were doing incredibly well. Colum was working in the practice, had a sweet Catholic girlfriend. Aidan was thriving at medical school.

'Oh, how I hate my smug sister,' Connie would scream. 'And the gall to say Nell is a worry.'

'The boys are much too busy to spend long with their aged mère et père,' Pat called out to Madame Martin above the chatter – everyone was talking at once. Madame nodded wisely back without understanding a word. 'Although Colum's hopefully keeping an eye on the house.'

No mention of Nell.

Pat was easy. She didn't listen or express any curiosity. She chatted on about the villa in Brittany, the local fifteenth-century church; the parish priest was a Monsignor and very modest and came often for lunch. They all understood each other brilliantly. The man had even visited Newcastle. They'd shocked him describing the changes: philistines in the council, corruption, lovely old buildings gone. Well, it would be all right with this conservative government. Pat was a bit more cautious about Mrs Thatcher.

Her aunt gave Madame, and everyone else, detailed information about Jessica's birth, assuming full understanding. 'Wasn't Connie quite delighted,' Pat continued. 'Having a girl.'

According to an overheard conversation between Maura and Pat, Connie hadn't been at all delighted. Her language during labour had appalled the midwife.

Did Madame Martin know there'd been a sister? Had Connie told her, one of those long summers when her mother and Madame leant on the fence, watching the hens, and gossiping? Connie had probably been crying about Claire; she definitely never cried over Jess. Or if she did it was with fury.

They had jugged hare and Madame Martin grilled a trout for Jess which was stretching being vegetarian but delicious. Pat had brought a fancy cake from a favourite patisserie in Quimper and a bottle of calvados, They all, even the Martin children, got slightly drunk. Pat nagged a bit about Jess going back to Moreton.

'You're still a child, Jessica, darling.'

When her aunt left early the next morning, the house felt unusually empty. It was Saturday and the summer-house garden much too cold. The leaves were changing colour. Neglected grapes withered on the vines, even the cows looked dumb and passive.

Jess had to get back to the shop.

Early on the Tuesday, one of the younger Martin child came running up the stairs. 'Jessie, Jessie.'

It was her mother on the phone. 'Hello, gorgeous sixteen-year-old. How does it feel?'

'Where are you?'

'Arles, I think.'

'That's not the South of Spain.'

'That's my girl, an A-student. The car collapsed just after the French border and it had done so well.' So, the 2CV had given up. About time. 'I got a lift to here, am waiting for money. I'll meet you in Derby. John offered that flat again for the winter, they still seem to want me back. You could study.'

'You promised London.'

'You should get some education, Jess, I should earn money.'

'Derby! I don't think so.'

'Of course not, who wants to be an idle student when they can work in a village butchers?'

Pat must have told her. Her mother was sounding very calm, almost human. Any minute now, though, she'd start nagging.

'What are you planning for today, Jess?'

'Just friends, that type of thing.'

'Look, think a bit about coming to Derby or going to Moreton; decide and send a message via your dad. I'll come straight away if you choose Derby.'

Fat chance she would pick that tiny flat, pompous neighbour, that ghastly school full of idiots and sadists.

'I love you. And Jess, I miss you.'

Well, that was so likely. It must be cocktails for breakfast in Arles. Jess grabbed her packed lunch and cycled down to the shop. Hard to feel upset when the sun was shining, the trees a brilliant red and orange.

Mid-morning Madame Martin turned up with letters and a parcel – she'd even brought Jess six yellow roses.

There were cards, one from Granny in Westport, another from Rory. There'd been a phone call from Liam: he had to go over to Howth, Grandpa was ill. He'd phone when he got back. Maura's parcel was a green cashmere sweater.

Once Madame had gone, Jacques arranged the flowers in a jar with water, put them by her cash box. 'How old are you, Jessie?'

'Sixteen.'

As they were locking up, Jacques paused, looking embarrassed.

'Would you like to go for a glass of wine?'

'No, but thank you.'

Once he had left, Jess pulled down the blinds. She put Maura's sweater over her T-shirt and jeans and walked round the silent shop, checking the surfaces. She took the chops that she'd already prepared, turned on the pan as the church bell struck five. She collected blankets from a cupboard and cushions, laid them out on the wooden floor. Should she put the roses there? No, too corny.

It was not too late to change her mind, her heart was thumping like mad. This was her birthday present to herself. It felt terrifying and exciting, she would do this then go back to her family. Back to boring Moreton most likely.

A moment later she heard the shop door click, could see René's reflection in the glass. Her heart was so loud, he must hear it. He paused at the door to the back room, looked around and smiled.

'Ah Yessie, I have a more private suggestion, don't you think?'

He switched off the pan.

'I thought you might be hungry.'

He took her hand and led her out to the back yard. One of the sheds was always padlocked, this evening it wasn't. One red rose in a vase, a bottle of wine with two glasses on a table, and a mattress on the floor covered with an embroidered quilt – it was beautiful.

René stood behind her and kissed the back of her neck. He pulled off her sweater and T-shirt, put them neatly on a stool. She wanted him to slow down but if he did he might change his mind.

He stroked her arms then stroked down her spine. She helped him undo her bra then she slipped off her jeans and knickers. She didn't turn round to watch him strip. She held her hands out in front of her and looked at them. They were a child's hands, pudgy fingers, soon they'd be quite different.

Jess heard him open the bottle. This was crazy. What had she been thinking? She was about to lean over and grab her pants when he was standing in front of her, holding out a glass of red wine. He was totally naked, muscular and hairy, black hair all over his chest. He was enormous. Like a bear. She swallowed the wine and he poured her another and she gulped it down, then he picked her up and laid her on the floor.

His chest-hair tickled. He was heavy. It was quick and it hurt. It really did feel like a rod burning through her body. The mattress was too thin and she'd got quite drunk – but there was no blood to mess up the quilt. Perfectly done.

46

Aidan settled down on the concrete step, put his head between his knees – the only sound the taxi accelerating away. In front were bushes and other blocks of flats, above a star-filled sky, a quarter moon. Midnight and still warm. Totally silent, the occasional rustle. Everything had gone smoothly. His ability to be stubborn had paid off with the customs people who couldn't believe that anyone would travel with no change of clothes, and only a few magazines.

Of course Nell wouldn't answer, if she was even there. For the next hour he pressed the bell every few minutes, thinking fondly of the bed waiting in London. Then he remembered the sheets.

Someone looked from a window on the top floor. 'My God!'

When Nell opened the door, she kept herself hidden. 'How did you find this place?' He started to stutter an answer but she pulled him into the hall. 'You smell.'

The cheek of it, it was if he'd popped round, slightly drunk, on the way home from the pub. Nell looked rather glamorous going up the stairs, wrapped in a silk dressing gown, slim and tanned. On closer inspection his sister was a wreck, her normally thick dark hair greasy and straggly. There was even a balding patch. The flat was modern, the air-conditioned cold a relief. It didn't have the musty heat that engulfed him at the airport, followed him since.

'You're brown, Nell.'

'Oh yeah? You're pasty and shouldn't be here.' She looked at him suspiciously. 'How did you know where I was?'

'I got a call.'

'From who? Not the despot?'

'No, I saw Dad. He didn't mention you.'

'You didn't tell them?' said Nell.

Of course he didn't. She could make him more welcome after the effort he'd made.

'A geezer called Femi wrote to Connie, said you needed help.'

'I don't need help.'

He followed her into the galley kitchen.

'What do I do with you, Aidan?'

Do with him? Nell started opening cupboards, banging them shut. He grabbed her hand.

'Are you really ok?'

She stepped away as he made to hug her. They stood examining each other then she put her head on his chest. Either he had grown or she'd shrunk. Feeling stupid, he patted her on her back.

He helped himself to a bowl of rice that hopefully had not been there weeks, followed her to the living area. Nell had slumped on the sofa.

'I'm pretty impressed with my detective work.'

She looked at him blankly as if he had just said he was giving up medicine, joining the police. 'Do you have money?'

'I changed loads at the airport.' More than he intended but he'd wanted to impress the beautiful young woman helping him.

Nell stretched out her legs as if admiring her toes. Her feet were filthy. 'The problem is my passport's disappeared. I need to get to England for a week or two.'

All she wanted was a holiday.

'Whose flat is this?'

'A friend, Femi, his American girlfriend. They're both away but she'll be back after New Year. I'm waiting for the embassy to call but so far nothing. I'm going loopy.'

It was as well that Aidan had turned up. This Femi had omitted to provide a number or even mention there was a telephone; he must have decided someone had to come.

Not surprising that the embassy weren't bothered; Nell sounded terrible, like one of those patients with endogenous depression. No endogenous anything allowed for in the British ex-pat. But she wasn't a British ex-pat, not really. 'I'll go and see them.'

'No, Aidan, better to ring. It's really not safe out there.'

So she was also paranoid.

'What about exams, Aidan? How come you've time to fly all over the world?'

Aidan went over to the sofa, sat in the small space Nell had left. He patted her legs.

'Fine,' Nell said. 'I'll show you the bathroom, and clean towels.'

The days passed for Aidan in a state of suspension, perhaps it was the brandy. There were full-length windows; he could stand for hours, stare at the other flats and the empty road. A larder was packed with food. He'd never seen anything like the freezer; the height of the vast fridge and more than full. Steaks and roasts and chickens stacked like toys, but real food. A walk-in cupboard had boxes of wine and spirits. Aidan had already checked the American's tapes. Since Nell seemed to share their landlady's taste, he insisted she keep it to herself.

'It's highlife,' Nell said. Which meant nothing to him, except it jangled his nerves.

She said help yourself, so he helped himself. There were cut-crystal glasses in a cupboard but he opted for a mug with *I luv Texas*. The chill of the flat was already a problem, he could feel his sinuses block. He smoked a bit, drank a bit, and since there were no books, started reading the *BMJs* he'd brought for Nell. Something reassuring in the research studies, the ordered calm as conclusions were made; something in the thought that his parents had once read these articles. Or his mother, anyway.

Nell had expressed no interest in anything medical. 'All that drug research is a luxury. People die here from poverty.'

'How about us taking a tour around the city?'

But Nell wasn't going anywhere.

Several days and two more phone calls to the embassy before the doorbell rang, and it wasn't a child selling tat. Aidan had begun to feel quite brave, going down and assessing if the small boy clutching bead necklaces or sacks of wooden sculptures was a cover for a deranged Jerome with an axe, more villains hiding in the bushes. There was no confusion about the grey man in the suit.

'Harrison.' The man held out his hand, his palm damp but firm.

'Ryan.'

'Always shake the patient's hand,' one consultant had advised. 'You can tell a lot.'

Aidan made tea. The two men sat in silence waiting for Nell to say something; she was collapsed on the sofa in the landlady's dressing gown, studying her bare feet as if they concealed an amazing truth. Aidan should have insisted Nell dressed properly. He'd found a man's shirt and jeans for himself in the woman's extensive wardrobe; either the woman was extremely tall or Femi was. All the shoes unfortunately were too small.

'So,' Harrison eventually asked Aidan. 'What do you think of Lagos?'

'Great. Well, I've only seen it once from a taxi.'

Harrison opened his briefcase. Good. Nell might sulk as much as she liked at the presence of colonial racists but he'd no desire to spend his life cooped up until an angry American walked in.

Nell was right. The embassy was reluctant to provide a new passport, let alone protect Nell from some vengeful Jerome.

'You sure he's dangerous, Nell?'

'No. But he's not well. He's been told lies. A mutual friend said I should be careful, and I need to go to England.'

'Wives do change their mind. We make a fuss, get them home. Before you know where you are, they're whizzing back to Lahore.'

Aidan looked at Nell to confirm his disgust, but, as usual, her attention was on her feet.

'Do you think there's any chance your sister would return to Jerome?' Harrison said, as Aidan went with him to the entrance.

Later, strengthened by brandy, Aidan repeated this to Nell.

'You only have Ifechi's word that you should be worried.'

'It's not just Ifechi.'

No point asking if Jerome had good reason to be angry.

'Jerome has no family. Just me. Then to be told I'd betrayed him. I have to get to England, have a break for a month or so. Come back here and work.'

Nell just wanted a holiday.

Madame Martin hadn't been surprised: 'Jessie, chérie, you need to be with your family for Christmas. They must have missed you.'

All the Martins seemed glad she was leaving. Since her birthday two weeks before there had been a distinct froideur, as Connie would put it. Her French wasn't good enough to make accurate sense of Martin family muttering – but definitely time to leave.

Your family. Some family. Her mother playing the delinquent somewhere. Dad still sulking after the dust-up two years before. She'd only been seeing a friend from school whose father was really, really ill – practically dying. She could hardly have abandoned her. Dad would probably lock Jess in her room, refuse a front door key. Imprisoned in suburban Moreton, how utterly gross. But Moreton was her only serious option.

Work had been fine as long as she avoided René which was not too difficult. He seemed anxious, then confused, relieved that Jess wasn't going to pursue him round the table in the back room; it wasn't for some reason remotely tempting. How could her feelings change so fast? He was old, and had a distinct belly. Yet just seeing him park the van outside used to make her go all soft and silly.

Now René stayed in the back when he came in at all; Jess remained in the shop with Jacques who seemed to have no idea that anything had happened and chatted as he normally did. All very French and civilised.

She'd have to grovel to Dad and Maura, start doing boring school work. No way was she returning to that convent. The train ticket that Connie had left seemed to have disappeared, Liam sent another. He'd phoned the night before she was due to leave.

'Your Aunt Pat and Uncle Dermot are back in England and he's in London, will meet you at Victoria.'

An escort to Euston. Yet again being treated like a baby.

'He's there on a course and to see how Aidan's doing, you're all the same, hopeless at keeping in touch.'

Dermot was leaning against a pillar behind the ticket collectors, reading *The Times* and smoking. He was the same as always, his belly almost popping the buttons of a crazy green-check waistcoat. Plus a red bow tie and heavy tweed coat. He looked like Toad in *The Wind in the Willows*, was shorter than her. She must have grown or he'd shrunk.

'Will you ever see the height and beauty of the child. What have you been eating? Foie gras morning noon and night?' He took her arm. 'Where's the guitar? Your father said you'd be loaded down.'

'I gave it to a friend.'

Jacques had blushed, but he'd taken it, promised to learn.

'A friend, ah hah,' said Dermot. 'Look, let's get a taxi to Piccadilly, have lunch at the Café Royal.'

'Aren't you on some course, Dermot? Going to lectures?'

'The innocence of the child, where are your priorities?'

One of the waiters seemed to think Dermot should order wine. At first Dermot refused. The man was horrible, it was good to see him back away.

'The afternoon's ahead of us, Jessie, must keep clear-headed. Even if I'm bunking off, you're part of my duties. I need to keep my wits about me.'

The vast dining room was all dark wood, green leather, crystal chandeliers, heavy cutlery, linen serviettes and muttering. It was gloomy and very grown-up.

'Why not have eggs florentine twice, Jess, if that's what you want. I'm for a steak.'

They didn't seem to like vegetarians in this place. Enormous roasts of beef and pork and lamb were being wheeled around on trolleys. Yuck.

'You can double up your puddings. They're always excellent.'

He'd been to this place before.

'Dad said you were in London to see Aidan.'

'Indeed, but the boy has gone gallivanting, no idea to what part of the globe. It's all fine. Very restless, your generation. Didn't I see him a few weeks ago.'

'Did you bring him here?'

'I did not indeed, filling his head with grand ideas.'

The eggs weren't remotely as good as Madame Martin's. Dermot was shovelling in some devilled mushrooms, they looked delicious.

'You know, Jess, Oscar Wilde used to dine near where we're sitting. They say Oscar could talk all night. Nearly a hundred years since, no-one to match him.'

That's what Dermot wanted, to be drinking with Oscar Wilde, part of that artistic set of 'wits and geniuses' as he called them.

If he liked this city, and the artist's life, why Newcastle and GP?

'Why don't you move down to London, and write?'

'Listen to her. And live in a garret? Talent, Jess. I'd no talent for it. And what I am good at and indeed what I want to do, is be a decent family doctor.'

'Dad never says what he wants.'

'Well, your father can be very trying. We have only the one life, Jessie. We need to get on with it, live it fully.'

Dermot changed his mind about the wine; he ordered the bottle the slimy waiter recommended. It was red, tasted wonderful.

'Now this is the thing, Jess.' Dermot poured her another glass. 'If you ever have regrets, do something else. Do you have plans? Didn't your aunt think you settled in Pontissy, we were surprised to hear you were off back to Maura and the father.'

Her uncle was spooning brown sugar into his coffee. He'd abandoned the peach tart which was as good as Madame Martin's.

What were her plans? To get out of Moreton as quickly as possible.

'You can tell me. Lips sealed. Was there a young man?'

Certainly not a young man.

'What was it like for Nell at my age, Dermot? Did she know what she wanted?'

Her cousin always seemed so focused.

Dermot huffed and puffed, debating if he should have a brandy and eventually said: 'Talk to your father, Jess. Don't let there be a distance between you.'

'Is Nell happy in Lagos?'

'Don't get to the point in life, Jess, when you wished you'd done it differently, and it's too late.'

Her uncle must be getting deaf.

'If you ever plan to settle, have children, be certain first that's what you want. Otherwise children can be the high road to disappointment and misery.'

It wasn't clear that he was joking. He must be.

They took a taxi to Euston, neither Maura nor Liam took taxis.

'You'll be sure to get a cab at the other end,' Dermot said, heaving her bag on to the train.

'I will.' There was a bus from the station that went to the beginning of the road.

Dermot slipped a roll of fivers into her pocket.

'How will you get back past the ticket collectors?'

'No problem,' said Dermot.

48

Jess poured herself more tea, another grim day of French verbs and calculus stretching ahead. Maura put down the newspaper, then studied Jess over her glasses. 'Did you talk to your father?'

That sounded ominous. Only back in this mausoleum a few weeks and she was meant to be *talking to* Liam.

They had made plans: Jess had been interviewed, forms had been filled in, a friend of Maura's was going to coach her for O-levels when Christmas was over. Talk to your father sounded more serious. And how could she, if he was in Ireland most of the time? Maybe this talk was what he was muttering about this morning while hunting for his glasses before leaving for the surgery.

'Please explain the butcher's shop,' was the first thing Liam had said when the three of them sat round the fire the evening she'd arrived.

All the answers she'd practised sounded pathetic: that she was broke, was curious, that she'd fancied the butcher. She would never say there was no other choice. She'd eventually decided to tell them what was almost the truth. Since she was forced to earn money, it was preferable to do something really terrible.

But before she could, Maura had interrupted the silence: 'How do we explain most things at that age? Remember yourself, Liam.'

Both had been clearly dying to ask about boyfriends but were too uptight, and had kept silent on the subject ever since.

Maura folded the newspaper, put it to one side. Jess reached over to take it but Maura shook her head.

'Not now. Listen, Liam was meant to find out if there was a relationship and if you were careful, but he's a bit distracted.'

What a joke, expecting her father to ask her that. And what would she say? She couldn't possibly tell them that she'd only had sex the once. But she hadn't been careful, and neither had René, it hadn't occurred to her – but you don't get pregnant if you just do it the once?

Maura stacked up the cereal bowls, 'How are your periods, Jess?'

The woman counsellor was ok and Maura promised not to mention their visit to Liam until Jess said she could. He'd been over in Dublin and was upset about Grandpa. Jess wanted to go with him and when Rory came back from uni for Christmas, he wanted to go over as well. Liam had said no.

'I don't think he has any right to stop me,' Rory had whined to Maura. Rory had also got angry with Jess, called her irresponsible, said she should inform the father. How naïve her brother was.

Apparently it was early and the whole thing easy. Maura and the woman seemed determined that she would not rush, must think about it carefully, and they seemed to expect her to change her mind which was crazy.

Jess wanted it over with as soon as the appointment was made.

Maura gave Jess an ultimatum about telling her father. Once he was back from another trip to Ireland, Jess followed him into his escape room which stunk of turps and oil-paint, and told him before he'd even noticed she was there.

He was upset. Slowly he put on his paint-spattered white coat, sat down on his paint-spattered chair and stared at his hands. He was silent for ages.

'But you're Catholic, Jess, you can't.'

'No, I'm not and neither are you, Dad.'

'I am, and so are you. You can't do this.'

What did he imagine he was saying? What a nerve.

'I so can.'

'Anyway you need my permission?'

She so didn't, was just keeping him informed. It was her body. From the way her father leant over and rocked around he was cracking up, or crying.

Had he imagined that sending her to that convent made her one of them? Bad enough to have to stand through endless assembly prayers, but he knew she'd made Maura write loads of notes saying Jess's beliefs meant she couldn't take part in anything too Catholic.

Maura seemed to quite like writing those letters.

'If I'm asked by Sister Anne, what beliefs are we talking of here, Jess?'

'How about the Incas?'

They had mentioned the Incas in geography. Any religion would do as long as she could avoid those scary priests whisked in to inspire terror and drive sin from the soul to make space for the call from God. Some of the girls talked about getting 'the call' as if it was sexy. It sounded grotesque.

Liam didn't seem to know what else to say. He got up and started shuffling paper on the incredibly untidy table. He lived in such a mess here, was so organised everywhere else. There were half-finished paintings, ripped canvas, open tubes of paint.

He began to get agitated as he started searching for something.

'Has anyone been in this room?'

Why would anybody want to come into this pigsty? He was checking through some charcoal sketches, looking more and more desperate. He turned and glared at her. Well, she hadn't done whatever it was.

'I refuse permission,' he said firmly.

So he wanted her to be saddled with a baby when his own experience of being a parent was utterly abysmal.

'It's not up to you, Dad. It's up to me.'

He waved her away in disgust and went back to his panicked search. Maura would arrange everything as per usual. At least neither he nor Maura was interested in details about men and how often. Surely he should be pleased, and anyway it was definitely her right, her decision. Having a baby with no house of your own, no father, zilch money. And she didn't like babies.

Jess found Maura in the kitchen.

'He's more bothered about something he's lost than about me.'

Maura looked uncomfortable as she glanced over from the sink.

'It's ok, I told him. But you're not to tell your best friend Sister Anne. Won't she crow.'

Maura agreed. Anything Jess decided was apparently fine, except she had to contact Connie.

How, exactly? Where, exactly?

Not a good idea, thank you very much.

'Connie's not to know, Mo. You must swear.'

49

It was only just dawn, a purple haze hung over the houses. The world around Aidan looked dream-like. He hadn't run for ages, every part of his body was aching. He was sweating but had begun to feel in his guts the familiar drive, a memory of going full tilt.

He'd taken a key, written Nell a note. When, after a few hundred yards, no one leapt from the bushes, he began to relax. Why hadn't he thought of this before?

As the sun started to move up and over the buildings, Aidan turned for home, jogging gently down the middle of the empty road. This couldn't be more different than the North Circular. His pulse was still racing – he was extremely unfit, all that lying in bed, months since he'd played squash.

There'd been no one around, then a family appeared from nowhere, and he followed them down a footpath between two mansions. They'd vanished by the time he emerged through the bushes.

He'd come straight on to water, had almost slipped in. It must be sea. It stretched to the horizon but was the palest lilac-green and utterly calm. The sky was misty and merged with the flat lagoon. Totally quiet, the occasional bird-call. He crouched and gazed into the clear water.

It felt like he stayed there for hours, watching the outline of fishing boats like Chinese junks gliding along the horizon. It must have been the running, he was light headed, out of his body, unusually content.

He jogged back to the flat, would not mention his euphoria to Nell. It reminded him of school retreats, that moment when the Host was held up in Benediction. Nell would only break the spell, confirm that he'd caught a cold, sitting around in a sweaty T-shirt and shorts. He'd say he'd started training, from now on would be away all day running – better not to mention the water, she would dismiss it as fantasy.

Harrison had arrived, the passport was being sorted, he was going to take Nell back to the hospital compound to pack.

'There's really no reason, there's not much there,' Nell said, behaving exactly like some dippy wife about to change her mind. Harrison would be appalled if he knew she planned to come back.

When Nell eventually went to find a clean T-shirt, Harrison said firmly. 'How is she?'

'A bit paranoid? Tells me there are men lurking in the bushes.'

Ola, the driver of the Land Rover, looked like a man who could take care of anyone. Harrison sat in the front, separated from them by a glass panel; the roof had been pulled over and secured. They were driving in a little bubble. Well, a fairly sturdy, largish bubble.

Ola had wished them Happy Christmas.

'When was it?' Aidan whispered to Nell. She shrugged.

She was relaxing slightly, no longer wringing her hands. Mum would wring her hands like that when getting Aidan to explain why he'd come back for the school holidays without most of his clothes, or why he'd wandered off while waiting in the pew for confession, or forgotten something at a friend's house, or had stopped piano practice to stare out the window. Well, he showed them all, no one expected him to get A-levels. No one imagined he'd be accepted into medical school.

The Land Rover stopped at the hospital gates. Ola spoke to the guard and they drove past several one-story buildings, following a tree-lined track. Nell sat forward, giving directions. The extensive grounds were green and manicured; there were rows upon rows of small huts, but Nell directed Ola to one apart from the others.

It was bare except for a cupboard, a narrow bed, a tiny bathroom which Aidan immediately headed for. When he reappeared, Nell was still standing looking useless.

'Right, Nell,' said Harrison. 'What do you need?'

From the evidence of the cupboard, all Nell had brought from the flat were a load of books, one dress, and a white clinical coat.

There was a knock, all three of them jumped. A nurse came in; she was young, short, severe-looking.

Nell took her hand. 'This is Nneka, a good friend.'

The two women stood looking at each other, saying nothing. It wasn't until Harrison coughed that Nell came to her senses.

'You disappeared, said nothing,' Nneka said to Nell, ignoring the rest of them. 'I thought something terrible had happened.'

'I'm sorry.'

The nurse shook her head. 'I rang Ifechi.' She spat out the name. 'He accused me of saying something. I didn't tell anyone, anything. Jerome's in an awful state.'

'I know, I know, I'm sorry. Jerome heard it somewhere and Ifechi mentioned your nun friend.'

'You trust Ifechi more than my nuns.'

Harrison was peering out the window as if checking for bandits. 'We should get on, Nell. Can you pack what you need?'

'Will you give these books, Nneke, to Joe in the canteen?'

What had possessed Nell, packing one dress and about fifty books? Aidan pulled the dress from the hanger before Nell could stop him. Since she spent most of time in the flat wrapped in a towel or in the American's dressing gown, a change of clothes seemed positive.

Nell grabbed Nneke's hands. 'I am so sorry.'

His sister still wanted to be forgiven.

Harrison briskly opened the door.

Nneka had arrived with a parcel. As they left, she handed it to Nell. 'Open it later.'

'I'll come back,' said Nell.

Hopefully Harrison hadn't heard that.

'I might not be here,' said Nneke. 'But I'll pray for you.'

Harrison hustled them out, Nneke waiting on the porch to watch them drive away.

'Not here? And she'll pray for me?'

Nell waved through the back window until long after the nurse was out of sight.

'Oh, Aidan, her party. That was a leaving-do and Nneke never told me. She must have decided to be a nun. All that gold goes to the church.'

1980

50

Another decade. Anne stood on the stage, gazing out at the assembly hall. From this angle she could see the dusty remnants of Christmas decorations still blue-tacked to the walls. The vacancy after the buzz of the end of term, the last carol concert. She could now only face the school when it was empty; for months had left any meetings with the girls or their parents to Sister Mary. They certainly wanted the capable sister to take over, why not give her the experience?

Maura had insisted on seeing her and was always on time. Better go down and face the woman.

It was pouring, Maura ran holding her bag over her head.

'You could have put your car closer.'

'But it's not my spot.' Maura looked at all the empty spaces then smiled back at Anne. 'Happy New Year.'

Uncomfortable to be scrutinised.

'Why were you constantly unavailable, Anne? You're pale, not looking after yourself – I should have insisted.'

They sat down in two of the many plastic chairs that littered the entrance, or atrium as Sister Mary called it.

For that matter, Maura was looking frazzled, not her usual serene self.

'Can we go up to your office, this place is freezing?'

The office was only marginally warmer, and Anne couldn't bear to be in it. She turned on the convector heater.

Maura pulled up her chair. 'I'll keep my coat if you don't mind. What's happening?'

Not much. That was the problem.

How to explain to a non-Catholic what loss of faith felt like. It was as if some vital part had gone; she would now join those like Maura who were not quite complete – she could hardly say that.

'How was your Christmas?'

'Subdued, Liam has just buried his father. Jess and Rory were around, some of the time. Well, not much of the time. They seem to find enough of a social life in Moreton.'

Anne looked over at the kettle. She could make tea, but then Maura would stay longer.

Maura rubbed her palms together. 'Is it because they've brought in Sister Mary, and told you nothing?'

What could she say? Her only wish was that Maura would leave and she'd be left alone. 'How about you?'

'Liam is more upset than I'd have expected. He and his father never seemed close.' Maura took a handkerchief, blew her nose then held her hands over the heater. 'He made sketches of the old man as he was dying.' She paused and looked at Anne. 'Shocking, isn't it? To distance himself. Exploit his own father. I encouraged Rory to destroy one, the best one. If the word best is appropriate.'

It was quite possible to imagine Liam doing that.

'How do we know people?' said Maura. 'I was beyond furious.'

Maybe the old man hadn't minded?

'Oh, ignore my wittering, Anne. Tell me what's happening with you? That's why I'm here.'

'There are things I should get on with.'

'Like what?'

Anne gestured vaguely to some papers on the desk. She hadn't asked Maura to come; she should be at home with her family.

Maura waited a few moments. 'Please, a hint you're all right.'

Anne had no intention of saying anything. Maura stood up.

'Ok, you win, but phone if you need anything. Or come round.' Maura paused and examined her again. After another pause, she buttoned up her coat, picked up her bag. 'Strange having Jess back. She's enrolled in the Sixth Form College.'

'Not going back to Derby with Connie?'

Where was Connie? There'd been no letters, not even a phone-call. Was Connie all right? A great friend she'd proved to be, to both Connie and Maura.

'Believe it or not Jess wants to study. We'll see how long that lasts.'

'But she's recovered after managing on her own in France?'

'Oh yes, it was caught early so dealt with quickly. We...' Maura broke off and her cheeks flushed. 'Sorry, Anne, forget I said that.'

What had Maura said?

That was it. Maura had said that. It was irretrievable, and quite clear. Impossible but quite clear.

'Are you alright, Anne?'

Anne had started shuffling the papers into piles: go now, Maura, get out.

'If there's nothing I can do?' Maura hesitated as Anne opened the door. 'Phone me. Once the holidays are over, we can talk.'

Anne followed Maura down the stairs, watched her run again to the car. She repeated the words to herself after Maura had driven off, then she went to the chapel.

It was not at all surprising. It was inevitable. She had been asked by Connie sixteen years ago to look out for Jess. She'd been a key influence. How spectacularly she'd failed; all this time consumed by her problems. When Jess was born, Anne's response to abortion would have been clear. It would have been murder – Maura and Liam had colluded in a murder.

But now she was no longer sure.

His daily run was making Aidan feel human again but Nell had gone back to pulling out her hair. Over a week since Harrison took them to collect her things, she'd have to stop ringing the embassy. They were probably short-staffed at New Year, would write Nell off as a nuisance.

'You weren't that bothered when I first came.'

'It's taking too long, Aidan. And Femi's girlfriend, her imminent arrival? What do we do?'

He'd forgotten about the girlfriend.

Harrison called in the next afternoon with Nell's passport and ticket. Aidan had bought an open return which he now regretted, maybe the embassy would have stumped up. Anyway Harrison didn't seem to think he could remain in Lagos, which was a relief.

Harrison paused. 'I met Jerome this morning.'

Nell appeared at her bedroom door. 'Jerome?' She was dragging a brush through her hair.

Harrison would clearly have been happier if Nell put the brush down, stopped looking so agitated. 'He threatened a member of staff. Some men that he's going around with are not ideal. He seemed erratic.'

'How erratic?'

It was Nell who looked erratic.

Some distraction was needed. 'I was thinking about a flight to Kampala,' said Aidan.

'Kampala?' Harrison beamed at him with relief. 'Oh, I think Lusaka a better idea. Idi Amin might have gone but not Uganda. Certainly not South Africa; I spent three years there, worst three years of my career. Dreadful. I'll give you some contacts. You'll like Zambia. They are lovely people. Much calmer than West Africans.'

Nell glared: 'A travel agency, Aidan, that's all you needed.'

Aidan went back to the lagoon just as the sun was coming up. One day left. He sat on the dry grass, let the warmth seep through him, his mind go blank. The water was quiet, barely lapping the sandy edge at his feet, a few bird-calls. A bubble of stillness. Maybe this was what those gurus were on about.

Images kept pushing in: his mother in tears in Blooms in Whitechapel. Mum was in London on a course, could only talk about Dad's ultimatum to Nell. As his mind emptied, there was more stuff: the noticeboard at the hospital, the examination pass-lists, the body odour and disinfectant smell of the wards.

These thoughts should float through and leave. But the memory of London was awful – all pus or sluice rooms or surgical spirit. The anxious faces of patients queuing outside clinics, the consultant turning to him for an answer in a ward round.

The more Aidan tried to empty his mind the faster it came. That pathology viva when the examiners handed him an alien lump of tissue, asked for his opinion. He'd dumped it back in the steel dish, ripped off his gloves, run for it. How had he managed to do that? One minute pretend to be the diligent student then run away?

Aidan folded his legs into the position that Camille took when she was meditating. She'd have said it was about levels of reality. The flat here was his only reality, but it was wealthy and American and he hated it. They'd drunk a lot, or rather he'd drunk a lot, smoked some of the dope in the kitchen cupboard. He wasn't used to dope, wasn't at all sure he liked it. There must have been a lot of drug trips with those swamis Camille was so fond of.

The aim was to keep his mind peaceful and empty but little niggles kept pushing through. Had he thanked Sam? What would Sam say when he described all this? They'd met at the University Chaplaincy, at a meeting to raise money for the African National Congress. Sam continued as a practising Catholic, despairing of

Aidan, who had speedily let his religion lapse. But he didn't despair enough to stop being a friend.

The seventies were over. Everything would be different.

Nell had not been helpful. 'What do you mean, you want to give up medicine? Of course, Aidan, you're now the lowest of the low, but it will get better, eventually. Now please swear that you'll never ever mention coming here to anyone.'

Well that concern hadn't lasted long. Too good to be true they might be talking about him for once. 'I'll tell Connie and Colum.'

'No one else.'

Nell hadn't even asked how he'd got the money; she'd have exploded if told about Dad. Nell, once his support, was useless.

Could he buy one of those boats floating across the horizon, just drift? Should he stay in Nigeria? He'd been away over two months, but it was hardly an escape, even if it did feel ages.

The sky was a luminous cloudless blue like that Mallorca bowl Mum brought back one summer. He would stay.

They left for the airport late the following afternoon having spent the morning cleaning, and collecting all their money. Aidan had changed a ridiculous amount at the airport – if that young girl hadn't been standing beside him, he'd have changed a tenth. If that. He'd put it in an envelope for the unknown American with a brief thanks and a scribbled note from Nell. Both were wearing their own clothes, now clean thanks to the amazing washing machine, and they had used the incredible shower for the last time. Again Harrison sat in the front.

'We're too cut off inside this,' said Nell.

He should stop finding her so infuriating. As the only sister, she'd listened to his anxieties about girls, instructed him in tactics. She'd spent hours giving advice when Camille dumped him; he had to pretend to be more upset. She'd gone away and he wasn't ready to tell her. But tell her what? That he might be more interested in men than in women?

But first, finals. Nell had kept the textbooks in pretty good condition, the skeleton had been intact. God, where was all that now? His room wasn't even locked; the others in the flat, crooks.

'This is why people prefer driving,' Nell said. 'Poverty's kept separate.'

It looked pretty unavoidable to Aidan.

'We get UN people at the hospital; they come in enormous four by fours. That's where they get that concern foreigners indulge in.'

Better not ask who the foreigner was.

Nell leant forward, rapped on the glass. Harrison slid it open.

'We're nearly at Dmapapa.'

Ahead was a roundabout, in the centre of it a circle of dried-out scrub. Suddenly Ola braked, a van-driver leant on his horn, a market woman, the bundle on her head obstructing all vision, weaved her way skilfully through the cars. Ola skidded slightly as they swung round to their exit. Half in the ditch, half on the road, lay a body – his face to the sky, features unrecognisable.

'There are often bodies,' Nell said.

'The police will deal with it,' Harrison replied with confidence.

'It can be weeks.'

Harrison clicked closed the glass between them. It looked as if the man had been there some time – swollen, discoloured, blotched purple and grey. They had dissected corpses in anatomy. Aidan had seen them in the morgue, examined them for pathology. He had sat with dying patients – this was different.

'It's the casualness,' said Nell. 'And unclaimed. Jerome always says don't look, they're unlucky.'

Aidan patted her knee and Nell pulled her leg away.

'Apparently, outside the villages there's a site for those in disfavour with the gods who can't be properly buried. This is like those places.' She grabbed his hand, squeezed it painfully. 'Aren't you glad you live in London?'

'Hold on, Nell, that hurts.' Aidan had only to think of England and feel exhausted.

Nell untied the parcel she'd got from Nneka. It was the ebony head of a woman, an ugly-looking thing and heavy. She started tracing its features, the sculpted braids.

Harrison slid back the glass. 'You're not disappointed, Nell? A job like yours is so useful. Do you like flying?'

'Hate it,' Nell said.

Nobody asked Aidan.

Harrison looked at the African head. 'Is that all you have?'

Nell nodded. If pressed to describe her expression, it was cautious. This was not all she had. All that locking herself in the bathroom – why had it taken him so long? That guff about going briefly to England.

They ducked under scaffolding, followed Harrison into an unmarked annex, an empty space with two chairs and a table.

'I'll see about the paperwork. At the last minute we'll put you on the plane.'

They watched Harrison leave.

'Will he contact someone about that body?'

'Probably not,' said Nell.

She looked exhausted yet had been doing nothing but sleep and laze around the flat.

What a great doctor he'll make.

'Is the baby Jerome's?'

At least she'd the grace to look surprised. Nell sunk further into her chair. 'Is it so obvious? Can you tell?'

'Not at all. You're thin, not the slightest bump. Are you sure?'

'Of course I'm bloody sure. I'm more than twelve weeks, otherwise I'd stay. I have to get home, get it dealt with.'

She wanted an abortion – that was the holiday she'd needed.

Nell had lured Jerome here. Now that it wasn't convenient, she was dumping him, planning to dump what was his.

'This caper, Nell, it's not about a real threat from Jerome.'

'Of course it is. It happened before I realised. The state he is in, he won't believe it's his.'

If Nell had mentioned the baby, that would have changed everything. It might have made Harrison think twice.

'Is it Jerome's?'

'Fuck you.'

How could women be so calculating? Meanwhile, Harrison had thoroughly disappeared, eating an enormous meal somewhere, having a cold beer.

Nell clutched Nneka's parcel more tightly.

'Don't waste your energy. Feeling sympathy for someone will stop as soon as they lose their temper, become violent. Don't preach till you've spent months in casualty, treating battered women. Or treat those miscarrying babies because their loved one punched them in their bellies, and then having to discharge them back to one of your *understandably enraged* bastards.'

It would be good to have something to hit.

'Look,' Nell continued, sinking further into her chair. 'I know I've been a pain, but thank you. I might not seem it but I am grateful. And I'm sorry, Aidan, for everything.'

She wanted absolution.

He stood over her. She'd the grace to study her finger-nails.

But it hadn't been Nell's fault. The bad memories from his childhood were the silences, secrets, the sense of loss – the cousin they should never mention. Not having any control, being sent away to that school.

Maybe he should do psychiatry.

'I would be a lousy parent,' she said. 'I don't want it.'

'Of course, it'll be a job getting everything together. I'll help, of course, will be an excellent uncle and godfather.'

Taking out the pram, dangling the toddler, buying train sets. It would be a boy. A boy? The chap in Carousel. Gordon MacRae, those braces. Nell had dragged him to a re-run in the flea-pit in north Newcastle as her fourteenth birthday treat.

Not a lot later, Mum had banned her from going to hear the Bee Gees. Nell had gone anyway – so much for Carousel.

'You won't say a word, will you?'

Nell was glaring at him.

'I'll find you and kill you if you breathe as much as a syllable to anyone, anyone, about this.'

Madame Martin shook out the tablecloth, Connie helping to straighten it.

'Jessie went to her father a few weeks ago.'

'I want to pay her bills, check the books she left in case some are useful for her exams.'

Exams. That was a word Connie hadn't expected to use in the same sentence as Jess. 'Liam seemed to think I should.'

Of course Liam hadn't given a fig about books, but she'd never come back here, the risk of bumping into Daniel was too high.

She needed to get a few answers. What had Jess been up to, working in that butchers? Bad tempered, totally vegetarian Jess. A vague image of a chunky rather sullen man, but he had sold the best steaks. Madame Martin didn't look ready to enlighten her.

'You are very brown, Connie.'

'Yes, I spent Christmas with a friend in Bali.'

Madame sniffed disapprovingly. Quite right too. After all, Connie had abandoned someone from the village; Madame used to scowl at Daniel in disgust but now clearly considered him a saint. And to make matters worse, with indecent haste, Connie had found someone else – she was a kept woman, a floozy.

What would Mamma have said: 'No better than you ought to be, and at your age.'

She'd send Laurent money when she had it. It had been wonderful, but enough with doing nothing, she needed to work, to keep busy. She had to see for herself that Nell was ok. Aidan had said they were safely back, sharing his room – not a happy thought.

'How much do I owe you, Madame?'

'Nothing, your daughter paid. She gave away her guitar.'

Madame definitely sounded chilly so it wasn't just about Daniel. Jess had been a problem. No point expecting to find out from her daughter how the summer had been; at best it would be something like: 'Oh great, you dumped me. Remember?'

Jess had already told Maura the guitar was given to some boy. Connie didn't even have his name. A boyfriend? Anyway Madame Martin didn't appear keen to talk, certainly not about Jess.

The books were in boxes in the empty cottage. As soon as Connie saw them she regretted coming. The bloody uselessness of it all, these novels, stories, meant to sweep you off to another world. Each tattered paperback made her want to howl. The yellowed, torn pages, some with the corners turned down. Who had scrawled *bollocks* across the cover of *Sense and Sensibility?* She could only see Rory and Jess lying in the hammock or almost hidden by the tall grasses in the meadow – Jess for once not moaning, Rory calm and content. The books were mostly in English, some she had brought herself, others were presents from Maura. Nothing, no matter how dog-eared, had been thrown away.

They'd hung on to these, and they couldn't hang on to people.

Liam had sounded awful on the phone, could barely say his father's name. The old bastard had been impossible, never talked, terrified of women. Yet Liam, who formerly appeared indifferent, was now devastated that the old man was dead.

He did offer the news that Jess had settled in peaceably. A miracle. Her daughter's rejection of Derby had not been surprising; her return to Moreton must be due to the tedium of earning a living. Jess was right, life was boring – and it was painful.

No, she must go back and get on with it. Essential to have a routine. She'd even been missing medicine, certainly needed to be doing something. She'd pay off her debts, check on Nell, see Jess and Rory. Find out if Jess was talking to her. Then go back and visit Laurent; she'd borrowed enough from him and from John. John had started getting tetchy and Laurent wasn't exactly happy at her disappearing only weeks after they met, or rather weeks after he had picked her up standing by the total engine failure known as her 2CV.

Arles was in all senses a diversion. Did she want it to be permanent? She already missed Laurent but not his complicated family, needy mother, snooty children, and that ghastly secretary at his law practice.

And Anne had disappeared. Liam could tell Connie nothing. Maura knew nothing, except the phone number of a priest.

'She left at New Year. Almost overnight,' Maura had said. 'No word to anyone, except presumably her superiors.'

It had been a bad line between Arles and Manchester, but the priest seemed to think he had the right address. The first thing would be to find out if Anne was actually there.

After one of Madame M's abundant suppers and eight straight hours of sleep, it was time for the taxi, train, ferry. The whole lousy business of going back.

Anne was indeed in Acton, doing casual work at a homeless hostel. Connie had to ring the bell several times before anyone opened the door. The man who did was probably psychotic. She found Anne in the kitchen washing up for what looked like five thousand.

'You should wear gloves. You'll ruin your hands.'

'I thought I'd successfully escaped you lot.'

Connie dragged her from the sink, hugged her; she could feel Anne's slight body relax. Nothing to the woman, even thinner if possible. Was she shrinking? Surely not at her age, not yet fifty.

They sat at the large kitchen table. The nun's habit had gone: Anne was wearing someone's discarded blue sweater, a black skirt that was too big and sandals with whitish socks. And she did have brown hair, it had been cut short. Without all that head covering, she was quite pretty.

'You look much younger without the veil, Annie.'

Anne had started stacking plates.

'Stop doing that for one moment.'

'Who told you I was here?'

'Your priest seemed relieved that someone was worried.'

'He's extremely ill.'

The priest was more concerned than Connie would have expected. 'It sounded as if he knows you well.'

'He used to come to the children's home to take Mass.'

Impossible to hear about priests and children without thinking the worst. Better to keep silent, from the tone of Anne's voice the man was a saint – how good to see her, it had been too long.

Anne began collecting dirty cutlery. 'He's the most spiritual person I know. Something unique about him, an aura of awareness. If only the rest of us could achieve that.'

If only indeed.

'I thought as a child he must be extremely old but he couldn't have been. He pushed to get several of us to grammar school, three to Oxford, as many as possible to have a decent education. Once received as a nun, I asked if he could be my advisor.'

'And what an achievement. Look at you now, washing dishes.'

Anne held out her chapped hands. 'He'd approve. He's an old man and ill.'

'Then visit him. I'll give you money if you've none.' Connie reached across and touched Anne's arm. 'Are you happy?'

'A great weight has gone.'

For goodness sake, working as a skivvy, this was crazy. Anne didn't seem ready to explain why she'd left Moreton so abruptly. Maura had made it sound dramatic, that Anne had a breakdown.

Anne went over with the cutlery to the sink.

'Did you remember the stones?'

'Of course.' Anne poured out the dirty water. 'Connie, have you any idea why Liam chose to garden after Claire died? It was something I've always wanted to know. Futile at the time, and so soon after her death. He clearly hadn't a clue what he was doing, probably wouldn't have been able to answer, but his restoring that garden became important to me. It was beautiful and hopeless. If we lost touch it was the one question I'd regret not asking.'

She did sound insane.

'Who else are you planning to lose touch with?' Connie brought over some dirty plates. 'Not me, I hope?'

They'd been so close. They had an agreement. Or did Anne now consider her too flighty? They had made promises, Anne had made promises.

'I thought Liam might give another perspective on losing faith. I haven't lost it completely but feel precarious. He always strikes me as someone who feels precarious, don't you agree? Anyway he was always preoccupied, we didn't talk.'

Connie had never thought of Liam as precarious.

Anne started rinsing plates. 'Are you staying in London? I do have to finish clearing-up, we can meet when I've more time.'

'For a couple of days, I have to find a flat for Nell and Aidan. At the moment they're crammed into Aidan's tiny room by the North Circular.'

'And Jerome?'

'I'll soon find out. Apparently Nell is pregnant.'

It was as if Anne had turned to ice. She was holding out the dirty plate as if playing statues at some children's party.

A mistake. Connie should have kept quiet.

*

Connie let herself into the flat and looked around. She made tea, had a cigarette, then took a mug in to Nell. Saturday. Only just arrived after another foul journey on the M1 and angry already. The new flat was a tip, both Nell and Aidan asleep. It even smelt of vomit. Her first week back at work. Why was she doing this, helping these ingrates?

'What is it,' said Connie putting the mug of tea on the floor by Nell's bed, 'that makes Aidan tick?'

Nell's reply was indecipherable, but she did at least stick her head out from the duvet.

'Don't mumble. Why is he lying on the bare sitting-room floor, snoring his head off?'

Nell shook her head sleepily, tried to sit up. Her dark hair was a mess. 'That's how he studies, on the floor. He made a chart of targets the day we moved in, got on with it.' She blew her nose on a grubby handkerchief, drank some tea. 'Keeps asking questions about my state of mind, making notes, says he's going to specialise in psychiatry. Then he might understand his family.'

Then eventually her nephew might be able to explain her own operetta of family dysfunction; how someone can love their daughter, and also hate her. Claire's dying was no excuse to have made such a mess, no reason to have Liam support another child.

At least according to both Anne and Liam, Jess was now fine.

What else? Nothing more could be done about Aidan; he seemed to be working. More worryingly, Nell had probably not been out of the flat, all that effort making appointments wasted. How was she going to be able to tell what Nell wanted?

'Have you been sleeping since I left?'

Nell stuck her head firmly into the pillow. She needed a good shake. They both did.

'Neither of you went to that junk shop, found furniture. Presumably Aidan still studies while squatting on the floor. You wouldn't get this tea if I hadn't brought a pack. No milk in the fridge, nothing in the kitchen but dirty mugs and mice droppings. The bed I left for myself, before going to earn money for the rent, did look civilised last Sunday, now it's been stripped.'

'Oh, Connie, this is your duvet. Aidan has your pillows. It can't be five days since you were here?' Nell struggled to sit up. 'I was cold, this flat is draughty.'

'I'm so terribly sorry,' said Connie.

Perhaps Nell could fly back to Nigeria since Palmers Green was evidently not cosy enough.

Her niece suddenly went yellow and Connie grabbed the bowl from the kitchen sink. She must not get irritated, they were doing their best, but they were both extremely irritating. She waited while Nell vomited, then handed her a damp flannel.

'How did your appointment go? What's the point paying phone rental when neither of you answer?'

Connie wasn't exactly screeching but could tell her voice wasn't soothing. Nell had pushed off the two duvets; was the bump more obvious? The child was so thin. Connie emptied the bowl into the toilet then gave it a scrub. When she came back Nell was looking more alert. Connie ripped open the curtains to let a blinding winter sun into the room.

'I missed the appointment.' Of course Nell had missed it.

Nell wasn't even sure about dates. She'd allowed Connie to examine her but that wasn't remotely precise enough.

'The days got muddled. Aidan said it was Tuesday when it was already Wednesday. I am really grateful, Connie. I know this place is costing a fortune, Aidan is really grateful too.'

Oh, fine talk. Connie sat down, put an arm round Nell's shoulders. The girl was shivering. She tucked the duvet around her. What could be done? No one was forcing her. She stroked Nell's hair: that's the first thing, wash Nell's hair even if the bathroom was freezing and there'd be no shampoo.

She should have come for the day. If only they could rely on Aidan. No, better to stay away. Nell might want to be mollycoddled but this decision was something she must make on her own.

'Aidan will give you some money, Connie, and he is studying. And he's been in to see people to book tutorials and stuff.'

Connie wandered round picking up clothes. They needed to do some shopping. 'You were all set.'

'I am all set.'

Connie had left them cash for taxis. Aidan had promised to go with his sister. And he didn't. The self-centred little sod.

'You don't want this abortion, do you?'

It was like being an unwanted puppy, Nell had been trailing after Connie since they'd got out of the tube. The café was in an alley off Long Acre.

Connie pulled up chairs to an empty table by the door. 'Stay put, I won't be long.'

Nell sat down as instructed. If only Connie could be in London all week, manage her. It was as if her brain had been beaten up; she couldn't follow any chain of thought. Words disappeared into mush until nights came with everything sharp, senses acute. And the nightmares. All she could remember of those were rooms with earth floors covered with heads, half-eaten faces. But that was more than enough.

'That sweet-faced man behind the bar will bring you a coffee. You sure you don't want to eat?'

Nell shook her head.

'Then I'll collect Anne from Stanfords.'

It wasn't until they'd got off the tube that Connie mentioned she'd promised to meet the headmistress.

'She's left the convent.'

'You never said anything.'

'Let's get out of the flat and buy some clothes,' was all Connie had said. No word about meeting the Moreton headmistress. No mention of meeting anyone. Connie had said nothing because she knew what would happen, Nell would not have come. One coffee now and she'd go. She might leave a note with the sweet-faced man – who in fact looked like a bulldog.

The man had forgotten her, kept looking over and frowning. Just as well there was no coffee, it would only make her nauseous. The toilet door was next to the kitchen. If she needed to use it they'd have to listen to her retching as they fried bacon and eggs.

No, she must stay here, stay calm. Rude to leave before Connie came, the table would be taken. Nell's scarf and coat had to reserve two chairs, the place was packed.

She couldn't get warm, had to keep standing up, closing the door. Didn't people think to shut it behind them? Everyone was hunched as they left, huddling out into Covent Garden as if heading for the Arctic.

She must leave this country as soon as possible. Be somewhere her muscles can relax. Not to Nigeria, not yet. To somewhere else where people glide as they walk, live in their bodies. Not London in February, everyone tight and anxious.

Twice Nell thought she saw Jerome hurrying down the road, then realised her mistake. Where was he? How was he? Despite constantly clearing a patch in the steamed-over window, searching the faces hurrying down the alley, Nell didn't, for an initial second, recognise her aunt.

Connie looked like those few tall women in expensive winter coats who strode through the shuffling crowds as if they were models. She had pulled a fur hat over her black hair. She looked very Italian.

Connie must have been wearing that hat when they left the flat. Why hadn't she mentioned that Nell looked ridiculous in Aidan's tracksuit and overcoat?

All she'd said was: 'It's not fair, Nell. You look wonderful, so tanned. You'd look stunning in a dustbin bag. I'll give you a trim and blow-dry tonight.'

If only her aunt wasn't such a liar.

Anne was unrecognisable. A tiny woman with mousey-brown hair. She was half Connie's height, dressed in a navy duffle-coat, baggy trousers, tennis shoes. What on earth did people think of the two of them together?

That night Claire died, a tall nun, black veil, black habit, thin white face, forcing her to pray. She had gripped Nell's arm and they had knelt. Nell had always told herself the nun was terrifying but her voice had been soft and the murmuring, the repetition of the litany, soothing. Anne had taken her hand and they'd looked at the pictures and talked about Raphael's *Madonna*. Something special about the strange woman – but prayers had not helped Claire.

The main association with Anne now was of dread.

Connie dumped her bags on the spare chair.

'Bought too many books but what a grand selection. I'm going to drive around France in the summer. It's a treasure house, you should have come.'

She took the sugar bowl from Nell, put it on the other side of the table. 'Annie, this is my favourite niece but of course you've met already. Have you had your coffee? Did you eat?'

Nell shook her head. Connie frowned and went to the counter. Anne paused a moment as if unsure whether to sit, after a few seconds she pulled out a chair. 'I thought you were her only niece.'

'I am.'

'Are you alright, Nell?'

'A bit cold.' Nell rescued Aidan's scarf before Anne sat on it. The nun was smiling in what she probably intended as a friendly way. She had very clear blue eyes, was looking at Nell intently as if taking in energy. Whatever she was thinking, it was unsettling.

As if released into action, the man brought across three coffees, Connie was busy examining the display of cakes. Nell buttoned herself once again into Aidan's coat. She would wait for Connie, then she'd leave.

Anne was watching her as she poured in the sugar. True, it was excessive, the coffee would be syrup. The nun was muttering.

'Did you say something?' said Nell.

'Only, how are you? And in Moreton they think you're in Lagos.'

Anne's voice was drifting in and out with all the other sounds, the roar of the espresso machine, knives banging on plates. So hard to concentrate. Connie was spending an age choosing food.

Everything began draining. How stupid to come here, how stupid to have stayed, wicked of Connie to have brought her to meet this woman. All Nell could do was grip the table until the risk of fainting had gone, her heart rate returned to normal.

Anne seemed oblivious, thank goodness. She was still talking.

'It must have been demanding. I've colleagues in Africa who are achieving heroic work.'

Was Nneka's friend a colleague?

Eventually, when her body returned to something manageable, Nell asked: 'Do you know any nuns in Lagos?'

'No, I wish I did. You sent your uncle such interesting letters.'

Liam was showing them to this stranger. Was there no one she could trust?

The man at the bar seemed to be telling Connie his full medical history. He'd pulled up his shirt sleeve; they were both studying his arm with great fascination.

Sweet coffee had been a bad idea. Don't think about it, and her stomach would settle. Don't let this woman suspect.

Connie said Anne had lost her faith, like falling out of love.

She'd fallen out of love with Jerome. Or had she?

Don't retch. Not here. Nell pushed her hands into her belly. What happened to Audrey Hepburn in *The Nuns Story*? Hadn't they treated her like a traitor?

The rebellion in her stomach was too powerful. Mumbling apologies, she headed for the toilet. Connie was explaining eczema to the man, a queue of people waiting to pay.

Before Nell had sat back down, Anne had a question.

'Why did you leave Nigeria?'

At least Connie hadn't told her. That would be unforgivable.

Why did Anne not say, leave Jerome? They'd been living in sin, or did the vows of chastity stop Anne even thinking about sex. It might have been different if she and Jerome had married. Would it have stopped him being suspicious? But it wouldn't have made her want children. Children got ill, they developed dreadful disabling conditions. They died.

Connie brought over a plate of cakes.

'I didn't ask either of you what you wanted because you're both self-denying puritans, would say nothing.'

She was speaking almost fondly to this nun. Did they know each other well? How come?

Anne looked quite attractive when she smiled, less forbidding.

'That's not altogether true. Contradict me if you like, Nell, but you seem to have embraced life.'

What did Anne mean? Was she doing that now, embracing her life while getting rid of another?

Anne had helped herself to a jam tart; Connie put an éclair in front of Nell. Nell hated éclairs – shiny and repulsive. She pushed away the plate, stood up.

'Sorry, I have to go. I'll see you at the flat, Connie.'

'But our shopping, Nell? You haven't a stitch and Anne needs things. That's why I dragged you both out.'

Connie paused, looked at her more carefully.

'Ok, go home. Keep warm, I'll be back soon.'

Not a good idea to get straight under the duvet as soon as she'd got in but Aidan had disappeared – Connie would be ages, taking Anne to buy clothes. Two years before, she'd done the same for her.

Nell filled a hot-water bottle, bed was the warmest place.

A few hours later, Connie exploded back into the flat, carrying several bags. 'I've got you loads. And I want to do a more thorough check, then we can talk.'

She stood at the bedroom door as if waiting for an objection.

'I went for a scan, Connie.'

'Did they really say only twelve weeks?'

She could hardly forget a thing like that. Some paper work was somewhere or had she thrown it away? A vague memory of being cold, lighting a fire in the dusty grate, looking for whatever was handy. Why couldn't she think straight?

'Depression, you are clinically depressed,' Aidan had said a couple of days before.

Her brother was probably too intent on his own studies to have passed on his brilliant diagnosis to Connie, who had no doubt deduced it already. Nell was still nauseous and that usually stopped after three months. The doctor had accepted her dates but what about the scan? Why had she not listened more carefully? All the decisiveness that had driven her since she'd realised she was pregnant in that hospital cabin in Lagos. Now she was mindless. Except she knew she wasn't fit to be a mother.

She had let Claire die. Too worried about disturbing her uncle.

Connie was still standing by the door.

'I forgot to tell you, Colum's getting married.'

Nell didn't give a toss about Colum. 'As long as Aidan doesn't mention me to Mum and Dad. No one must know.'

Connie shrugged, went back to the kitchen. So Colum was going to marry his good-Catholic horse-adoring vet. Nell climbed out of bed, pulled on Aidan's coat. 'I thought you'd bring the nun back, you seemed very matey.'

'Sad to see her like this.' Her aunt was putting tea-bags into a canister. 'She helped me.' Connie stopped stacking away groceries, looked around as if realising something. 'I was about to add, she encouraged me to have Jess. Which is kind of true.'

She went to the fridge, poured Nell a glass of milk. So good at caring for her, Aidan, Colum. Useless with her own children.

Nell put the milk out of sight. 'How is Jess?'

'Anne didn't say. My darling delinquent is settled with Liam and Maura, apparently everything's calm. Isn't that unbelievable?'

Connie filled the kettle, rinsed two mugs, put them on the table with some short-bread. The sight of biscuits made Nell nauseous.

'I talked to Anne about you.'

What had Connie said?

'She won't tell anyone.'

What did Connie mean? 'You are joking, you must be?'

Connie had told the nun about the pregnancy? How bloody outrageous. 'How dare you, Connie.'

Don't scream. Calm down. If only the shivering would stop. Nell was ready to punch her aunt, kick her out the flat. But she couldn't tell her to get the hell out, Connie was renting the place.

She ran back to her room, slammed the door shut. No bloody lock. Leave tonight. Nothing to pack, she'd wait for Aidan, borrow money. Go.

She climbed into bed, pulled up the duvet.

Connie knocked and came in, without waiting. She didn't look remotely contrite.

'This is for your consideration, Nell. Anne knows of an excellent charity. It would be a compromise.'

'Get out!'

PART THREE

2000

2000

55

Spring at last. Through the open windows came a lingering chill of winter behind a warmish breeze carrying the smell of Arles: the fruit market two streets away, a car's exhaust as it reversed at speed, and, with imagination, a motor-boat chugging down the Rhone.

She should shower. No, that would mean leaving Laurent, this warm bed and, if Connie was lucky, finding her slippers. If not, padding down two treacherous flights of cold stone in bare feet. Laurent's house was ancient, narrow and built around a courtyard, had too many stairs. She moved herself free from his arm, stretched down, hauled up the duvet.

'Was that ok?' said Laurent.

'Mmm.'

Pleasure should get more out of reach but so far, all good. Desire was a running breath through the day and, with this lazy life, satisfaction readily available – was it enough? On the few occasions when she'd gone on a binge, Laurent had called it her *noir*. He'd waited till she'd eventually come through. Somehow he'd taught her to treat wine and life with more respect. But she was restless. She felt too young for no more medicine, too young to be retired. The French *retraite* was a better word with its echoes of school girls muttering prayers, the candles, the silence; its suggestion of reflection.

According to Laurent: 'You'll learn to enjoy idleness, Connie, when you get to my advanced age.'

In August, she'd be sixty-seven. Laurent was seventy in six months. Unbelievable. She was not meant to have lived this long. But Laurent was a good role model, never idle. If he wasn't working on the house, he was gardening, or worrying about his olive trees. They would probably stick it out till the end.

'Why?' Laurent had said when Jess had asked if either of them was likely to look for another relationship, implying that they were being a bit boring. 'It's all too tiring,' he'd added. And he was right, getting to know people was tiring. This was enough.

Jess was probably joking. She had a nerve, had been with James for years. Was her daughter happy? She rarely emailed. Occasionally she'd phone in answer to a message. Jess worked too hard, was thirty-six; she should be considering having a child.

Laurent ran his fingers up and down her spine. 'What are you thinking? You seem suddenly full of purpose, very worrying.'

'About Maura. I haven't heard since she promised to talk to Liam, he should be the one to help, but is he any use?'

Of course he wasn't any use. Maura might be back in hospital.

'Liam doesn't trust me enough to say how she is.'

Could she trust Liam? He was so remote compared to Laurent who was a great mountain of energy and sensuality. How lucky that Laurent had waited while she commuted between England and Arles, between medicine and idleness. But that was now over with: stay here, stay away from hospitals – stay away from Maura.

They had put Claire in a room of her own, in a full-size hospital bed. She'd looked so tiny, not like her baby Claire at all.

'What are you deciding?' Laurent swung his legs to the floor.

Connie reached over and stroked his back: a broad back, black and grey curly hairs. She'd ask Jess if she could stay in the flat – absurd to be scared of your own daughter. About time Connie made sure things were really fine. Jess had a new flat with a spare room, no excuse. Maybe her daughter would say she couldn't.

'Are you homesick, Connie?'

'I need to get up.'

Homesick? Westport, Dublin, Moreton, London, Derby, Arles?

No home to be nostalgic for. This was Laurent's town. It didn't help that her French wasn't up to complex conversations. His friends liked their chat indecipherable – if they did know English, refused to use it on principle.

Laurent stood up, tied on his dressing gown. What a giant, well over six feet. He smiled down at her, those deceptive brown eyes. Could any man be trusted? But they'd stuck it for twenty years. Not bad to fancy someone after twenty years: your car gives up, you put out your thumb and look what treasures fall into your lap. What deliciously disreputable behaviour; how much it had delighted him to shock his intensely conservative family.

'I said to Maura, I'd go back.'

She had done all she could. Families, what a toxic creation and what a pig's ear she'd made of hers; even her mother gave up on her after Claire died – much safer to forget Maura, not interfere.

'You'll get the blame, whatever.' Laurent bent down, picked up her slippers, threw them to her side of the bed. 'You deserve it.'

No obligation, family or not. Neither Liam nor Maura had any claim on her. Connie was an ex-, an ex in all senses. Staying here would mean not getting it wrong, no reminders of her poor mothering, no regrets. What bliss.

But Maura had insisted that there was nobody she could turn to. There must be. Maura had appeared so sociable, all those people she worked with; Jess claimed she was always getting post and phone calls. Where were these friends now? Maura had been busy but perhaps not gregarious, cool and so ruddy competent, always the teacher. And now she was putting that same firm competence into dealing with this.

'Maura has been too pre-occupied making Liam happy.'

'And looking after your children, Connie. You abandon them and she takes over.'

Connie hadn't abandoned anyone. Laurent leant down and

kissed the top of her head. 'It's amazing they still speak to you.'

He sounded sad. He was fond of her two, they seemed fond of him. But his own children rarely got in touch, both were in Canada near his ex-wife. Had Connie driven them away? No grandchildren. Which as far as Connie was concerned was a relief. Did she dislike children? It was more that they made her anxious.

Rory worked too hard, but when he did take holidays he came to Arles. Jess was fairly polite when they met up in London, or more accurately Jess was charming to Laurent but prickly with Connie. At least with Laurent, Jess could talk law; his variety was so different from hers. Jess had nothing to say to her mother. Connie irritated her.

'So, I get Madame some tea?' Laurent lumped himself down on her side and tweaked her nose.

'I need a pee,' said Connie, burrowing further under the sheet.

She couldn't just lie here, wait for a phone call from Brighton, even if that was the wisest thing to do. But by supporting Maura, she'd infuriate Liam, infuriate Anne, infuriate all of them. How to justify being Maura's ally when it went against her oath, her training. But she'd also been trained to listen, and be realistic.

She would have to talk things through with Anne, Anne who, according to Maura, had refused to listen to Maura's clearly stated wishes. Maura had to summon Connie to help when she realised Anne would not. What to do, where was the much-vaunted wisdom of age? Oh what a hypocrite. Do something.

Connie pushed down the covers and sat up. Laurent kissed her and she traced her fingers over his full, sexy, lips.

'You once told me, Connie, getting the blame usually means doing the thing that is more important.'

He was right, there wasn't much choice. And this time, she'd talk to Anne, brave her wrath.

56

Liam leant against the sea wall; he was alone in a bubble of sound and light, the waves folding over the shingle slow like him in the May sun.

'I need your help to die, Liam,' Maura had said.

What did she mean? An injection? A pillow? The visit this morning had been the worst yet. Normally they whispered because of the other three patients; this time Maura's voice was loud, clear, still echoing in his head. Maybe he'd imagined it as loud. There'd been no rustle from the other beds. He couldn't reply, and Maura had drifted off to sleep. The whole visit was a nightmare, even before asking for help she'd been sombre, absent. He'd denied her with his silence. If she were to ask now, he could offer nothing.

Yachts tacked towards the horizon. She wanted to sail away. Instead of helping, he'd got angry.

'Has the consultant been?' Liam had hissed in her ear. 'She wants you to have more chemo, doesn't she?'

Of course the consultant did. They'd readmitted Maura because they wanted to keep her alive. Liam wanted to keep her alive. Chemo might give her several years, anything might happen.

The yachts were racing each other around a row of buoys. How pointless.

He hadn't told her about his four am walking up and down Sandford's beach front. 'Can I help you, Sir?' from the policeman.

Had he no home to go to, a respectable, elderly man like him? The police bothered about wandering pensioners, ignored clumps of half-naked drunken teenagers. 'You're not meant to be out at this hour,' the policeman was thinking. For God's sake, was he supposed to be tucked into bed at nine-thirty in a home for geriatrics or standing around a piano in some beach front hotel singing *My Old Man Said...*

Maybe it's good the police were alert. Maura would have laughed at how sweet they were, those children calling out as he passed. 'You ok, Sir?' Those kids were the vulnerable ones. What a relief not to be that age.

Just before he'd left, Maura had grabbed his hand and whispered: 'Liam, it's enough.'

He'd tried to pull away.

'I don't want chemo. It makes me feel awful, I want to control what's happening. You have to support me.'

Who could advise him? Maura was the only one and she was the one he'd denied. He knew what she was intending. When Papa was paralysed after the stroke, got pneumonia, Liam had known to tell the super-keen registrar there was no need for antibiotics. But Papa was old, Maura wasn't even sixty. And more chemotherapy might save her life, this was different.

He'd already talked to Vijay. Having Maura's GP as one of the family had not been any help – Vijay was sympathetic but useless, the consultant no better.

More than halfway home from Brighton, he'd stopped the car. To stand in the spring sunshine, feel the salt breeze, let the warmth soak in. Staring at the water, all his life staring out.

Why not hire a boat, take off into the ocean? Maura saw no reason why people don't face into land, make a line along the water's edge watching the beach, cliffs, people, busyness. Whenever they had a few days away, it was Stratford and Shakespeare for her, the nearest decent waves for him.

Now she wanted to walk into the water.

A text pinged through from Rory. 'Love to M.'

His son didn't say when he would visit.

'Rory's an anorak,' Maura had said too many times. 'You should be worrying about him, not Jess.'

A gentle tick from the cooling car and a shuffle from the waves dying on the shingle. Maura's nun would be on her way to the café, assuming he'd be there. She'd been immediately recognisable, hovering outside the ward this morning – still had that nun hover, a blend of humility and rigidity. He knew she'd kept in touch with Maura. They even had a couple of boxes in the garage with Anne's name on them. On many occasions Maura had driven for the day to Birmingham or York or wherever, had never invited him.

Had Anne recognised him? She'd looked a bit unsure. Twenty years. Jess, just back from France, had moved in. Then Anne disappeared, according to Maura, was wandering around Britain. When Maura went into hospital for surgery, Anne suddenly turned up, started visiting. Liam had on several occasions just missed the woman – she'd been avoiding him?

Maura claimed to be happy to see Anne, but there'd been some rift just before Maura came home. No contact since, as far as he knew, until a few days ago. Good. Impossibly hard to think of sharing Maura with anyone, let alone one of those who believe they know the answers.

After he'd left, Anne would have gone into Maura's room, preached to the barely conscious four women about the afterlife. Some vague memory from childhood, having the sanctimonious pray all over you. The dip of the head to show that they care. Someone he needed, someone he loved, had died. His mother had died.

A windsurfer was in trouble. When he'd told Maura he'd just seen Anne, Maura had said: 'Be nice. Anne is lonely. And stop calling her that nun, she's not a nun anymore.'

The windsurfer had been struggling with the sail, but at last managed to pull it upright.

57

Anne tried to stretch out her cup of tea as long as possible, Liam was an hour late. He'd said he knew this café in the Lanes; it was one both he and Maura liked. He'd described the smell of roasting beans puffing from a vent above the door.

A shock seeing him today at the hospital – he'd aged, hair white, face lined, back slightly stooped. But he was smart in his grey slacks and sweater. She must have become used to the appearance of the residents at the hostels and half-way houses, forgetting not all people look like that. What would Liam think of her? Even Maura had noticed that Anne's red track-suit, T-shirt, were tatty.

Well, they were clean.

'You could have trimmed your hair with more than kitchen scissors,' Maura had said.

Not if you didn't have any money.

'But you're being the mendicant pilgrim very convincingly, Anne. You never age, the same expression as when we first met. How do you do it?'

What might that be? Resignation? Resign now, leave the café?

Some months ago, they had argued. Maura was being defeatist, Anne had got furious. One afternoon, Anne had turned up at the hospital and Maura had gone. No warning. Only a brief message: Maura had been sent home, everything was fine, she'd get in touch and they could meet. Nothing more. If Anne hadn't called the Sandford house a week ago, got the cleaner, she'd never have known Maura had been re-admitted.

Liam was at the cafe door, gazing around the crowded room. Spotting her, he seemed disappointed; clearly he hadn't been late enough. The coward.

He hung his tweed jacket on a chair. 'Can I get you something?'

No apologies.

'Thank you but nothing for me.'

He came back with a cappuccino and sandwich for himself, a fussy ice-cream for her. She disliked ice-cream.

'Tutti frutti,' Liam said.

So that was what he'd prefer.

'I need to talk to you, Liam.' She must not sound agitated. No matter how upset, she must seem calm.

'About what?'

'Maura.'

How to put it in a way that wouldn't make him get up and leave? After all she was blaming him as well. Liam had turned his chair so as not to see their reflection in a mirror.

'It's Connie,' said Anne eventually.

Liam was removing the tomatoes from his sandwich. Those long slender fingers. He stopped when he saw Anne looking, then moved his mobile closer to his plate.

'In case the hospital calls,' he said. 'What about Connie?'

'She's not encouraging Maura to fight. It is possible to cure this cancer, isn't it?'

He didn't answer but had certainly heard her, it wasn't too noisy a café. Fragments of conversations: muttered anger, resentments spitting out around them between the intermittent roar of the espresso machine. Maybe he thought he'd missed the diagnosis; any kind of question from her would be painful, but Connie had to be stopped.

'Can we change the subject?' he said eventually.

She'd not be brushed off that easily. She took a spoonful of ice-cream. There was a layer of fresh raspberries, it was delicious.

'Why are you smiling?'

'Catching the sight of myself in that mirror,' said Anne. 'Seeing my grandmother.'

'You said all those years ago it was your grandmother you

missed when you were a child.'

What had possessed her to confide in him?

Difficult to remember her grandmother's face. The only thing that was vivid was the smell of moth-balls and aniseed. The old woman must have died before the war ended. She'd only visited the orphanage once, not long before they were evacuated.

'She was probably younger than me now. Brought me a bear she'd knitted, I loved that bear.'

Liam picked up his empty cup, went to the counter, came back with two cappuccinos. Had it not occurred to him to ask? If he was so irritated by her, why come? But she had to get him on her side.

'Not for me.'

Liam put both in his place.

'For some reason,' Anne went on. 'My grandmother is my most vivid memory.'

He burst out laughing. 'That's so familiar. I could have driven home, got the newspaper, come back. You'd carry on exactly where we broke off. Don't you remember?'

No, she didn't remember.

'I never knew,' Liam said, 'why you left Moreton. Maura had no idea. It must have been Jess.'

'It wasn't Jess.'

Anne put down her spoon. It was detestable, the trivial chat being spilled out around them, the hoots of laughter. Liam assumed she'd left because of his daughter. She had been appalled at their decision and prayed for the child. But she had respected their right to make it. Had any of them respected her? As far as Liam was concerned she was a nun. He kept his distance.

'I can see you huddled with Sister Jude, Liam. The pair of you grinning over some joke, managing to exclude me completely.'

'I miss Jude, should never have let Gerry take back her care.'

Sister Jude hadn't settled into the new school, was no support to any of the nuns. Her death, the following year on Easter Sunday, had marred what should have been a celebration, their first Easter in the new building.

But that was self-deceiving. The truth was she'd resented Jude. But why still feel bitterness after all that had happened since?

Jude had known how to love, a gift that was increasingly unreachable? She mustn't start feeling self-pity, not with all this suffering happening to Maura.

'I was in a bit of a state,' said Liam.

He was sad. He had every cause to be sad, then and now. If something wasn't done, Maura would never fight back. She must be encouraged to have treatment but would only listen to Connie, too much time had been wasted. If only Anne had realised in January. Maura was recovering from surgery and had said nothing about a hospice, had said nothing about Connie coming over from France to help her look.

'I didn't realise Maura stopped her treatment, Liam. She looked so well when I first came, I took for granted she was better.'

Now Maura was back in the ward and failing, letting go. Wasn't Aidan's friend, Vijay, her GP? Could Aidan not help if Liam was so useless? Maura was slipping away, Anne had done nothing.

She scooped out the remains of her ice-cream, caught Liam watching. It was an unreadable expression; was he afraid of her?

'Maura is fond of you,' said Liam.

He looked as if that was surprising, yet she'd introduced them, known it would work. Maura, dependable, loyal, not a religious or spiritual bone in her body. Maura had been lucky for Liam, lucky for Jess and Rory. And she'd been lucky for Anne.

Maura stayed on teaching at the convent because Jess was there, and she'd become a good friend. Father Willis once asked why Anne hadn't organised a Catholic. 'Because it wouldn't have lasted.'

Liam must promise to stop Connie interfering, must help Maura survive. But how? All Anne could think of was her grandmother's knitted bear, the smell of moth-balls, that bear's black-button eyes.

She was boring Liam, had got nowhere. He was touching his mobile, fiddling with the salt. He would always connect her with that night, Nell calling him from the stairs, the Canon rattling on about nothing.

Liam pushed back his chair. 'I have to go.'

Maura smiled at Aidan over her reading glasses. 'Who let you in?'

Aidan closed the door gently; the three other patients were asleep. Liam had said Maura was mostly sleeping but she was wide-awake, propped up by pillows, papers and diaries all over the bed.

'You look great.'

'Liar. I bet Liam said I was depressed.'

A week since he'd seen her, Maura was not looking good. Times like this it was a blessing to have done psychiatry.

They'd visited Sandford regularly for Sunday roasts, but it was Vijay who a year ago suggested to Maura that she drop into the practice. 'She's normally energetic. Hasn't been to see me for ages.'

'Liam wouldn't have missed that,' said Aidan, when they'd got back in the car.

They'd all missed that. Aidan drew the curtains round the bed, pulled up a chair; he took Maura's hands in his. Her nails were painted bright red.

'Terribly sluttish, aren't they?'

'What's with all these papers, Maura? Are you working?'

'I'm sorting, so I don't leave a mess.'

'You're hiding the evidence.'

'Exactly. I don't want my ears metaphorically burning while my body does. Saintly Maura deceived us all, the witch.'

'Stop that crap.'

There were more and more wonder drugs, no reason for her not to live for many more years. But Vijay was not optimistic.

'Take a look, Aidan. Help me have the courage to destroy it all.'

He picked up a bulky envelope from the box by the bed and pulled out a letter. 'It's to you from Nell. Did you and Liam ever know about the adoption?'

'None of us knew, Nell told me five years later. Liam still

doesn't know. Why the secrecy, Aidan? We could have done something to keep the child.'

So could he. But it hadn't occurred to him, exams had been all consuming.

'Why did Nell decide to tell you then?'

'She wrote several times after Dermot died in '85. She was thinking of working in Zambia, a locum at her practice was setting up a clinic.'

'She never mentioned it to me.'

'Because she didn't go. That's when she told me about the baby. Look, I'm fed up with these. Take them away, bin them. I don't want Liam bothered.'

'In this for 1980, you say Connie describes me as weird!'

Cramming for finals while looking after a pregnant sister having a breakdown was weird? 'I was heroic.'

'You're still heroic, and handsome, Aidan. And clever. You should stick to being an analyst, give up the hospital. It's too stressful. And you always look so smart, Rory is such a tramp, your Vijay not much better.'

Rory and Vijay could afford to look like tramps, he couldn't.

'And don't give me that guff about appearances and being a consultant. And you've gel in your lovely black hair!'

'Have you quite finished, Auntie?'

Maura laughed and rapped him on the head with an envelope.

Aidan rifled again through the journal. 'Connie told you I was making notes?' He paused. 'She's right, I did make notes – thought Nell might be a useful case-study.'

'What a callous brother you are.'

Had he been callous? Or single-minded.

'It was a difficult winter,' said Maura. 'Jess arriving pregnant.'

'What!'

'Keep your voice down, they're all sleeping.'

Aidan went to the sink, washed his hands. 1980. Jess was pregnant? His baby cousin had been barely a teenager. While he was rescuing Nell in Lagos, Jess got pregnant?

'I regret not telling Connie,' said Maura.

Connie should have been told.

What a contrast, the freedom given to Jess, Rory, compared to his, Colum, Nell's teenage years: Mass, Sunday Rosary, confession, clergy in and out of the house.

He checked his reflection in the mirror. More grey hair than black. He should point out the thinning patches. Maura always used to praise his thick curls, not thick any more.

'Vijay rescued this box from the house without telling Liam,' said Maura. 'Can you do something? Calm your uncle? Apparently he's questioning the treatment.'

Aidan sat down again.

'I can't offer you coffee, I'm afraid.'

'Oh, Vijay banned coffee years ago.'

Vijay had replaced Aidan's coffee machine in his office with a Japanese tea-pot, matching bowls, kettle and several packs of green tea. And the man trusted him not to cheat, send for an espresso.

Maura fumbled in her bedside cupboard, took out a piece of paper. There was a name and address.

'I want you to see if Anne needs help. I mentioned it but Liam will do nothing. And bin this box of stuff, please. Oh, and call Nell. Tell her to visit.'

Nell wouldn't visit. She never visited anyone, never phoned Aidan. She didn't want to know about his or Colum's life. She went into Sanghi's practice each morning, saw a few patients, referred the complicated ones, disappeared home.

'When Liam is sorting out stuff, can you go to the house? There are two boxes in the garage that belong to Anne. Get them to her.'

'Will you please stop this, Maura.'

Maura smiled and grabbed his hand. 'How are the patients? I mean the NHS ones, not your private pampered ones?'

'Fine.' He paused. 'Well, as long as I can ignore the fact that my hand-picked staff are about to be dispersed by some teenager of an inept manager. That our excellent system taking the emergency team into the crisis will be reversed. That the consequent figures showing the reduction in occupied beds is about to be of historical interest only.'

'Is that all?' said Maura.

'Pretty well. All we've achieved is under imminent threat of being wrecked. Otherwise, everything is fine.'

'Has Vijay succeeded in getting you to meditate, Aidan?'

59

The adoption people needed another interview before any possible meeting. Nell took the letter over to the sitting-room window; the hawthorn behind her patch of garden was beginning to flower. It was going to happen, she would meet the child, meet Jerome's daughter.

How to explain to a social worker that decision made twenty years ago? Perhaps the more inadequate she came over the better? However lacking they would consider her, it was too late to do any parenting. Did they know she'd been responsible for her cousin's death? And that Claire kept returning, asking her to do something. Easy to imagine the report: this woman is totally unfit to mother a child, a child who in another week would be twenty.

Her life had been in a limbo, now was the reckoning. For twenty years, Nell had seen that rejected child in every three, four, eight-year-old. Each June birthday had been awful. She'd made sure that the other doctors in Sanghi's practice treated the children; she didn't want to be the first to diagnose a leukaemia, miss meningitis. The noise Claire had made in that dark bedroom, her sweaty ashen face. Those children in Lagos expecting Nell to save them.

An abortion would have freed her.

The office was in an anonymous block off the Caledonian Road. A matronly woman with a reassuring smile and blonde cropped hair greeted her at the reception, led her down a narrow corridor to a neon-lit room. The furniture was plastic wood, cream paint on the walls. There was a bulky filing cabinet and shelves over-loaded with files. 'Can I call you, Nell?'

Before she could answer, the social worker said: 'I'm Amy.'

Amy moved a pile of folders to the side of the desk; opened one and looked at Nell over her glasses. 'You told my colleague that you have no questions?'

None at all. Her mind was a complete blank.

'Ring me at any time if you do.'

Of course, she had questions. Millions of them.

'Rose has been asked to bring someone,' said Amy, 'but her mother's about to go into hospital.' Amy paused. 'An ovarian cyst.'

This was such an unlikely conversation; Amy seemed to think there should be a response. Was she expecting a medical insight about ovaries? That open folder? Would there be photographs? Take a deep breath, stay calm.

'Right, if you'd prefer she brings someone, there are siblings.'

Amazing, Nell needn't say anything.

'I'll give you these leaflets and photocopies to look at later.'

Amy was examining her; eventually she spread the papers over the table. Nell was being judged – she'd better smarten up or this would never happen.

'Can I get you some tea?' Amy said.

She was rightly looking at Nell as at some unhelpful teenager.

'And you, uh, you should bring someone too.'

Who? Why should she? She'd dumped the child on her own, lived with the consequences. Now she needed some kind of support? Or was it protection? Would Rose get angry? Would Rose hate her? And if not, why not?

Connie phoned to say she'd got the message, was coming round. Nell opened red wine though it was hopeless for her stomach. Connie arrived an hour late with a bottle of brandy. Nell hadn't told her when she called that Lola/Rose had got in touch; she meant to but couldn't get the words out.

'Thanks so much for this, Con. I could only think of you. Laurent said you were in London.'

'I asked Jess if I could stay and she agreed. It's as if I'm with my mother, not daughter, and have to behave. She leaves me with her bloke, some innocent ex-hippy called James.'

The last time Nell had seen Jess was at Dermot's funeral: Jess had linked arms with her as they'd wandered from the church. 'Do you remember anything about my glorious arrival? Connie and Liam never mention it. I had to beg your mother for baby pictures.'

'You cried.'

And so did Connie. All the time. But not helpful to say that.

Jess had stopped suddenly to examine a flower below the hedge. 'Cowslip, isn't it lovely? Do you think it's there by accident?'

Those weeks at home in Newcastle, after Jess was born, had felt forever. When Connie wasn't crying, she was an absence. Even while they were having meals, baby Jess for once asleep, Connie was cut off, a black emptiness at the table. Then a visitor would call and Connie almost her normal self. A relief to the whole house when Liam arrived to take them back. 'I can't remember much. Your father turned up just before Christmas and you all left.'

Better for both Jess and Rory to be with Maura, and better for Liam. But she couldn't say that, it felt a betrayal of Connie.

They'd stopped at the church entrance by a row of empty black cars. 'I hated you,' Jess had said. 'Mum was nice to you lot.'

Before Nell could think of a reply, they'd started to transfer the flowers. Her father had died. She'd had to abandon a child. Her father was gone. It wasn't his fault. She mustn't blame anyone but herself, certainly not the dead. If only Jess would shut up.

'Tell me, Nell, what do you remember about my sister?'

Her first impulse had been to walk away, but Jess looked as sad as Nell felt.

'She wouldn't stop talking. Claire would beg for a story, roll around giggling before I'd even started.'

And then Nell couldn't stop crying, great noisy chokes of grief, and Jess had stared horrified. They hadn't met again since.

Connie was pouring herself wine.

'Is this about Maura? Have you visited?'

Nell loved Maura, didn't want to see her like this. But of course she would go.

'It might be months, though it could be sooner,' said Connie.

Her father's funeral had been when? Fifteen years ago? Jess had just finished her degree, was starting articles; since then she'd sent Nell occasional invitations for supper but was only being polite.

'Jess is never home. Isn't she a bit old for gadding about?'

'Fourteen-hour days facing abusive husbands, even murderers? You call it gadding about. What example have you been, Con?'

Connie straightened her green silk scarf, tied it more tightly. 'A brilliant one, frankly.' She lit a cigarette, a smelly French one. 'How is work, still the same place?'

'I do short weeks.' Nell got up to open the window then settled on the rug in front of the electric fire.

'Can you turn that on? It might be June, but it's freezing. So what about the rest of the time?'

Connie's voice had taken on a shrill tone, similar to Pat's the week before. Her mother had phoned for a talk and ended up criticising Nell's lack of oomph. 'You're wasting your life.'

Nell switched on the fire. 'You were often part-time, Connie.'

'I was always full-time, just not all the time. So, I'm not here because you want to know about Maura?'

'The baby has got in touch.'

'What baby?'

'She's twenty. And called Rose.'

'That baby! For a moment, you sounded like a zombie movie. Oh, my god, how wonderful.' Connie swooped down and hugged her. 'That's bloody brilliant. What a miracle.'

Connie was kissing her hundreds of times, had become very French. Nell extricated herself. Why did Connie assume this was good news? It was wonderful and it was terrifying; Nell had done something appalling, now she had to face it.

'Rose wants to meet.'

'Of course she does. What else? Do you need me with you?'

'She might come alone. I don't want her to think me a sad, old granny in need of support.'

'You're barely forty, Nell. Leave the old lady guff to me. Oh, this is so fabulous.'

No point saying she was already forty-seven. Nell shoved a can of peanuts in her aunt's direction.

Connie took out a note-book and pen. 'What can I do?'

She hadn't talked to her aunt about any of it since then. A vague memory of refusing to see the baby; Connie was the one bottle-feeding and cuddling until the nightmare day the agency took it away. The incredible pain of labour, much more than expected, Nell had done enough deliveries. Then swollen leaking breasts and, once Connie had made certain that this was what Nell wanted, a blur of signing papers. Before and after that, despair. There was a vague recollection of Connie calling it, Lola.

'You weren't in a fit state, darling. Maybe I shouldn't have influenced you against a termination but you were further along than you thought.'

If only she could remember.

Connie had stopped her, and a few cells had become a child. But then Connie could have kept the baby, or helped her keep it? Who else could have helped? Mum? Dad? Hardly. Jerome was no use, he would never have believed it was his. Nell had been abandoned just like Lola was abandoned.

Connie tossed a peanut in the air, caught it in her mouth. Her aunt didn't care. And this hadn't been some stranger, it was her and Jerome's daughter. What rejection the child must feel.

'Exciting isn't it?' Connie beamed. 'Oh Nell, you weren't fit to make any kind of decision.' She missed the next peanut, picked it up, popped it in her mouth. 'Look at our family. Your mother and I brought up by Jansenists, taught to believe an all-seeing power knows each time we drop something.'

It had been too much of a coincidence, Anne suddenly turning up, knowing an adoption agency.

Connie pulled off her scarf, folded it carefully. 'I probably did pressure you but would do it again. Your dates were a muddle, Aidan more than useless.'

'It was Anne, she ruined everything.'

Connie opened the note-book, pressed back a new page. 'No. She made suggestions, but I had to decide for you, you were profoundly depressed and that scared me.'

'What's with this making notes?'

'Helps me focus. Aidan gave me the idea – always writing things down, don't you remember?'

Her aunt was taking too much space, there wasn't enough air in the room.

Nell stood up. 'I'm tired, Connie, I'll phone.'

Connie picked up her bag. 'Darling, it is good news.'

'No one must know,' said Nell, collecting Connie's leather jacket. 'No one. You have to swear.'

There'd been that same waiting room packed full of patients, Nell trying to get past the crowd to find the screaming baby. She was wearing a T-shirt, nothing else. This time she'd managed to find the crib. It was in a garden under a bush of forsythia, inside it a baby's head. Only the head, a hydrocephalus, the baby's eyes open.

She couldn't get back to sleep, would not describe this to Aidan. He'd reduced her recurring dream of the nun on the beach with Claire, to being *merely interesting*. He'd wittered on about Anne being the idealised mother, Nell trying to bury her in the sand. What would he make of this?

She walked up and down in front of the window. The children downstairs had lit a bonfire the night before; smoke was still lifting around the leaves of the beech by the gate. It mixed with the early morning mist that clung to the neglected section of garden that Nell was responsible for. Ownership of that patch had felt important when she'd bought the flat, now the weeds were waist-high and, according to her neighbours, contagious.

This was a bad thing. If her mother did one of her rare visits, she'd be appalled; Nell's garden had been a useful crutch for their conversations, Mum would even turn up with plants. But since getting the request for a meeting with Rose, Nell had abandoned it, abandoned her mother. Pat wasn't to know any of this.

Why had Connie allowed Anne to interfere?

Nell made coffee and sat on the edge of the sofa cradling her mug. She looked around the living room, the debris from the night before. 'Get a cleaner,' her mother would say each visit. 'You work. Give someone a job, it's unsanitary.'

As far as she knew, Pat had not been to see Maura – her mother was becoming increasingly isolated. She'd be furious about the garden, must not know. The children next door could light bonfires illegally but Nell must keep order, only grow regular plants that knew where they came from.

When she got home from work there was a message from Amy on her answering machine with a date to meet Rose.

60

Liam pulled the curtains around the bed to block out the fat man visiting the very old lady in the corner. The man, probably her son, spent each visit in silence, reading the same page of the *Daily Express*. Today he was wearing an orange track suit, orange buttocks bulging over the black plastic chair.

Liam took Maura's hand, launched into his usual ramble. 'Do talk even if she's asleep, she can hear you, Doctor,' the ten-year old nurse would repeat each time. 'It does perk her up.' At least the child called him Doctor, not Liam.

'Aidan phoned yet again. I was about to go to bed; he keeps such late hours. I suspect he thinks it's therapeutic for me to talk.'

Maura's palm showed a long healthy life-line.

'He told me Nell had a child and it was adopted, and you knew.'

They'd kept it from him. Women's business, apparently.

'You never said a word. Aidan seems to think that Anne stuck her oar in.'

He shouldn't sound annoyed, nor bother her with Aidan's paranoia. Aidan was a psychiatrist, his job was to imagine paranoia. But Maura had known about Nell, not told him. Shouldn't he be the one to be paranoid?

Nell had come back to England at almost the same time as Jess. It was just after Christmas: Maura had described the absurdity of workmen taking down decorations while anti-abortion protesters from SPUC heckled her and his daughter outside the clinic. No one had said that Nell had returned. Had Nell come to have an abortion? If so, what had happened?

Liam ran his fingers along Maura's arm, reached for some hand cream, massaged it in. She used to be so muscular, off to the gym three times a week, lifting weights.

It had never made sense why Nell stayed in England, got that job with Vijay's brother.

Maura was mumbling something but was asleep; they all were, the woman in the opposite bed was snoring.

The consultant had collared Liam before he could get into the room: 'You know Maura needs us to have a talk?'

Liam had nodded, tried to look sympathetic.

'I am sorry, Liam, but Maura is very clear. She said you would back her up.'

The consultant had paused, a professional and meaningful pause. What did she expect him to say? 'There is more we can do, Liam, as you know, but your wife isn't interested.'

So it was going to be left to him.

'Do you think it might be time, Liam?'

What? The right time to put a pillow over Maura's face?

'There are days when your wife's positive, we're sure we can help. But Maura says she wants some peace – that you'll confirm it.'

'I don't think I'm ready.'

He would never be ready.

Liam held the cream to Maura's nose.

'Good smell, isn't it? Roses, I think.'

As if he'd know. What a useless gardener. He tried a bit of weeding now Maura wasn't home, didn't want her coming back to anarchy. She was the one who persisted with the salt-saturated, windswept patch behind the bungalow. Yet, he'd transformed that convent garden in Moreton. Why in God's name had he done that?

'Did I tell you I went to the book group, gave your apologies?'

Maura opened her eyes slightly.

'Gillian and Bernard loved *The End of the Affair*, the rest hated it. I said you loved it because I thought you'd find that Catholic angst about adultery hilarious.'

There was an enormous crash outside the door but the man reading the *Daily Express* didn't stir. Liam went to have a look. An empty corridor. The poor old bat next to the toilet, who groaned all day, probably all night too, carried on moaning.

'After hearing about Nell from Aidan, I phoned her this morning.' Liam sat down again by the bed. 'It must be years rather than months and of course I didn't know what to say. I was total discretion, thought better not to mention anything, rattled on about the wretched Greene novel. Just as well it wasn't about abandoned babies. Or maybe it was? Nell had even read it, said she found it dated. Dated! She said she'd try to come down and visit you.'

There was a flutter from Maura, she opened her mouth slightly. Liam lifted her up, put the beaker of water to her lips. Maura sipped a little then sank back. She was so light, nothing to her.

'Next month's your favourite, a Margaret Atwood. Nell had read that too. Should get a life that girl, at her age. If I buy the audio-book, you can bone up before the next meeting, put on your usual impressive show.'

He lifted Maura again, tried to help her drink.

'Bernard will hate it, he grumbled yet again he hates women writers. He's getting worse you know, I think he might be banned.'

'He should be banned,' whispered Maura. 'Bernard is a bore.'

She was getting the knack. Anne leant on the edge of the spade, shoved down hard, loosened up more soil. She took a deep breath, pushed again. Reach the end of this section, have a tea-break, then put in some summer bedding. These months in this hostel were her first chance to garden. Ever. You couldn't count the convent all those years ago: doing a bit of weeding, trailing after Liam.

It was becoming obvious why this could be addictive. Her seedlings were coming through. The roses were about to flower, the last of the rhododendrons had given up, after an extraordinary display of reds and purple. She rubbed her back, dug in again. Almost sunny, the promise of rain had disappeared.

Someone noisy in a vivid blue scarf and leather jacket had burst through the kitchen door, and was waving. That couldn't be Connie walking towards her? No phone call. No warning.

No sign of her since January, Connie driving off with Maura. Some phone messages which Anne had ignored. Who had let her in? Connie was too confident to be excluded from anywhere. She was now standing, arms crossed, in front of Anne, beaming.

'You're glowering, Anne. Do you hate me so much?'

No, not at all. Anne put down her spade and they hugged. Connie kept her arm around Anne's shoulders as they walked to a bench beneath a cherry tree. It was a relief to sit, be again separate – easier to then remember what to say.

'My god,' said Connie. 'You and me in a garden, you even have saints. But where are the grottoes, the secrets?'

There was no romance here, a rectangle with an absurd statue at each corner. Its ugliness was a complete contrast to the garden in Moreton. Anne woul never have learnt to love that one so much if it hadn't been for Liam. Why had she not mentioned it when they met in the cafe? Seeing the garden being wrecked as crocuses came through the following spring had been agonising.

Anyway, this one might be ugly but she was learning to love it.

'There's no money. I have to go round the garden centres begging. Come and admire my vegetable patch.'

Connie was tugging out weeds from under the bench. 'You didn't reply to my messages. Maura said you moved here last winter, I wanted to see you. What terrible sin have I committed?'

She should have answered.

Connie stood up. 'Let's look at those vegetables.'

She must not get distracted from challenging Connie, Connie had such an ability to seduce.

Maura had said she was better, and wanted time alone with Liam. It wasn't Anne's business. But then to hear Maura was refusing treatment. She had to stop Connie, supporting Maura's obstinacy was tantamount to murder; Maura was in no state to make a decision herself.

Connie didn't look as if she felt guilty, was gazing at the bedding plants lined against the wall as if this was a social visit.

Connie and Maura were so different. The two women had never been that friendly; Anne had been closer to each of them, until now, now that Maura and Connie shared their own secrets. Both would have discussed her, and despaired: the Oxford graduate, the headmistress, the lost nun going from town to town, surviving by doing menial work, moving on. Each place had been a refuge. Maura regularly nagged Anne to get an address, claim benefits, stop this penitential wandering, Connie was the same.

She didn't want to. Travelling around had been liberating.

Connie was looking at the ridges of soil and plants in the potato patch as if expecting something to happen. Anne rooted around in the earth, pulled out a small potato, handed it to her.

'I planted a few early ones, a bit soon but not bad.'

Connie studied the potato as if it might explode. Anne couldn't say: Do you really want Maura to die? And of course Connie didn't.

Anne collected two sets of cutters from the wheelbarrow. 'Come and trim the clematis, it's rampant.' She led the way to the back wall. 'Liam believes that Maura can fight this.'

Connie dragged down several dead stems, ripped them off. 'Is this place a psychiatric hostel, Anne? How ill are the patients?'

'Worrying enough not to want back in the community.'

She was being fobbed off. Everyone, including Connie, no doubt considered her much the same as the residents. No harm in that, pride had never been one of her vices. Or had it?

One of the older men was staring from the kitchen window. What would he make of this exotic visitor?

'You and Maura never seemed close?'

'We aren't. She insists there's no one else. I've been a taxi-driver, getting her around.'

'You know she needs chemo, yet you put her in touch with that quack homeopath. You helped her find a hospice in January.'

'She asked to see the quack. As for the hospice, you know Maura, she's an organiser, likes to be prepared.'

'You should have forced her to have more chemotherapy.'

It was unforgivable.

Maura had known Anne wouldn't do what Connie had done.

Connie threw the cuttings into the basket, linked her arm through Anne's.

Anne felt immediately insubstantial. That was so familiar.

'Are we going to fight all day about this?'

Anne let Connie steer her away from the clematis. She wasn't sure, she certainly was angry enough. They'd fought about Nell's pregnancy, Connie had given in. Somehow during the argument in the jeans shop in Covent Garden, she'd not mentioned to Connie that Jess had an abortion – deliberately avoided mentioning Connie's daughter.

Had she decided that her silence would be punishment for Connie's appalling mothering? What right did she think she had? Inexcusable. Did Connie know now? But did it matter? It was years ago, no longer important.

Now, Maura, and another probable death. They had met at a death. It hadn't occurred to her before. Did Connie resent Anne for being in the house when Claire was dying, for distracting Liam?

'While you carry on telling me off, Anne, let's look at those monstrous saints, work out how to subvert this place. Make it more therapeutic for patients.'

Anne followed Connie to the far corner and one particularly ugly statue of St Peter.

She had achieved nothing.

62

James snuggled back, made to start again. 'We can be quick, Jessie.'

No, they couldn't. 'Make coffee while I use the bathroom.'

James checked the clock. 'You're a monster, the crack of dawn.'

Jess carried an extra-strong espresso into Connie who had taken over the spare room. Alarming to have her mother occupy part of the flat as if this was how they normally behaved. But hearing her say that she wanted to stay had been rather comforting.

That was until seeing this mess, a dirty wine glass on the table, clothes all over the floor.

Snorts and snuffles came from beneath the duvet.

'Con! Wake up.'

No sign of movement. Jess started to pull off the duvet, then, seeing her mother had nothing on, left the bedclothes where they were, yelled again. 'Coffee is beside your book. I leave in twenty minutes with you or without.'

'You cow,' said Connie, hauling back the covers.

One thing about her mother, she could shift when she had to. In slightly more than an hour they were at Crawley.

When Jess had got home just before midnight, it looked from the mess in the living room that her lover and her mother had shared a meal, abandoning the clear-up to her. Well tough, James' mess, he tidies. James might think he was being valiant but he'd never been asked.

'Why so early?' Connie was trying to put on lipstick using the passenger mirror.

'I have to get back, I've appointments. Did you see Nell?'

'You know about the daughter?'

'Nell has a daughter!'

'Twenty years ago. Can you please slow down, we don't have to stay in the fast lane.'

'No one tells me anything.'

'And still for some inexplicable reason not to be mentioned.'

She never saw Nell so that would be easy. 'Where has she hidden the child?'

Connie covered her eyes as Jess accelerated back into the middle lane. 'She gave it for adoption, she wasn't well. But the girl has got in touch so, I suppose, everyone, including Pat, will know. '

Nell had given the baby away? How could anyone do that?

'Pat and Dermot never knew,' Connie added.

'That's terrible.'

'Yes,' said her mother.

What did Connie mean, not well? Why had Connie not encouraged Nell to keep it?

Twenty years ago, Connie was driving from Derby to spend weekends in London. 'Your mother popped round,' Maura would announce when Jess got in from college. 'In a rush as usual to get to London. Don't ask why, maybe some new lover.'

Maura always said *Your Mother* when she was exasperated. Had Maura known? Nell might be more normal if she'd kept it but that could have been disaster for the kid: Nell as mother, Pat grandmother, total nightmare. Dermot was ok. He was fun.

Maura had said he was racist, he probably was.

Connie hadn't gone with Jess to Dermot's funeral. Liam cried. Her father had cried. Nell had wanted to sit next to Jess and chat, then she'd also burst out crying. Jess had tried to summon a few tears. She did feel sad and Dermot had been good to her, but she couldn't.

Hadn't he once said: 'Don't have children.'

Twenty years.

Her child would have been almost twenty. Unsettling to imagine a toddler version René: square, podgy, arrogant. Chewing on rare steak, slashing randomly at innocent animals. How daft she had been, but what a sexy man. Her choice was ideal, no regrets.

What would life have been like if she'd kept it? Probably still living in Moreton with her father and Maura, working at the checkout in Safeway. Why did Nell go ahead with the pregnancy then have it adopted? That must be the completely worst scenario. Nell could have easily taken care of a child, but to give it away?

Should she try now? James would be delighted. That would be the only reason, to make James happy. Otherwise – no, thank you.

Presumably no one had told Connie about the abortion. For once, people had listened to her. Maybe her mother wanted a grandchild. What would it look like? Like Connie? Or Liam? She'd certainly inherited her father's pale skin and red hair. Liam looked so old: freckled, wrinkled face, watchful expression. At least she had Connie's brown eyes. What else had she inherited? Depression? Liam once said that Connie was depressed after Jess was born. But Jess never got depressed, life was too busy, work too absorbing. Nell probably did. Was it anxiety about Nell's off moods that made Connie care more about her niece than her daughter?

Connie was awake and hunting in the glove compartment.

'What can I expect, Mum?'

'You don't ring Liam?'

'He always says Maura's shopping or gardening and things are fine. I was at their house a few months ago, the surgery and radiotherapy seemed to have done what it should. Since then work's been hectic.'

'The woman virtually brought you up, I thought you were close.'

How did Connie manage to make everyone else responsible, not herself?

'We are close.'

She threw a pack of chewing gum at her mother. There were rarely any questions from her parents about the office – if it wasn't medical it didn't count. Ten hours yesterday trying to get a place of safety order for a terrified young mother and her two children.

Jess braked as they turned into the hospital car park, taking a space that a 2CV was about to occupy. Her Espace might look clunky but it was nimble enough.

'That poor man,' said Connie.

He should have been quicker, people who owned those cars deserved no mercy. But, of course, they'd had one in France. Maybe they were really too late, she wouldn't have to face a dying Maura. No, that was a terrible thought.

The air was lush with the heat of the summer morning. The hospital grounds were lined with trees, the lawns just mown.

'Don't you love that smell.'

Connie was hunting for her bag in the boot, not listening.

Jess slotted in coins for a parking ticket – oh, to lie down, stick her nose in a mound of cuttings.

Connie had disappeared. They'd picked such a beautiful day, it was going to be full of death. Best not to think about death, her own, Maura's, anyone's. Too many hospital waiting rooms, too many surgeries as she waited for one of her parents to finish work – the stink of surgical spirit, unwashed bodies. That's what had been brilliant about Maura, a perfume of chalk and furniture polish, no trace of sickness, no over-scrubbed pink hands. Usually there was ink on the edge of Maura's right index finger, but that, like the emerald green nail polish or the sapphire blue, had been reassuring. Law could be smelly: sweaty arm-pits, desperate clients, over-heated offices, but it wasn't as bad as medicine.

Connie had disappeared.

There she was. Over by the entrance talking to a small woman with short greying hair, who looked vaguely familiar. Connie seemed cross, glanced up as if not expecting her.

'It's the fifth floor, room sixteen.'

Clearly there'd be no introductions.

Maura opened her eyes, took Jess's hand. 'I'm so pleased you came, darling. How are you?'

Jess kissed her on the cheek. Maura's skin felt sticky.

'Absolutely fine. More to the point, how about you?'

'A lot of the time I'm out of it,' said Maura. 'Your father has been staunch, is here every morning. He'll be in soon, waits till the main fuss with the nurses is over. He stays even when I'm snoring.'

'I bet there are queues of friends.'

'I've no energy, Liam keeps everyone away.'

Jess went to the window, trying to ignore the three other patients. She wanted to close the curtains round Maura's bed – all too public, privacy not allowed. She couldn't do any kind of cheerful chat. Maura looked awful, talking seemed a struggle.

'But the latest thing,' Maura whispered.

Jess had to go back, crouch by the bed.

'Rory has been visiting. Did you know he's about to give up the job, give up work completely?'

Rory had said nothing, Connie never mentioned anything. What would he live on? But Rory assumed people were psychic, found out things without being told.

'Not a clue. At least we know gossip central is here.'

Maura was playing with Jess's rings – the opal had been a Christmas present from her and Liam. Would she remember?

'Shame on you, I don't gossip. Was that right, Jessie, really? Do you ever regret it?'

'What?' Jess paused, trying to make sense of the words. Maura looked feverish, her voice rasping.

If only Connie would come, suggest something to make Maura's breathing easier.

'I did influence you, Jess, all those years ago. Twenty years.'

Maura had always influenced her. Not always successfully, it had to be said. 'Connie told you about Nell, Jess?'

'Her baby?'

That's what this was about, Maura must mean the abortion. Jess hadn't thought about it for years, now twice in one day. Maura was gripping her hand. How did someone so frail, find such strength?

'You know very well how I was, Mo. Not a thought in my head. Once they told me, I was desperate. You got me educated, gave me a life. Insisting on me having the test was genius. I'd no idea, only fucked the once. That doctor was brilliant.'

Jess gently unclasped Maura's grip, her fingers were losing all feeling. Odd to remember the doctor. She'd been chatty but, once she'd put on her gloves, become focused and serious. As if there'd been two people. Like going to the clinic and watching Connie: the mother Connie, scatty, irritating, and then the doctor Connie, substantial and professional.

'You were completely brilliant, Maura, a godsend. I was a kid, stubborn, stupid. I thank you every day since.'

Maura was still staring at her intently, trying to winkle out any doubts. After a moment she sank back against the pillows, satisfied.

'You were a pain in the neck up to then, Jessie, you know that.'

Connie came through the door balancing three beakers of coffee. 'Who's a pain?'

'You are Connie,' said Jess. 'We were just talking about you.'

Where had this church sprung from? Liam had probably registered it as he drove to Waitrose, but not really – red brick, Victorian? The sign outside did not talk of the Coming and Retribution. Only a list of Mass times. It was RC.

Several weeks since he came this way. Just driving. He'd been driving and saw it, and the door was open.

Liam parked, looked at himself in the driving mirror, practised smiling. Was he fit to bump into a priest? After sitting with Maura all morning, his back ached. He paused at the entrance: the familiar pews, pulpit, plain windows, there was no stained glass. The faintest hint of incense mingled with the damp.

Jess and Connie had been to see Maura the day before; he'd missed them by minutes. All these random chances. Was ovarian cancer random? A higher occurrence with nuns? No, that was cervical, he should warn Anne. Did they suggest ovarian occurred more in women who did have intercourse but never had children? Maura was in her twenties when they met, she had time for babies.

He reached for holy water and smiled – the reflex of it. The splash of his fingers in the font echoed through the emptiness. That's a perfectly bitter smile, he told himself. Guilt. By God, the boy does guilt well.

When Maura told him, he'd not looked up the most recent research papers; he'd not done a thing. He was no longer registered as a doctor, refused to behave like one. He didn't want to know. Maura had said he should stop being stupid; Liam had listened, nodded and they'd gone for a walk by the sea.

He didn't like going when she saw the consultant. She'd eventually asked him not to; she'd be more concerned with him, than taking in what was said. It turned out she'd been a couple of times with Connie. Maura had never mentioned Connie.

Liam knelt down in the back row. The church was indeed empty, no one stealing the pews. Little else to steal. No one arranging flowers, no one cleaning, no women rather. Always women busying around these places in his past, men coming only for Mass, aloof behind the altar rails or hovering with a cigarette at the entrance.

That time he went with his mother when she took flowers to the church, she'd used an old pram, he'd helped push it.

His father never mentioned his mother. Liam had found a few photographs in the bottom of a clothes-press in the spare room. He'd stolen them, waited to be accused, his father said nothing.

Aidan had once asked him if he'd ever felt responsible for his mother's death: puerperal sepsis, mother and his new brother dead. That wouldn't happen now with antibiotics.

'I was five,' Liam had answered.

Aidan had said nothing. Like all those analysts, he said nothing, which of course was very eloquent.

The church was cool, airless. No page numbers for hymns above the pulpit. No open Gospels. No organist practising on the balcony. There was no constantly burning light over the altar, no one was home. He stood in front of a marble Pieta and tried to pray. He'd pray for Maura, pray for Jess, he'd pray for Nell and her daughter. He'd say a Hail Mary for his mother.

He couldn't remember the words.

Rose had an urge to polish and tidy yet no one, not even the social worker, was visiting. Mum would soon be home but she'd never notice. Even after the thorough clean, the flat stayed a mess. So many photographs: Mum, Arnst, herself, Jarene, several of the other children Iris had fostered. That holiday in Jamaica took most of one wall. Rose would happily have junked the couple of Rothko prints she'd given her mother one Christmas, but Iris claimed to love them. How likely was that? Birthday knick-knacks, Iris refused to throw away, were crammed onto shelves. That calendar Arnst got from school – some teacher's softening-up strategy – was three years out of date. And a waste of time with Arnst.

This was lousy timing. When she'd first made enquiries all was well, Mum was fine, Arnst not going walkabout. But it took ages to organise the meeting. Mum helped with the forms but when the contact confirmation came through she was in hospital.

Rose took one last look round the flat, checked herself in the mirror. Mum better get home, re-braid her hair.

Now she was late.

Once she got out of Swiss Cottage tube, Rose half-jogged to the traffic lights then slowed down. Amy was fine, but this wasn't going to be a chat with Amy on her own. What an idiot to come alone. The hotel was off Adelaide Road. There were fountains and lots of glass, Amy's office would be better. There was a car-park. They might come by car, she could spot them first.

Obvious who it was, that middle-aged white woman – Amy said she was a doctor in her forties, Irish parents. She wasn't short, but a good few inches shorter than Rose. She had come with someone; an older woman climbed from the passenger seat, long grey hair looped into a bun, sun-wrecked face. Let them go ahead. Wait till her heart stopped thumping.

That woman driving a small innocuous car, that dull-looking woman had carried her, delivered her, dumped her. The older one was already heading for the entrance; the other gazed carefully around the car-park before clicking the remote lock. She was wearing glasses. Was Rose going to need glasses?

Impossible to know if she'd been seen, but probable, only the one black, twenty-year-old, lurking outside the hotel. Had she been adopted because of her colour? A drunken one-night stand? That dreary-looking woman hadn't realised the man was black? Maybe Amy was wrong, and it was just a casual relationship.

Rose made herself go in. The two women had disappeared. The entrance lounge was deeply carpeted, everyone flashily dressed as if this was Park Lane not North London. This was one of those times she should have listened to Iris, could have done with her mother to remind her, first impressions are crucial. 'Make an effort to impress.'

Before she could get the attention of the man at Reception, Amy was touching Rose's arm. 'I thought you'd bring someone?'

'Sorry, Mum isn't out of hospital.'

She could have insisted on Arnst or a friend from work. Pedro would have been delighted, act protective. But, if Iris couldn't come, it was better alone. This way she could back off, pretend nothing had happened.

'We're over in that corner. You ok, Rose? Shall we carry on?'

Of course. Get on with it. Nod enthusiastically. Act calm.

Several armchairs were grouped round a low table near floor-length windows that faced on to more fountains and a garden. The two women got to their feet. The older one smiled and ignoring Amy's half-protest, hugged Rose.

'Nell was right. It was you outside.'

The same heavy perfume as Iris: Joy by Patou, that fancy smell Jarene gave Iris last Christmas. 'You robbed a bank, Jarene?' Iris had said, but she still wore it.

'I'm Connie, your great-aunt I suppose, God help us. And this is Nell dithering.'

Rose sat down, tried not to stare: Nell was thin, her dark hair greying, pudgy pale face. She had no make-up, square spectacles, and she kept her eyes fixed on her hands. They were clasped so tightly over her knees the knuckles were white.

Amy opened her folder. 'First, of course, I want to welcome everyone.'

There was a brief pause then Nell blurted out: 'I need to go to the toilet.'

'You need to what, you ninny!' said Connie as Nell nearly fell over the table in her haste to get away.

Was Nell that appalled at the sight of her?

'I'm sorry,' said Connie. 'It's the shock, that you're beautiful.'

'We should wait for everyone before we talk,' said Amy.

Connie made a face. Once Amy turned away, Connie did a mock yawn then winked at Rose. What had she meant, beautiful? Perhaps she'd been an incredibly ugly baby: let's get rid of this one, she's horrid. Or maybe Nell hadn't realised what colour the baby would be, but she was a doctor, must have taken a look.

'You're lucky to have inherited your father's height,' said Connie.

'We should really wait until Nell gets back. I'll find a waiter, organise tea.'

They smiled at each other as Amy disappeared.

'I'm sorry Nell is so nervous. Tell me about yourself.'

Rose hesitated. 'Did you meet him?'

'Briefly. Before they left London. He was completely charming. Very attractive, and he loved Nell. They loved each other.'

But not enough to stay together, bring up their child.

Connie reached over and touched Rose's arm. 'You're gorgeous.'

Was Nell opting out already? Rose would have to make do with this unlikely old woman.

Amy came back with a waiter, Rose ordered an espresso; Nell appeared, her skin sweaty and pale as if she'd been sick. She seemed to have lost her spectacles, was fretfully gazing around as if another abandoned child might pop out from somewhere.

Then Nell looked directly at Rose. 'We should have waited until you could bring someone. I'm so sorry.'

'Calm down, Nell,' said Connie. 'Rose seems fine. I'll go and search for your glasses.'

Rose felt far from fine. How could she be disappointed when she hadn't expected anything?

Nell continued to stare. 'You must be terribly disappointed?'

How could she answer? One minute, normal, the next a blob of jelly. 'No, I shouldn't have said that,' Nell continued. 'Of course you are.'

'Well,' said Amy briskly. 'I think Rose must have some questions.'

Everyone talking for her. Rose did feel disappointed. Had she really hoped her mother would be black, that the agency had made a mistake? Probably. Always there was a voice that wondered if her mother might be like Iris. That black mother would never have given her away. This Nell came from an alien world, one she had no wish to be part of.

'If you'd thought...' Rose managed to say, before they were interrupted by the waiter reaching over with their coffees.

It wasn't that she wanted an explanation. Yes it was. She wanted Nell to explain why an affluent middle-class woman would give away a baby.

'What were you going to ask, Rose?' said Nell.

There was a brief reprieve as Connie arrived back, having found Nell's spectacles in the toilets. Now everyone was wanting her to say something. All sorts of questions that Amy hadn't been able to answer. Where did Nell come from, how had she met Jerome? Nell was so withdrawn, even the older one, Connie, would be preferable.

What had she expected? What had this woman done for her? It was Mum, Iris, who had given her everything, fed her, clothed her, fretted about them all. It was Iris who worked all day in the laundrette or supermarket or went cleaning, Iris who spent every evening cooking, clearing, sorting, appeasing.

She wanted them to explain.

Vijay's practice was on the edge of Brighton in the centre of a large council estate. The surgeries looked very smart. Connie parked Jess's car by a wall that was covered with either a mess of graffiti or some expensive street art. The estate was fifties, this practice most definitely not fifties. Vijay had warned it was post-modern ironic; what did the locals make of such post-modernity in their NHS?

She'd be able to get Vijay's opinion, find out what chances for survival Maura had when Connie first visited. Had Maura been completely honest?

The waiting room was pink, a double-height ceiling with stairs at each corner to a balcony. At the centre of the ceiling was a large glass dome. Someone had been having fun, but it must have cost a fortune. Who were they kidding, where was the familiar reassuring grunge?

Anne thought Connie had acted in bad faith. What did that mean? What else could she have done but listen to Maura and help?

She checked the turquoise notice-boards, same boring details of flu jabs, times for baby clinics. The receptionists wore shirts in a nursery-school range of colours but still looked as harassed as those she'd worked with. And the twenty or so waiting were as despairing as in any other surgery.

Vijay appeared almost immediately. He beamed and rubbed his hands. His shirt was bright blue. They hugged and the receptionists pretended not to notice.

'It's even beautiful, Connie, when the sun isn't shining.' He took her arm, led her out into the courtyard. 'Let me show it off. Down this west side we have osteopathy, physiotherapy.'

'How did you get them to agree? It must have cost a fortune.'

They stopped by the central fountain.

'They love it. So does our bank, especially because they bleed us empty with interest. The extra things pay rent so it's no more expensive than the average group practice, just more fun.'

'Any women partners?'

'Of course. Three men, two women. We could do with having Nell, she's a hard worker.' Aidan would have told Vijay about Nell's baby; he'd have known the whole time, and said nothing. 'I saw her last week when I visited Sanghi, she was in a bit of a state.'

He'd disapprove of the adoption, of course. Everyone would. And they'd blame Connie. More blame. Time she went home.

Connie couldn't go back to Arles just yet. How was Nell going to know how to be with this lovely but vulnerable girl, not continue to alienate her? How would Nell explain that the grandmother knew nothing and, because Nell was a coward, must know nothing?

Tempting to go to Newcastle, tell Pat the whole sorry story.

'How do you get on with Pat, Vijay?'

'I don't, we rarely see her. Aidan talks occasionally on the phone; she's aware of course of my existence, nods politely when we cross paths. That's it. How can it be possible, you're sisters?'

Because Pat was the oldest and had taken her role very seriously; she'd accepted everything the priests said and accepted from very early on that her baby sister was deeply sinful.

Vijay opened an opaque glass door next to the chemist on the eastern side. 'I have to reveal my secret place, my indulgence.'

It was a small white-painted room: the only light came from the entrance, laid out on the floor were grey cushions, a low table with a vase of flowers, heaps of stones, candles, incense sticks, and a small golden Buddha. Above it was a black and white photograph of an old man with a long beard. Connie looked again at the table; the stones were rough and chipped. There were several, she picked up one, slipped it in her pocket. It was warm in here.

'Are you ok? Is the incense too much?'

The room smelt of freesias. As they were leaving, Connie paused at a landscape by the door.

'A present from Liam,' said Vijay. 'He says it's abstract but basically a view of the sea from their house.'

It was a few streaks of paint of the palest green, beautiful and incredibly sad. How had Liam achieved that with something so minimal? She looked again at the room, the table, the stones. Anne must still have them.

'Do you still go to that monastery, Vijay?'

'Whenever I can. Aidan won't take holidays that aren't sailing so it's my only escape. Let's go to my office, have tea, you can say what's bothering you.'

His room was on the ground floor behind the reception; he had a kettle and a very beautiful Japanese teapot. From the look of the dried leaves he spooned into the pot this was not going to be a much-needed double espresso.

It wasn't easy to know what to say.

'I'm out of touch with medicine, Vijay. When Maura contacted me, said she was refusing further treatment, I accepted it.'

'Why should you not?'

'In your opinion, will more treatment prolong Maura's life? Would it have six months ago? Is there still a chance that chemo might help her?'

'Oh, Connie, you know as well as me that's an impossible question. It's down to Maura and her consultant.'

Should she explain that – even if Anne didn't mean the trips to Switzerland in the news, or a serial killer like Shipman – Connie was being accused?

This was wasting Vijay's time.

'I'd assumed Maura would be a survivor,' said Connie. 'The one clinging to the cliff, not letting go. That she'd want to stay alive as long as possible, but know when she'd had enough. When she told

DON'T MENTION HER

me that was it, I believed her.'

Vijay looked cautious. She should be talking about this to Liam not him, but that would be impossible. Was Anne right, she was no better than a murderer? Even if she did nothing but drive Maura around looking for a hospice, she was guilty of neglect.

'More tea?'

Connie shook her head, watched him get some for himself. She hadn't expected Vijay to make her feel better, that she must do on her own. 'I'll go back to Arles, leave people in peace.'

An unlikely couple, Vijay and Aidan. Aidan was a good foot taller and lean. Something soft about Vijay, Aidan was more of a greyhound. And Vijay's manner was gentler, Aidan could be quite aloof.

'I remember my mother wanting so much to die, Connie. It felt to us like being abandoned; I can still hear my father howling after she'd gone. It's my first memory. Her decision was fine, anything that is a free choice is fine. We have to help as best we can. You know that.'

Rose had made it clear – a half-hour walk, no more. Iris was due home. No way was Nell going to be allowed near the restaurant, Pedro would get nosey, become possessive.

Rose got off the bus in time to watch Nell park by the entrance to the Heath. There was no embarrassing shaking of hands, no hugs. Once they were through the gate, and Nell had stopped worrying that it was August and unpredictable, might easily rain, and neither of them had an umbrella, they set off up the hill.

'Tell me about yourself, Rose? That might make it easier.'

Easier!

Try not to get angry. Stupid to have started this, but too late to stop now. Always better never to expect miracles than discover what a let-down life can be.

'What do you do, Rose? Amy wasn't sure if you were studying.'

No way would she mention dropping out of college.

'You said you'd be happy to talk about Jerome.'

She could hear Iris. 'Calm down. You don't have to yell.'

They were walking quickly, Nell was getting short of breath.

'I know, Rose, I'm nervous, that's all.'

Nervous. So she was here to reassure this person. How simple. Give the baby away, when they're over eighteen say, ok, I'll take a look. See what sort of mess the thing turned out. But be nice to me because I'm scared.

They walked back along a muddy track towards a pond.

'You're a doctor, how come you got pregnant?'

Nell stumbled, and Rose grabbed her arm.

'Amy said it was an accident. She told me you were Catholic.'

Amy hadn't said anything about accidents, but how else could she get this woman to talk?

'Not remotely Catholic, and I'd campaigned for free choice. I'm sorry, it's a bit of a blur.'

So she'd wanted an abortion. What happened? Probably taking loads of tablets, doctors always did. The foetus, Rose, was plugged full of toxins.

It would be better to sit somewhere, Nell sounded puffed out.

'Do you go to church, Rose?'

What business was that of hers? Did she want Rose's opinion on abortion? It was tempting to elaborate on bizarre evangelical practices, but why bother? Why tell this person anything about herself, or her family? It already felt she was betraying her mother. To say that Iris was Catholic but had taken them all to the Spirit of Christ church because she hated the silence, dismalness of Catholic churches in Kilburn. That would be unfair.

They found a bench half-way down the hill, watched a dog chasing a swan. The owner was standing on the muddy bank, dragging on her cigarette, half-heartedly calling: 'Bobby, Bobby.'

A crowd of anxious walkers had gathered.

'You said you met my father here in London. Why did you go to Nigeria?'

Good how easily she'd let out the word, father.

'It's been a long time, Rose.'

Nell was talking so quietly it was heard to hear.

'Fine. Well, it's been my lifetime.'

'I'm sorry, Rose. You're right.'

It was as if Nell was practising her name, kept repeating it, and it sounded wrong. They paused to watch the exhausted swan distract the dog away from its mate and cygnets.

'It was seeing you that first time – you look gentle, like him.'

Gentle? What did that mean? Now was not the time to tell Nell she used to make money as a bouncer, until Pedro stopped her. They both stared at the drama in the pond.

'I wanted to leave England, more than Jerome did, I was already cut off from my family.'

This was what the woman remembered, some family.

Nell stood up. 'Let's go, they've rescued the dog.'

It was the swan needed rescuing. They should kill the bloody dog, and its owner. As Rose took off down the slope, she could hear Nell screaming: 'Watch out!'

The dreadful woman was cooing over the German Shepherd as it shook water over the rather uncertain observers.

'What the hell were you bloody thinking?'

Rose didn't care if she was yelling. People backed away.

The woman snarled: 'Fuck off, black bitch.'

Should Rose deck her? Not a good idea with that dog. Someone was grabbing her arm, nearly pulling her over.

'Come on, Rose,' said Nell.

'It should be shot,' Rose threw back at the owner. 'You too.'

'My God, calm down.'

Nell had suddenly become more substantial as she hauled Rose up the path. Everywhere, so many bloody dogs, so much dog-shit.

Eventually, Nell said. 'I'm sorry, you need to hear about Jerome.'

'Isn't he more important?'

'He didn't know.'

She hadn't even told him. The fucking cheek.

Nobody wanted to know anything or tell anybody anything. For all anyone cared, she could be dead – Jerome probably was dead.

Nell had asked her nothing.

All the questions she'd expected, vowed never to answer. Had she been happy? What job did Iris do? Had Iris been a good parent? Where was her adoptive father? And Rose's siblings, what did they do? What did she do? Ok, so when the social worker asked, she'd lied about waitressing. She'd lied about giving up her degree. Would she tell the truth? No way would she mention Pedro.

Sunbathers were already spread over the grass like squashed

flies. Normally summer was the best time of year, today it felt stale, the smear of too many people, ice-creams, noisy grubby little footballers. They found another bench.

'I'll try and explain,' said Nell.

Ok. Now the pain of having to give away a child. Jarene had warned her there'd be buckets of regrets, that whenever Nell held a baby, she held her own. Marked each year as the solid weight of the year-old became the wriggling energy of the two-year old. Swinging a three-year old in the air, finding her too heavy.

'Five years after I gave you away,' said Nell.

No remorse then. How naïve to expect more. Yet, so many children in Iris's house to cuddle – how could Nell not be heart-broken to miss that?

This was a waste of time. She stood up.

'Look, Rose, please wait.' Nell grabbed at her jacket. 'I'll try to tell you what I know.' She paused as if struggling to speak. 'Ok. I was feeling better after a several dreadful years, and it seemed the right time to look for Jerome.'

Rose perched on the edge of the bench.

'I'd applied for a job in East Africa. I wanted to talk to him before moving from London, in case he ever came to England. Tell him about you. So I flew to Lagos.'

This was going to take forever. And it would be bad news.

Nell paused again. Did she expect to be helped? Too bad.

'I tracked down a friend of his, Ifechi, he gave me Jerome's address.' Nell blew her nose. 'He's living near Enugu.'

So Jerome was alive.

Nell put down her cartons of vegetable juice. Maura looked weak but focused. 'It is so good to see you. Thank you, darling.'

'I'm amazed they let me in, so late, I said I was your GP.'

'They're agency. I'll swear you are, Vijay will swear too.'

The other three patients were sleeping. Nell closed the curtains round the bed. She pulled up a chair, poured out some juice, gave it to Maura.

There was no space on the bedside table. 'You've so much.'

'Help yourself. Grapes are lovely but I do prefer this stuff.'

'It was recommended by someone at work. Are you in pain?'

Maura shook her head. 'Did you see your daughter, darling?'

How on earth did Maura know? What was the point in asking people not to say anything? Aidan must have told her. Or Connie.

'I don't know why I don't leave secrets in an open box, labelled "Tell everybody".'

'What a terrible idea to keep them sealed up. Why do it?'

'Rose looks like her father.'

She held Maura's hands around the cup.

'Well, I think,' said Maura, then she paused to sip her drink, 'that's meant to be common. Genes and things.'

'She's stunning. That was a shock.'

Nell took the cup away, kissed Maura's fingers. It had been a shock. And Rose had taken one look at Nell, been disappointed. Not surprisingly.

Today's walk had been disastrous, ending with Rose rushing off as if Nell was unbearable. But it wasn't fair to dump this on Maura.

She plumped up the pillows. 'Is there anything I can do?'

Maura smiled. 'Be content, Nell. That's all.'

How could people be content, the world was a terrible place? And everyone wanted her to smile all the time. Well, she couldn't.

'The first time we met was a disaster. I hoped today would be better but it wasn't. I suppose Connie told you how pathetic I was.'

'She did pop in – before returning to her paramour – said it all went fine and Rose is lovely.'

'Well it didn't, but she is lovely. What's Connie's paramour like?'

'I've no idea. She keeps him well away.' Maura shut her eyes.

Nell was about to stand up when Maura grabbed her. 'I suppose you had to answer lots of questions from the child.'

'Not really,' said Nell.

'She must have so much to ask, the poor mite.'

Nell released her hand and Maura sank back.

'I've had enough of this, darling. It's time.'

Maura seemed to doze off. Nell waited a few moments then went down to the main hall to try and get them both cappuccinos. The café was closed. She managed to find enough coins for the machine but had to queue. The reception area had the panic of a railway station when the last train has been announced. None of the usual slow amble of those with little else to do, or the urgent shuffle, drip attached, to get to the outside world and a cigarette.

When Nell returned to the room, Maura and the other women were fast asleep. Nell kissed Maura, squeezed her hand, poured the coffees into the sink, and left.

68

Rose ran up the steps, stopped when she saw Arnst. Her brother was crouched under the front window-ledge. The passion she felt for him: those bony hopeless shoulders, neglected ringlets. And the same wrinkled sweater even if Mum had just ironed it.

'You are late,' Arnst muttered.

No point asking. 'Come on,' said Rose. 'Are they back?'

He shrugged. She grabbed his arm, hauling him up the stone steps. Why all this again? Arnst had proved incapable of retrieving keys thrown from the window, if left, could spend hours kicking at leaves, covering any trace until a diligent burglar spotted them months later. One evening, when Iris couldn't find any spare child to go of the two that were hers and the two being fostered, she had to drag herself down. She then tied a key inside the only jeans Arnst would wear. Such an impressive knot it survived the washing machine. With each new pair the ritual of the key.

Rose gave him a quick hug – he was right, it wasn't there.

'I borrowed a mate's clothes.' She pushed him through the front door into the hall. 'Haven't seen you for weeks, Rosie.'

'Some of us work, get up at a normal time.'

Better not to tell Arnst she'd been staying at Pedro's. Her brother was a sieve.

Once inside the house, with its high ceilings, wide staircase, Rose paused. When she'd left here yesterday, she'd known nothing about a father. Now there was an address.

No familiar smells: running back from school, their flat at the top of the house, promise of roast chicken even four flights down. Although most of Iris's children had in theory left home, the flat was still a base. And that wasn't because of its comfort, Mum was incapable of making a place homely. It was chaos, but not enough money around to make that chaos cosy.

But Iris could cook. Plenty of semi-attached family from children that she had fostered called in for meals, and always some drama – someone leaving someone, babies left for Iris to watch over. Or as Jarene would say, neglect. Jarene was the oldest, initially a foster-child, but one who stayed put.

'Super-glued herself to the chair, age seven, not budged,' said Iris. 'The day your useless dad, her useless dad, walks out, our Jarene hasn't budged.'

Jarene was doing a PhD in Birmingham; even so, she spent most of the time in Iris's best chair, improving her score on Tetris.

Rose had no recollection of her adoptive father, Jarene claimed he wasn't worth the space he took.

'Why adopt me, why adopt Arnst?' Rose had asked her mother. 'You had perfect Jarene. Once you married her dad, wasn't that enough?'

Iris gave some flip reply about getting muddled with the forms. Jarene had said Iris wanted her own proper family.

Passing all those closed doors, wishing their flat was not at the top. 'Didn't you ring the bell? Maybe they're already home.'

Arnst shook his head. 'I knew you'd come.'

Had he been in trouble?

Iris's shopping trolley was in the hall next to a plastic bag with the hospital's name, her anorak on a hook. Jarene had put her own linen jacket on a hanger.

'Where you been?' Iris said as they went into her bedroom.

She looked behind Rose at the door. 'Is that Arnst skulking?'

'You look sweet too, Mum. I thought you was in hospital.'

'Then what dragged you home?'

Iris pulled herself up in bed, threw a copy of the *Daily Mirror* at Arnst. 'Do something useful. Go make us all a pot of tea.'

Rose hugged her mother. Iris felt less solid.

'You're a bit more skinny?' Iris tapped Rose on the bum.

'Or am I getting blind.'

'You're right, Ma. She's anorexic,' said Jarene from an armchair, without raising her eyes from her game.

Rose had to follow Jarene at school, two years between them, impossible to catch up – never the star that she was. Jarene's mother was dead. Always the chance her father would claim Jarene back. Then he married Iris, adopted them all. And disappeared.

'Did you see her yesterday?' Iris asked. ' A sweetie like me?'

'Did she mention any father?' Jarene said, without looking up.

No way would Rose answer that yet. She wanted to imagine her own version Jerome before people started diving in, giving advice.

Nell had gone to Lagos, tried to track down some nurse and failed. But she'd found Ifechi and talked to Jerome on the phone.

She hadn't gone to Enugu to see him. She hadn't even gone to Zambia. After talking to Jerome, she'd realised she needed to stay in London.

Why?

What was possible to gather from Nell's half comments and general reluctance, was that Jerome had his own children. His own family. He didn't accept there'd been a child. Or, more precisely, he didn't accept that this daughter was his.

69

Liam paused outside the corner shop. Buy some cigarettes? Get in the car you fool. Go and tell Maura you like the look of the hospice. Tell her you approve of it. Well, he didn't.

The signature witnessing Maura's living will was Connie Dillon. He'd blamed Connie that time they'd bumped into each other, accused her of encouraging Maura to give up treatment. He hadn't meant it. But it was true.

The hospice was loathsome, all that deep carpet and gravel drive, soft bustle and pretend caring. It was a good half an hour from Sandford. The hospital was so much better with buckets of disinfectant failing to conceal a general panic.

Connie had helped his wife, his ex-wife had helped his wife to die. They had chosen this place; Maura had put her name down in January, told no one. Well, she had told someone, Connie. They'd gone out searching just after the operation when he was away in London. Months ago, Maura had deceived him. She had given up.

He would never give up. Maura had kept it from him, then she'd asked for help. No, she'd asked for permission, and he'd denied it.

Apart from the odd hiccough, the hospice was a smooth conveyor belt to death, professionals who knew what to do.

If only Maura believed in something afterwards; he had no such solace but how much easier if she had. The room they planned to give her was airy, comfortable. A big window overlooking the lawn could be left open, the air full of salt and sea. If Maura was able to appreciate it, she would appreciate it.

Liam got into the car.

Everything was draining, a cold sweat from head to toe. Nell gripped the edge of the computer. Wave after wave taking all that had life with it, leaving her an empty shell.

She phoned through to Madge to shift the final two patients, took off her glasses, sat with her forehead resting on the desk. Breathe slowly, it was simply a panic attack. But the main feeling was terror, she was suffocating.

Her surgery door opened, a mug of milky tea placed beside her head. 'Dr Sanghi has seen to them; he's off somewhere in a rush. Do you want a diazepam?'

'I had some already.'

'I've left a pack here.'

Nell drank a little of the sweet tea, took two tablets, put her head between her arms. This must stop, these episodes were scary. No point phoning Aidan, he'd call this something else, but it would amount to the same. Anxiety. Aidan had stopped suggesting analysis, would only tell her off for taking too many pills.

'You haven't had one of those funny turns for years,' said Madge, as Nell stood at the reception desk, doodling circles on a prescription pad. 'Why not talk to Aidan?'

'What did you say to Sanghi?'

'You might be going down with flu. Is it Rose? You need to make up your mind.'

Madge took away the pad and pen, gave Nell her glasses. She was the practice manager, Nell's main ally in life. 'Do you want to contact Rose again or not?'

It wasn't about Rose. 'My aunt is dying.'

'Same difference, as my niece would say. Invite Rose here. From what you say, she sounds delightful. Let her see where you work, introduce her to Dr Sanghi. He'll do his reassuring number.'

Rose would see all this: dry rot and damp and dead mice under the floor boards.

'How long has it been since you saw her?'

'A month.'

'Imagine what she's feeling.' Madge picked up the half-empty mug of tea. 'Fine, you don't want her to feel pestered, but this is ridiculous. Give the poor child some affection; tell her whatever she wants to know.'

Madge disappeared into the back office. How could someone be so infuriating, and so right? Nell sat on one of the plastic chairs, her head spinning.

'Stop sulking.' Madge reappeared with her coat on. 'A life-time of sulking is enough.'

Madge had been mothering her since Nell started this part-time job fifteen years before – the same year Dad died. It began as a locum, a few months to make some money before going back to Africa.

But she couldn't go, the child was probably living in London.

Madge covered for her on the gloomier days, convincing Sanghi and the two male partners that she was indispensable. She kept quiet about Nell's occasional panic attacks, arranged for her to see the more tricky cases: the persistent chronics with nothing much wrong who could surprise you, get something major. Nell was the one helping the practice nurse with difficult cervical smears. Madge even made sure that Nell did her postgraduate training more promptly than the others. She defended her to patients when they complained that the lady doctor was remote. Madge had created a functioning doctor who wasn't about to pester Dr Sanghi to be made full-time, let alone a partner, but sometimes Madge could be exasperating.

'You look grey, Nell. Do you want me to call a taxi?'

According to the Edwardian mirror hung on several nails for security over the grubby teddies, broken Barbies, ripped picture books spread all over the floor, Nell looked ashen. She took off her glasses and pulled out some grey hairs, tugged at her limp black hair. It wasn't so black any more, a sort of mousey-brown.

Madge was banging shut filing cabinets. Everyone else had gone home, time to switch on the answering machine, lock up. 'You know, Nell, if your aunt's dying, maybe you should talk to your mother?'

'Pat and Maura never got on.'

Madge was pushing her out the front door.

'I don't think Mum sees Maura as a real aunt, more like some trollop who stole her brother-in-law.'

A few days later, Nell arrived home to find a young black man sitting on the door-step. It had been a busy afternoon, everyone complaining about the late-summer heat-wave. He didn't look familiar, wasn't a patient. Untidy Rasta hair, about eighteen. The most bright, delightful smile.

He stood up. 'Nell?'

'Yes?'

'I'm Rose's brother.'

Nell sent him out to the garden and collected a tray with orange juice, can of Coke, biscuits from a forgotten cake-tin, and carried it down the four flights. The boy had stretched out on her favourite deckchair, almost hidden by the waist-high grass, dried-out flower beds, sprawling hydrangea. His name was Arnst.

Rose had mentioned a brother. 'How is Rose?'

'Haven't heard from Rosey for a while.' Arnst helped himself to two biscuits. 'She's so busy.'

'Don't you both live with your mother?'

How easy to say that.

'Sure, of course,' said Arnst. 'Well, sometimes.'

'Is Rose ok? I mean, do you think she's ok?'

'Sure. Rose's always fine. She takes life very calm.'

Calm would be useful, a hot irritable day like today. Nell needed to change her sweaty T-shirt. 'Did she know you were coming?'

He hesitated, then smiled. 'I found your address in her diary.'

Not much could be said to that. And such an innocent face.

'Why did your mother call you Arnst?'

'Cos Ma is totally crazed, and didn't like my baby name, which was Henry, and I guess she wanted me beat up at school.'

He started pacing around. Everything on her side was an overgrown mess. He picked up a couple of apples from under her tree, bit into one.

'Is it all yours, Nell?'

'Just the half on this side, it ends at that sort of hedge.'

'It don't look like a hedge, it's well neglected. This part's better.'

He was admiring the impeccably boring garden bordering hers.

What did he want?

71

'It's so ordinary,' said Jess as she parked in the gravelled forecourt.

'You've got to admit, pretty imposing,' said Connie.

Jess should have said imposing, then Connie could have offered ordinary.

'And Eastbourne of all places.'

A boring double-fronted house, not remotely a mansion. But a palace was never going to be much use to Maura. A woman, in a pink velour track-suit and name tag saying Ellie, showed them the room.

Maura was asleep. The place stank of lavender air-freshener.

'Let's leave.'

'We've just got here, Jess. Find yourself somewhere to sit.'

Connie took the shopping bags to a small fridge under the window while Jess pulled a chair up to the bed. After a few moments Maura opened her eyes and smiled. 'Hello, Jess.'

'A room of your own, Mo. Mmm, very smart.'

Maura was murmuring something. Despite being sent pleading looks for help, Connie pretended to be stacking away jars and packets. Maura's breath was metallic, she was struggling to talk: 'Have you seen your father?'

'Not yet,' said Jess. 'I'll phone.'

'Please, darling.'

Connie brought Maura over a juice and sat in the opposite chair. Time to leave them to it.

The house was hushed as if everyone, including the staff, were asleep. There was a door to a balcony at the end of the corridor. Below, a man was sweeping up leaves, a group of people were playing croquet.

This place was awful. It might be luxury after the hospital, but it reeked of surrender. Sitting on a wall, watching the game, was the woman who'd been talking to Connie when they visited Maura at the hospital. Of course she'd been familiar, it was the headmistress from Moreton. What was Monster Anne doing down there?

There'd been no point rushing back to the room, Connie and Maura were whispering; Maura's hair was almost gone, Connie's as abundant as ever. Connie looked twice the size of the woman in the bed.

Jess stood at the door and watched. Connie was rubbing oil into Maura's arms and shoulders. She used to do that when they were in France; would stand behind her while Jess was dipping her baguette in milky coffee, and massage her shoulders. One morning Jess said that it hurt. Connie had never done it again.

Jess raced ahead out the front door. Once they were back in the car, she rested her head on the steering wheel.

'How do people manage?'

'Sometimes, they don't.'

Connie reached over and stroked her hair, Jess shook her away.

'I don't want to leave Maura again, then wait for the phone call. How long do you think?'

'Not more than a couple of weeks.'

'She was fine. Whose insane idea was it for her to move here?'

'Hers and the doctors. You might as well be warned, everyone blames me. They think I encouraged Maura to give up.'

How did her mother manage to be always, but always in the wrong? How can you compete with someone who behaves even worse than you do?

Why had Connie been meddling?

'I saw the woman today who was fighting with you in front of the hospital.'

'Not fighting. A discussion. Surely you recognised her?'

Yes, even though the best policy in those days was to avoid

looking the terrifying thing in the eye. Word had got round that she was Medusa – one look, you're stone.

'Anne called me a murderer,' said Connie.

That was a bit over the top. Real murderers came into the office pleading innocence, aggressively demanding a defence. Connie was unpredictable and selfish but she had more goodwill than Aunt Pat, or even Jess herself.

Maura would know what she wanted. Surely she must still want to live?

'She loved the juiced veg that cost a fortune.'

'Maura barely touched anything. She's signing off, slipping out.'

There was no tissue when you needed one. Jess straightened the driver's mirror. It would be dreadful for her father, he'd collapse.

'Maura was clear, she'd written her instructions ages ago,' said Connie. 'Can you keep missing work? No one to take your clients?'

Maura had always been around, solid, dependable. Now she was about to disappear. Jess gripped the steering wheel. They owed her loads of leave, she hadn't had more than a week off for ages.

Maura had been the boss and for most of her teen-age, Jess had hated her. Those times staying out all night, which Rory said Jess only did to get a reaction, and that the parents had been far too soft. It had felt beyond grim, living with a teacher. And one who was always lecturing.

'Don't let Pat's lot influence you,' Maura would mutter when they went to Newcastle and Rory had agreed to go to Mass with his cousins. 'All religions are means of restricting thought, Jess. Most murder those who dissent. Remember that, when the others are being indoctrinated at school.'

The same school where Maura had taught for years, where she'd stood on the stage in Assembly with the other teachers. According to Rory, she'd only stayed there to look out for Jess. Maura had written the letters to Sister Anne that helped Jess skip the worst bits of brain-messing-up. And Jess's response?

To repeatedly get into trouble.

Jess had taken her for granted. And now all this fretting about the abortion, Maura, who'd been such a support, so clear all those years ago.

Should Jess tell her mother?

Connie leant over, touched her clenched hand. 'Ever planning to drive this thing?'

They were still in the parking space outside the hospice.

Jess put the gears into reverse, backed out.

'I'm not returning to London. Can you take the train? You've got the keys for the flat. I'll phone Dad, stay there. Book myself a B&B for tonight.'

Jess brought over two glasses of Merlot from the bar. 'Sorry about the choice, otherwise it's Riesling.'

'Fine.' Connie sat back on the padded leather. 'I think Anne is planning to visit Maura as often as she can.' She started fiddling with the combs holding up her hair. 'The chance of extreme throwing around of oils.'

How could her mother be flippant?

'From my memory of religious instruction, it's gentle dabbing and a sacrament. You're being profane, mother. A mortal sin.'

'Bugger that.'

Jess looked at her watch. Eight-thirty. While she was with Connie she couldn't think. Connie had wanted to stay the night, suggested a twin-bedded room – Jess had said no.

Her mother reached over, ripped open a bag of crisps.

'You might bump into her, a chance to meet again the guardian of your youth.'

This was what was meant by a cold sweat. That was why Maura had gone on and on in the hospital about the abortion. Anne had been there in Moreton, found out, was rootling it over with Maura.

Telling Connie about the pregnancy never cropped up. Not that it was any bloody surprise. Connie wasn't around, she'd dumped her daughter then fucked off to Bali with some pick-up.

'Your nun's been filling Maura's head with poison.'

'If you mean religion, Maura's too rational.'

Telling Connie hadn't seemed the most important thing. In fact Jess hadn't wanted to. 'The bitch has been messing up Maura's mind, wants her to dredge up the past.'

'What do you mean?' Connie knocked over her glass. 'Oh, fuck.' She started mopping up wine.

Jess pulled tissues from her bag, took over the cleaning, her mother continuing to uselessly dab around the edges. Connie had abandoned her; she couldn't expect to be told everything.

'That time when I came back from France to Dad and Maura's, I had an abortion.'

Connie stared for a moment then touched Jess's hand.

'You were a baby.'

One old enough to be left on her own.

'I always assumed you'd be careful.'

Jess collected the soggy tissues, packed them into a glass.

'That's disgusting.' Connie frowned at the mess. 'I'm sorry you couldn't tell me.'

Her mother was expecting more. She wasn't going to get it.

'Maura mentioned it to me, I think Anne had reminded her.'

'Anne knew?'

'Maura let it slip by mistake during a conversation, then Anne disappeared. Whoosh.'

Jess collected the glasses, went across to the bar.

'This must have been before Nell got back to London,' Connie said when Jess returned with a bottle of wine. 'You were sixteen, Jess. Anne told me nothing. Neither did Maura.'

It wasn't that anyone was being secretive, it never cropped up.

'What about James the hippy?' said Connie. 'Doesn't he want children?'

'You know very well, he's not a hippy. He's a librarian.'

James might have his black hair in a pony-tail, that did not make him some relic from the ancient past. Just when she was beginning to feel guilty, her mother could be infuriating. James even deluded himself Connie liked him; he thought her mother was fascinating.

'You'll soon be thirty-seven, you need to be sure,' said Connie.

Blame Jess's job. Anyone who listened to what she did day after day would never want children – the hatred in some families.

'I'm better clearing up other people's mess than providing disasters of my own.'

'Not a disaster for everyone, Jess.'

'Look at you and Pat.'

'Don't scream.'

She wasn't remotely screaming – just when she was saying something important.

The barman was glaring but the only other customers were two old men sitting alone; one had his nose buried in his pint, the other was gazing up at the silent TV screen, at blobs chasing a football.

'Are Pat and I such lousy mothers?'

There wasn't much debate about Connie, and now that Dermot was dead, Pat was more interested in the Church. On the couple of occasions that Jess had seen her, her delight with Colum and his horsey wife was the main topic of conversation, when it wasn't about bishops.

Connie had done a rubbish job, if job was the right word. The fill-in schools in Tottenham and Derby had been nightmares; when Connie did deign to visit Moreton it was to see that headmistress.

Connie took a gulp of wine. 'It was better for you both that I kept away.'

What self-delusion.

'I do think Rory likes me.'

'Well, I kind of like you,' said Jess.

Did she like her mother? She wouldn't give her any medals. Everyone blamed Connie's behaviour on the death of Claire but that should have made her try even harder. Whose idea that none of them should even mention Claire's name? At Dermot's funeral, Nell had said that even before Jess was born the cousins were banned from bringing up the subject. It would cause too much distress. No one wanted distress.

'What about poor Dad swapping all sorts of possibilities for a dull marriage to Maura?'

'Who said it was dull?'

'She gave everything up to look after us, well me, mostly. And now that vile nun is making her feel guilty.'

'She gave up nothing. Don't think you know it all, it's what Maura wanted, and Liam loves her.'

All that walking about on tip-toes, her father doing his suffering artist act – why had Maura indulged him? She'd probably have been a much better painter. And now this grim nun was making Maura feel guilty. Maura of all people. Why did her mother deny the obvious? Moreton was excruciatingly boring; Maura must have climbed the walls, going into that school day after day, coming home to Liam, his silence, his bloody oil paints. Maura had been a total martyr yet was always preaching: women should do this, do that. Meanwhile Connie had dumped her shit and gone.

'You know Maura loves him, he loves her. In no way is it dull for either. Life isn't always as it seems.'

'So, you chasing off after some bronzed smug French midget only appeared to be selfish and insane.'

Connie looked at her for a moment then stood up.

'Anne is not the enemy, but I agree Maura can do without any guilt-trips. Speak to your father. I need to go for a walk.'

Connie didn't appear for breakfast, she wasn't waiting by the car. Jess went down the street to the flower shop; she was not going to apologise. When she returned there was still no sign of Connie. The man at Reception handed her an envelope. 'Sorry. Forgot about it.'

'When did my mother check out?'

'I was in the kitchen. Could ask my wife, well before breakfast.'

Jess sat on the wall outside, read the note.

'You're better off doing this alone, Maura would probably prefer that. I'll phone in a couple of days. Give my love to her and do speak to Liam. Ask him, or try and get Anne banned yourself. I love you. I love you very much.'

Jess threw the roses into the back of the car. She wouldn't have bought them if she knew her mother had deserted her again. They were a mad price, but they smelt wonderful.

72

One of these times, Jess would walk in and Maura would be dead. She was fast asleep. Rory was looking out the window, he came over to hug her.

'You're a godsend. I'd a row with Mum, now she's disappeared.'

'What's new?'

She touched her brother's face. His glasses were surprisingly trendy: he was normally so shabby, preferred schoolboy specs, bits of elastic band holding them together. 'You look wonderful.'

Had Rory been crying? He did look wonderful, and for once was wearing really smart clothes. His hair was still red but darker and flecked with grey. He was tanned, almost handsome. Tall, geeky Rory had lost all trace of clumsiness. Why had it taken until he was forty, why hadn't some stunning PhD swallowed him up?

'I made all sorts of resolutions to be civil, Rory, then lost the plot. She should be a granny, it would make her do something. Why not have babies, take the pressure off me?' Jess stuck the roses into an abandoned vase. 'You're the one who needs children.'

'Connie, a granny? Would she even notice the infant? Plus, I fail to see why I should swell an over-populated world to satisfy you.'

Was her brother satisfied?

Rory nodded at the sleeping Maura. 'Apart from this, what else is important?' He pulled up two chairs. 'Let's sit with her.'

There Jess was, assuming it was her tragedy, it affected them all.

A relief to wait in silence, looking at the sleeping woman, and forget about everything outside. They sat for nearly an hour.

Maura woke a few moments after Rory had left.

'You missed Rory, Mo. He zoomed down in his flash car. And you slept.' Maura looked confused. 'Your son, Rory,' Jess said loudly into her ear.

Maura muttered something, impossible to tell what.

'What did you say, Mo?'

'Liam frets about you, never Rory.'

Had Maura said that? Was she always going to be the bad child?

'Are you in pain?' Jess took the vase with roses over to the sink. Maura shut her eyes.

'They sort it for me.' A long pause. 'They'll help if necessary?'

'Help?'

No way would Jess go down that path. 'Oh, you mean help?' She began pulling off leaves. 'Are you frightened?'

Maura opened her eyes, smiled. 'Of course, but not of dying.'

'I was surprised Dad arranged this place so fast.'

There was a splutter, Jess put the vase down, grabbed a tissue.

'It was your mother, Jess. She came over, hired a car.'

'When?'

'When I asked her, months ago.' Maura struggled to lift herself. 'Jess?'

She was going back to that again.

'Mo, I've told you and told you, I was sixteen.' Jess pitched the crumpled tissue at a waste-bin and missed. 'I confessed to Connie.'

'It's not a sin, darling.'

'Not telling her before felt bad.'

'I'm glad you did,' Maura whispered. 'You were so young. It was difficult, with your grandpa dying. A strange time, with Anne leaving the convent.'

Jess took a comb from the side table, tried to smooth what remained of Maura's grey hair. She rubbed Maura's head gently, massaging the patches of pink scalp.

'While on that subject, we thought Anne should be discouraged. Making you go on about the past, that's not you.' None of it was remotely to do with that nun, the nosey cow. 'Could I ask them not to let Anne in?'

Maura stared at her as if she was suddenly a stranger. 'Anne is peaceful to have around.' Maura must know the woman was a religious screw-ball. 'How is James?'

'I haven't a clue. All right. He usually is.'

'Poor Liam. Your dad so wants to be a grandfather.'

'He so doesn't! Look, this isn't you. That nun's been doing her voodoo all over your sick bed.'

Maura began to laugh, it quickly turning to a cough. Jess helped her sit up. 'Pull yourself together, Mo.' She gave her a sip of water. 'We need you.'

Maura was mumbling again. She couldn't possibly have said: 'Anne would be a great support for your father.'

*

Connie got out the bus by the car park then walked to where a fence marked the edge of the cliff. A forbidding drop, yet people did it. There was a brisk breeze from the sea; winter was going to be early. At least in Arles it might still be warm.

She had done what she could. Or had she done more than necessary, that's what Anne had implied?

She'd stay away until a few days after the funeral. Laurent wouldn't expect to go, she'd successfully managed to quell any such expectation. He had been full of enthusiasm to travel over when Dermot died. 'So far I've only seen your children but I want to meet Nell, Pat, the whole lot of criminals.'

'Jess and Rory are the only ones relevant.'

'And they'll appreciate having their mother there when their uncle is buried. Funerals are about celebrating family and survival.'

Not the ones she'd witnessed: her father drunk, her mother joining in the keening – even if the corpse was no relation. Having to put on a grieving face, being seen to grieve. To be at Claire's funeral had been inconceivable.

'No, Laurent,' she had said. 'No funerals.'

This visit to England had been worst than useless. Jess quite understandably loathed her, and she was right – Daniel had been short. Laurent was not short.

No one had thought to mention to her that her sixteen-year old daughter had needed an abortion. They'd obviously believed Connie was so detached from mothering that her daughter's welfare was beneath her consideration. But would Connie have told her own mother? Absurd. Then why the self-pity?

Did Jess hate her that much? There was good reason, Jess might have discovered Connie wanted to abort her. Divorce for Catholics had been a dire enough sin, but an abortion was infinitely worse – worse than taking your own life.

Anne and the other nuns had offered novenas. Anne was so angry with her now, Connie wouldn't merit a Hail Mary.

What would Rose think if Nell ever told her what she had planned? Absurd, it was like despairing those zillions of wasted spermatozoa. No, far worse to give Rose away, and Connie had been as guilty. She'd only just met Laurent, had been appalled at the thought of taking responsibility for a baby, or Nell for that matter. It would have been a mess. But she could have done it.

And now, instead of supporting her daughter, she was running away again.

A bit further on, the unprotected drop to the sea was dizzying. Could she do it, or too cowardly? It wouldn't be quick, would take attention from Maura, and she hadn't told Anne. She reached into her pocket, touched the stone. A vow was a vow.

Eventually, she turned away from the wind, headed towards the café. Rory never made her feel this bad and there'd been so many times when she'd failed him. He visited Arles often, usually accompanied by some version of his great passion, Ondine. Jess had brought James once because James had never been to France;

she and Laurent had talked law and bored everyone silly.

Both children were so agonisingly vulnerable. Easier to forget all that when in Arles, the distance helped. If she went there now, she could stop this harangue in her head, all the ways she'd failed.

How self-flagellating was that? She hadn't failed anyone. Failure would have been staying with Liam, both of them spending a lifetime in mourning. He carried that five-year-old boy who had lost his mother everywhere, and refused to talk about it. He would never have talked about Claire. Neither would Pat and Dermot. No, she had been good enough. She'd always worked hard, always loved the children; between her, Maura and their father, they'd been loved, clothed and fed.

The café looked uninviting and there were too many people; the best thing was to get away. She'd walk back down, take the bus to Newhaven, get the ferry, a train to Avignon, then Arles. All she needed was with her. She wouldn't have to see anybody.

Maura needed to face this alone, if people would let her.

Liam drove down from the hospice and parked in Burlington Place. Walking towards the sea, he found himself humming; anyone passing would think him glad to be alive. The *Happy Heart* mile beckoned and the October sun was faint but at least trying to shine. Who had he once heard sing *Burlington Bertie*? Surely not his father?

Jess wanted Anne to stay away from Maura. Why?

Liam hadn't had coffee. He took the road up to the café, apprehensive at the thought of seeing his daughter, of her moving in. 'Cappuccinno, Elsa, please. Strong as usual.'

Elsa made her amused face as she turned to the machine. He'd been saying that each day for the last week. But it was comforting, that nod of hers. He helped himself to a cheese sandwich.

Jess arrived with a bounce and exuberance that could only be marvelled at. This beauty was his daughter, this red-haired joyous delight had come from his genes. Jess shook her head when he gestured for her to slip past the others. Liam shrugged, went to a table away from some tennis rowdies.

She was queuing for ice-cream, had slung her leather jacket round her shoulders: a skimpy halter top, tiny skirt, bulky trainers. Wasn't that outfit a bit young? Her red hair was tied in several plaits. It must have taken ages. What did the clients think? A solicitor, nearly forty?

She always gave him a hard time for looking boring, should blame her step-mother. Maura saw to all the shopping. Maura had seen to all the shopping. Would Jess take over? Should he offer to pay for her ice-cream? When was it time to let them take control?

With Jess it had been aged five.

Rory must be over forty. No wife, no children. Liam got up as Jess put her tray on the table; she came round and hugged him.

'I'm sorry, Dad.' She sat down in the opposite chair.

'I'm useless, Jess. Can't help her.'

'What can anyone do? It's vile.'

'Maura asked me to help, Jess, I ignored her.'

'Don't be daft.' Jess tapped her bowl – this clearly wasn't a conversation she wanted. 'Doesn't it look beautiful, strawberry and pistachio ice-cream. I hope you're fully prepared for me moving in?'

'Of course.' He'd made up a bed, what more did she need?

'How old are you exactly, Jess?'

'Dad?' She waited, smiling, was expecting him to get it right. 'Thirty-seven in two weeks. So you're not taking the tablets.'

Soon it would be difficult for her to have a baby but then again Maura never had her own, she was a better mother than Connie or Pat. What a mess those two had made.

Jess looked around the crowded cafe then turned back to him. How uncomfortable the way some women stare as if checking the ways they can improve you, wiping improvements over your skin like moisturiser.

'Let's walk up and get the car.' He helped her with her jacket. 'Nell rang last night, promised to visit.'

'Has she not been?' said Jess.

'She never mentioned it, nor did Maura. Have you seen her?'

Did Jess know there was a child?

'Nell's almost a recluse,' said Jess. 'It's hard for her. Vijay's brother exploits her totally, still an assistant and probably very good. GPs don't necessarily need buckets of empathy, do they?'

They most definitely didn't, the less the better. The Nell of twenty years ago, in the early letters from Nigeria, had too much.

Jess had linked her arm into his. 'But why fret about Nell? Connie does enough for all of us.' She stopped walking. 'Oh, I get it. You were talking about Rose? Connie told me. Isn't it great?'

What was he anticipating? Disapproval? Jealousy?

'I'm not sure I'm meant to know, Jess. No one said. I don't think Pat has been told. Good of Nell to phone, but she didn't mention any child. Can you keep it to yourself?'

He stopped to blow his nose. They stood to one side while a crowd of children giggling in French, spilled down the path.

'I want to talk about that nun,' said Jess.

Good. She'd changed the subject.

'Isn't Anne no more than a homeless stray?'

'Mo seems to have lined her up for you, Dad.'

Liam stuffed away his hankie. Jess was capable of saying the most childish things. 'That's not funny.'

She had looped her arm more firmly through his, did she think he might fall? As they reached flatter ground, his breath returned to normal. This was the bit he dreaded, seeing the wall that led to the large detached houses that included the hospice. Jess was exhilarating but she made him uneasy. And she was moving in.

His daughter bent down and picked up some weeds. She held out her palm. 'It really is camomile.' She crushed the flowers. 'So late in the year. Smell them.'

Where was the car? 'Bugger. I'm sorry, Jess. I didn't park here. We have to walk back.'

They paused by the fence, looked along at the white cliffs, the symbol of most people's England. Was a sense of place more about people than houses? He'd always seen houses as the reality, people ghosts flitting through. But Maura was more substantial than that. Would he lose that certainty of home when he lost her?

He'd been settled in Moreton. No, he hadn't, he'd been tied to the place. Was his home, Ireland? Connie had once told him that he wasn't truly anything. 'You're from the Pale, Liam, listen to your accent. You're not Irish like me, rooted in penal laws, in hedge schools. Those years boarding made something else of the boy.'

Jess frowned at a woman passing with an over-trimmed poodle.

'Dad, do you have many memories of your mother?'

Well, that came from left field, or whatever the saying was. Did he? Another thing he'd never talked to his children about. Maybe Maura or Connie had given Jess details, at some point she and Rory must have asked why their father didn't have a mother.

Where's the missing grandmother?

'No, not a lot.'

A sense of someone. Mainly that one walk to church, a pram full of flowers. But it got muddled with photos: studio numbers mostly with a potted plant on a lace-covered table. His mother as a child with the same frown as Jess had now. That graduation picture of her from the College of Surgeons; he always had it in the surgery next to the one of her on a bench beside a bus stop in Stephen's Green. She was laughing, hands gripping the wooden slats, kicking out her legs and laughing. But of her, her touch, nothing – maybe something from those last months when she'd been pregnant, he'd just turned five. That pram of flowers.

'I remember Grandfather, but only just.' Jess said this crossly as if it was Liam's fault. 'I was never told anything about him. Though I do remember a funny smell in his house.'

'Turf smoke, burnt rashers, old age. A good man. He looked after me fine, never grumbled about his teaching job, scrimped to send me to boarding school. Not a talker, though.'

Surely he could remember more about his mother. He was the same age as Claire. Had it been good for Claire, those brief years that in the end were all she had?

'Jess, Maura asked me to help her, and I didn't. What should I have done?'

74

Iris had sent four photographs and a note apologising for missing the meeting with Amy – there was a postscript reminding Nell to drop into the flat any time. The photos were now on the sitting-room mantelpiece. Two were of a toddler in a park, laughing at some huge man in a bright patterned shirt. In one, the man held the familiar-unfamiliar child aloft; in the other he was watching a black woman with a striped woollen hat push the swing. This was Rose, that must be Iris. The third was a child of about five playing on a beach. The last one was an end-of-year school photo: a poised, sweet-smiling girl of about nine who looked like Nell at that age, but had the eyes and softness of Jerome.

The child looked happy. The child looked healthy. Why feel so heart-broken? This was exactly what she'd wanted to avoid. Were there more? There must be, everyone kept photos; Pat and Dermot had albums and albums of them, had even taken movies.

What would have happened if she'd told Pat she was pregnant?

Iris's invite sounded vague. It was up to Rose.

When she'd phoned Liam, he'd given details of the hospice; said it wouldn't be long. She'd go at the weekend.

There was a ring on the bell. Ignore it.

Another more persistent ring. Nell lay back on the sofa, shut her eyes. The bell again.

It was Arnst. Weeks since she'd seen him or Rose. No reply to her messages, no return phone-calls.

'Can I come up?'

'The buzzer doesn't work. I'll be down.'

It was a miracle to see him standing there.

'You ok?' Arnst even looked concerned.

'Well, actually, I'm not sleeping. But I can still get in to work.'

'I'll make you some of the tea Mum does when any of us can't sleep. It's the goods. She grows it in the allotment.'

'That would be fine, anything would be fine.'

'I been thinking about that job you offered,' Arnst said.

Nell couldn't remember offering any job. They had certainly talked about the garden which was a mess but it was winter now, no one used it. She followed him out to the back; he was holding a canvas bag over his shoulder. It was as if she were the visitor, Arnst showing her around. 'You got any tools?'

'I used whatever was in the shed.'

He dropped the bag, pulled out a trowel and some secateurs.

'I'll get those plants for tea from Mum, put them here. You want me to mow?'

Didn't grass stop growing in autumn? And the lawn was communal, not her responsibility.

'It would be nice.'

It was crazy and not possible but that mess of a garden might get sorted, there was even the chance she'd see Rose again. Arnst looked full of energy. It was contagious. Was he drunk or high? Was she picking it up? But he seemed sober enough.

'How much will you charge?'

'We can fix that,' said Arnst.

'There's a decent mower, the keys for the shed are on the hook by the back door.'

'Sweet,' said Arnst.

Liam pulled his chair closer to Maura's bed. He had done what he could, or that's what Jess thought. The move from hospital to hospice had been completed gently; they were relying on experts, the goodwill of strangers.

There were freesias on the bedside table, a note from Aidan.

'Don't you dare leave me, Maura,' he whispered.

She was terribly thin. No muscle, nothing on her arms, they stretched over the sheet like pins. She'd lost that recognisably Maura round face – a remnant of the woman he loved. He'd sat by so many patients when they were dying. It was true, they faded away, light leaching out until the last gasp or shudder and flight of the soul.

He squeezed her fingers but there was no response. Her breathing sounded painful; he unhooked the aspirator, cleared saliva from her mouth. This was not bearable.

'Jess has settled in. Rory phoned, is coming this weekend, alone this time. I told him he should get a dog, just as you said. I don't think Rory dog-owner material.'

Jess had brought in photos, put them round the room. Why had he not thought of that?

'He's already told you he's stopping work. What will the boy do? Should I worry, Maura?'

What about Maura's family? That sister Maura used to visit, what happened to her? When her mother died, Maura contacted relatives, a couple of cousins came down on the bus for the funeral. No nephews, nieces. Maura's whole life caring for children, other people's children. His children.

Impossible to speak to someone so far away, indecent to be light-hearted. It was thought to be important not to be gloomy, imply everyone would be fine. That she had their permission to leave. Well, actually, she hadn't.

He rubbed Vaseline over Maura's cracked lips. 'I bumped into that nun of yours. Jess is a bit worried Anne's a bad influence. Can I ask her not to come?'

Maura frowned.

'Tell me, Maura. Jess is worried.'

'She's fine,' Maura seemed to mumble. But what did she mean?

'Anne said she used to stand outside Lower Six, listen to your Prelude, or Hopkins. You did Hopkins better than anyone, she wished she'd taped you. Did she tell you we saw each other?'

No reply. He'd told Anne not to visit. Was he tricking Maura, asking such questions?

The nurse came in and Liam went to the balcony at the end of the corridor, stared down at a clutch of staff and visitors smoking in the garden.

Liam was leaning on the sea wall stubbing out an absurdly expensive Dunhill when he saw Anne.

She was distraught. 'They've asked me not to come.'

'I told you, they're restricting visits. Maura is very weak.'

Anne must have taken the bus from Brighton, walked up the hill. All that effort to be turned away. 'Do you want to find a café, Anne, have something to eat?'

She nodded, and he led the way to the nearest greasy spoon.

'In future,' Liam said, before she'd even sat on a chair. 'I could give you an update by phone.'

Anne stared at him as if he was talking gibberish. She'd hung her plastic shopping bag on a coathook near a couple of workmen forking up egg, bacon, sausage. The food didn't look tempting.

'Why, Liam? I only want to visit Maura briefly and pray.'

'She's a contented atheist, no fear of the absence of an afterlife.'

Was fear the right word? Who was he talking about? Him or

341

Maura? The teabag had left a puddle in his saucer.

Anne poured a sachet of sugar into her milky coffee. 'You think I'm hoping Maura has a last-minute conversion?'

Of course not.

'She told me, years ago, she liked the idea of the Last Rights. It doesn't mean she isn't an atheist but she does appreciate ritual.'

'Well, Maura never told me.'

Was Anne lying? His toasted bun was inedible, Jess sitting on his shoulder, muttering in his ear. 'Don't trust her.'

'The hospice insists just immediate family.'

'Ah, family,' said Anne, as if it was some exclusive club.

Well, maybe it was. He'd always felt excluded from any he'd witnessed. End of term, they'd cluster round the other boys at school: self-satisfied and smug, tweed-suited fathers smelling of cigars, fussing mothers, an over-abundance of jostling siblings.

The profound embarrassment of noticing his own father, all alone, standing back from the crowd, waiting quietly.

She finished her egg and chips, took out her purse, put it on the table; it was pink plastic with a stud fastening. A child's purse. 'Do you think I'm whispering propaganda into Maura's ear?'

No, but that was what Jess had in mind.

'You wanted to stop Connie helping Maura,' said Liam.

'She, of all people, should have encouraged Maura to fight. Connie's always had such strength, a great will to live, even at her darkest. How could she not recognise that battle in Maura?'

'Connie's a doctor. A good one.'

And the only one willing to do what Maura asked. And he couldn't accept it either. Was he like Anne, seeing Maura's surrender as almost a mortal sin?

'Did you ever speak to Maura, Anne, about Jess's abortion?'

She looked surprised and shook her head. 'Why should I, it's years ago? And anyway, no one actually told me.'

She snapped shut the stud on her purse. She had surprisingly beautiful hands and filthy fingernails, was now playing with the puddle of tea on the table. 'I want to say good bye to her, Liam.' Bloody hell, if she wasn't back fiddling with the purse.

'My confessor once said I needed to learn to mourn.'

So Anne had a particular confessor. What did she have to confess? He finished off the rest of his bun. She was tapping the salt cellar on the table. He moved it and she touched his copy of *The Guardian.*

'I can't read newspapers. Not any more, the world is so terrible.'

Liam suddenly saw himself by a dank pond in a convent garden, fishing out sodden newsprint. He shivered.

There were moments when he was with Anne that felt charged. Being with her was quite different than being with anyone else.

He was going mad. Grief was driving him mad.

Maura's breathing sounded so painful, Jess couldn't stand it. The room was too full: Aidan, and his partner, saying nothing, Liam muttering away to Maura, Rory looking awful and nearly groaning. She must get away.

There was a lounge at the end of the corridor with almost-comfortable chairs and a coffee machine. Jess had only just sat down with a plastic cup of a dark-brown liquid when she was interrupted by Aidan's Vijay.

'I have to pop back briefly to work, Jess. Wanted to check you were all right.'

He pulled up a chair – a good looking man, a bit chubby but attractive. And he wanted to be consoling.

'I'm fine.'

Had he seen her crying?

'It's a lousy business. If there's any way I can help?'

All these doctors convinced they were God. But he was Maura's GP so this must be more difficult.

Connie had once said she was glad to have stopped general practice, shifted over to locums and clinics. The family doctor was meant to care for the patient from birth to death, twenty-four hours a day. And most deaths happened in the middle of the night. Not good.

But general practice had changed, a different doctor each visit, Vijay wouldn't have to do night-calls like Liam and Connie.

'If you get a chance, Jess, have a chat to Aidan.'

Why? Because Aidan was a psychiatrist, might know how to help her feel better? That was unlikely.

The last time they'd talked at any length was at his father's funeral, in the evening they'd all gone to the pub. Aidan had asked questions, mostly about why Jess chose law, but any idiot could see he was more interested in her childhood, and, of course, how damaged she was. She barely knew him, unlike Nell, he rarely came to Moreton. Nell was easier, Aidan was intimidating, a bit flash. Flashy cars, flashy clothes, and that alarming ability to remember exactly what you said and repeat it back.

Vijay kissed her on the head and left. It might be quieter in the garden. She took her cold cup of coffee, went down the fire-escape from the balcony only to find Rory sitting on a bench, lost in his own world, earphones in, bent over a copy of *Nature*.

She banged him on the shoulder. 'What are you listening to?'

'Bartok.'

Wasn't that all jangling and folk tunes? Better to keep silent, not expose her ignorance, Rory was such a nerd about music.

'Did you sort out that fight, Jess, you had with Mum?'

'How exactly when I haven't seen her? She's back with her lover, drinking champagne.'

Jess took up an abandoned rake, started piling up dead leaves.

'I wish you could be kinder to her,' said Rory.

Why? Connie had left them yet again, left Maura.

'How is it living with Dad?'

Weird. She'd expected the house to be as normal: Liam's pictures on every wall, a few bits of driftwood, their father's rubbish that he called *found sculptures*. But the walls had been stripped, everything stacked in a junk-room. The place was now so bare it was clinical, no evidence that he'd ever painted anything, ever. Liam said that he'd tidied when Maura moved to the hospice.

'Don't you think he's a bit too calm?' said Rory. 'Do you remember the terrible state he was in when Grandpa died?'

Not really, it had been quite a busy time. Coming from France, starting Sixth Form, her dad travelling to and from Ireland, not wanting anyone with him. Rory had turned up briefly from uni, went back before he could do much more than say Jess was a trollop, should tell the father. Her brother had always been in his own world.

'Didn't he do some sketches,' said Jess, piling the leaves in the centre of the lawn. 'And you had a row, said he shouldn't?'

No making sense of that row. Jess had even asked Maura, she said it made no sense to her either. Much later, Maura brought it up again. 'Jess, go easy on Liam. He's in a state about his father. If there's anyone to blame, it's me.'

Maura, as usual, taking responsibility.

Rory shoved the magazine in his raincoat pocket and stood up.

'Dad insisted the old man was happy to be sketched. Can you imagine it? Those drawings were unbearable, he exploited Grandpa. And then wouldn't let us come with him to the funeral.'

'That, I do remember.'

'Don't get carried away, leave some grass.'

Rory headed for the staircase.

That was what Liam had been looking for when she'd told him about the abortion. He'd been distracted, yet still managed to come the heavy father. At least he hadn't done pictures of Maura; he'd stopped painting when Maura first got her diagnosis, but still left stuff in every room. Until now. A white wall blitz of denial.

Jess had visited when Maura was just out of hospital, when she seemed to have the all clear. They'd walked round the house together, Jess spooked as always by the weird Indian mandalas.

'Long before my time,' Maura had said.

'Dad was definitely taking something.'

No sketches of Maura from even before the diagnosis. Most painters used their women as models, but not her father. No portraits, no air-brushed pictures of his darling daughter. Maybe Liam's subject was actually death. Those landscapes, they were mostly landscapes, maybe they were all places lost to him. Perhaps he was always painting loss. Well, get a life, Dad.

How could she even think that while Maura was dying?

A call from the balcony – Rory summoning her.

Maura's breath had become even more gruelling, short breaks of nothing, then a deep rasping inhalation. They stood in silence around the bed: Aidan, Jess, Rory, Liam, Vijay, watching her struggle, as if no one dared touch her.

Then Maura abruptly opened her eyes, looked at them all and took a deep breath; Liam leant forward, grabbed her hand. She smiled at him for a second then she left. So clearly, so obviously, Maura died. Jess had never seen anyone die.

The life force did really leave the body.

Aidan was organising them. Jess agreed to meet everyone at the house, she'd go for a walk by the sea first. It had surprised her that she'd managed to get the words out semi-coherently.

It was windy and the waves rough, she was drenched with spray. No one around, she could bawl as much as she liked. Aidan had taken Liam; Dad was on auto-pilot, couldn't be trusted to do anything, let alone drive.

Jess's first instinct had shocked her, it was to phone her mother. She'd rejected the idea immediately – a betrayal of Maura, one mother gone, she picks up another. But it was what she badly wanted to do.

She could hear Maura: 'Ring Connie, darling, tell her.'

Connie was in the Arles house. 'I was waiting for your call. Do you want me to come over after the funeral?'

'Yes, please.'

Aidan squeezed Rory's arm as they joined the queue filing out from the chapel. 'Let's investigate those flowers, can't all be for Maura.'

Considering how much he was earning, odd that Rory was so shabby. Even Vijay had muttered while waiting for the service to start: 'An anorak and jeans? The man must have a dark suit and tie? What do they wear to these fancy shareholder meetings?'

Rory was on the list to give a reading but at the last minute opted out, Jess had looked unsympathetic.

'You'll give up work, Rory, head for the horizon?' said Aidan.

'That's what I'm planning, if I can ever get it together.' Rory stopped to shake hands with some elderly women. 'From Maura and Liam's book group,' he said, re-joining Aidan. 'They've been bringing Dad cakes.'

A small woman in a tattered fur coat was heading straight for the row of wreaths near them; Rory would recognise Anne, they'd be stuck. 'Let's scoot over here,' said Aidan.

Rory was interrupted again to shake hands with a couple.

'You know all these people?'

'Those two used to live next door in Moreton. Twins. Maura had been a second mother. What happens now, Aidan?'

'We mill around, chat. Go to the house, mill around and chat.'

'I don't want to chat. Let's get away.'

'We can't.'

Liam was failing to make conversation with his Italian neighbours, the only people brave enough to have sung. Vijay was with Jess, deep in conversation. Aidan had never thought to introduce them; Jess clearly found Aidan boring but might now, with the discovery of Vijay, be more willing to visit.

'Still no sign of Nell,' said Rory. 'Did she go to Dermot's funeral, I can't remember.'

'God, yes, or Mum would have killed her.'

They found a bench behind the chapel. Rory was wearing trainers, scuffed trainers. Affluence that did it. No worries.

Rory had always been an interesting cousin, didn't seem to have ghosts lurking around to prevent him from being professionally successful. Maybe he'd had analysis and told no one.

'Dad never took me to his father's funeral, Aidan. He went on his own, not even with Maura. He didn't take Jess and me much to see Grandpa, a couple of times at most, a nice old man, so bloody lonely.'

Aidan picked up a discarded Coke can, dropped it in a bin.

'We should be finding the people who need lifts.'

Rory had sunk further into his rain-jacket. 'Dad got a junk shop in to clear the house in Howth; put it immediately on the market, not one pot or vase as a memento for us.'

'They'll be getting anxious,' said Aidan.

'He watched Grandpa die and he drew pictures. He brought some back. Nothing else.'

So, Rory had lots of ghosts.

'Come on,' said Aidan, taking his cousin's arm. 'They'll worry we abandoned them.'

*

Nell waited until the last of the cars had left; the free spaces had been taken quickly by the next lot disgorging more dark-clothed bereaved, then she went into the chapel and knelt in the gloom at the back. There were pale beams of light from the windows. It was cold, it was late afternoon, it was almost November, but the sun was trying to shine.

So many chances to talk to Maura had been missed. She could have said goodbye properly, said thank you. Hard to remember

Maura that last time, during those few minutes in the hospital. She'd asked about Rose, had seemed already somewhere else. No trace of the glamorous woman who'd married Poor Old Uncle Liam. Their wedding had been very quiet, according to Mum who had talked about it in hushed tones as if there were something not quite right, no guests at all. Certainly no nieces.

Another coffin had appeared at the front, pews were filling up for the next session; people tripped over each other as they found a place in the gloom. Did anyone plan to turn on a light?

Someone was behind her, a faint hint of musk. A hand on her shoulder.

Nell jumped out her skin. 'What the fuck.'

She'd been mistaken for someone else.

'I'm sorry.' The voice was vaguely familiar, sounded amused. 'Just wanted to offer my sympathy.'

Whoever it was moved towards the door. Nell took a quick look. The woman was slight and short and wearing a fur coat; she was probably the only person in the place who was warm. But how shocking, a fur coat. No one now would dare to wear fur. It was as if she'd walked out of the past.

*

Aidan picked up a spare loaf and looked for a knife. Easier at this sort of thing to be useful. Jess pushed him away. 'Talk to people.'

He'd given a lift to a couple from Liam's book group who refused to come in for a drink. 'We don't want to disturb your family. It was a lovely funeral, so sad,' the man, who was called Ernest, or Bernard, had said.

'Sort the drinks,' Jess said to Rory as he came into the kitchen with two ex-teacher friends of Maura.

Aidan shook hands with the teachers because no one else was

about to, showed them where to get wine.

Jess had linked arms with her brother. Uncanny how alike they were: Jess had cut her red hair into a bob, Rory's red was becoming less vivid. His face was ageing into the good looks of his mother, but he had Liam's edginess.

Jess went back to smothering egg mayonnaise on bread.

'Wasn't the service beautiful,' said Rory. 'Are the Italians here?'

'In the garden. Why didn't you say your piece?' said Aidan. 'And where's that smart suit you were wearing the other day?'

'Maura always liked these jeans.'

So that was why Rory was scruffy, he must tell Vijay.

'Look, Rory, take Aidan next door and mingle,' said Jess. 'Dad wanted one of you to bring Anne, did you?'

'Your headmistress?' said Rory. 'No. Did she want a lift?'

'Dad thought someone should ask her.'

Aidan followed Rory, both of them carrying bowls of food, into the sun-room where Vijay was sitting with Colum. 'Did you give your favourite nun a lift, Vijay?'

'Was thinking about it, Aidan, but she disappeared.'

So they had all avoided the woman.

Colum stayed firmly in the most comfortable armchair while reaching out for a sandwich; his brother was looking quite portly, more and more like their father.

'Oh, don't get up, Colum. Where is Fiona?'

'And hello to you, too, Aidan. Freezing in the garden with Liam and the neighbours.'

Another good reason to stay inside. Aidan always managed to feel uncomfortable around Colum's wife, partly because there were dogs involved and she wasn't impressed with the care he gave his.

'You only have a flat, Aidan,' Fiona said each time he and Vijay visited. 'It's cruel to keep a dog, you even hire a dog-walker. Do it properly. You and Vijay could, at the very least, get a garden.'

Well, they couldn't all have a converted farm and several acres.

Colum never joined these exchanges; he watched from the margins, playing with whichever of their labradors was nearest, enjoying his pose as host. At least, they'd left the dogs at home.

It was so dark and dismal outside Aidan couldn't make out the sea beyond the road. Liam was pouring whiskey, Fiona giving a speech, probably saying that some people shouldn't have animals.

'I wish I'd made time to visit Maura in these last months,' said Colum. 'She was always good to me.'

Colum and Fiona should have children. They badly wanted them, and would be good parents, and they had that huge house.

Jess came in with a tray of canapés, put it on the table, dumped herself on the sofa next to Rory. 'Make sure everyone has a drink.'

She had dressed for the funeral as if going clubbing. Bright green sweater, short skirt, Doc Martins. How old was she?

Her birthday must be any day. He'd been playing with the neighbour's youngest son, returned through the kitchen to collect a missing piece of Meccano. The house was full of panic, the hall full of patients, wet stuff on the lino under the kitchen table.

'Have either of you talked to Connie?' said Aidan.

Clever of his aunt to put her foot down, no funerals.

And now his mother also realised they could be avoided. Or was it only the ones where Vijay would be included?

How long before he could get Vijay out of here? Go home.

Breakfasting together was something Liam couldn't avoid, Jess would stay in the kitchen until he got up.

'You were wailing again last night, Dad. I was worried the Italians would ring the door-bell, offer solace.'

She was fumbling with her bag, probably looking for her phone. Before Liam could put his cup back in the saucer, she was up and at the counter, doling coffee grains into the cafetière.

He shook out the newspaper. 'What are your plans?'

Jess switched on the kettle. 'Don't you need me?'

'Need, no. It's lovely, but three days since the cremation? Aren't the clients stacking up?'

'Mmm.' Jess looked at him curiously.

At least there was no oozing concern. Each day since Maura died, his daughter had willed herself to stop grieving. At first she looked as if a bomb had hit, gradually she'd toughened up. 'Maura's clothes. Will you manage that?'

One thing Sandford didn't lack was an efficient system to get rid of unwanted effects. 'No problem.'

'And you don't mind, really?' She looked relieved.

Nothing required from him then. Good. He wanted to be alone with Maura's absence, get to know this version of loneliness, the one where he'd lost hope.

'I don't mind, really.'

Jess tried to pour him more coffee. 'You don't plan to see that nun again, do you?'

If he did it was none of his daughter's business; she had no intention of letting him read his paper.

'I once saw her arguing with Connie outside the hospital. What do you think it was about?'

Without waiting for an answer, Jess got to her feet.

'If you're sure you can manage, Dad, I'm off to pack.'

Liam picked up his coffee, followed Jess into her bedroom. She began opening drawers, folding clothes. Now she was going, he didn't want her to leave.

Jess glanced over. 'You ok?'

Her voice had become brisk, she was already at work.

She came over, took the cup, put it down and held him tightly. 'I'll be down often to check you're behaving.'

He tried to hug her and she hugged him back. Was it normal, this appalling sense of loss? It now felt like it had never gone away, that summer after Claire had died, all that absurd gardening, those months of splitting with Connie; Connie would say that he never returned to normal.

He couldn't do this without Maura. Perhaps he should contact that analyst Aidan had sent him to? The young man had said almost nothing, only the occasional grunt? Had Aidan decided that having a mother die when you were five, having a daughter die when she was five, was more than bad luck, needed years of analysis. Not the real truth – that it was simply bloody unfair. Liam could not be considered responsible for his mother's death, how about for Claire's?

He was holding Jess too hard, he let her go.

Jess stood back and smiled. What was she thinking? He'd told her so little about anything, about Claire, about the split from Connie, about her own birth.

'You really ok?' She gave him back his cup, folding his fingers around it. 'Will you be able to get back to painting?'

He shouldn't mind that she was talking to him like a child.

'I should imagine so.'

Jess looked relieved then started hunting for some lost shoes. Painting was behind him, he'd never touch a brush again. Funny to think about that therapist, he'd given up after a couple of months.

'I think this can be helpful, Liam,' the man had said. 'Please reconsider stopping.'

But he hadn't. The analyst clearly expected him to be obsessed with his mother's death, Liam barely remembered his mother. Had he mentioned the pram full of flowers? It shouldn't have happened. If they had had access to penicillin, it wouldn't have happened. Plenty of nuns around in those days. Black shrouds.

That's what he remembered: Connie away in London, Claire upstairs in her bedroom, Rory sleeping in his. Nell was meant to be with Claire while Liam poured whiskey and listened to that dreadful canon wheeze on and on, and Anne, the new young headmistress, had folded and unfolded her hands, leant forward on the chair and nodded and nodded. Nell calling him from the hall, like a ghost as she waited on the stairs, him not understanding, her apologies for being a disturbance, seeing his daughter, his panic call for an ambulance. His car away for repair. Nell's white face, the stairs, the canon, the nun, hovering in the hall, the canon muttering prayers, rushing ahead to start his Ford Anglia.

'Dad!' yelled Jess. 'You're spilling your coffee.'

It was winter, but Arnst had managed to put colour into Nell's garden, the chrysanthemums and cyclamen almost vulgar in their bright reds and pinks. He often didn't tell her he was there. She'd look down and something would have changed.

Maura was dead. It wasn't possible. Nell had kept Rory's message. He'd called several times. 'I'm sorry, Nell, couldn't get a reply. Maura died this afternoon. Phone one of us.'

They'd think she hadn't bothered to turn up for the funeral.

Maura was no longer around. On Nell's shelves were books that had arrived birthdays and Christmas since Maura became officially Liam's wife. Liam was Nell's Godfather and Maura said that, even if she didn't believe in God, she'd take it seriously because Liam never bothered. Three rows of books. When Liam was with Connie, there'd never been books. Among the novels were non-fiction: *The Dialetic of Sex*, *The Female Eunuch*, *Sexual Politics*.

'You never read Simone de Beauvoir? What do they teach in that Sixth Form?' Maura had given Nell her own copy; there it was with the others, a battered paperback of *The Second Sex*. What a lousy example of a feminist she was now.

What would she do if Rose never got in touch? What would Maura have done? What made a good mother? Pat had tried, had cared for them, loved them, but if Mum had been told about Rose, she'd have refused to accept her. Or would she?

Why had Nell let Rose be adopted? Would Pat have allowed that to happen? All she could remember was the flat in Palmers Green being so cold, the hospital too warm. Everything was sweaty and she couldn't understand anything anyone said. 'You can keep her, Nell, cancel the adoption. It's only paper-work.'

Whose voice? Connie? The nurse? What did they mean paper-work? A paper baby ready to be torn up. They could see how dangerous she was. All those children who had died, how she'd pretended to do something and known it was useless; leaving them at the side of the road waiting for her to come back. And she had never come back. They were still waiting, she was not coming back.

'If you don't change your mind soon, Nell,' the voices had said. 'The baby will be fostered, then adopted.'

That would be safer for it. Nell would have a new start. Get out of this country with its freezing flats and cold people. Impossible to look at a baby's face, not imagine it eaten away.

Madge had once said that perfect mothers were the less likely ones: the overweight in the waiting room, gossiping, longing for a ciggie, not the skinny middle class staring at children with anxiety. Not the selfish, neglectful ones like Nell.

The next evening Connie turned up and collapsed on the sofa. 'I'm a wreck. Give me a drink, your bus drivers are maniacs.'

Nell fetched a bottle of whiskey. 'When did you get here?'

'Two days ago.'

Connie could have come earlier, gone to the cremation.

'I'm staying at Jess's. Aidan and Vijay were meant to come for supper. Vijay cancelled, Aidan left for his train early.'

Was there a problem between them? Vijay had come into the practice the day before to collect Sanghi and he'd looked uneasy. When she'd mentioned it to Madge, there'd just been Madge's usual optimism that no relationships survived for ever.

Connie poured whiskey for both of them. Connie never used to sleep over with Jess, several times she'd suffered Nell's sofa.

'A great relief to have James around, Jess still treats me like an unexploded bomb. Tiptoes around, peering out the corner of her eye as if any moment I'll become dangerous.'

Her aunt was dangerous. And why was she here?

Connie raised her glass. 'Are you ever going to sit down?'

She wouldn't show Connie the photos of Rose. Connie had not helped. How could she not have helped – to have done nothing?

Nell brought over bread and cheddar, put them with crisps on the coffee table. 'I'm sorry about the funeral, Jess must be furious.'

'Don't be silly, Jess doesn't do furious. She rages then forgets.'

They'd despise her if they'd known she'd skulked outside.

'So, Nell darling, you're free now.'

What did her aunt mean, free?

'Listen, you've met your daughter, employed her brother. You're able to travel, find work wherever you like.'

Still giving advice, suggesting Nell disappear now she'd just discovered Rose. How quickly Connie had become the wicked witch. Go where? How long for, and how about Rose? Did Connie mean to stir up trouble? She imagined she was being helpful.

That was why she'd come, she was tidying them up. In that case, was Connie right, and what could Nell do?

'Auden said people who read murder mysteries are interested in blame?'

'Implying me, Nell?'

'Well, to be honest, I was thinking more about me.'

2001

80

The first week in the year and Aidan was about to cancel appointments. Was this a resolution? It felt quite liberating.

The ward sister stood blocking his way. 'Where do you think you're going?'

'I have to meet someone.'

'You're joking, Aidan. Now, when we've one of your morning meetings that mean we're here an extra two hours, I have to get in cover? I don't think so.'

'Well, I do. You can manage without me.'

She was going to wrestle him to the ground in the hospital corridor. She certainly had the muscle, but she paused, seemed to take in what he'd said. Of course they could manage; it had never happened before but was a hopeful sign. She stood to one side; Aidan waved farewell, headed for the stairs.

'Ring Anne. See her, Aidan,' Maura had said yet again, during one of the last visits when she was lucid.

Maura clearly thought this nun needed Aidan's professional help. That was two months ago, he'd forgotten all about it. Work put it out of his mind until this morning and the email from Rory. Rory's intention to sail round the world was actually going to happen. The boat was already moored off the coast in Portugal; he was joining some others, the trip booked for the spring. He wasn't doing it alone. That was what Aidan wanted, to sail away alone.

Rory had mentioned Anne. 'Didn't she look small? I remember her being much taller in that nun's habit. She always seemed powerful when she visited the house, scared me shitless.'

What should Aidan have said to her? 'Do you want a lift? Maura gave me your number.' She had looked innocuous, an oddly dressed old lady. He'd always imagined her as a fully-inhabited nun – could see her flying down the A2, the whole works: butterfly wings of white cotton sticking out from the head-dress like those holy sisters in Rome, a diabolical leer on her face.

Vijay was sitting in front of the open fire with his mid-morning cup of green tea, reading *The Tibetan Book of the Dead*. 'Aren't you meant to be chairing your meeting?'

'Why don't you give up on that tome? I've left them to it, arranged with Maura's nun to go for a walk.'

At least Vijay was here, he'd been going to London more often than usual. Good to come back to the flat, find someone home. No, it was good to come back and find Vijay home.

'I've the rest of the day clear so can get this done. Have you seen my trainers?'

'You never met up with the woman?' Vijay stood up to help search. 'Despite Maura begging and you promising.'

Where was his new rain jacket?

Vijay blocked his way. 'Why the sudden rush, Aidan? Maura gave you that address months ago?'

He wasn't going to say it was the email this morning from Rory that reminded him.

'I suppose it's a good sign,' said Vijay, retrieving the jacket from behind a trench coat in the cupboard. 'You act so indispensable at the hospital. And now at last are doing what Maura wanted.'

Vijay could have chatted to Anne at the funeral, he was standing next to her. He was the one who'd thought she looked interesting.

'Your shoes are under the kitchen table.'

'Thank you. Now can I use the bathroom or are you going to follow me there?'

'I'll follow you there,' said Vijay. 'I can't believe you did nothing, the only thing Maura asked.' Vijay stood at the basin, checked his chin in the mirror. 'You were avoiding Anne, Aidan. She's strange. You don't like strange people, especially strange women.'

Vijay was being unbearable. And Anne was hardly that strange.

Aidan shoved Vijay to one side, washed his hands. Then he paused, pulled Vijay back and held him so they could see each other in the mirror. Not bad. He kissed the back of Vijay's neck.

Vijay was not to be deterred. 'Give the nun some decent clothes and she could be a university don.'

'University dons look more homeless than the homeless.'

'Just have a gander at her eyes. Listen to what she says, the woman is interesting. Why did you ignore Maura's request?'

'Rory is going to sail round the world.'

'Ah hah, that's what this is about.'

*

The walk from Eastbourne to Beachy Head was one of the things Anne wanted to do before moving away, Aidan's invitation was welcome. He wasn't enthusiastic about driving from Brighton to go tramping up a hill. It was January, it was cold, might rain. But Anne had insisted.

He was going too fast. 'It's a beautiful car.'

'A second-hand Rover, not at all special.' Aidan put on some Bach. 'I didn't recognise you at the funeral.'

What a liar. He'd been standing with Rory, they'd walked away the minute Aidan spotted her. Aidan had said nothing, but Rory had nodded and smiled.

'Why would you, Aidan? I don't think I met you in Moreton.'

Of course they had met in Moreton. Why had she lied?

What made this boy suddenly decide to do what Maura had asked, and what had Maura been plotting?

Aidan parked and they set off. As the first slope flattened out, they sat for a rest; it had begun to sleet, she was making him suffer. She pulled a mackintosh from her backpack, wrapped it round her shoulders. Maura had talked about some schoolboy and here he was: tall, expensively dressed, handsome, and a consultant. He also had the best haircut she'd ever seen on a man. Was it dyed, his black hair streaked blonde? Weren't the Ryans all dark?

He was too pretty. Hadn't she read that most psychoanalysts were narcissists?

He helped her zip up her bag. It hadn't just been the prospect of a walk. When Aidan turned up, suggested coming back later, she'd been curious. Connie was back in France. Maura gone. She had no links to this family. Would talking to him clear her head?

But it now seemed unlikely – he was Connie's family, not some detached psychiatrist. Sitting next to him on this bench, did such a confident person consider getting old, ever pause to consider the sanctity of life?

Looking over at the Channel in the almost snow, with a few hundred yards further on, the cliff edge that was a regular witness to people's desperation.

'So Maura thought I needed a psychiatrist?' Anne pulled up her hood. 'Isn't it a bit late? I'm sixty-seven.'

'I've no idea what Maura had in mind. Was relieved to find you still there.'

They'd both get pneumonia. 'Only just. I plan to give my place to someone else.'

He zipped up his jacket. 'Now you do sound like a nun.'

'I haven't been a nun for twenty years.'

And she was only leaving because she was restless. Gardening at the hostel was not enough, she wanted to move on. It might be her last move, exciting to imagine where she could go.

'A long time since I first met your family, Aidan. Did Liam mention me?'

'You called in bulldozers. Every summer, when he and the landlady in Norfolk discussed her plants, he'd repeat your crimes.'

Not her bulldozers, she'd been a servant of the school, did what she was told. 'You enjoyed those holidays?'

'I liked Mrs P,' said Aidan. 'We kept in touch with Christmas cards. She gave up on Norfolk, moved here. I, or rather we, spent a few weekends at her B&B in Bexhill.'

'You have someone, Aidan?'

'I was seeing this conversation as more professional than that.'

He was attempting to dry his face, did think this was about him being the psychiatrist. Was he right?

'Shall we go on? I mean if you're up to it.'

He got to his feet, then tried to help her, which was ridiculous. What had made her mention Vijay?

'You haven't met my uncle again, have you, Anne?'

'Reminisced about bulldozers?'

She offered him a mint. He shook his head and started doing leg stretches. He was meant to be an expert at being silent, at listening, but was impossibly restless. This walk was not going well, she'd enjoy it more on her own but could hardly ask him to walk ahead. Anne repacked her bag.

'I don't think,' said Aidan as he helped her put on the back-sack, 'it was a great idea getting together rain or shine, mostly rain, every August. Connie disappearing once Liam turned up. No one mentioning Claire's name – generally speaking, a bad idea.'

Why was this family so addicted to keeping secrets? Of course Maura had told her about Vijay, Aidan knew she knew.

'Did it occur to you, Aidan, that Maura might have given you my contact details so I could be of use to your family? That was what Maura needed from me.'

*

They both had the fish and chip special in the restaurant by Beachy Head, Anne letting him pay without a murmur. All this time she'd been seeing herself as the therapist, he and his damaged family the ones to be helped. Maura, Anne, were in cahoots. And what a crafty woman. All those innocent questions when she knew more about him than he did himself.

Anne was examining her fried haddock and mushy peas in forensic detail. She seemed extremely happy with the chips.

Why was he not back at home spending Saturday with Vijay?

She went back to collect more cutlery. What did other people make of her, so shabbily dressed? Yet there was something contained and alert about the woman, Vijay was right.

Anne looked cautious, still, while surrounded at the counter by greedy, grabbing hands. She'd pause, then carefully select; negotiated the crowded tables on her return with equal care. She distributed the forks, paper napkins, sachets of tomato sauce as if they were very precious. She looked so delighted at the meal in front of her, she was probably starving.

Was this person really a monster?

'What sort of use to our family did Maura have in mind?'

'Some plan, Aidan, Maura always had plans.'

Anne organised the food in front of her, started to eat. Her manners were fastidious; she was chewing her haddock with the awareness that Vijay would preach as the only desirable way. 'Slow down with that, Aidan. It took hours to cook, and please put away the journal.'

'Why did Maura ask me to speak to you?' said Aidan. 'Not Colum, or Rory. Rory's almost her son.'

Anne shrugged. She was looking at him with a professional

pose, head tilted slightly to show attentive concern. Well, enough of this, he wasn't going to have her judge his family.

Most of the other diners were obese. Some dreadful children were racing about, kicking over chairs. There were tables outside and play equipment, but it was too cold, the ground muddy. The parents could at least keep their kids away from human beings.

Anne finished her fish with enthusiasm then went back to the counter to return an unused sachet of tomato ketchup. Aidan was feeling more and more cranky. What a waste of a day.

He abandoned his meal, which was inedible, went to collect them both a bowl of salad. He realised, as he rejected the Iceberg, Anne was right, Maura did have a plan. She didn't want him to help Anne after all? Maura wanted Anne to help Liam. Aidan had to put Anne and Liam together.

The young girl picked up the prescription: 'I know you haven't much time, Doctor. I'm sorry to keep you late.'

She had just had a miscarriage, needed to talk more, but Nell had three people waiting. Work was getting busier and stressful. How come she was enjoying it?

'You don't like time to think,' said Madge.

Madge wanted Nell to make decisions. Sanghi intended to retire. Vijay's cloak and dagger meetings had been advising his brother on alternatives, Nell was being asked if she wanted to be a partner. Did she? The thought of taking responsibility for any of this made her panic. She pressed the buzzer to Reception.

The next patient had just left when Madge put her head round the door. A phone call.

'I'll ring back.'

'It's about your flat and the police.'

It was someone called Pedro. Arnst had been arrested. Rose had never mentioned any Pedro. Nell rang Jess.

Nell followed Rose up the four flights of stairs. The same climb as hers but this wasn't her purpose-built block, it was a substantial mansion.

'At least my sister Jarene's away, she can be a bit of a pain.'

Strange to see Rose in her own environment, she even seemed nervous. Well, she should take a look at the state of Nell, palms sweating, heart racing. Rose turned at the second landing and whispered: 'Arnst has made a cake which will be inedible.'

Should Nell pretend the cake is delicious? It was meant to be a thank you from Arnst, so she had to. What could she talk about to Iris? Amy had suggested they meet ages ago but it never seemed to happen. Now it would. Iris knew what Nell had done twenty years ago, must think her a terrible person.

Rose said they'd lived here all her life. How had Iris dealt with shopping, prams, babies up those stairs? When Iris opened the door it became apparent. The woman in front of her was another Madge: a manager who sorted life out, same strength and energy.

'Hello, Nell. You're so welcome.' Iris took Nell's hand in both of hers. 'I got your message, am sorry about Jess.'

Rose steered her through the door, took her coat, gave her an armchair in the living-room.

'We did try, Mum,' said Rose. 'Nell had just collected her, when Jess's phone went off. She had to rush back to work. I haven't even met her.'

It was true, Jess had been happy to come. 'I want to see them. Arrange it again, next time I'll switch off my mobile.'

Rose bent over and whispered: 'The cake looks doubtful. But he does want to get it right, I'll go and check.'

She'd left Nell on her own with Iris. Don't panic. There was muttering from the kitchen, a kettle boiling, plates being collected. Now was the time to say something, might not be another chance.

'I know it's inadequate.' Her voice sounded strangled. 'But I have to try and thank you.' What Nell really wanted to do was prostrate herself in front of Iris, weep with relief and gratitude. 'It sounds pathetic, but Rose is such a lovely person, she's so lucky to have you as a mother.'

What was she trying to say? This wouldn't get rid of any guilt.

'Well, listen to you,' smiled Iris. 'Rose has always been a pleasure of a daughter.'

Rose returned too quickly with a tray, cups and a pot of tea. What more could Nell say? It was hopeless, the whole thing wretched and sad. But she must not cry.

Jess should have been here, that would have made it easier. Jess had rescued her, that irritating child had saved her, saved Arnst.

Rose poured tea and sat beside Iris on the sofa opposite Nell; Arnst had peered round the door and waved, then disappeared.

'He's thinking about smothering it with icing,' said Rose.

'We're so grateful to you and Jess.' Iris handed Nell a cup. 'He has a bad history with keys, that boy.'

Nell should be the one apologising, her fault not telling people about Arnst and the gardening, inevitable that some time he'd turn up when Nell was at the practice. He often came when she was working, why hadn't she warned people earlier?

He'd forgotten the key, climbed over the fence; apparently he'd even been sleeping some nights in the shed. Neighbours reported a break-in, the police were there in minutes.

'The others in the house have seen him hundreds of times, clearing leaves, planting, cleaning.'

They were racists, and busybodies. But she should have told them. Jess got Arnst off the charge, then advised Nell to introduce him to everyone in the building. It had been fine; even though no one apologised they were content to have the garden dealt with.

'It only takes one,' said Iris, offering her a plate of tuna sandwiches. 'This Jess is your cousin? Her parents are Catholic but divorced?'

'Mum,' said Rose. 'Don't be nosey.'

'Well, you go on about Connie.' Iris turned back to Nell. 'She wants to help Rose with her college fees, isn't that too much?'

Connie interfering again? She'd said nothing about helping Rose. It hadn't occurred to Nell to offer support, it was too pushy to suggest any such thing. Amy warned her about not expecting to be close – here was her aunt barging in, throwing money around.

Nell explained how her aunt and uncle had divorced after their child died. 'I was ten, was staying there when it happened.'

'I'm so sorry, you poor little girl,' said Iris, reaching across and touching Nell's knee. 'What was her name?'

Nell's mouth felt full of wool, she couldn't answer.

'It's brilliant, a masterpiece.' Arnst pushed through the door, holding an iced cake above his head.

He put down the plate, started cutting slices. Then he looked around, uneasy. 'All of you so quiet? It's not that bad.'

'Claire,' Nell said. 'Her name was Claire.'

She took a slice from Arnst, put the plate down before she could drop it. They were waiting for her to say more. How could she explain about the snow, that Connie was away, Claire was ill, and she had to tell Liam? And that she hadn't straight away. How could she stop crying?

'I don't know why I didn't check Claire earlier. I should have.'

'Oh, you were a child,' said Iris. She came over to Nell, gave her a hug, and Nell didn't shrink away. She didn't want to shrink away.

Aidan was outside when Nell got back to the flat. She'd hoped he wouldn't come, or at least be late. She needed time on her own.

He helped her carry up the shopping. 'Waiting then following you up loads of stairs seems familiar, doesn't it?'

She was not going to go there. She double-locked the flat's front door, took the bags from Aidan, and his coat. Very smart, she checked the label, Burberrys.

'Why lock it,' Aidan asked.

'I lock everything.'

Aidan stretched full length on the sofa. Her brother was too big for her room – too tall, too smooth, too well dressed. This was the first time he'd visited, and she'd lived in the flat for ten years.

Why had he come? Was he here to talk about their mother? Pat was becoming a recluse yet complained as much as ever. 'You and Aidan are so anti-social?' she'd said on the phone on Christmas Day. 'Why can't Aidan be chatty like Colum or Vijay?'

Pat mentioning Vijay, let alone praising Vijay, was unheard of.

Aidan leant over and turned on the fire. The flat was far too warm. The sooner she got this over with, the sooner he'd leave.

Nell tore off packaging, put the meal in the oven, then poured them both wine. She crouched on the almost-impeccable carpet in front of the sofa. It was rather good, having everywhere so clean. She'd have another frantic go in a week or two.

'We're lucky Colum and Holy Fiona live near Mum. It frees us.' It felt as if Iris had given her some kind of blessing. She could do anything she liked. 'You can tell Mum I've gone back to Africa.'

That was what Connie had meant. Of course that's what she should do, write to that Zambian clinic. But what about Rose? How could she leave after being welcomed by Rose's family?

'Will you contact Jerome again?'

Why not? Jerome might have disowned his daughter but she could send him Rose's address, leave it to him.

'I'm hungry, Nell, shall we go out to eat?'

'I've smoked salmon, while we wait for the casserole.' She'd made an effort, he could pretend to enjoy it.

She went to deal with the rest of the shopping, sliced the bread too vigorously and cut her finger.

'You said on the phone, Aidan, it was important.'

'You look better than for years. Is it Rose?'

Nell hunted through the kitchen drawer for surgical tape.

'I had tea today with her mother.'

'And?'

She didn't wish to chat with her brother about Rose's family. It would diminish it. 'Vijay told Sanghi the surgeries need cheering up, he thinks I should become a partner.'

'Don't let them paint it pink or fill it with Vijay's freesias.'

'Is everything all right with you two?'

'The man's doing too much supervision: cares more about archetypes and the collective unconscious than general practice and kids with measles who didn't have their MMR.'

Vijay was too good for her brother, but that was hardly news, everyone agreed. Except Maura, who thought Aidan did no wrong.

'Can you deal with that finger? It's disgusting.'

It was only tissue and a bit of blood. And already clotted. She put the soda bread and salmon with slices of lemon on a tray beside him. Aidan was running his hand down behind the cushion; he pulled out a hair brush. 'Didn't know you used these.'

Still OCD, but he would say it was not obsessive or compulsive to be orderly and clean. Of course, he and Vijay had a cleaner.

'We need to talk.' Aidan was using his calm professional voice. 'You realise Liam will be on his own.'

'I'm alone.'

'You like being alone, Liam doesn't. As far as I know he's never lived on his own. And he is being pursued,' said Aidan.

Did she like being alone? People could be irritating; Aidan had started taking hairs from the brush, was throwing them in the waste-paper basket. A relief that she'd emptied it. He sat forward.

'You were staying in Moreton that time, Nell. The nun was there all night. What was she doing?'

'Praying, I suppose. I was in bed. She was walking around the house, maybe looking at things.'

Aidan had pulled a piece of paper from his wallet, started ticking some notes.

Nell took his pen. 'Stop, you make me nervous.'

'Whenever there was a crisis, it had some connection to Anne. She even knew the nun in Pontissy. That weird job Jess had, one designed to send her straight home. There's more, and it's tricky.'

He was going to talk about Lagos.

'Do you remember when we went to get your things? The nurse said a nun told Jerome you were having an affair.'

She remembered nothing except the sculpted head which was

now on her bedroom chest of drawers. Fine, if Aidan kept to the subject of Liam, not fine if he was going to bring up Jerome. Even if Nneka did say something, it didn't make a link with Anne.

Nuns were everywhere, thousands of them, mostly harmless.

What was it Anne said when they'd talked in the café in Covent Garden? 'I did ask. Anne didn't know anyone in Nigeria.'

Aidan sat back. 'Liam probably said he was worried.'

'That's absurd and you know it.' Nell hunted through the cupboards, found a half-bottle of gin.

Would Aidan agree that if Pat had known about the pregnancy, she'd have helped Nell keep the baby? Pat wouldn't have let her grandchild be adopted.

Why had she trusted Connie?

'Anyway,' said Aidan, holding out his glass. 'Was it witnessing Claire dying compelled Anne to insulate Liam from grief?'

'Does it matter?' said Nell.

'She's pursuing him. Liam's lonely, and a softie. Do we want her in our family, replacing Maura? Anne as our new auntie?'

82

The hostel was on the Hove road; it was like a grand country house. Liam rang the bell. A lot of land lurked behind those high walls; there were pediments and buttresses, gothic balconies and steeples, roofs with pointed bits. Inside no doubt would be grimy corridors, boiled cabbage, panic clatter of someone running.

A relief to make up his mind, he'd been looking forward to this: the first step in moving on, leaving a house where Maura kept turning up. People were kind, but enough with chicken pies and hotpots delivered by over-chatty friends checking his state of neglect. He wanted done with making himself eat stale remains of Victoria sponge, listening to small talk. The Italian neighbours had been magnificent but he never wanted to see a lasagne again.

Anne would not console, she was familiar, she knew him. She had known Maura. He'd do this, then plan for something different.

Anne opened the enormous door; she seemed to have shrunk.

'I was admiring the outside. Where are the gargoyles?'

'Look at the garden before mocking, but of course you've come at the completely wrong time, everything is frozen.'

He kicked the black bags he'd taken from the car.

'There's a couple of boxes Maura had in the garage with your name on. I'll bring them another time if you still need them. Where do I dump these?'

'You have sorted things.'

Of course he had. It had taken all his energy and he'd had to force Jess and Rory to help. He should have hired a clearance company, not tried to hold on to anything. But there hadn't seemed any hurry and he'd wanted to live for a while with Maura's things. 'I left in a couple of party frocks to keep you cheerful.'

Anne looked at him, one of those infuriating concerned looks. Even from her. But it went quickly and she returned to her familiar efficiency. 'You're ready, Liam, to see what I've done in the garden before handing it on to others?'

'You have to leave?'

'Of course, it's a year, but I've transformed what was an appalling wilderness. Although you're going to have to use your imagination.' She gave him another of her looks. 'I got your letter but it wasn't necessary to apologise, you were under such stress.'

No excuse. To exclude her like that from seeing Maura when she'd only meant well had been unfair.

'Come on now. I want to show how you've been an inspiration.'

She walked ahead of him down the corridor. She had cut her hair properly for once, was wearing a baggy purple sweater that looked almost new, and a respectable pair of black tracksuit pants.

'Come on now'. The same voice. And the same walk. He could see her ankles, the glimpse of white stockings, her black habit, reflections of stained glass from the high narrow windows on her white starched bib, on the white lining to her veil. A feeling of lightness, that's what he was feeling. It should have been the familiar muffling of grief, but it wasn't.

Anne turned suddenly, staring back as if she was also remembering. An old woman's face. This was a stranger, an old woman in ordinary clothes.

No, this was no stranger. How good to see her.

'Leave the bags over there. Do you want tea first?'

'No, thanks,' said Liam. 'I'm ready.'

It was early spring in an ordinary garden, snowdrops along the borders, crocuses peering through the lawn. She'd left the lilac un-pruned in front of a St Francis in one corner, and the statue was almost concealed. A bench had been moved to be hidden by a hedge. There was cherry blossom just beginning to emerge, in a few weeks the garden would be wonderful.

'You plan to abandon this?'

'I can have pleasure in the summer, imagining it.'

He should paint it. Most of the trees were bare. Was Rory right, he was obsessed by winter? Liam had cleared everything into a junk room but Rory had wanted to see the old work even though Liam had no intention of going back to any of it. 'What are these, Dad?'

'Mandalas. A nun I knew said monks make the actual ones with coloured powders, then they blow it all away.'

'The only portraits you've done are of Grandpa dying.'

Rory had forgotten the sketch of him stuck up for years in the Moreton kitchen. None of them had liked being sketched, unlike Papa who'd said he didn't mind at all; it meant Liam could sit with him for hours, both silent, the scratch of charcoal, rasping of his father's breath, the occasional cough or clearing off a throat. A chance to look at someone he loved who was leaving for ever, to look at death. He hadn't with his mother, hadn't with Claire; he had refused to with Maura.

'The best one went missing.'

Rory was clattering his way through the canvases.

'Maura told me that she destroyed it. Did she? That woman would have hung for you.'

Rory had smiled. 'Of course I did, and would do it again. It felt wrong, making false images, not respecting Grandpa – several commandments were broken.'

Not true. The sketching had been evidence of Liam's respect; it made the silence easier between them. Waiting for the inevitable became bearable, Papa had appreciated it.

Anne had crouched down, was examining some pruned rose-bushes. The Sandford house was on the market. Liam didn't need to take anything from the garden. Soon he had to decide between Ireland and Moreton. More likely Ireland, Moreton was too painful.

Was it Aidan's fantasy that Anne had been some Machiavelli, that she had tried to interfere with Jess's life and Nell's?

'You helped Connie, Anne. How did you manage that?'

Anne stood up and frowned. 'When she was still your wife?'

Liam nodded.

'Aidan has decided that I interfered, hasn't he?'

He had indeed. Aidan had a list.

'He thought you might have contacts in Nigeria.'

'If only nuns were that influential.'

Anne took a brush, started sweeping up leaves. 'You remember the cairn of stones in the convent garden, the one at the centre of a pattern? It became more obvious as you cleared the weeds.'

He had stood on the wall that last time with Mr Drummond. The untidy pile of stones had been annoying.

'Connie and I made it for Claire. Some of the stones were Claire's, making it was part of an agreement Connie and I had. I know it sounds pagan, I didn't know how else to help.'

His garden? They'd already been in there plotting before he even saw it. How had they known in all that wild confusion where the centre was?

Anne was right, Connie had been more than a worry. And he'd been unable to do anything. He should be grateful, he was grateful.

'I've got plants that will go to waste, Anne. I'll bring them over, help you put them in.'

He would come again. Anne would make him tea. He'd bring sketchpads and charcoal. He would draw this.

PART FOUR

2013

2013

83

Anne closed the laptop. The email had arrived several days ago but neither of them had checked, only opened this morning because Anne couldn't sleep and it was too dark to go out. But dawn at last.

She took her mug of tea to the yard behind the cottage. Her favourite place was the bench by the shed, from there she could see through the open gate the ruby glow of fuchsia in the lane beyond, her small garden beyond that, the scent of wet stone, burning turf and honeysuckle.

Why had Connie decided that she wanted them now?

It was still early. Anne could collect them in one go, recover as many as possible. It looked as if it would be a mild July day, no rain expected. She'd make the route a loop, that way she'd reach enough places. As she removed each of the offerings she'd leave a flower, offer a prayer at each shrine for any that had gone missing. That would be enough.

Anne put water and rain-jacket, three apples and tissues into her back-sack then filled it with flowers; she'd gone round her garden cutting the best of the roses. She left a note on the table for Liam. It was only six, he'd not be up for another hour. She had no map but would remember most of it – there'd be no buses but she'd look for a lift if necessary. Drivers always picked her up. They assumed she was a nun in mufti even though she hadn't been seen in a habit for more than thirty years. She never disillusioned them. They accepted her silence, keen to get their credit in heaven.

Connie was leaving France and coming to England. This was only the third time Anne had heard from her since Laurent died three years ago and Connie moved to the trailer park near

Perpignan. Email apparently meant going to a café a kilometre away, and Connie had never been keen on emailing. Nor was Anne and who would she email anyway? What had Connie's last letter said? It was the usual, Anne should visit her since Connie refused to come to Mayo.

It would be a joy to see Connie again. Fifty years, and hard to stretch memory that far, almost impossible to recognise the person Anne had been, but the very thought of Connie gave a sense of exhilaration.

Some of the shrines were small, almost secret, a few were ones Anne herself had made when out on her walks. Several were full-size statues of Our Lady with marble steps. Some she liked and visited often, others were kitsch – in fact most lacked any beauty.

At first she approached warily, anxiously scanning the pedestal, the surroundings of the saint or the Madonna, for her offerings. Often they had fallen into the grass but eventually, when the ones she recognised from their markings had indeed vanished, instead of giving up, she went to find another.

It took longer than Anne anticipated, by four in the afternoon she was hungry and tired, her back-pack heavy, and five miles from home. She was too old for this, had overestimated her strength. That was one thing Connie had said in a letter, after Laurent died: how hard to accept their bodies wouldn't behave like they used to.

This last shrine was small, a picture of Our Lady behind glass together with a red night-light long since extinguished and a few dried-out flowers. It was not at a junction to anywhere. No houses in sight and the lane that used to lead to the road had been ploughed over; wherever it once went disappeared into the earth.

The road was quiet; Anne sat for a rest on a low wall, finished her water and the last apple. Well, that was tempting fate. But fate was on her side, the first car slowed down before she even thought to lift her thumb. The middle-aged couple looked cautious as they took in her tiredness, her clothes. But again her calmness seemed to convince them she wasn't a threat, and that she was holy. And they delivered her to the door.

Liam was locked away in the back working so Anne made herself a cheese sandwich, turned on the computer.

Connie's email had been brief. The Subject: 'Do you still have them?'

Anne pressed Reply, typed 'Yes' and pressed Send.

Rose slipped the key into the ignition. Hire cars were exciting, the nearest she'd get to a new one even if this was only a Micra and the brand-new reassurance came from a chemical cocktail to seduce buyers. The flight to Knock had taken an hour and a half. One minute she was on a bus to Stansted, then here, surrounded by moorland, heather. Or was all this bog? Connie had said on the phone it was bog around the airport – the Google description of Irish bog made it look as if it should be avoided.

'Are you sure?' Connie had said. 'It's a hell of a journey.'

Why was she here? Because Connie had asked; she partly owed her career to Connie. She owed Iris, and she sort of owed Pedro – that was it. Or did she now owe Jerome? If she hadn't arranged this weekend away she'd probably be dragged into another shopping trip. It wasn't clear if his wife, or Jerome for that matter, accepted that Rose was his daughter. But they were in London for a conference and wanted to spend money on her. 'At least one expensive outfit,' said Jerome. 'Nell always dressed like a tramp, don't copy her.'

'What's he like?' Iris had asked.

'Quiet. And not sure about me. But she is a whirl of energy so no one gets a word in.'

And the new things were wonderful, and such luxury. Neither Iris nor Nell went in for luxury.

Where were the wipers, and the main road? Left, as she got out of the airport gate, or right? The few getting into their cars looked in a hurry and irritable; Rose had expected it to be relaxed, people chatty. This was more stressed than Harlesdon.

People must go mad in this emptiness.

Connie had wanted some black pudding.

'I'll try.'

Iris had said: 'I want a little statue or something.'

'No chance, Mum.'

She was driving through a mist of rain. Pedro had told her that if she waited a few weeks they could make it a trip but Connie sounded more urgent.

As soon as she could, she parked half in the ditch, checked her mobile. Zilch reception. The car had a TomTom, or whatever they called it; she'd no clue how to use it, hadn't wanted to ask.

This countryside was unfamiliar and empty, the road barely wide enough for two cars. At least there was no traffic. Where had the motorway marked on the map vanished to? She could break down, be lost for ever. Murdered, and left in some boggy hole by racist locals. One Indian woman at Knock airport and an African priest; that was it, all the rest were white.

August, but the fields were the same misty grey as the sky, almost no horizon. A sweet stench, a sickening one. It wasn't silage. This wasn't like her brief summer job in a city farm; though there might easily be pigs hidden behind the stone walls. And mad pig farmers.

She couldn't live in a place like this, ever. In fact better to turn round, get back to the airport, take the next flight home. But first, somewhere to have a pee.

It took a while to find enough shelter that wasn't in mud. And she was wearing her new trousers. The trees were low and windswept, the hedges shrunk. Her luck that if she stayed by the car, someone would come along as she squatted down. It was like Jamaica. You get a spot you think is safe and private, as soon as you're in the middle, children erupt from nowhere.

Infinitely preferable to be in Jamaica at this moment; the wind made a spooky howl and there was a sodden quality to the earth, in everything around her, even the stone wall that she'd used as cover. The drizzle seemed mild but it was soaking into her rain jacket.

'There are more schizophrenics in the West of Ireland than anywhere else,' Iris had read out from the book she'd taken from the library.

'Are you worrying about my genetic make-up, Mum, or my chance of being stabbed when I get there?'

'It completely defeats me what you think you're up to.'

Rose had shrugged, carried on chopping tomatoes.

'You'll miss two days of that summer school. They won't like it, having to get cover. Bad enough you skipping shifts in that wine bar. Everyone's looking for a job.'

The wine-bar was pleasure, and her inability to split from Pedro. She didn't want to split from Pedro. If he had managed to get the weekend off this trip would have been fun. He made things enjoyable while Iris was becoming more and more anxious, just when there was less to worry about.

She wasn't even being much of a grandmother: Jarene was in Hull, her two children secure in nursery, full-time co-ordinating something in education that Jarene had explained and Iris didn't understand.

'This government privatises anything good we have.'

'Trust her, Mum. Jarene will do what she can.'

Arnst was working. Nell had helped him set up a gardening company before she went to Zambia, now he had his own flat, girlfriend, baby. They could all breathe again.

At least the car started. Continue straight, at some point she must reach a sensible road. The road, when she found it, was a dual-carriageway and empty.

The cottage was in a tiny hamlet hidden between several round bald hills and, as Connie had said, *Nephin* was written over the door. Despite knocking and yelling, she couldn't get herself heard. Liam had no mobile.

No matter how hard she banged, no one answered.

An old man appeared from the next cottage. 'You'd be better walking straight in. Aren't they as deaf as posts, the pair of them.'

What did he mean by the pair of them? Connie had said go and see Liam.

An old lady peered from the half-opened door, holding a lethal pair of scissors. 'Come in. Put your jacket on the hook, sit down. Keep quiet as you can.'

The tiny woman pushed Rose into a small cluttered and over-heated living-room; she'd been wrapping a box. She pointed to a closed door, an empty chair. Rose sat down.

Who was this person? Too old to be Liam's carer? Her spiky grey hair cut by very blunt scissors, a sweater and skirt from a charity shop. But her eyes were bright blue and curious and she had an amused expression as she examined Rose; she seemed to find what she saw delightful.

The cottage was not as full of junk as seemed at first, but junk fixed on to wood and hung on the walls. Text written up the stairs, canvases stacked facing away from the room. There was barely enough space for the table and chairs.

Connie had simply said: 'Please visit Liam. Something I'm at last getting back that's too precious to post.'

Liam, apparently, was asleep in the next room. Not at any price to be disturbed. The woman returned to the table, sloppily sellotaping brown paper around the box, then tying it with string. Presumably the package from Liam to Connie.

It would be bliss to have a glass of water, a cup of tea. But maybe not. The place was not only small, but smelt of something sweet and not very hygienic. The kitchen was part of the living room, had an ancient black range that was hot despite it being officially summer outside. The thing leaked smoke. The grime was recognisable from visits to clients when Rose had thought about social work, done some volunteering.

Connie had asked her to check for holy pictures. No religious images anywhere. She'd warned her not to stay the night. 'Get yourself booked into a B&B.'

The parcel was being thoroughly wrapped, Rose wasn't going to be told what was in it. Another plane-trip before the train to Devon and meeting Connie. Hardly a terrorist threat, but what to say when asked if anyone else had packed anything? Maybe it was booby trapped – something of the rebellious teenager about the old woman.

'When do you expect Liam to wake?'

The woman squinted over at her and whispered. 'Do you want anything? Coffee, tea?'

'No, thank you,' Rose whispered back.

Liam was more lively than expected.

'Look at that, you're a fashion model,' he said accusingly as he emerged from the bedroom.

Perhaps she shouldn't have worn her new clothes. No point explaining to Liam, or the woman, about Jerome's brief appearance in London.

'I thought you were a bouncer and a black belt. You should be all track suit and muscles. '

Connie must have mentioned it.

'I used to be a bouncer to get cash for uni but I'm finished with that. Who told you?'

'Anne,' said Liam, without looking at the old woman who was putting her packaging material into a large chest, and didn't react.

Was this old woman, Anne? The ex-nun Nell had described? Was she in contact with Connie? Connie had given the impression they'd been close, they couldn't be less alike.

'Well, that's a relief,' Liam continued. 'Mind you, the clubs here in the West might be as risky with drugs as you're used to over in

London. Knives and the like.'

'Liam, you are making no sense,' said the old lady.

'A big trip for us to go into Westport,' Liam continued, ignoring the interruption.

Us. So they were together. This Liam seemed so different from the elderly retired doctor she'd expected. She'd imagined a country gentleman – corduroys, cashmere sweater. This man was as scruffy as the woman, if not more so. But for all his wild white hair, paint spattered sweater, filthy trousers, broken sandals, he didn't seem eighty. Anne didn't seem eighty either.

'Connie,' Liam went on. 'How's Connie? I heard something, but we're all old. We were never there, never in her place in France. Did you ever visit it, Rose?'

'Yes. I think it suits her.'

Rose wasn't going to give details about the battered caravan, the trailer park with its improvised bar and couple of tables outside; Connie sitting with the same old men, drinking Ricard, playing cards. Nell had warned her that Connie sometimes drank too much. Everyone there drank too much.

'Come on Rose,' Connie would say. 'You always look inscrutable, it's a talent that shouldn't be wasted. I'll teach you poker; once this lot are plastered you can win us some money.'

The men had looked drunk already, and penniless.

Presumably Liam was imagining some luxurious gite.

'Anne told me the place was a tip,' said Liam. 'Full of wild dogs.'

How on earth did Anne know? The old woman had settled in an armchair, was examining her.

'And so you were at college, Rose?' said the woman. 'A degree in English. Do you enjoy teaching?'

Yet again, Connie must be the source. There'd not been enough money for college until Connie gave her some and paid off her debts, but she needn't have told people.

'If she offers, why not take it?' Iris had said. 'A good job, then it's find a steady young man.'

Iris must have known about the mess with Pedro. 'How's that manager of yours, that jumped-up barman?' Iris had once asked with her carefully prepared super-tactful I'm not really curious face.

Liam took a battered brown hat from a hook over the stove. 'Let's go for a walk.'

She followed him into the small crowded hall, he turned round a couple of paintings. 'These are landscapes.'

They didn't look like any landscape Rose had seen. The first had a mucky grey, blotched background with a brilliant turquoise streak along the diagonal. It made no sense, but was beautiful.

'Done just outside the door,' said Liam.

'It's lovely.'

Rose took some from another stack; a few were portraits of the old woman in her Oxfam clothes looking quite content, she was even smiling. There were several charcoals of a man in pyjamas on a bed. One was especially striking; Rose crouched for a closer look.

Liam grabbed it: 'Not that.'

He was shoving it back just as the old woman appeared.

'Let her see properly. A fine piece, isn't it? He always thought he and his father had never been close, but something was special between them when he drew that.'

The sketch made Rose uncomfortable.

'Rory wanted them destroyed,' said Liam. 'Accused me of worshipping images, ignoring reality.'

'The boy was fond of his grandfather and you do avoid things,' said the woman. 'You still do. I came to tell you to take a better raincoat, Rose. Protect those good clothes.'

She lifted an enormous ripped mackintosh from a hook then disappeared back into the living room.

Liam was rooting around, he'd found more abstract work. Rose hadn't expected that. Beauty.

'This is why we came, Rose. The country around is endlessly interesting. She can go off on her walks, I can avoid everyone.'

One of the paintings was more like a photograph: a careful representation of a winter garden, a long lawn surrounded by a path and high brick walls, statues in the corners. There were a few trees, a few evergreens. In the background – with photographic accuracy – was a forbidding Gothic-looking building.

'This needs some imagination,' said Liam.

Yet it was detailed and precise.

'I was thinking of somewhere else altogether. Maura had died a few months before.'

He unhooked a stick. 'Shall we go?'

Rose put on the rain coat, stuck her head round the door to ask if the old woman wanted to join them. She'd already settled in an armchair with a book.

Nell had once said that Anne was responsible for her split with Jerome.

'Sorry to bother you but in case I forget to ask. Did you have a friend in Lagos, a nun who was worried about Nell?'

The old woman looked cautious. 'I've no idea what you mean.'

They had left the few houses behind, were walking down a hill and along a stream towards a small wood. No one was around.

'What if you became ill, it's so remote.'

'I'll ignore that question,' Liam said cheerfully. 'How is Connie?'

He'd asked that already.

'Fine, I think. She's very tough.'

What made Rose say tough? Was that the same as independent? She meant independent.

Liam stopped by an oak, stroked the bark. 'We never thought she'd make it. For fifty years I've waited to hear something. Now the woman will soon be eighty. A miracle, isn't it?

Connie not make it? According to Nell, she occasionally mixed alcohol and tranquillisers, but never when Rose was around.

They had started up a steep slope and Liam was marching ahead. He was fitter than her.

'Anne was more help than I was,' Liam called back.

'When was that?'

Liam turned, surprised by the question. 'After Claire died.'

Connie never mentioned Claire; it was Nell who said there'd been a daughter. What else had Nell said? That the family should have talked about it. That Nell should have talked about it – which daughter did Nell mean?

'Was it Anne who told you she'd helped Connie?' said Rose.

Liam chuckled, walked back and tucked his arm through hers.

'Nell isn't keen on Anne. You young people are so suspicious. Let's go up this other track, take a gander at the ruined abbey. Did you go to Aidan's leaving party?'

She hadn't known about it, had never met Aidan.

'Both of them disillusioned with the health service, packed up early, gone sailing. Vijay loathes boats.'

They paused at the top of the slope, looked down at the ruin through the trees. The clouds had gone and sunlight filtered through the branches. The great stone walls had collapsed, settled into a green that had defeated them. The air was soft and animated. Leprechauns, fairy rings, changelings.

Iris had read out everything to her that Rose should expect.

Liam smiled at her expression. 'It's not safe any nearer. Shall we go back and get some tea?'

So when he and Connie were still married, that time after their daughter's death, Anne had intervened. Was Liam implying Anne had somehow saved Connie from hurting herself? But that didn't mean he had to end up shackled to that strange woman. Or that the woman back in the cottage was Anne, not some housekeeper.

Liam's parcel was unwieldy and heavy; the woman had fixed a string loop to make it easier to manage but it didn't. Since Rose was about to fly it was crazy not to check. Re-wrapping would be no problem, it couldn't be messier.

Rose stopped at a newsagent in Knock, bought sellotape, and a luminous Madonna for Iris. She was starving even though she'd eaten several slices of seed cake and four scones, all baked apparently by Liam. He'd poured the tea while Anne put her book away, interrogated Rose about teaching. The old woman was quite knowledgeable and sharp and did keep nodding as if in approval, so maybe Rose hadn't sounded too ignorant.

She found an open café and, after eating the Full Irish All-day Fry, went to look for her hotel; the waitress had packed her some black pudding. The streets were crowded: it was going back fifty years, the women middle-aged in head-scarves and buttoned-up coats despite it being summer, the men in soft hats as if just off to the races, and so many nuns in full nun habits. And priests, priests everywhere, rushing around gleefully as if on holiday.

Once in the hotel bedroom, Rose cleared the dressing-table of holy knick-knacks, started to unpick the string. Under the first layer of paper were a couple of closely-written unsigned pages. Liam had written to Connie.

The first paragraphs talked of frequent visits from the parish priest and refusing to go to Mass or have confession and eventually turning him away, then some gossip about the alcoholic postman and his wayward wife. There was a section about the neighbour's grandchildren helping to put in seedlings, then driving to Westport, running out of petrol. Nothing that Liam could object to her reading. The tone was affectionate and witty. Westport had been dire, like it always was, but this time they both struggled up Croagh

Patrick and would never do it again. They had kept their shoes on and were overtaken by barefoot ninety-year-olds. It was the bit about the French trailer camp, and then memories of some man who had died, that began to sound more and more unlikely. So L was meant to be Laurent? Connie had told Liam all this stuff about Laurent? Details of how much she missed him?

Rose checked again for a signature. Nothing. On the front of the parcel was written Connie Dillon. On the back, the Mayo address and a name, Anne Klima. Not Liam.

It was from Anne. The letter was from Anne. The parcel was from her. What could have been packed by an elderly woman in Ireland to be sent to another old woman staying for a week or so in Torquay? This was unlikely to be gold bars or Semtex; Rose stopped her unpicking, tied back the string.

Her clothes still carried the turf-smell of the cottage. She put the parcel in her overnight bag, took a shower. So Anne was funny, and clearly liked Connie; they probably liked each other. It was Anne who refused to go to Mass, had turned away the parish priest.

Why hadn't Connie mentioned that the parcel was from Anne?

The holiday flat in Torquay had an almost-view of the sea. It was ugly-modern, the rooms bare and unwelcoming. At least it wasn't a B&B with fussy curtains, padded satin bed covers, harassed owners doling out full-English breakfasts; Connie having to smile a lot, say good morning to miserable strangers, then disappear all day.

Control this misanthropy in case Rose or Jess picked it up – yet what madness had possessed her? The town was full of elderly couples and families whose boredom was infectious; a mostly grey sky, a typically wet August. She knew no one. Easier for both Rose and Jess if she'd rented a room in London. But this needed to be done somewhere she was quite alone.

The state of being alone was more intense than Connie had expected, and without any soft corners where she could curl up. Movies were of no interest. For the first time in her life she couldn't imagine buying a cinema ticket with the confidence she'd be transported to another world. Foreign places on her own had once been exhilarating: find a café, order a coffee, watch people. But not here, the cafés were too slick-fake-comfort or too greasy.

At least she could swim. She'd told Rose on the phone to pack a swim-suit. 'You have to. Even if it's bucketing down.'

Rose hadn't sounded enthusiastic. The last time they'd seen each other was two years before when Rose came for a long weekend to Perpignan. Connie had picked her up at the airport. Rose had gazed with horror at the assortment of trailers, miles from anywhere. 'I understand now why you don't reply to letters, Connie. They could easily go astray.'

'Not true. I'm usually outside and the only visitors are the postman and croissant van, that abundance of excitement is never missed. It's not so bad, and cosy in winter.'

'Your caravan doesn't look as if it will survive the first breeze.'

Connie's spare camping bed was comfy enough but even when she'd taken Rose to the impromptu bar they'd fixed up near the entrance, introduced her to friends, Rose hadn't looked reassured. She'd even moaned about all the barbed wire. But at least they'd gone swimming.

Time in Torquay seemed endless; that should be a good thing but it wasn't, it was intolerable. She'd adopted a restaurant for her evening meal so at least there'd be someone who knew her. She went to the hairdresser but that was a waste of money so she skipped the manicure booked next door. She found a good quality tweed coat in Help the Aged and sat in the gardens near the Marina, wrapped up as if it was winter, and watched people. She went to M&S and bought food.

For the first time in her life, Connie was early to meet someone; Rose was glowing with energy and beauty and dressed inadequately for Torquay weather in a pink silk shirt and fitted trousers. It was not her usual scruff and clearly pricey. Her hair last time had been long and braided but she'd shaved it off. She looked wonderful.

'You are positively beaming, Rose. It must be Mayo.'

'Oh, completely, what an unmissable trip.'

So, it had been grim.

'But,' Rose continued. 'It's wonderful to see you, it's been ages.'

They hugged and Connie took a look into Rose's bulky shoulder bag; the parcel with eccentric wrapping was definitely Anne's. 'So that is it?'

Connie let Rose go; she mustn't let the child see how wobbly she was. That parcel looked so insignificant.

'Surprisingly heavy,' said Rose. 'Anne's name's on the back, not Liam's. Is that right?'

'Yes.' Connie paused and looked around. 'Bit public to start ripping open here, let's go home. I probably even forgot to tell you, Anne would be with Liam.'

She'd deliberately not told Rose. Heaven knows what Nell would have said to Rose about Anne – it might have put her off.

'You did forget, Connie, I'd no idea. Could hardly say who is this strange woman? You said collect a parcel.'

'I did indeed.'

Connie took hold of Rose's elbow, steered her to the exit and the taxis. Of course she should have mentioned Anne to Rose. But it was difficult to imagine her ex-husband sharing his life with a woman Connie could still see walking towards her in full nun's habit holding two mugs of tea.

She had tried, had sent several letters of advice in response to Anne's anxious questions. Laurent helped – they'd been efficient marriage counsellors.

'I thought you'd get on with Liam.'

That was true. And she'd suspected Rose would get on with Anne, they could talk teaching.

'He was very sweet, we went for a walk. His paintings are beautiful.'

'Good, there you are. See, we're not all useless.'

She found a taxi, directed it to the flat. Rose looked done-in.

'It's just along the front, but you Londoners give me such tantrums if you have to walk anywhere.'

'I am not Jess.'

No, Rose was not her wonderful but volatile daughter. If Connie had asked Jess to go to Mayo, she'd say no at first, then get suspicious and insist on knowing what was going on. She tolerated the craziness of her father living with her headmistress but would have to know everything about the parcel. Jess's interrogations could be ruthless. Rose on the other hand gave out a sense of acceptance and concern that Connie had first seen in the brief glimpse of Jerome all those years ago: Nell crashed out on the sofa at that dreadful party, Jerome looking down at her. Rose would consider the parcel personal, and only Connie's business. She'd ask no questions.

'Maybe it was a daft idea,' said Connie. 'But why not? You know so few of Nell's family. Nell's pathologically antisocial.'

The taxi pulled into a space in front of the flat.

'Why didn't you ask Jess to go, Connie, or did she refuse?'

That made Jess sound unhelpful; it wasn't accurate but Rose would find out for herself. 'Jess wouldn't have gone. The woman expelled her from school twice.'

She'd put Rose in the room with plenty of windows; if Rose leant out over the balcony, she could just see the sea.

'Come and have something to eat, I've a hundred salads and three hundred varieties of sandwich and I'll make something resembling coffee.'

When Connie had visualised this meeting it had seemed so much easier.

'Why did you invite me here, Connie? Just for the parcel?'

'For me to see you. For you to enjoy the weekend, and to meet Jess at last.'

Connie poured boiling water into the cafetiere. Now that she'd started all this she might as well continue, Rose could condemn her later.

'To hear if you're enjoying teaching, find out about that rascal Pedro. If you've made up your mind.' Connie collected two cups. 'I needed you to go to Mayo, Rose, and I'm so bloody pleased you did. That parcel was something I wanted to have for a long time.'

Then why was it weighing her down? It was still on the floor by the front door. All so immeasurably sad. When should she open it? Maybe it wasn't a good idea to wait for Jess; Rose hadn't asked much, still might not. It would be simpler.

'Why did Anne have whatever it was you wanted, Connie? And, why now?'

She managed to evade the question, dumping food on the table and distracting Rose with talk about food fads, challenging Rose's conviction that the sandwiches were full of chemicals.

She had filled a backpack with towels. 'It's only five, let's swim.'

'Are you serious? I've been travelling all day. A bumpy bed in Knock last night, I'm knackered.'

Best thing was to give her no choice. Connie pulled Rose out of the chair.

Rose was unimpressed when they got to the beach. 'The water looks freezing. It's nearly evening, a north wind. How can you bear the cold? At least your French sea was vaguely warmish.'

Connie quickly stripped down to her very faded bikini. 'Get in quickly and you'll love it.'

'You have a terrific body, Connie.'

'Well, it has every bloody thing wrong with it.'

She shouldn't have said that, but Rose didn't seem to have heard; the child was preoccupied with avoiding getting wet. Connie had promised herself not to soften, not to talk. It was her business, inevitable there'd be something amiss considering her age; in a few days she'd be eighty. My god. Nothing more boring than hearing the aged groan on, especially one who'd convinced people, as well as herself, she'd no intention of getting old.

This was a celebration as well as an acknowledgement. Would Jess and Rose see it as she did, a tying the string on a complete life while she was able to appreciate it, and mourn.

Pat's voice in her ear: 'Attention seeking as usual.'

She raced ahead into the sea, dived under.

Rose was still holding the towel tightly round her sensible one-piece suit. What a waste of a perfect body.

Connie swam back. 'It's warm as toast!'

Rose cautiously dipped in a toe, felt her way forward.

'This is melted ice straight from the Arctic, Connie.'

'Just go under and swim, count to twenty. It will be fine.'

The sea was still only as high as Rose's thighs. Connie left her to it, allowed the water to embrace her body. The bliss; it was there inside her muscles, that craving for seawater since her childhood.

After a bit she could hear Rose duck under and gasp with the shock. Count to ten, it will get warmer, but Rose was already splashing her way back to dry land. Reluctantly Connie joined her; the poor girl looked numb.

While Rose towelled herself, Connie stood with hands on her hips, staring out to sea. 'Odd isn't it? So many whales beach themselves – no one knows why.'

'By accident?'

Rose was trying to dress without being seen. Oh, please flaunt yourself, Rose. Give us a glimpse of beauty.

'Put something on, Connie. There's a bitter wind.'

Connie pulled her sweater over the wet bikini.

'You'll get pneumonia,' said Rose.

'That's not how people get pneumonia, but you're young and too thin, so dry yourself properly.'

Connie put her hand on Rose's shoulder, steadying herself as she pulled on her jeans.

'Your hands are ice, Connie.'

'So namby pamby, your generation – you ought to have been ducked daily into the Atlantic from Easter on like Pat and me.'

They would go to her pizzeria for supper; Connie should have done more research before settling for the place. She'd chosen her favourite deep-green silk dress, even put on make-up; ages since she'd tried anything more than the occasional splodge of lip-stick.

'Why didn't I bring more clothes?' said Rose.

'With that outfit? I'm so relieved to see you spending at last. It's a bring-your-own place. We're celebrating; I've these bottles from

France, a very good Pinot.'

The waiter welcomed them as old friends so it had been worth her loyalty even if the food wasn't great. He ushered them to the window, away from a young couple, the only other customers.

'How many times have you eaten here?'

'Three, four, give me a chance. Only arrived a week ago, a quick trip to Moreton then here. I hate fish and chips; hope you didn't want that.'

'Not my favourite, but why Torquay?'

Was this drama what she wanted? Wouldn't Rose be furious?

'No idea,' said Connie. 'I'd never been to Torquay in my life but I'm getting to know it. Useless at sleeping so I go for a walk around three in the morning.'

'The town must be empty.'

'It's packed. The shopping area behind the Marina has crowds of half-naked boys and girls – drunk, noisy, presumably happy. Was that you at their age? Forgive me, is that you still?'

'Oh yes, half-naked and drunk every Saturday night.'

'Excellent.'

'You didn't explain, Connie, why Anne had what you wanted.'

Connie poured more wine. 'We'd better decide what to eat.'

She couldn't answer; it would involve too many questions. But was she right? Was this going to be cruel? An unfair burden for both Jess and Rose? At least they'd now meet. She'd give details of the alternative future when she emailed, but they would be angry. Jess would certainly be angry.

Rose couldn't sleep. Connie had left some novels by the bed. 'In case you wake early.' Several Patricia Cornwell, two Val McDermid.

The beating of waves on the sea wall was unmistakable. She could hear Connie walking around the flat, a couple of times a kettle was boiling. The night before, in the hotel in Knock booked on the internet, it wasn't the lumpy mattress but the silence that had kept Rose awake.

To want to swim had been bizarre. Unsafe for a nearly eighty-year old to go jumping into freezing water. Not exactly the Caribbean. 'Listen to yerself, Carrybean. Say it properly,' Iris would yell. 'You not carrying a thing, Rose. You and your posh voice.'

Why didn't she hate Connie, a woman who'd encouraged her biological mother to have her adopted? Her whole life marked by that decision to give her away. Always making up for it: trying to please, rushing here and there, feeling responsible. Being a good person. The years helping Iris through various fostering crises, Rose had carried Arnst.

Like that all her life, this weekend no different. Did she delude herself that she loved Connie? Had Connie bought Rose's affection? Had Jerome bought her forgiveness for his scepticism?

And was that so bad? She had Pedro. Iris was taking it easier. Arnst seemed happy. If he had discovered gardening earlier he might not have had such a rough time, not given Iris total constant stress. Since Rose introduced her to Iris, even Nell had softened.

'Will it be dangerous for Nell in Zambia?' Rose had asked Iris.

'After Harlesdon? You joking girl?'

A relief that Jess had not made contact, it was enough to include Nell and Connie in her life. The years had been busy: a degree, a job, a flat. Once Connie had retired, she was never in London – Rose had to go to France.

She switched on her mobile. Two texts from Pedro. She'd leave on a morning train. After all this travelling: Jerome, his family, Ireland, Liam, Anne, it was much too tiring to deal with Jess.

She had to decide. She loved Pedro, he loved her. It should be enough. She sat down at the kitchen table. 'I've to get back for supper with Iris.'

'Jess is coming specially.' Connie passed her a plate with eggs, bacon and black pudding. 'You've got to stay a bit longer.'

Connie was being very sociable. 'I thought you rarely saw Jess.'

'Yes, well, of course I see her. She couldn't come yesterday, James' birthday – they booked some theatre.'

Nell once said that Jess might be a workaholic as a sort of defence.

Once in London, she'd phone, arrange to meet up for a drink. Better than here with Connie.

'You look exhausted, Rose.'

'Are you going to open the parcel?'

Connie pointed to a pile of folded brown paper. 'I have already. Or at least unwrapped it.' Her hands were shaking.

Connie picked up the box that Anne had parcelled so badly. A delay when neither of them said anything, then Connie gently tipped the contents on the floor. It was full of small stones.

No wonder the woman at the x-ray machine in Knock airport had looked at her oddly.

'Stones?'

'Anne didn't show you? They're Claire's, Anne's had them for fifty years.'

All that fuss for a pile of pebbles. 'Why did she keep them?'

'We made a pact while I was pregnant with Jess – Anne and I.'

Iris's voice was in Rose's ear. 'They're all mad.'

Connie picked up a few, held them in her palm as if alive.

'Claire collected them, hid them in her bedroom. She painted several, stuck plasticine over some, filled in holes. But more were hidden all over the school garden.' Connie poured them both coffee. 'Claire was taking them from the grottoes, she promised not to do it again.'

'Why were they with Anne?'

Connie looked over as if not quite understanding.

'We built a cairn, put these at the top. I hadn't meant to get pregnant – an act of madness. Anne promised to make sure the baby was ok. She persuaded me to live: I suppose you could say we had an arrangement. She'd keep the stones until I was ready. Nell never talked to you about Claire?'

'She told me your child died.'

'Nell had come to stay. It must have been wretched.'

That crazy tea-party when Arnst had made a mess of the cake and Nell broke down. Iris holding her, Nell crumpled up in tears. It was the first time Nell had seemed human.

Connie reached across, stroked Rose's cheek. 'I'm sorry to dump this on you. I was a mess, making that pact helped, making that cairn helped. Anne rescued the stones from the demolition mob. And looked after them until I was ready, just as we agreed.'

Rose went to take a final look at the sea, then they walked together to the station. Connie had slung a bag over her shoulder. What had Connie meant by ready? Anne must have known what the parcel meant but had said nothing. But she had said something. Just as Rose was leaving, Anne had taken her hand: 'Give Connie my love. Please tell her that even if I'm now as God-less as she is, I'll be praying. She'll understand.'

It must have been the praying bit that made Rose blank out the old woman's words.

'Are you doing anything special on your birthday?'

Connie smiled, put the bag down on the platform. She took out a beautifully wrapped package, cradled it for a moment and handed it over.

'Take this. I'll treat myself, celebrate survival and having choices. I'll send you an email.'

'Is this what I think it is?'

'Most likely,' said Connie. 'In case Jess doesn't make it. I realised it's better you have them. I know it's primitive, and fully apologise in advance.'

Did she mean that getting the stones meant the arrangement with Anne was over? Anyone who swam in that freezing sea with such pleasure was not about to do anything drastic? But the train was due, Rose had to text Pedro.

Connie hugged her tightly, kissed her, then walked away quickly. Rose had an urge to call out, but the train had arrived.

She knew what was in the box before she opened it. Stones, some coloured, some small. She counted them. There were fifty.

ABOUT THE AUTHOR

Jane Kirwan is both Irish and British, writes poetry and prose, lives in England and the Czech Republic, has degrees in both English and Dentistry. And she is Libran.

OTHER WORK PUBLISHED

Stealing the Eiffel Tower
The Man Who Sold Mirrors
Second Exile (with Aleš Macháček)
Born in the NHS (with Wendy French)

ACKNOWLEDGMENTS

Thanks to all first readers – current members
of ReWord, former members of Clink – plus Nan McNab and
Eloise Millar. And thank you to Jill Foulston for her brilliant editing
and William Marshall for spotting the howlers.

Bluedoorpress.co.uk

Made in the USA
Charleston, SC
29 July 2016